LORDS OF IRON

THE DARK AGE CHRONICLES, BOOK 3

MJ PORTER

Boldwood

First published in Great Britain in 2025 by Boldwood Books Ltd.

Copyright © MJ Porter, 2025

Cover Design by Head Design Ltd

Cover Images: iStock and [Collaboration JS] / Arcangel

A CIP catalogue record for this book is available from the British Library.

Paperback ISBN 978-1-83617-526-1

Large Print ISBN 978-1-83617-525-4

Hardback ISBN 978-1-83617-524-7

Trade Paperback ISBN 978-1-80656-155-1

Ebook ISBN 978-1-83617-527-8

Kindle ISBN 978-1-83617-528-5

Audio CD ISBN 978-1-83617-519-3

MP3 CD ISBN 978-1-83617-520-9

Digital audio download ISBN 978-1-83617-522-3

This book is printed on certified sustainable paper. Boldwood Books is dedicated to putting sustainability at the heart of our business. For more information please visit https://www.boldwoodbooks.com/about-us/sustainability/

Boldwood Books Ltd, 23 Bowerdean Street, London, SW6 3TN

www.boldwoodbooks.com

For Mr Duke, Windy Woody, Sulky Sid, Whirling-dirvish Socks and Sunny Skye

MAP OF C6TH BRITANNIA

CHARACTER LIST

The Eorlingas, a native Brythonic tribe from the west of Britain, close to the River Hafren

Beli, warrior of the Eorlingas

Bronwen, Meddi's mare

Edern, leader of Villa Eorlingas, now dead

Elen, Edern's wife

Gwynmarch, horse

Idnerth, warrior of the Eorlingas

Idris, warrior of the Eorlingas

Kenal, warrior of the Eorlingas

Maccus, Madog's son

Macsen, Madog's father

Madog, tribal chieftain of the Eorlingas

Marchell, Meddi's servant and former seeress

Meddi, seeress of the Eorlingas, former wife of Edern

Merin, Madog's father's father

Rhiann, Madog's wife

Sian, a woman of the Eorlingas

Terricus, charcoal maker now turned bladesmith

Tudwal, warrior of the Eorlingas
Twrch, warrior of the Eorlingas
Urien, warrior of the Eorlingas

Wærmund's *comitatus*
Bægmund, warrior of the Gyrwe
Bucge, warrior of the Gyrwe and seeress
Cynin, warrior
Dewi, warrior
Eastmund, warrior of the Gyrwe
Eli, warrior
Freki, wolfhound
Goddæg, warrior of the Gyrwe
Heafoc, warrior of the Gyrwe
Hygebeorht, warrior of the Gyrwe
Locinna, warrior
Maggenræd, warrior of the Gyrwe
Mato, warrior
Nothelm, warrior of the Gyrwe
Osfyth, warrior of the Gyrwe and hunter
Rhun, warrior
Totia, warrior
Wædel, warrior of the Gyrwe
Wærmund, warrior of the Gyrwe and son of Wihtlæd

The Gyrwe, a tribe from the east of Britain, formerly a *comitatus* **invited to Britain after the end of Roman occupation by the sixth century**
Alric, warrior of the Gyrwe
Burnoth, warrior of Wihtlæd
Cenbryht, warrior of the Gyrwe
Waga, father of Wihtlæd

Waga, Wærmund's younger brother
Wihtlæd, Wærmund's father

The Beansæte, a native Brythonic tribe that borders the Eorlingas
Hedrek, their leader, now enslaved by the Eorlingas
Centus, blacksmith, now dead

The Hicca – a tribe in the middle of Britannia
Boddw, their leader, now dead

The Wæclingas – a tribe in the middle of Britannia
Isarninus, their leader
Iuti, Isarninus' son

The Færpingas – neighbours of the Eorlingas
Prasto, their leader

The Wocingas
Riderch, their leader
Gwener, Riderch's wife

The Husmeræ, neighbours to the Eorlingas
Cadwysti, seeress
Tangwysti, new seeress
Padern, leader of the Husmeræ

The Stoppingas, neighbours to the Eorlingas
Ladus, their spokeswoman

The Tomsæte, a tribe in the middle of Britannia
Sennicus, their spokesperson

Blatero, warrior

The Sweordora, a tribe that borders the Gyrwe
Dægbeorht, their leader

Within Uriconium
Diseta, translator
Gildas, a holy man
Gwladus, of the Wreocensætan
Katourn, bladesmith

LOCATIONS

Villa Eorlingas – based very roughly on the Frocester Roman Villa, but closer to the River Hafren

The home of the Husmeræ – based on Great Witcombe Roman Villa, Gloucestershire

The home of the Wæclingas/Isarninus – settlement close to Verulamium, now St Albans

Corinium – Cirencester

Glevum – Gloucester

Uriconium – Wroxeter, the archaeology reveals there was a building phase taking place there throughout this period. That's unusual at this time when most former Roman settlements were decaying. I've decided to name it Uriconium and not Viriconium because I came across the name Uriconium first

Verulamium – St Albans

Watling Street – Roman road (although evident in the landscape from the Bronze Age) running from Dover to Wroxeter (and further north)

Fosse Way – Roman road running from Exeter to Lincoln

Icknield Street – Roman road running from Bourton-on-the-Water to York

BRITANNIA AD541

Rome's reach disappeared from Britannia over a hundred years ago. In its wake, the sophisticated warrior and political society that allowed a far-distant emperor to govern the unruly province has slowly crumbled with the attendant loss of its currency, skills, political elite and, of course, brave warriors who once fought against Britannia's enemies: the Picts from the far north, long held at bay by the snaking walls crossing the north of Roman-held Britannia.

Quickly, the skills and ideals of *Romanitas* have become subsumed by the basic need to survive amongst those who still inhabit the island of Britannia. Some have taken advantage of the weakness of others, although with the magik of bladesmith and ironworker lost to all but a few, the majority lack the required weapons or the desire to wage bloody wars against their ancient enemies. The blades they have are old and tired, riddled with rust and lacking the keen edge to make warfare possible.

Instead, the men and women of Britannia inhabit the cities abandoned by Rome, forging a living from the soil, reliant on barter. And for those who shy away from the haunted ruins and the lost Roman gods, the even more ancient hill forts of an age before Rome came offer the promise of their protective ditches and ramparts, as well as their familiar gods. Others shelter in the remnants of a once rich and prosperous agricultural landscape doing all they can to grow enough food to survive, daily reminded of all they've lost, as they build ditches and embankments to protect themselves from those desperate enough to risk all for enough food to eat despite the lack of good weapons.

To the east, new tribal warriors have emerged, who were once strangers to Britannia, and herald from the northern lands of the Continent. They're not strangers to war. They have come to protect those too weak to fight but with the wealth to pay them in the immediate aftermath of Rome's departure. With a century of no coinage the *comitatus* now lay claim to that which they were once paid to protect.

This is Britannia, a century after the withdrawal of Rome and a century before the emergence of the kingdoms of the Angles and Saxons.

This is the true Dark Ages.

THE STORY SO FAR

Meddi of the Eorlingas grieves the loss of her mother, dead at the hands of the machinations of her despised sister, Elen. Elen was once wed to the man who killed their father, stole their villa and killed Meddi's daughter. Elen is busy collecting allies to her cause, with the intention of taking Villa Eorlingas from Meddi and her brother, Madog.

Wærmund of the Gyrwe has sought to reclaim his lost treasures from a man who betrayed him, Isarninus. But while he has sharp iron blades to kill his enemy, Isarninus' son has allied with Elen, the woman who almost killed Bucge. And Wærmund fears another of her allies might be his father.

1

MEDDI OF THE EORLINGAS

Dawn crests the horizon in a welter of flaming reds and yellows, smoke swirling sporadically from the celebratory fire we feasted around last night. But my heart feels leaden. I gaze down at the still face of my mother, Marchell, the former seeress of the Eorlingas. I wish to cry but the tears will not come.

My brother's a constant guard at my side. Alongside him stand Urien, Tudwal, Kenal and others of the Eorlingas. Sian sobs quietly, unable to stop, while Terricus, Hedrek beside him, stays apart from our small party, their heads bowed low. I sense Hedrek's searing gaze but ignore it.

Of us all here, Hedrek knew my mother for longer than I did. He and Urien both did. I should acknowledge his sorrow, but I feel hollowed out. A husk. I thought myself made whole once more, my scars miraculously healed. I didn't know it would cost me my mother.

My hands pulse uncomfortably where I extinguished leaping flames amongst the mane of one of my precious horses during last night's attack, but they're not painful enough to drive away the sorrow sinking into my belly.

My mother is gone.

My father is gone.

I know my sister, Elen, is to blame for all of this. Somehow.

I believed her dead, but I can't any more. There's no other reason for our mother to have been targeted in such a way. If our enemy had come for our new iron blades, or our horses, I could have understood it, but not this. Never this. My mother is gone from my life.

'Meddi.' My brother's voice is insistent. I know he recalls me to the here and now, to what must be done, but I don't wish to stand aside from my mother's body. To do so would be to accept she's journeyed to the afterlife, to forever be with our ancestors and gods. 'Seeress,' he tries again, coughing aside the smoke we've all inhaled throughout the night.

It's been a terrible experience, our triumph turned to dust, our people attacked. I should thank my horse-god so few of the Eorlingas died, but of the two who did, one was my mother, and the other a fine warrior with a burgeoning family. I know only too well the grief those children will endure throughout their lives, from this moment onwards. They have their mother, as I did when my father was killed, but still, the loss of a father is traumatic enough. It will mark them throughout the coming years of their lives. They'll always be different to those who have both a mother and a father.

'Seeress,' Madog tries again. Now I lift my head and note his expression. Grief softens his taut features, the ash of last night's fire sliding down his face like mud under an onslaught from a flooded river. He grieves Marchell, even if she wasn't his birth mother. In all honesty, Marchell was to all intents and purposes his mother. She ensured he lived after the death of his mother. Marchell was everything to him, as she was to me.

Laboriously, I stand, and puff out my chest, seeking the clarity of my position, the strength of who I've always been. I have survived. I will survive this. I don't want to, but I will do so. My mother's final words begged me to protect the Eorlingas, as she once failed to do when the bastard Edern overran Villa Eorlingas, taking anything and everything he wanted. Including me. I have protected Villa Eorlingas. I hope my mother will be proud of me. I wish, however, I'd protected her as well.

'People of the Eorlingas,' I croak, and then cough, clearing my throat of the ash and smoke, and the grief clogging it. 'People of the Eorlingas,' I begin again. 'And the people of the Husmeræ and the Stoppingas, we've been attacked, viciously, our revered seeress, Marchell, has been taken from us, as has Idnerth, our fine warrior. We'll grieve for them. But, in this moment, we must praise our warriors, and extend our thanks to those who fought at the side of the Eorlingas – our neighbours and friends.'

My words are greeted with silence. I'm aware everyone watches me. I cough again. I need to drink.

'Tonight, we'll send Marchell and Idnerth to their gods. If there are others who've perished from amongst our neighbouring tribes, we'll send them on their way as well, with all honour and respect.'

A low murmur greets my pronouncement. It's unusual to mix tribes in such a way. We all have our own gods. Our own ways of grieving. But, in this, I won't have it any other way.

'Those of our enemy who lost their lives,' and I growl angrily now, 'they'll be exposed for the carrion crows to pick clean, and their bones bundled into a hole in the earth, never to walk with their ancestors.' Silence greets this proclamation. I square my shoulders once more, allowing strength to flood my body with the righteousness of those words.

'It will be done,' Madog intones, his words respectful.

'It will be done,' Padern of the Husmeræ echoes.

'It will be done.' Ladus of the Stoppingas adds her voice to mine.

I eye the three of them. Padern and Ladus are tribal leaders of their people, but they've been assaulted, just as the Eorlingas have.

'Tomorrow, we'll seek vengeance against the bastard Færpingas,' Madog announces decisively. 'They presented themselves as our neighbours and allies, and were anything but.'

I nod.

'We'll join you,' Padern of the Husmeræ agrees.

Ladus nods, as I meet her eyes. 'We'll support you, but lack the warriors to reinforce your numbers.' Her words are edged with grief at the admission.

'We welcome all who will stand with us,' Madog confirms, his words thrumming with conviction. 'For those too young, too old, or lacking warrior skills, you'll aid us in other ways. We'll stand united, against this foe.' His words thunder, and behind them, I hear his rage and fury. I nod, tears finally sheeting from my eyes to drip onto my ash-stained breastplate.

'We'll seek vengeance,' I affirm, my thoughts tumbling to Elen. We'll not find her in the settlement of the Færpingas, south of here. It'll not be that easy to track her down and end her life. But I avow, looking down into my mother's unseeing face, that I'll do so.

Elen, my bitch of a sister, will die. She simply must. This time. I will not be dissuaded from it as I was last summer, when Madog decreed I shouldn't kill my sister, and his half-sister. Now, if we don't ensure her death, Villa Eorlingas, our home, will never be safe and secure, despite our iron blades.

2

WÆRMUND OF THE GYRWE

We travel for the remainder of the long day before I deem it safe enough to stop and cremate our two dead warriors.

We're a sullen bunch, even with Dewi and his three warriors amongst us. They grieve their lost man, as we do Bægmund, who left the lands of the Gyrwe as my warrior, and has paid the ultimate price.

We've lost so many since leaving my homeland far to the east. I fear I may still lose more of my valuable warriors before our vengeance is complete. And it is *our* vengeance. It's not only mine. Bucge and Osfyth hunger to satisfy their blood feud against the bitch, Elen. Heafoc and Eastmund are as resolved to banish the spectre of my father's presence throughout their lives, while I wish to do both. Elen was never the answer to our questions, I now realise. If anything, she only made our quest to make a name for ourselves much worse. I should have been wise enough to understand solutions to problems are never that swiftly resolved. But I was young, and impetuous. I've paid dearly for that.

As we stand, in the gathering gloom, the small flames growing bigger on the funeral pyre of scavenged wood, I turn to Dewi.

'Tell me what you know of Elen,' I demand. He recognised her. He said as much. His face twists with fury.

'She's a manipulative bitch and certainly no seeress, although she wears the symbols of one. She's the daughter of a former tribal leader of the Eorlingas, who make their home close to the River Hafren.'

He pauses then. I want to encourage him to speak more openly, and quicker, but I've waited over a year to know the truth about Elen. I can wait a few moments longer.

'Her father was murdered by another ambitious man, Edern, and their tribe dispersed, if they were lucky to escape, or imprisoned under his rule, if not. But not Elen. No, she waited for her sister to be taken by this man as his wife, and then, when she produced a daughter, not the desired son, the sister was banished and Elen took her place, encouraging Edern to more and more dishonest tricks. He took all from me and my family. He ransacked our settlement, stealing our wealth and leaving nothing in his wake, aside from me, a small boy. He killed my parents. My sister. My brothers. I vowed vengeance against Edern and his bitch of a wife. I've not yet achieved such, but I've never forgotten my vow of vengeance I shouted to the gods on that fateful day. I'll aid you though, now. I've hungered for her death throughout much of my life.'

'So, why is she no longer with this man, and calling this place her home?' I can't help thinking how much better it would have been for me, and my warriors, had Elen never stumbled into our encampment when we first fled from Isarninus.

'He's dead, and the tribal villa once more in the hands of the rightful ruler, the son of the man Edern killed. I've heard of it from the traders visiting Verulamium. It pleased me. I'd wondered what became of Elen. I'd hoped her dead as well, but I have my answer now. How do you know of her?'

'We discovered her, a year ago. We thought she was our ally. She betrayed us.'

Dewi's face creases in fury. 'She has no honour. She thinks of no one but herself, and believes everyone else will bid to undertake her will.' He spits the words. 'You were unlucky to encounter her in the wide expanse of this island we call our home,' he mutters.

'She was bloody lucky to survive the wound I gave her,' Bucge growls angrily. She remains furious. I know she blames me. I assured her Elen was dead. I'm astounded anyone could survive with the amount of blood sheeting the ground in the woodland clearing where we left her for dead on our original journey to Uriconium.

'She has the luck of the gods,' Dewi complains, but without anger. 'And your father?'

It seems this is a time for sharing confidences.

'He's a warrior from the east. He's the leader of the Gyrwe.'

'And why does he hate you so much?'

'I killed my younger brother. He was a weak man, much loved by my father. My father thought me Woden-cursed and a useless warrior.' I indicate the mark on my face, my eyes daring the other man to show fear. Once more, Dewi surprises me by laughing, his eyes switching between me and the mangy wolfhound, Freki, who stalks my steps.

'He was a fool. You fight like Woden.' His grin broadens. 'And you have the blades of gods too.'

The smell of burning flesh floods the air, the sharp pops of fat bubbling from beneath skin, making me grimace. It is the way of our people to inter the dead. It hasn't been possible on our journey to Uriconium, or now in the wake of our departure from Verulamium.

'I do now,' I confirm. 'Perhaps, I wasn't as good as I believed myself when I attacked my brother.'

'And Isarninus?'

'He held us captive and stole our treasures, including my ancestor's sword.'

'Hum,' he muses. 'It seems we can do much good for one another. I hunger for vengeance against Elen, and you against her and your father. My men and I will fight with you. We will, if you'll have us, become part of your warrior band.'

I nod. 'We'd welcome your numbers, but know, I'm the leader of our *comitatus*. I lead. No one else.'

'My lord,' and Dewi bows respectfully, his three allies following suit.

'You'll pledge to fight at my side.'

'We'll fight at your side, until Elen and your father are dead. You have our word on it. We'll swear it, if you prefer. After that, well, we'll see. If, as I suspect, Wærmund, your reputation grows to match your battle prowess, we'll stay with you, always.'

The words reinvigorate me. I thought to seek my revenge on Isarninus. It hasn't gone how I hoped it would. But, perhaps, this is merely another part in my journey to earning the high regard of Woden, my ancestor.

I hold the gaze of Heafoc, my oldest and most staunch supporter, of Bucge and her talent with the skills of seiðr, of Osfyth and her hunter's instincts, of Eastmund and his lethal ability, of Maggenræd and his fierce resolve, and I nod to each of them. We're all that remains of those who initially fled from the lands of the Gyrwe when there were twelve of us. We've survived because we're the strongest, and we'll become even stronger. Dewi's easy acceptance in joining us assures me of that. I'll claim the reputation once enjoyed by my father.

I'll become a warrior of Woden.

3

MEDDI OF THE EORLINGAS

The celebratory fire is far from extinguished when I light the funeral pyre to send my mother, Idnerth and two warriors of the Husmeræ to their gods.

It's been a strange day, sluggish at times, too fast at others. I've spent much time tending to the bodies of the deceased, while my brother and his warriors have stripped the dead enemy. As I requested, they've been taken outside the boundaries of Villa Eorlingas, and away from the streams we use, to be picked clean by the carrion creatures. In time, we'll return for their bones and inter them beneath the ground. It's not the way of my people to treat the dead like this. It's the only punishment I can assign to our enemy for what they've done.

The warriors of the Færpingas who came to Villa Eorlingas are all corpses. None have lived to hurry home and tell their families of what they've done. Tomorrow, Madog and his warriors will travel that way and exact their retribution on those who live. It'll not be like with the Stoppingas earlier in the season. No. The Færpingas will lose all they have. They'll be lucky to keep their lives, although my brother will not become

Edern, despite his rage. He'll know who to punish and who not to punish.

With the crackle of the flames taking hold, I fixate on my mother. I don't wish to remember her like this. I wish to remember her wise words, gentle admonishments and the bond we shared, even if I bucked against it for over half of my life. I can't claim that time back, but I can remember it, if not fondly then comfortable in the knowledge we were together.

I know that, while moving the bodies, Madog and Padern have spoken at length about their intentions towards Elen. I also comprehend they've discussed the work of Terricus and how it can benefit the Eorlingas and the Husmeræ, as well as the Stoppingas. I realise my brother will accomplish much, provided he's successful in stopping Elen from moving against us again. Edern ruled our neighbours through fear. Madog will unite with them in a common pursuit. I sense the relationships will be more productive because of that. I'm proud of him, even while I weep for my mother.

I'm adorned in white chalk and black charcoal to highlight my eyebrows. My greying hair's also coated in charcoal and I've not removed my breastplate all day. I stand proudly, the double-headed horse torque around my neck. I try not to cry, to be the seeress of our people, but in this, I'm a daughter first. Tears track down my cheeks although I don't sob. Instead, they fall without cease. I'm barely conscious of them.

I feel the loss of my mother as a terrible weight on me. Every time I enter my workshop, I expect to find her there, bent over her collections of herbs. I anticipate hearing her voice, berating someone or other, or offering them advice. I'll not hear it again, unless I commune with her through our god, and that's always been more her skill than mine. Or rather, it was.

A small, sticky hand slips into my motionless ones. I turn,

glimpse the saddened eyes of young Maccus. He's so small, only having celebrated his first year earlier in the season. Yet he's wise. Perhaps wiser than all of us.

He stands with me, deep into the night, when I'm sure he should be sleeping. I'm aware of Madog behind me, keeping his own guard, and perhaps ensuring his son doesn't fall asleep on his feet.

I take strength from Maccus. He's the hope for the future of my people. As we mourn those who went before him, I feel the heaviness within me lift. My mother exerts no burden on me to seek vengeance for her death. I've placed that on myself. I'll fulfil it, but I also realise, as I watch the yellow and red flames leaping and dancing in the gentle breeze, as they consume the physical forms of those who died here, in the ice-cold heart of the flames' hottest elements, I'll only survive if I release that need for vengeance and revenge. I'll atone for my mother's death but it need not scar me physically, as Edern's marks on my body did before I was healed.

With the rising of the sun, in a fiery red glow on the far horizon, I bow my head one more time to my mother, and then turn aside from the funeral pyre, pulling young Maccus into my arms. He's swaying on his feet.

Gently, I pass him into his father's arms, and stride towards my workshop, bending low to enter it, and running my hand over the lintel, as I always do.

I swallow against my grief, eyes peering into the gloom where my mother was always to be found. I expect the place to ring with the silence of her absence but, instead, warmth wraps me, and I offer a soft smile, and take to my bed.

It's been a long few days. Our triumph, I feared, turned to dust. But that isn't the case at all, and when I've rested, I'll make my mother proud, as well as my father, for I'm Meddi, seeress of the Eorlingas, and beloved by the horse-god of our people.

There's much for me to do, and I'll see it done knowing I'm watched by dead parents. They'll give me the strength I need to accomplish all that was taken from us during their lives.

* * *

The following morning, I join Madog and Padern where they prepare to ride towards the settlement of the Færpingas. The funeral pyre still blazes intermittently.

'We'll inter her when you return,' I inform my brother. He inclines his head in understanding.

I eye the warriors of the Eorlingas and those of the Husmeræ. In total, there are fifteen of them on fine horses. The force is perhaps not the largest, but with the blinding, shimmering edges of their blades, there need not be many to overawe those who lack such keenness to deliver a lethal strike without exerting too much of themselves.

I'm not alone in gathering to watch the warriors ride out. I share a look with old Kenal and young Tudwal, my escorts from earlier in the season. Tudwal sits his horse competently, and Kenal has always ridden well. I understand both have prevailed upon Madog to allow them to join the coming attack. I also know Madog was pleased to welcome them.

'People of the Eorlingas, Husmeræ and Stoppingas,' my brother shouts from the back of his horse. 'We ride to avenge those taken from us by the deceit of those who took our hospitality and turned it against us.'

His words garner a murmured response. Even now, there's disbelief at what befell our celebratory harvest feast.

'Know we will return to you as victors.' And so spoken, he

casts a final glance in my direction, and turns his horse towards the open gateway allowing entry and exit from the double-ringed ditch protecting the core of Villa Eorlingas.

There are many keen to keep guard duty in the absence of our warriors, and Madog has tasked our oldest surviving warrior to ensure there's a rota of people on duty. Even as I watch, the warriors turn towards the east, to where the Færpingas settlement is. I know no fear. My brother, and his allies, will triumph. It's only a matter of time.

I turn aside from observing my brother's progress, and my steps take me to visit my horse, Bronwen. She was mighty during the terrible fight, leading the other mares to ensure we prevailed. I glimpse her now, and wince to see the livid burn mark on her neck. I tended to it yesterday, but evidently more needs to be done.

I hear a soft voice, and smile despite myself. Maccus is with the horse he's determined to claim as his own. Gwynmarch. The beast much is taller than him. While Maccus is still a young child, only just losing the chunkiness of babyhood, Gwynmarch is lean and spindly. The two will grow together, until they work as one.

'Maccus,' I call to him. He grins broadly on seeing me, and reaches out to take my hand.

'Come, see.' I stand tall for a moment, seeking his mother, but Rhiann is not to be found. Maccus has escaped her. For now.

'What is it?' I ask, curious.

'Look,' and a small, chunky finger points to where he means. I smile softly. Gwynmarch is surrounded by the other young horses. They're all long-legged and spindly, like young trees before their roots begin to expand. 'They will be friends,' Maccus crows. My smile broadens at his obvious delight, and then I hear Rhiann calling for her son.

'Go, quickly.' I push him aside. With a lingering glance at Gwynmarch, his warm hand leaves my cold one, and I feel bereft once more.

Having tended to Bronwen's burn, I take myself to Terricus, where Hedrek and Sian work with the bladesmith. The three of them have been labouring hard for the last two days. They're keen to ensure our new allies have good blades to take with them when they leave. The Stoppingas, under Ladus, need to return as soon as possible because they left many of their people behind to tend to animals and crops.

'Mistress.' Sian breaks the silence between the three of them. I sense the scrutiny of Terricus and Hedrek. 'Do you need me, now...' and her voice trails away. Sian still struggles to name Marchell's death.

'No, I came to ensure you had all you needed.' I incline my head towards Terricus. He nods, but his face is pensive.

'We'll soon need a new source of the iron you discovered contained within your horse-shaped object,' he admits. 'I've been busy working with what there was, but there's little left now.' As he speaks, he holds up a small lump of the item, and it is a lump, perhaps a leg, or a head, the only element remaining. Not that the small horse-shaped object was very large in the first place.

'Do you understand what's different about it, yet?' I question him.

'It's not from the ground near here,' he murmurs. 'It's not like the ironstone Urien found for me. It's similar, but different.' I consider this, and then turn, surprised to find Ladus has crept up without me noticing.

'Mistress,' she speaks respectfully.

'Ladus,' I reply. Her eyes are keen. She's been gifted with one of Terricus' blades, but there aren't yet enough to give her more than one. The warriors have others Terricus has forged.

'Forgive me, mistress, you were discussing ironstone?'

'We were, yes.' I feel my forehead furrow.

'I suspect we may be able to aid you there. We've many such items amongst our own treasures, if you seek similar to that Terricus holds. I know of at least another three of those small horse shapes. I'll ensure they're brought to you.' I wait, expecting her to say something else, but she doesn't.

'Do you know where they came from?' Terricus asks eagerly. But Ladus is shaking her head.

'I don't. I suspect those to the far west, towards the sea there,' and she points where she means, 'may have more knowledge than we do. They've held to the old ways for longer than we have.'

'Then we must go west,' Terricus announces decisively, a look of determination on his face.

'Perhaps not you,' I counter, but he shakes his head.

'No, it must be me. I understand what I need. I'll know the correct questions to ask.'

I fall silent at this. We've only just ensured Terricus has the material he needs to make the blades so important to us. I don't welcome the thought of him leaving Villa Eorlingas.

Ladus surprises me by laughing softly.

'Not yet, my young friend,' she calls to Terricus. 'I'll have the items brought to you, and then you'll see if they're the same as those you already have. If they are, you'll have what you need to last this winter. It's not the time to be travelling.'

Terricus swallows down his complaint, and bows his head towards Ladus respectfully. I feel a swell of gratefulness towards her. Too much has happened, too quickly. I couldn't determine how to prevent Terricus leaving us, but Ladus made it sound easy.

'Now, mistress,' Ladus draws my attention once more, 'I've

come to bid you farewell. We'll travel to our home, and ensure all is well. I wished to thank you for your warm welcome and to extend my sympathies for the loss of your mother. May she walk with the gods in the afterlife.'

I swallow against a swell of grief, and extend my arms to grip Ladus tightly on the shoulders. 'You have the thanks of my people for aiding us in our time of peril. We'll not forget such bonds formed under terrible circumstances. And remember, if you suffer throughout the winter, you and your people will be welcome here. We'll feed you and keep you warm.' A sudden pensive look on her face makes me think I've said the wrong thing, but then her face transforms into a smile.

'You're wise, Meddi of the Eorlingas, and you're generous. We'll be friends and neighbours from this day forth.' And with that, she bows, and strides from me, back rigid, chin raised.

I admire Ladus. She's a firm woman and will keep her people safe.

I'm sure of it.

4

WÆRMUND OF THE GYRWE

With our dead sent to the afterlife, we follow the by now familiar path towards Uriconium. We move quickly, our desire to be far from Elen and my father's warriors at Verulamium ensuring none wish to linger. I sense we're being hunted. I suspect the others feel it too. But will the enemy truly seek us out? After all, they have the hilltop site above Verulamium to keep them safe. They must suspect we'll not be able to overawe them. We'll ensure we can. In the future.

At the settlement we once attacked, I call a halt. Eastmund rides to my side, his gaze appraising. On our return to Verulamium we avoided the place, but now I feel the urge to visit it. Do I wish to apologise or make good on what happened here? I don't know. But I don't ride past it. Instead, I encourage my horse towards it, and the animal obeys my command easily enough. Heafoc remains at the rear, with Dewi, who wisely says nothing, even if he is confused by my actions.

There's a single trail of smoke rising into the air from one of the houses. The ditch encircling the settlement is unprotected. I think the people here must all be dead or have fled. But then the three old men I encountered last time walk towards me, their ancient spears held tightly, their eyes filled with rage and fury. Behind them, I see the youngster I bartered in exchange for East-mund's life. I halt my horse's advance. The three men's faces show uneasy flickers of recognition. I swallow against my grief for what happened here. It shouldn't have come to it. They should simply have allowed us to take what was needed. It wasn't my finest moment. I accept that. Warriors need not take all from everyone in order to be the bravest.

Hastily, I turn and fumble within the sacks on my horse's back. They don't contain the treasures I hoped to regain from Isarninus. But I do have items these people can barter for, if they leave here. Carefully, with Eastmund a presence beside me, the others further back, I dismount, and hold out the items Dewi bartered in exchange for the knives. It's the wealth I have. I can't give them a horse, as we're using them all. I can't give them food. I do have treasures that might prove more useful to them. The brooches glisten and sparkle. They remind me of a shimmering pool of sunlight on water. I shake the fanciful thought aside.

Aware of the ring of silence within the settlement, I keep my eyes on the three men and the small boy, conscious others have come to witness this. No one, aside from the three men, has their hands on blades. They're a poor people, lacking good food. It's my fault.

Slowly, I lower my haunches to the ground, and lay the brooches out on the ground. I hear someone's hiss of surprise. Immediately, I stand, and slowly walk away, my back to them. If they wanted to, they could kill me, here and now. I suspect they'd rather have the riches.

I mount up, and turn my horse back towards the road, but a clatter of blades has me turning back towards the settlement. The young boy runs towards me, his hand outstretched. It's Dewi and his warriors who hold their sharp blades menacingly. But there's no need.

I bend low over my horse's neck and take the offering from the boy. He gives it to me with a broad grin on his face and then gruff voices no doubt calling him to return; he does so. I look at what he handed to me and close my fist over it. It's his treasure. He's gifted it to me. Already, the young boy is wiser than I am. It's a lesson I must learn well.

'Come on,' I urge my warriors. It's only later that day, when we shelter in the remnants of another abandoned settlement, that Bucge comes to me. We have a roaring fire blazing, burning the wooden struts from a tumbled-down building, and the heat warms my face.

No one else has truly spoken to me since we visited the settlement where I left the brooches. My warriors have been conversing amongst themselves, just not to me. No one has asked me what I was given. No one until now.

Silently, I place the object in Bucge's hand, and she twists and turns it, examining the depiction of what I believe is meant to be a wolf, from many angles. I suspect it's no more than a boy's treasured toy, but she surprises me.

'It's an emblem, of their people. I'm sure of it. It's a means of welcoming you amongst them. Don't disregard this. It will aid you, if we ever meet them again.'

'Why would he welcome me after what we did?'

'He's but a boy, he either didn't understand the symbolism, or he did. It may be the means of forgiveness. It may be his way of thanking you for ensuring he lived.' She shrugs, her familiar face cast into shadows by the leaping flames, and the advance of the coming night. There'll be no moon tonight. Clouds cover the sky, but I don't anticipate it will rain. Not yet. There's no sharp scent of coming rain.

'Then I'll keep it safe,' I murmur, strangely comforted. I'm not riddled with doubts for what I was before meeting Isarninus and my father's warriors on the hilltop, but I realise I am changed. I don't wish to become Isarninus. I don't wish to become my father. Freki keeps me constant company. His loyalty, and this gesture from the boy I saved, even while killing others of his settlement, has made me alert to the many ways a man can be a warrior. And the many ways a man can be a man. I must be better. The small emblem, I decide to entwine with other such trinkets around my neck. That way, it'll be kept secure.

'When we reach Uriconium, what will we do?'

'We'll seek out new warriors. We'll rebuild our strength. And then we'll pursue our vengeance against Elen and my father.'

'And then what?'

I allow a soft smile to touch my pensive lips. 'We'll then become something better. We'll build our own tribe.'

'Where?'

'Ah, Bucge, my friend, I don't have the answers to everything. But I will, in time.'

She nods, and her face softens in the glow from the fire. 'Your father was and is a fool. You're Woden-touched, not Woden-cursed, never doubt that, my friend.'

* * *

The following day, we arrive at the location where we fought the warriors who attacked us, and where Elen deceived us and wounded Bucge. I sense Bucge wishes to see the location. Silently, we make our encampment beneath the trees. The rain's been relentless throughout the day, my confidence it wouldn't rain misplaced. My clothing's wet, my horse sodden, and my wolfhound, still not recovered from the privations he's endured throughout his life, looks more than half starved with his fur sticking to his slim body. With a fire spitting fitfully, I turn to Bucge, and without speaking begin to walk towards the roar coming from the river. Freki shadows me.

I have my blades with me. I'll not take the chance that, somehow, Elen has beaten us here. It's entirely impossible, but the unease remains. I'll not be caught out twice in the same place. I know, behind us, Heafoc speaks with Dewi about what's happening. The two have struck up a firm friendship.

Silently, we walk through the shush of the branches and leaves swaying in the storm. Water occasionally lands on my face, but the brand I carry lights our path. I'm careful to ensure it doesn't gutter. It's been overcast, and beneath the branches the light's already poor, although there should be some time before the sun sets. It's been a dank and cold day, but my body warms with my steps. With an unfailing path that astounds me, we arrive at the opening beneath the trees where Bucge and Elen fought. I stand aside then, still beneath the shielding branches, with the brand held to the side so Bucge can see.

She limps into the clearing. I consider where her thoughts have taken her. Does she enter the place reminded she once arrived here without a limp, and the terrible wound that will forever scar her? I don't know. Neither do I break the silence between us to ask the question. She'll speak if, and when, she wants to do so.

I watch as Bucge hunkers down, running her hand over the damp grasses where she fought, and where I left Elen, believing the bitch was dead. I'm still astounded she survived. In all honesty, I'm amazed Bucge lived through her injuries, and she had me and her fellow warriors to help here and the ministrations of a healer within Uriconium. Elen was entirely alone.

Freki goes to her, nose busy sniffing the many scents.

A soft cry, and I have my seax out before I even consider it, dashing towards Bucge.

'Be still,' she speaks quickly, one hand reaching to calm Freki who growls. 'I'm not under attack. Get under the branch before the brand gutters and we're left fumbling around in the dark.'

Quickly, and biting back my immediate retort – I'm the leader of our *comitatus*, not a child to order about – I do as she requests. She remains where she is, busy with something I can't see very well. Freki stays with her.

Eventually, as I'm growing cold once more, and the smoke of the brand's making my eyes itch and my throat raw, she strides back towards me. As with the small boy I encountered, Bucge holds something in her hand. She opens it to show me.

'What is it?'

'Something that belonged to Elen, I'm sure of it.'

It seems to be nothing of import, just a small object, perhaps of metal. Maybe it even fell from the shattered sword remnant when she attacked Bucge. It could be a small fitting, although – and I furrow my brow at the memory – I'm sure it was more rust than iron. Maybe, then, the small object which catches the mellow yellow of the flickering brand is something else, something she prized. 'Are you sure?'

'No, but I suspect, and I'll keep it until I encounter her again and end her life.'

I nod, and don't deny the rage thrumming through her voice. I respect Bucge. I won't say I doubt she can beat Elen's warriors. But, with our aid, Bucge will have her vengeance.

'Come on. I'm bloody starving,' she calls, and quickly we retrace our steps, the sound of the river receding behind us, while the drumming of the rain intensifies. My clothes are sodden, my hair dripping, and like Bucge, I'm hungry. The smell of damp dog floods my senses. But of course, nothing is ever simple. The sound of raised voices has me once more reaching for my seax, while Freki growls again, but I'm too late.

Bucge and I have been hunted, and cold blades at our throats assure me these people mean to seek their vengeance against us. Whoever they are.

5

MEDDI OF THE EORLINGAS

Sian calls to me through my open doorway. I've flung it wide open despite the drumming rain falling without cease. In all honesty, I'm tempted to stand in the rain and allow it to wash away my grief, but I know better than to do so.

'What is it?' I reply, lifting my voice above the sound of the pounding rain.

'The Færpingas settlement burns.' I stand aside from what I'm doing and, swirling my cloak around my shoulders, I step into the deluge.

'It must be a mighty fire if it burns so brightly in this weather it can be seen from here?' I murmur in surprise. She doesn't reply. There's no need. With weather such as this, I would expect everyone to be indoors, but that's not what's happening. Indeed, I'm about the last to be informed, as I hurry towards the gated enclosure and up onto the built-up rampart. I suspect every member of the Eorlingas is standing, turned towards the east, to where black smoke rises menacingly into the dank air. It's as though it's a cloud made of ash, not rain, oscillating close to the ground. Perhaps it doesn't rain there. Or maybe my brother has poured oil onto everything, determined to make the flames catch, despite the weather.

No one speaks. No one even comments about the heavy rain falling without cease. Instead, as we did with the funeral pyre for my mother, and the brave warriors of the Eorlingas and the Husmeræ, we stand and keep a watch until at some point late in the afternoon the torrent ceases, and the low-lying cloud begins to rise higher. It's only when a thunder of hooves draws our attention, I appreciate my brother has returned to Villa Eorlingas, abandoning the Færpingas settlement to burn in his absence.

He and his warriors, alongside those of the Husmeræ led by Padern, ride through the enclosure entrance. They show no surprise at seeing our guard. They have three spare horses with them. All three are laden with whatever they've taken from our friends-turned-enemies.

'The warriors are all dead, not that there were many left behind,' Madog informs everyone confidently from atop his mount. 'We've news to share of why they attacked us. The surviving women have requested sanctuary amongst the Stoppingas.' I grimace at this, but understand it. They must have heard of how Ladus and her women survive without the men to cause problems, including being swayed by an errant seeress.

'That will be for Ladus to decide,' I announce.

Madog nods, before dismounting. I see a brief wince on his face at the movement, and my eyes sweep him from head to toe, but he seems well enough.

'Come, we've much to talk about,' he announces, even while the other warriors are greeted by their families, and those of the Husmeræ joke amongst themselves at a task accomplished well and treasures stolen away.

Quickly, I follow Madog's great strides towards the interior of Villa Eorlingas. I momentarily pause at the entranceway, allowing my feet to absorb the familiar feel of the coloured stones beneath them. Then I hurry to catch Madog. He's pacing within the main room of the villa, the painted walls dulled by the greyness of the rain-soaked day.

'Tell me,' I demand. He shakes his head angrily, before coming to an abrupt stop in front of me.

'The women knew little, other than their leader had been promised great wealth once our mother was dead.'

'So, it was a specific attack on Marchell?'

He nods, lips twisted with fury. 'It was, yes. I also believe you were a target, if not me.'

'And it was Elen who gave the instruction?'

'It must have been. The woman said their leader had been to Verulamium to trade recently, and came back imbued with some secret he'd only discuss with his warriors. This must be what the secret was. The bloody bastard.'

I'm shaking my head, as angry as Madog. 'So even from such a distance, she imperilled us and enacted her commands, while she waits, days' travel from here, for her orders to be completed?'

'Yes. We must send to Verulamium for answers.'

'No.' My response tumbles from my mouth without thought. Then I consider what I've said, while Madog's eyes blaze with fury for my rejection of his idea. 'No. Elen has shown herself to be more powerful than even I believed. We mustn't seek her out. Not yet. We need more warriors. More blades. More everything.'

'It'll allow her time to build a greater following of her own if we don't react immediately.'

I pause, considering his argument, testing it to determine if he's correct to remain resolved to hunting her down straight away. 'Will it? She gave her commands to the Færpingas when they visited her. There are no instructions to any others. News will travel of what happened here, and others will be even less keen to follow her orders. There's already the example of the Stoppingas to stop foolish men from doing as she dictates. When more hear of our vengeance against the Færpingas, they'll realise even acting out Elen's directives far from their homes will not keep them safe.'

'Will it? We've much wealth now, and people are greedy for knowledge they didn't earn and for the treasures others have collected.'

'But we have many, many blades, sharp enough to kill with a single stab wound. Did the Færpingas benefit from the same weapons we had? I don't believe they did.' Now Madog's face clears, thoughts no doubt tumbling through his mind. He's been angry, furious, wrathful, but he's an intelligent man. Anger will only get him so far.

He offers a wry smile. 'You're most wise, seeress.'

The use of my title pleases me. I stand a little taller. I've vowed to be more astute, and aware of the forces swirling around us. Am I already doing so?

'Then what do you suggest?'

'We need more warriors, more allies and even more blades forged by Terricus. Elen might have no one at her side, although she must have won someone's aid, or she'd be dead, as we believed her to be.'

'Do you think she's blessed by the gods?'

'Not at all. I believe she's stubborn, and defiant, as all are in our family.' I offer him a respectful incline of my head. He nods in agreement, lips twitching beneath his drooping moustache.

'The Husmeræ are our allies already, and the Stoppingas.'

'Yes, they are. We'll need more. There are many tribes between here and Verulamium. We must come together. We'll triumph against whatever it is Elen hopes to achieve. We can win them to our cause with the promise of sharp blades.'

'She may get to them first.'

'She may. How long, though, until she learns of the failure of her scheme? Until others do? Winter's almost upon us. People will not be travelling as far from home.'

A flash of unease on Madog's face has me glaring at him.

'What?'

'I fear someone may already be on their way to Elen. A youth, little more than a boy, I didn't demand we stopped him when he tried to escape. He was the son of one of the warriors.'

I breathe deeply, driving my spurt of anger away. 'It's done. It can't be undone. We'd never find him, not now. Anyway, he might not survive. It's many days' walk to Verulamium, through all those tribal areas. I take it he had no horse.'

'No, no horse. Just his legs.'

'Then we'll have to hope he doesn't make it to Elen before the weather becomes too difficult to travel, but let us assume he does. I don't believe Elen will come this way, immediately. We have until the better weather, I'm confident of that.'

'And in that time?'

'We seek new allies, and make good on what we already have. Ladus suggests she has more of the horse objects that helped Terricus produce such fine blades. She will share them with us, and Terricus can make more blades, to entice allies to our cause. And to make our enemies fear us more.'

'Then that's what will be done. Elen will face our wrath and atone for her actions. Her death must follow.'

'And it will. Remember what we have. We have Terricus, and our blades, and the might of the Eorlingas. We're not the same people Edern once overran. We've learned much, and we'll always survive. We'll ensure Elen's resolve to overwhelm and destroy us comes to nothing.'

He grunts, and turns aside, but I don't miss his wince.

'What have you done?' I question, concerned for his well-being.

'Bruises, nothing more,' he concludes, but my eyes narrow.

'Show me,' and so he does. I concede, it is little more than bruises along the base of his spine and his left leg, but they're painful, all the same. 'Tonight,' I inform him, with a sympathetic wince as he covers his green and black skin. 'We'll send Marchell to the afterlife.' He nods, face clouded with grief. The exertions of taking his vengeance against a feeble enemy aren't enough to stop him sorrowing for the only mother he ever knew.

'It'll be done with all honour,' he states, before pulling a disgusted face. 'The enemy dead aren't a pleasant sight.' I swallow my nausea at the thought of the suppurating flesh outside Villa Eorlingas.

'It's all they deserve.' I harden my resolve, knowing what it is he wishes to do. 'It's how our enemies are treated. Think of what was done to our father.' His fierce gaze meets mine, and he shrugs, accepting my will.

'I only hope we don't encourage the wolves closer. I don't wish to fight such beasts even with our better blades.'

'They'll stay away,' I announce staunchly, although I can't guarantee that.

'Seeress,' he concedes, but he does so with a smile. He doesn't believe me, but the dead must be left as they are. Only those of our people and those of the dead Husmeræ are to be accorded great respect. Not the Færpingas. Never them.

6

WÆRMUND OF THE GYRWE

A strangled cry erupts from my mouth, even as my blade is taken from my hand by one of the enemy.

I eye the man before me. In the shadowed half-light beneath the spreading boughs of the trees, I see he's not a warrior. He's slight. Yet they've overwhelmed us because we dropped our guard. Even Freki didn't know to alert me until it was too late. What sort of *comitatus* are we?

A gabble of voices, and I feel a knee in my back as I'm forced forwards. I catch sight of Bucge. Like me, she stands with a blade at her throat, and a fiery glow in her eyes, burning me with its intensity. A yelp, and I hear my wolfhound rushing through the undergrowth. He means to escape. I don't blame him.

I can't believe this. As we step into the scant remaining daylight, free from the trees, my eyes are everywhere. How have we been overwhelmed? There are more of us than there used to be when we last came this way. With Dewi and his warriors, we now number ten, not including my wolfhound. We should have triumphed.

Voices call one to another, using words I don't understand.

My eyes tell me everything I need to see. The fire smokes, something's fallen into it, but I don't believe it's one of my warriors. Instead, all of them – Heafoc, Dewi and his three allies: Osfyth, Maggenræd and Eastmund – lie on the ground, hands being bound behind them, even as they endeavour to fight free. But our enemy, whoever they are, have taken our blades. I'm menaced with the finest blade I've ever seen, or owned.

'Why didn't you fight?' I roar to my warriors, only for dazed eyes to look my way. Heafoc bleeds heavily from his forehead, blood running down his nose to trickle into his mouth. Osfyth fixes me with an angry glare, which assures me they did fight.

A smack to the side of my head with the hilt of my own seax has me wishing the blade at my throat wasn't there. I feel the sharp burn of a slicing cut, even as the man who holds me captive grumbles to the one who hit me. I don't understand the words. I suspect the one berates the other.

'They came out of the woodlands,' Eastmund roars, only to be clobbered on the head with one of our shields. His head slumps forward and he's silent. I step forward instinctively, only to stop. The blade bites once more into the skin around my neck.

The horses are being saddled by our enemy. I look to my beast, sensing some unease, but the animal doesn't try and skip out of the way.

'By Woden,' I growl, angry almost beyond coherence. How has this happened?

I'm forced close to Heafoc. My hands yanked behind my back, the blade moved just in time because I feel a boot on my arse, and tumble forwards, landing so the air's knocked from my body. I've no means to stop the fall with my hands tied.

The smell of grass tickles my nose as I cough and try to inhale, twisting and turning angrily, but now one of our enemies sits on my back, pulling my hands to twist them uncomfortably tightly. I grimace, and meet the resigned eyes of Heafoc.

'Leave it,' he cautions me. 'We'll get another chance. But not yet.' He's the next to receive another strike to the side of his head from a seax hilt. The blow has his head thumping to the ground. He's still. Only when I realise he's still breathing do I stop wriggling closer to him.

I take a deep breath and endeavour to heed his words. These aren't the men who once owed allegiance to Isarninus. Neither are they men who pledged themselves to my father, for they speak the wrong tongue, and wear their hair entirely different. They've no horses either, as shown because one of our beasts is far from happy at the smell of shed blood. He bucks the damn fool who tries to mount him.

Who they are, I don't know. But it seems they know who we are. Suspicions begin to form in my mind.

'Uriconium,' I shout, just to see what they do. Every eye looks my way. They reveal fear. I absorb that.

These people have managed to overwhelm us, somehow. It's embarrassing. But they're clearly not warriors, or at least not very skilled ones. We'll win free from them, as Heafoc said. We just need to await our chance.

Not that Bucge seems as keen to acquiesce to the demands of our captors.

'Untie me, you bastard,' she roars. I peer upwards, the grass continuing to tickle my nose now my breathing's been restored. She's doing her best to evade the enemy. Somehow, she's escaped from the blade held at her throat, but now three of our foes surround her. She has only fists and feet with which to defend herself, although Freki's returned. I hear his snarling from nearby. She only needs a chance and, I'm convinced, the beast will risk his life to free her.

I don't believe it'll be enough, however, and I don't intend to lose either of them.

'Bucge, stop it,' I huff, but my breath still hasn't recovered enough for the sound to reach her. I wince as she punches one of our enemy. The man folds to the ground, almost as I did. Another roars something I don't understand, but which becomes very obvious as he flings himself at Bucge. She goes down in a tangle of fists and legs, but she's still fighting.

I wish I'd manage to escape as she evidently did. Then I could aid her. A boot in my face assures me those who keep guard don't appreciate my involvement, even though I'm trying to help them.

Bucge surges up on her hands and knees, her attacker below her, and now she rains fists down onto them. Blood flies into the air.

'Bucge, you'll kill him,' I shout, this time able to get more volume. If she hears me, there's no let-up in her frenzied attack.

The man next to me hurries to aid his ally. I turn from side to side and realise there's no one keeping watch on me. Tensing every part of my body, I roll onto my back, and then rock myself to my feet. I sway slightly when I'm standing, sweat beading down my face as I taste nausea. What should I do now? Everyone's focused on Bucge. She fights like a vixen. I need a blade to release my hands. Then I can free the rest of my warriors. I'm not alone, Eastmund's also managed to get to his knees. He turns towards me, a question on his lips I don't know the answer to.

My hands are too tightly bound to be able to work at the knots. I look towards the unhappy horse. Immediately, I know what I need to do. The foeman trying to mount is back on his feet but he's not looking my way. If anything, his determination to exert control over the horse has made him ignorant that he and his warriors are under attack.

I stagger towards him, almost losing my balance in a smear of horse shit, but just regain my feet in time, legs tensing uncomfortably, and jarring my back. I knock him aside with my body, jolting every part of my stomach. He falls with a cry of outrage. Discarded on the ground is a seax. I bend low, scoop it into my bound hand with some difficulty, and turn, just in time to see Eastmund's following me. He comes towards me. I turn my back towards him, and feel for the knots. If one of us can get free, the rest of us will be released as well.

'Be bloody careful,' he growls, as I smell blood and realise I've cut him. Below us, the downed man's staggering upright. I kick him, while Eastmund yelps.

'Sorry,' I huff, mindful time's short. If Bucge's overwhelmed, they'll come for us as well. At last I sense the hempen rope give way. Eastmund turns to take the knife from me and carefully cut my bindings. I grimace as my hands come loose, unsure what to do first. 'Free the others,' I decide, aware blood dribbles onto the seax. I bend low, and punch my enemy in the face. He deflates, as I surge into the saddle of the unhappy horse who belongs to Heafoc. I direct the beast towards where Bucge still battles our enemy. I can't see her amongst the welter of feet and punches, and neither can Freki, although the beast is moving closer. He just needs a chance to strike. I shake my head, astounded Bucge's managed to hold off all seven of them, even while I'm still angered my fellow warriors were unable to do it themselves.

The animal takes my commands easily, and surges into our foes, one unfortunate crumpling beneath the horse's hooves. I forge a path to Bucge's side. I don't have a blade, but Bucge's managed to take one and now she darts forward and backwards, using me and the horse to shield her as she raises welts and bruises on our feeble enemy. Her nose bleeds, her lip as well. I think a tooth or two dangles from her open mouth.

I dismount quickly, and scoop a blade from a motionless

hand, and join her in combatting our adversaries. The first man I face gasps with horror, thrusting his hands before him as my seax blow comes closer. The blade slides between his hands, and only stops short of entering his open mouth because he thrusts it aside, blood streaming from both hands. His cheek bleeds as well.

I hear the angry cries of my fellow warriors, and the shrieks of the enemy. It seems we will overpower another force, here, in the same place we've already killed foes who thought to over-whelm us. I don't spare a thought for who they are. They simply need to die. Chest heaving, I thrust the blade against the same man, and he endeavours to skip aside, only to tangle his feet in the juddering legs of a man dying from a slit throat. He slams to the ground. My blade follows him down, but Freki's there, jaws clamping around my enemy's leg.

I realise Dewi's before me, standing between me and the man I wish to kill. He's talking quickly, in one of the other tongues he knows.

'Stop, Wærmund. Stop. These are the men of the Tomsæte, they foolishly thought to have vengeance against you for killing their leader here, earlier in the season, but they've changed their minds. Now. I've heard of them.'

'So?' I pant, desperate to kill the bastard who made a fool of my *comitatus*.

'They've need of a *comitatus*, like yours. They can pay. And as you can see, they're not the most skilled at fighting, even if they're stealthy.'

'What?' But I stand back, blade in hand, my eyes scouring from the cowering man to Dewi. He has a blackening eye, puffy, and swelling shut, even as I watch. 'Here,' I snap to Freki, who releases his grip slowly, as though testing my resolve. 'What?' I repeat, aware all of my warriors, aside from Heafoc, who's still on the ground, are free.

'They need your help to fight an enemy who thinks to overwhelm them after you killed their warriors earlier in the year. You killed the leader of the Tomsæte, here. That was who you burned. That was who Elen allowed to attack you.'

'Why would we do that?' I growl, thinking quickly and deciding there's nothing to be gained from such an arrangement. Better to kill them all.

'They're very wealthy.' Dewi's asked the man on the ground, and he gabbles quickly in reply.

'If they're so damn wealthy, why don't they have better warriors?' I shout.

'Their leader was an arrogant arse. He thought he'd never be defeated. You fatally showed him the error of his ways.'

'So you know these people?' Quickly, I retract my blade and, chest heaving, I address Dewi, while Freki comes to my side.

'I've heard of the Tomsæte, yes. They're a prosperous tribe. They've suffered from an unwise, if honourable leader.'

'Why do you say that?'

Dewi fixes me with astute eyes, and a slight curve to his lips. 'They came to defend their allies from an attack by yourselves. The people from the villa you so recently offered retribution.'

'Ah,' I huff, realising some of these men can live after all. 'Everyone, leave them. Gather our blades, and aid those who might be wounded. Osfyth, check on Heafoc.' But at my words, Heafoc lets out an almighty groan and starts to work his way upright. His eyes lack focus, and so he remains on his knees. 'Who are their enemy?'

'A tribe to the east of them. They think to take their riches for themselves.'

'Are they good warriors?' I direct towards the man on the

ground, who's only just lowering his hands from protecting his face, although his leg bleeds copiously from where it was bitten. He replies quickly to Dewi's question, and Dewi listens attentively.

'They lack the blades you do. There are, however, many more of them.'

'How many more?'

'Double your numbers. So, twenty.'

For a moment, I pause. My intention was to return to Uriconium and attract more warriors to my cause. But, perhaps, this might be better. These men have shown themselves to be clever and devious, if lacking the overall ability to keep us as their prisoners. I could use warriors like that. I might, therefore, be able to entice one or two of them to my cause, and at the same time, fight against these other enemy and be paid to do it. Having the funds to make our stay more welcoming within Uriconium would be good.

I look to Bucge, who breathes heavily, and occasionally kicks one of the foemen on the ground whenever he stirs.

'What do you think?' I question her, for of us all, she's fought them the most.

'They have potential,' she grudgingly admits.

'We'll go with them, and see if they truly have the wealth they state they do,' I decide quickly. My breathing's almost returned to normal, but my shoulders remain tight, and my knees ache from where I first crashed to the floor. My neck's pulsing, although it no longer bleeds.

Dewi describes what's happening to those we fought, and those who are able stand and eye us pensively.

'Explain to them their allies attacked us and we beat them in a fair fight. Tell them, we've offered the original settlement recompense and they took it.' I sense some of these people don't wish to forge an alliance with us, but now I watch them, I appreciate they lack all forms of protection. Indeed, some of them look footsore, their feet encased in sheep's wool. Have they been looking for us since the summer? It seems possible, I suppose.

I stride towards Heafoc, and offer him my hand. He takes it willingly, and staggers upright, assessing the enemy, and our own forces.

'Bollocks,' he exclaims, running his hand over the back of his head, wincing as he does so. I want to question how the enemy managed to overwhelm the rest of the *comitatus* so easily, but I don't believe that's the most important question. Not now.

'Come, fine warriors. We'll see what the Tomsæte have to offer us. If they're as poor in wealth as they are in fighting men, we'll kill them all and make our way to Uriconium.' I'm not at all surprised Dewi doesn't translate those words. I doubt I'd want to hear such a threat when I'd been so roundly defeated either. A yip from Freki, and I take it I have his agreement as well.

7

MEDDI OF THE EORLINGAS

The night's dark and the brands and fires only drive so much of it back, and only for a short time. I'm pleased the steady downpour has finally come to an end. I'm busy with my rites, finding it strange to be performing them alone. In the past, I've always had Marchell to ensure I fulfilled the requirements correctly. Now I must perform the rights for her. I hope I manage to do so.

With my face whitened and my breastplate and ancestral torque in place, I walk reverentially towards the grass mound where my father's essence is interred, as is that of our ancestors. My hair's been darkened. My face shines as the brightest thing, even more easily visible than the flames of the fires.

There's not even a gentle breeze. Instead, the night's still, as though in expectancy for what will happen here.

My father's remains were entombed upon a ceremonial shield. My mother, as a seeress, will be placed into the hallowed space already prepared with the symbols of her profession. She had her own spangles and talismans. It's only right they rest with her in eternal slumber. I've already placed her fine cloak within the hollow, alongside other items she'll need in the afterlife, not just grains and wine, but three small pouches containing her favourite herbal remedies for easing birthing pangs, relieving bruising and for making the transition between life and death easier for those old beyond their time.

The men and women of the Eorlingas stand silent witnesses. There have been fresh tears, but now even Sian waits, shoulders back, defiance on her face. I don't ask her to assist me. She's not a seeress, but I'll need to find someone new to begin training. The Eorlingas must have a seeress. Sian's too old, older than me. I fear Madog's daughter is far too young for me to wait for her to come of age to aid me. Neither do I believe Rhiann, my brother's wife, wishes to take up the position. I never wished to be a seeress either. Until... well, until I did.

But those are concerns for another time. Tonight, I remember my mother, and all she did for the Eorlingas. I've mourned her, and watched her earthly remains turned to ash in the funeral pyre. Now they'll finish their journey.

I raise my voice, summoning my ancestors and horse-god to this place, hopeful once more my horse-god will walk at my side, and in doing so, honour my mother. I stare around me, looking up at the starlit sky, devoid of all clouds, the rain chased away, perhaps by my horse-god, and focus on the path ahead. The way's been lit for me. I needn't fear not being able to see what must be done.

In my hand, I carry the remains of my mother in a precious and rare pottery jug. I know she loved this jug, with its decoration of a fearless woman riding a wild horse. It will now be hers forever. Above those remains, I've added a collection of loose tiles from our horse mosaic. I don't wish her to forget she's one of the horse people of the Eorlingas.

As I come closer and closer to the barrow, I hear the death song of our people, led not by the men, but by the women, who honour my mother with their ululations. The men add a deeper timbre to the song.

Tears sheet from my eyes as I lower the remains of my mother into the barrow, not far from where my father also lies. My arms ache with the weight of the jug, although it wasn't heavy when I began my steps towards this destination. Around me, I sense the presence of my ancestors, and all who've gone before us, but I don't see my mother, or my father, which saddens me. I sense the rage from those who are in attendance for what happened to my mother.

With steady hands, I place the jug into the waiting hole and bow my head low. The words I mutter invoke my horse-god. I vow to seek vengeance for my mother's death. While the sky above my head is cloudless, with no hint of rain, I hear a solitary answering crack of thunder. Startled, I look up, as the sky mourns for my mother just as I do.

Immediately drenched in the unexpected deluge, I turn and face the people of the Eorlingas, the Husmeræ amongst them. Our allies have bled for us, and vowed to fight at our side. In every single person's eyes, even young Maccus, my nephew, I see they understand we've been answered by our horse-god and ancestors.

We'll seek vengeance against Elen. In doing so, we'll have the might of our god to accomplish it.

With firm steps, I stride within the villa building, to where we'll drink to the memory of my mother, Marchell of the Eorlingas. She accomplished much in her long life. I'll ensure her legacy continues and none forget all she did for us. When Edern took Villa Eorlingas, she kept the survivors together. When Madog's mother died, she kept him nourished and ensured he thrived. When Edern took all from me, she healed me, and endured my silent fury for almost two decades. Her death has united the Eorlingas once more. Her life ensured the Eorlingas survived. Her death will ensure we thrive.

* * *

The Husmeræ leave us. There are no firm plans. Not yet. We must survive the coming dark time of winter, and then return to our endeavours to end Elen's life. Padern's a wise man and he, like me, cautions my brother to wait.

But waiting has never been Madog's strength.

'Train the warriors,' I inform him on a cool day, some weeks later. The bite of winter is in the air. The animals have been culled and the meat salted or smoked. The horses have been brought into the close paddock, with a building to shelter them from the coming snows. Even Terricus has taken to wearing a long tunic as he makes use of the supplies Ladus has sent to us. True to her word, she too possessed some of the small horse-shaped objects similar to the one Urien gave to me at the beginning of the previous summer. They are the same. They enable Terricus to continue apace.

'We are trained,' is his snapped reply.

'No. You can never be trained enough. You must always practise. My skills as a seeress must be constantly repeated to ensure I don't forget anything important.'

Madog sighs dramatically, but departs to do as I instruct him. Only then do I allow myself to sink to my stool and consider my words. I'm as impatient as Madog, despite my instructions to the contrary. The urge to find Elen claws at me.

I've ordered Madog to be patient. I've agreed with Padern's determination it's the correct action to take, but still, the need overwhelms me. I wake each morning considering how I'll feel when I slit Elen's throat, and the image follows me throughout the day as I check on my horses and tend to the people of the Eorlingas. It's almost the best time of year to be harvesting roots, but my impatience makes even the thought of that task unappealing.

'Mistress.' I turn and smile at Sian. She dips her head and waits outside my open doorway. She's always respectful.

'Sian.' I speak perhaps too gleefully, pleased to be distracted from my thoughts.

'Terricus has fashioned new blades, using the supplies from the Stoppingas. He wished me to inform you he's pleased with the quality. He can continue and produce more blades, but we must arrange for more charcoal to be made.'

I nod, jumping to my feet. I welcome having a task to consume my thoughts. 'I'll speak with Urien and Lord Madog.'

'Very good, mistress.' She bobs again, but doesn't immediately depart. As I emerge from my workshop, I almost collide with her.

'Sorry,' I murmur, but she still doesn't move, instead her eyes stray to the door frame, beneath which she knows my daughter's remain are interred. 'What is it?' I question. She offers me a wary glance and then must decide to tell me what worries her. She sighs heavily.

'I think Hedrek should have his chains removed, mistress. He's proven to be helpful. And skilled.'

I shake my head, dismissing the suggestion without considering it. But Sian hasn't finished.

'Mistress, Terricus is a free man and entirely loyal to the Eorlingas. Hedrek remains unfree, but also loyal. I wouldn't wish his loyalty to be tested by those who fill his head with promises if he should escape from here.'

My forehead furrows. 'There have been no visitors recently. Who would do such as this?'

She offers me another worried look. 'I fear it will happen. I fear he'll do it just because he could. But he's a good man. Remove the temptation and he'll be one of the most loyal of warriors for Lord Madog.'

I open my mouth, and then snap it shut again. I don't know what to make of the suggestion, but better to consider it than dismiss it out of hand. 'I'll speak to Lord Madog,' I confirm, and a small smile plays on her lips. A white-hot rage ignites within, but I immediately douse it. If Hedrek and Sian are friends, or more than friends, it doesn't truly concern me. Maybe they both do deserve to be happy in their final years on this earth before they go to meet their ancestors in the afterlife. Perhaps.

8

WÆRMUND OF THE GYRWE

Conversation between us and the surviving members of the Tomsæte is entirely reliant on Dewi. Unlike Elen, I don't distrust him. The Tomsæte sit with us that night, wary around the hearth fire, but eager enough to take the food we offer, even if they resent those of their friends we've killed. Through Dewi, we learn it was their people we encountered here during the summer, when Elen showed her disloyalty by giving no warning of the approaching attack. Do I grieve for the men we killed? No. They weren't the best warriors. But I do recall the wealth we took from the dead. If these people truly have more of the same, we'll replace all we were forced to abandon within the home of Isarninus, and have yet to reclaim.

That night, I stay awake for much of it, Freki beside me. Eastmund has the first watch, Bucge the second and Heafoc the final one, but they're not alone. The Tomsæte keep a watch too, and when I wake from a brief doze, with the hint of dawn on the horizon, it's to a heated argument between Heafoc and his counterpart amongst the Tomsæte. They both shout at one another, but of course they don't understand what the other says. Bloody fools.

'Shut up,' Eastmund calls angrily, turning in his cloak as though that will stop the debate. Only the sound of blades being pulled from sheaths forces Eastmund upright, lips pulled back from his teeth in a grimace of hatred.

I endeavour to leap upright and thrust myself between the two men, but succeed only in tangling my feet so I fall once more, only just avoiding grazing my chin on the stones surrounding the hearth. If Heafoc sees my elegant tumble, he doesn't show it, his face remaining etched with fury. Freki nuzzles me with his long nose, and I push him aside.

'What is it?' I glower, shaking my head from side to side, and blinking as I lean back on my folded knees to gaze at the pair. The rest of the Tomsæte have also leapt to their feet, and stand to the side of their ally. I must remember their names. 'What is it?' I demand when I get no reply. Heafoc's shouting so loudly his words are incoherent.

Dewi's the one to bring some much-needed order, him and his surviving allies who can speak more than one tongue.

'The Tomsæte fool accuses Heafoc of theft. Heafoc accuses the Tomsæte fool of being an idiot.' I narrow my eyes, looking between the two, and then listening to Dewi speak with the Tomsæte. I'm sure he tells them something different, but his expression gives nothing away.

'What did Heafoc seemingly steal?'

'A seax.'

'But Heafoc has his own seax?' I question, confused.

'He does, yes. The Tomsæte practises trickery. He says he won it in battle against Heafoc.' Gritting my teeth at such a rude awakening, I stride towards the two, this time staying well clear of any bloody trip hazard.

'This?' I point to Heafoc's blade, and the angry Tomsæte nods urgently. I shake my head, and turn to Dewi, in the hope he'll explain what I'm saying. 'This is Heafoc's blade, forged in the fires of our bladesmith. If you want a blade such as this, you must pay us for it. Or take it from Heafoc's corpse.' Heafoc flashes me an ire-filled look for suggesting the Tomsæte could kill him. I shrug my shoulders. It's the way of our people to take the blades from our defeated foes.

The man, named Sennicus, which reminds me of the names of those we met within Uriconium, speaks ever more frantically, as Dewi sighs.

'He says it would have been the case if not for the woman.'

'But the woman, or rather, Bucge, did intervene. So Heafoc was in no risk of being dead,' I debate. 'Tell the damn fool, he'll have to earn such a blade. It's not his by any right.'

Again, Dewi does as I ask. I sense this could go one of two ways. We'll either descend into another bloody fight, which the Tomsæte stand no chance of winning, or the arse will back down. Of course, no warrior likes to back down. The tension between the two sides is almost palpable.

'I'll kill him,' Bucge menaces, as helpfully as a slick cowpat underfoot. I turn to glare at her. She shrugs her shoulders, lacking all contrition.

'Don't tell him that,' I mutter to Dewi, but the other surviving Tomsæte understand her intent well enough. One of them speaks urgently. When Dewi doesn't tell me what the conversation's about, but the other three men stand down, I know one of his own tries to get Sennicus to calm down. This isn't going to end well unless he does. We might have been caught off guard yesterday, but not now.

Eventually, after a protracted debate, Sennicus scowls and steps back, hands to either side, not in defeat and certainly not deferential, but enough to show he won't continue the argument. I exhale a breath I didn't know I was holding.

Osfyth breaks the silence again. 'Are you sure about this?' And I know she's questioning the decision to help the Tomsæte.

'Well, it rather depends on whether we make it to their settlement with any of them alive, doesn't it?' I retort, tired, frustrated and wishing my mouth didn't taste like rust and salt. I've evidently bitten my tongue, and now the blood flows down my throat. It's an unwelcome reminder of how easily all men bleed. I have to hope it won't be our blood being spilt should we make it to the Tomsæte settlement in one piece.

* * *

I'm surprised when we do make it to the Tomsæte village in one piece, aside from the odd exchange of barbed words, having burned the dead. Instead of turning towards the setting sun, and Uriconium, we turn towards the rising sun at a crossing of two roads, and only a day later arrive at a settlement very similar to that which we attacked, and to whom we've made recent retribution. Smoke clouds the sky directly overhead, with the heady aroma of hot food and fresh bread.

Not that we're allowed within the village, seemingly sited between two wide flowing rivers, and with a small ditch enclosing it. It's not a hill-fort settlement, which assures me we won't be fighting either up or down a steep slope when we have to defend it. This, I believe, is what we need to do to win our payment.

'It stinks,' Eastmund mutters. Of us all, he remains the most uneasy about the plans to aid the Tomsæte. His ill-humour increases even as his bruises and cut hand heal.

'So do you,' Osfyth mumbles in reply. Here, with the settlement before us, unease is once more growing. It's not as though we've cloaked ourselves in martial glory of late. Yes, we triumphed against Isarninus, but we were then beaten back by Elen's new-found allies. What we really need is a mighty victory to earn our name as a warrior band worthy of rewarding with silver.

'They can't be wealthy. Living here.' Eastmund ignores Osfyth's taunt and refuses to be consoled.

'Just because you can't see the treasures on display doesn't mean they're lacking,' I respond, but I do share Eastmund's misgivings. The men we've encountered don't have horses, admittedly, that's because we sold them in Uriconium when we overwhelmed their leader. These men have walked to and from the place we met them. While there are fields that have perhaps grown good crops through the summer months, I see no sign of grazing animals. They implied there was great prosperity. I remain to be convinced of that. Although, well, if we did fight their leader earlier in the summer, he certainly possessed wealth, even if he lacked the ability to defend himself and his allies. 'We wait,' I comment, looking to Dewi to see if he might tell me what Sennicus said before departing within the settlement. I cast a glance behind me. We can leave here if we want to. We'd be able to move far more quickly than the horse-less Tomsæte. Then, we could make it to Uriconium and do what I initially proposed. We need more warriors. There are so few of us now, it's almost embarrassing.

'For how long?' Eastmund continues to complain.

'Until we know their intentions,' Heafoc interjects. Despite the argument between him and Sennicus, he does seem prepared to allow them to show what they have.

I move my horse closer to the settlement, with its ditch and embankment, and narrow my eyes. Freki comes with me, nose to the ground.

'Is that a sign of burning?' I point to where the grass is blackened, the ground beside it, bare of even the smallest of weeds. Heafoc nods.

'So, they have an enemy, that's not a lie.'

'I'm sure they have many enemies,' Heafoc confirms.

Reaching for my seax, I feel comforted with the promise of the blade on the handle I grasp. The Tomsæte have so far revealed nothing of an equal keenness. The blades created by Katourn remain the best I've encountered during my life.

More quickly than I expect, Sennicus returns to us. This time, there are more men and women escorting him than we've encountered so far.

'Who are they?' I demand.

'They're the elders of the settlement,' Dewi offers. 'Sennicus has to get them to agree to his proposal.'

The six men and women are far from being elderly. I appreciate the term is perhaps more to do with their position of respect within the tribe than their age.

'And does he have it?'

'It seems they're keen for you to fight their enemy, yes,' Dewi quickly confirms, but then pauses.

'But?' I demand, aware Eli and Cynin have shared an uneasy look.

'But they're far from convinced of the need to recompense you. They seem to believe you owe it to them for killing their leader and warriors.'

Osfyth's sigh is heartfelt. My eyes travel between Sennicus and those who escort them.

'Then we'll leave.' And I gather the reins to lead my horse

away, but Sennicus shouts my name. 'What?' I'm growing increasingly frustrated by the delay. The weather's turned decidedly cooler during our journey here. Thoughts of the warmth from the bathing house at Uriconium are appealing.

'He offers you shelter throughout the winter in exchange for aiding them.'

'We don't need shelter. We have somewhere to go.' Dewi's quick to repeat this. Sennicus gabbles in return.

'He states wherever you mean to go will cost you valuable coin, which you don't have. Here, it would be all part of the trade.'

'So what?' Eastmund spits angrily. 'We get to risk our lives for them, and in return we get a mattress stuffed with more lice than straw, and some grudgingly provided food?'

I don't stop Dewi repeating this. A flicker of fury touches Sennicus' lips, while the elders also speak amongst themselves, hands raised, voices low or raised, depending on whether they argue for us, or against us, or so I suspect. It feels too much. I must convince my allies to stay here, while Sennicus must win the support of his elders. It would have been easier to slit the Tomsæte's throats close to the woods and have done with it.

Three of the elders surprise me by offering the briefest of smiles. Another gabble of words.

'Sennicus assures that while the Tomsæte settlement may not benefit from every comfort of Uriconium, it certainly doesn't provide its visitors with lice-laden mattresses or poor-quality food. Indeed, they have many cattle, recently slaughtered, and a certain sort of pig that makes for some delicious meals too. He welcomes you to come within and enjoy their hospitality, and then you can decide on the truth of his offer.'

It's hardly a tempting offer, only then it is.

A chill wind springs up, bringing with it a driving rain more hail than water, all blowing directly into our faces. My horse nickers unhappily. Freki emits a feeble howl.

'What harm can it cause?' I turn to face my allies, but none of them reply, hoods covering faces. No doubt, I'm not alone in thinking it best to be indoors than outside in weather such as this.

9

MEDDI OF THE EORLINGAS

For the next few days, I keep a wary eye on Sian and Hedrek, but I detect nothing untoward between them. Yes, they share some jokes and laugh together, but Terricus joins them, as do some of the youths Sian's teaching about the properties of charcoal. Urien and his fellows are busy with their task of producing enough charcoal to allow Terricus to continue his endeavours. Convinced all is well, I take myself to where Madog plays with his young son. The two laugh together, as Madog shows Maccus how to groom the foal, Gwynmarch, Maccus has determined should be his. I smile to see them together. It pleases me to know Maccus is as fond of the horses as I am. It bodes well for the future of the Eorlingas.

'Sister.' My brother notices me quickly, and turns, his lips lifted into a smile. 'Maccus was telling me stories of how he and his horse will be faster than all the others.'

I assess the young animal's build. He has long, thin legs, but moves confidently. He's entirely comfortable with Maccus and Madog so close to him. His mother is perhaps not so keen, but she merely maintains a wary guard, as all mothers must do when their children begin to grow.

'I think you might be correct,' I confirm. 'Although none is as fast as Bronwen.' As though summoned, she trots towards us, intelligent eyes assessing the small group. She stops short of the foal. She knows better than to anger his mother. I walk to her, and run my hand over her long nose. The hay-smell of her is pleasant.

'No,' young Maccus says slowly and with consideration. 'He'll be even faster.' He giggles once more. He's a beguiling child, and shows no fear of me, his aunt, but more importantly, his seeress. Maybe he's too young, or perhaps he simply recognises the family connection.

'I doubt the seeress came to talk about horses.' Madog pushes his son towards Gwynmarch, and assesses me carefully. 'Or perhaps she does,' he concedes, when I offer nothing else.

'Horses are the source of our strength and wealth, alongside the new blades, of course,' I quickly qualify. 'But, young Maccus must know all there is about breeding horses and ensuring they develop a good temperament.' As I speak, I catch sight of my burned hands which are now healing. They've been painful for the last few days, distracting me from other tasks, but at last, they're on the mend. It reminds me I would do anything for these horses.

'They are,' Madog confirms quickly. 'But they can also be fun,' he chides me.

'Yes, they can, provided we're always careful and never reckless.' At my words, Madog lifts Maccus onto Gwynmarch's back. Some might think it foolish when both are so young, but it's the way of our people. Much better for the horses to be used to us from a very young age. Not that Maccus sits there for long, and not that his father releases his hold on him. We're not that fool-ish. 'I did wish to speak to you,' I eventually say, when Maccus is once more on the ground, hurrying to find some oats for his horse to offer as a reward for his calmness.

'We have the charcoal in hand,' Madog quickly interjects.

'It's not about that, well, not directly, anyway. Sian suggests we release Hedrek from his bonds. She says his loyalty will be more greatly gained if we show our trust in him.' Madog's face flashes with fury, his immediate response very similar to mine.

'And you believe the idea is a good one?'

'I believe it may be, yes. I've been watching him. As Sian says, he does seem entirely reconciled to our tribe. His skills are valu-able. We don't wish Elen to have any excuse to turn him to her bidding again.'

'I'll think on it,' Madog confirms. And then his face furrows. 'There's something else, too. I understand Terricus made the remnant of our father's sword into a seax, but I believe I should also have a sword. What do you think?'

'A sword made with the same technique?'

'Yes. As you know, Ladus has provided more of the special ironstone contained within the horse objects for Terricus. I don't think every warrior needs a sword, not when they have seax, and better spear heads these days, but a sword for the leader of the Eorlingas would be a sign of our intentions towards any enemy.'

'It's not a bad idea,' I agree slowly, reminding myself of Maccus' assessment of his horse. 'It would mark you as a warrior of old, like our father was, although with a much sharper blade. It will be up to Terricus to determine if he thinks it possible.'

'It will, yes.' Madog nods eagerly. I see he already imagines himself with a sword on his hip, or wherever it is a sword should be lodged by warrior men. 'Perhaps just for ceremonial purposes?'

'No, if you have a sword it must be deadlier than the seaxes, otherwise it's a waste of precious resources and Terricus' time.'

'You're correct, mistress,' my brother admits, a rueful expression on his face. 'And of course, with it,' and his voice turns darker and filled with menace, 'I can ensure our most lethal enemy meets her death.'

'No,' I retort, surprising myself with the vehemence in my voice. 'No,' I say more softly, and understanding flashes in Madog's eyes. 'It's for me to do, and I'll not argue about it.'

'Of course, seeress.' Madog bows, all amusement fled. In that moment, he reveals himself a man wise beyond the winters he's lived. In that moment, he reminds me that I've forged my brother with the iron resolve of a man who'll ensure the Eorlingas thrive rather than survive. But first, well, first there's the issue of the bitch, Elen, to resolve. While I cautioned patience, I must confess it sits ill with me. The sooner she's gone from this world, the better for us all.

* * *

Hedrek's freed in a quiet moment between Madog and him. I observe it, clad in my seeress' garb so he understands my part in it. He cries soft tears, and some might think it unsightly for a man to cry before his lord, and previous master. I realise it reveals Sian's wisdom in seeking his freedom. Hedrek and I have a long and twisted history. I owe my survival to him. I also owe him my hatred for releasing Elen. I think there's no one else within the Eorlingas, aside from my brother, who despises Elen as much as I do, ever since she abandoned Hedrek on her release. Hedrek will be our firm ally from now on.

'Terricus.' My brother strides towards the bladesmith. A flicker of uncertainty covers his face, quickly banished as my brother explains the new task to him. Hedrek makes his way to my side when he understands Madog won't prolong granting him his freedom, other than he must have his chains removed by Terricus when the two have stopped talking.

'I owe my freedom to you?' Hedrek questions.

'Yes, but also no. To Sian. Tread carefully with her,' I caution him. Sian's witnessed Madog's conversation with Hedrek but has returned to her task of sorting the supplies of charcoal. A flicker of surprise touches Hedrek's lined face at my words.

'I believe she still hates me.'

'Then, Hedrek, after all these winters, you're still unable to understand a woman.' Laughing, I stride back to my workshop. This morning, early, I journeyed to the local woodland in search of herbs and roots. I must begin preparing them. All around me, I'm aware of the busy activity within the villa. Of the youngsters cleaning the muck from the animal paddock, of the cries of fractious babes being consoled by mothers, of the clanging of weapons where Urien trains those who think they can fight for our people, alongside the smell of good food cooking. The wind is far from gentle this day. It carries with it the taint of the sea as it whirls inland, clothing left to dry after being washed swirling in the air, as though people wear the clothing. I allow a smile to touch my cheeks once more, reminded all over again my scars are healed. I consider if I'll ever stop being surprised by that.

I run my hand over the lintel above the door to my workshop and enter its comforting embrace. My mother's essence remains here, but it soothes now, rather than distresses me. Still, it's a rare day I don't hear her in my mind, gentle words telling me of her skills, or admonishments when I make a mistake in preparing the lotions and potions required to keep the people of the Eorlingas hale and well.

I'll never not miss my mother, and my rage for her murder

will only be quenched when Elen has been hunted to her death when the winter is gone, but here, in this space, I hardly feel Marchell's absence at all. She's all around me, and my smile broadens. I might even talk back to her on occasion. I'd dare anyone to question me when I do, I really would.

10

WÆRMUND OF THE GYRWE

The interior of the settlement is pleasant, and we're given good beds, while the horses are housed outside the walls surrounding the dwellings, in a small paddock area that's demarcated by thick, prickly hedges. Freki stays at my side. We don't have much time to enjoy the comfortable surroundings, or the good food we're served on arrival. The following day Sennicus comes to us, face reflecting his uncertainty. I listen to his words, and wait for Dewi to tell me of the problem.

'The enemy have been sighted.' Dewi yawns languidly. 'Sennicus suspects they'll attack today.'

'Remind me again,' I direct to Dewi, 'why the tribes fight?'

I anticipate a quick answer from Sennicus when Dewi relays my question, but it seems to be long and convoluted. Dewi's face twists in thought as he absorbs everything Sennicus tells him. I look to Rhun and Cynin as well. They listen carefully, but show no signs of concern.

'It's little and nothing,' Dewi eventually announces. 'They fight over land and the best cattle and oxen, and steal when they can. At the moment, the enemy sense the weakness of the Tomsæte. That's why they've determined on an attack.'

'And are they good warriors?'

Dewi pauses before conveying the question. His shrug tells me much although, again, Sennicus speaks for some time.

'Then we'll defeat them,' I assert confidently, preparing myself with seax, byrnie, shield and spear, and offering East-mund a kick where he lingers in his bed.

From outside, I hear an increasingly querulous conversation between some of the Tomsæte but pay it no heed. We're not here to talk, but to fight.

Quickly, my warriors and I are armoured and equipped with our battle gear. We stride into the settlement proper. We've gathered a crowd of spectators, amongst them those who were with Sennicus when they almost overpowered us. They wear decent enough equipment, but I know they have blades similar to those we possessed before meeting Katourn within Uriconium. Yes, they could kill their enemy, but it would take a great deal of luck as well as physical prowess.

I allow Sennicus to lead me towards the heavily defended entranceway. The trail of manure on the ground assures me they've brought their previously grazing animals within. Perhaps they even did so before rousing us. I'm pleased to see our horses remain outside in their enclosure. In future, I must be wary of being separated from them.

Sennicus points. Dewi's ever-present at my side, but I don't need him to tell me what the Tomsæte warrior is doing. The enemy draw closer. Slowly, I count them, a stir of anxiety stalking me until I'm convinced the force isn't larger than ours.

They carry something before them. I consider it. I might get something similar to that. I narrow my eyes to try to determine what it is. Is it a dead animal raised on a pole? Bucge's the one to provide the answer.

'It's a depiction of a bear,' she informs me. 'Not a very good one, admittedly.'

'What's it made from?' It's not linen because it remains rigid in the gentle breeze.

'Some sort of metal,' she confirms. She's busy preparing herself. Osfyth's beside her. Indeed, all of my warriors, and those who joined us alongside Dewi, are ready and prepared. We've not so much been offered water or food with the dawn, and we're expected to fight. As though hearing the complaint in my mind, three women step forward carrying bowls of honey-sweetened pottage and offer them to us. I eat quickly, enjoying not having had to cook the food and endure Heafoc's poor attempts at pottage before joining the coming fight.

'There are fifteen of them,' Heafoc informs between mouthfuls. The pottage is hot. There's also water to cool our burning mouths. The food barely fills my grumbling belly but I don't ask for more. I don't wish to feel too full. It would dull my actions. I need to be sharp when I encounter the foes of the Tomsæte.

'And there are ten of us, as well as the warriors of the Tomsæte,' I counter, stretching my neck from side to side. It's been some time since I slept on a soft mattress. I can't say my body's enjoyed it, which surprises me. It just shows, a man shouldn't grow too placid. Not if he means to be a violent and deadly defender of all he holds dear.

Heafoc turns to eye the warriors I mention. Sennicus stands proudly with his blades. Three of the others look a little suspicious. The final member of the Tomsæte is broader than Sennicus and muscled like an ox. I hope that means he can stab effectively with his blunt weapon. I realise it would aid our temporary allies if we shared some of the remaining seaxes from

Katourn with these warriors. I only hope they don't cut themselves with them.

'We have more blades?' I direct to Heafoc under my breath.

'Three,' is his quick reply.

'Then we offer them to those who look like they need them,' I confirm. He grunts, but whether he agrees I'm unsure. He does, however, fulfil my request and quickly Sennicus and two of his allies have the better blades. The man who doesn't benefit from one of our blades looks angry, but the large, ox-like warrior shows no concern. I consider why I've not seen him before. Perhaps he never leaves the settlement, or maybe he's the tribe's protection in the absence of the others. 'Tell them to fight at the end of our shield wall, as you do,' I direct to Dewi. He nods, and assesses Sennicus and the others once more. His eyes remain blank, but I'm unsurprised when Sennicus and one of those with the seaxes are advised to keep Dewi company. The other three, including the large warrior, take to the far side, where Cynin and Rhun mumble under their breaths.

I bend to Freki, and rub my hand over his nose, where he remains at my side. He's rarely far from me. I suspect he doesn't even trust Heafoc to look out for him, which surprises me. I rely on Heafoc above all others.

'Come on then,' I announce to my collection of warriors and allies, striding towards the guarded entranceway, hardly pausing for the gateway to be opened, so I can stomp over the ditch surrounding the enclosure. It could do with being much deeper to dissuade a foe from attacking, I muse, eyes on my feet and not on the coming fight. The enemy, I notice, aren't expecting to meet a force such as the one I command. They wait on the far side of one of the converging rivers, uncertainty revealed in the way the warriors stand too closely together. The foeman who holds the bear-shaped emblem, much easier to detect now I'm closer, also wears a shimmering helm of copper. I can't imagine it will do much to protect his head from our blades, but he certainly looks the part with his battered breastplate, and some contraptions on his lower legs. If his knees weren't knocking together in fright, I might be worried.

I run my gaze over my horses, pleased they're all still there, and haven't been stolen away in the night. In future. I'll need to remember to keep them close. I bend to Freki, and point.

'Stay here,' I urge him, not wanting him in the heart of this battle. He, I fear, isn't a warrior. A whine, and the animal slinks away, tail between his legs. 'Is there a way to cross?' I direct to Dewi.

Sennicus' words only just reach my ears, for he speaks in a low voice.

'The water's running shallow,' Dewi replies quickly. 'It's easiest to surge across the river than seek the bridge, which would allow our foes to anticipate our arrival more easily.'

'Do the enemy know that?' I counter. I feel foolish standing here, facing a terrified opponent who've purposefully placed a river between us.

'No,' Dewi offers the single-word answer.

'They don't intend to fight,' Heafoc quickly surmises. 'Or at least, they didn't,' he counters. I nod. The enemy might be fearful of us, but they're making up for it by shouting what I assume must be insults, showing their naked arses, and generally acting like warriors who appreciate we can't get to them anytime soon. This seems ridiculous. I flick a glance along my row of warriors, grateful they look the part, and while I've no experience of these members of the Tomsæte, aside from when they temporarily overwhelmed us, I suspect they can fight well.

'Well,' I huff through tight lips. 'Let's get this over and done with. Advance,' I call, my voice so loud I see Heafoc wince at my side. I offer him a grin. He replies with a grimace, and as one, we rush towards the gentle incline of the riverbank, and as the cold water rushes around my ankles, I detect the taunting cries of our foes turn to ones of fear, and some of them must hurry to cover their naked arses. From within the settlement of the Tomsæte I hear shouts and cheers, but the battle hasn't even begun yet. We still need to end their lives and in that way the reputation of my *comitatus* will grow and flourish.

As the cold water reaches my crotch, I consider whether this was really the best way of setting us on the path to victory, but there's no time for recriminations. We must overwhelm the enemy.

I surge up the steeper riverbank on the far side, water dripping from my trews, my feet squelching within my boots, and wish we had used the bloody bridge to keep my feet dry.

'Shield wall,' I bellow. I feel the shields of my allies being slid into place along the fifteen-warrior-long wooden fence, and allow a wolf-grin to touch my cheeks, reminded of my wolfhound, to the other side of the river, awaiting my return. As though summoning Freki, a haunting howl ripples the air, even as the banner man of our opponents emits a shriek and dashes back amongst his fellow warriors. 'Advance, my brave warriors,' I shout. We surge into the enemy, our steps fluid and fast-paced. It takes only a moment, as we press against their weaker shield wall. I appreciate the fighting might be bloody and not without risk, but they're no match for the *comitatus* of Wærmund, the wolf-lord.

* * *

Bruised, but not bloodied, I walk the slaughter field when the enemy are all dead. I seek the bear banner. I'm curious about it.

Perhaps I could have Katourn make us something similar, only with a wolf emblem, not a bear.

Sennicus limps at my side. He speaks quickly, so quickly Dewi struggles to decipher the words, but I understand easily enough. He's pleased with the result, jangling with the joy of such a victory. He hardly seems to notice two of his fellow warriors are dead. Not the large man. He's slumped though, blood sheeting from a wound on his upper arm. No, the two dead men are, surprisingly, those who were gifted the better blades. The one with the dull blade yet lives, his face shining with triumph. In that, I made a mistake. I'll learn from this. A sharp blade doesn't make up for lack of skill in the shield wall.

'Ah,' I cry with delight, finding the metal object wedged under one of the dead. I kick the man to roll him out of the way. I grimace at the shocking state of his throat, his head almost coming clean off. I didn't do that to him. I suspect the work of the larger warrior.

Bending, I lift the metal frame, or at least what remains of it.

'By Woden,' I mutter, disappointed at finding it so battered. I test the structure with my fingers and quickly realise why. The metal's thinned with age. Still, it gives me an idea of what I want. I feel it would be better to take this to Katourn rather than try to explain it. Sennicus, it appears, has other ideas. He attempts to snatch it from my hands eagerly. I resist him. 'Dewi, tell the bloody fool this is mine.'

'Ah,' Dewi comments. 'I recall now there was something about this in the story he told of why the two tribes hate one another.'

'What?' I glower at him. My body's starting to cool after my exertions, and I still need to return over the river, which means my damp legs will become wet again.

'This is some ancient relic. It belongs to the Tomsæte, or it did. Or something. Their leader gave it away, or lost it in a wager, I can't remember all the details. It was a long and complicated tale.'

'But I want it. No, I need it. My *comitatus* must have such as this.'

'That might prove problematic,' Dewi continues. 'He really was quite insistent.'

'Fine,' I huff with a grimace. I don't want to start another fight over a piece of metal that's certainly seen better days. But I do want something similar. Osfyth and Bucge are making short work of taking all the treasures these dead men had. Not that their treasures are particularly inspiring. Some of the shields are worth keeping. The blades can be melted down and made into something more useful. The breastplates they wore are mostly dented or filled with holes now.

From across the river, I see the people of the Tomsæte have erupted from their settlement and watch us. If that's all of them, the tribe isn't large, perhaps similar in size to that of the Gyrwe, and nothing compared to the vast number we encountered living within Uriconium.

'Is that all of them?' I ask Dewi.

'No idea,' he murmurs, bending to pick up something shimmering from the ground. He turns the rounded object over on his hand, and shows it to me. It's as dull as all the other metal on display, but I recognise it quickly enough. I've learned about these in my time away from the land of my birth.

'It's a coin.'

'An old one, yes,' Dewi agrees. 'He must have worn it as a talisman.' I look where he points. A hole's been punched through the metal and the rough edges smoothed away. I can't tell how it's fallen from whatever it was attached to. It wasn't yanked. Perhaps it came from the mostly headless corpse.

'Come on. There's not much here,' Eastmund calls in an aggrieved tone. 'I'd welcome a fire to dry my wet clothes.'

'Is that really it?' I question Dewi. 'Is this the total of the enemy they wanted us to fight for them?' He relays the question, as we make our way back towards the river. I've no intention of tending to the corpses. The carrion creatures are welcome to them.

'It's one thing to face an enemy with skilled warriors, and another to do it when your leader is dead, and your best men alongside him.'

'Ah, yes,' I murmur, reminded we killed the leader of these people. It seems bizarre to me they welcomed us so warmly and that we've faced no recriminations for those we killed on meeting a few days ago. Ahead, I hear a howl from my wolfhound, and narrow my eyes, turning angrily to Sennicus. 'What by Woden is this?' The people of the Tomsæte have retreated within as we've recrossed the river. The clatter of the gate being closed grabs the attention of all of us, as does Freki's distressed cry and the nicker of our horses from where they're still enclosed outside the settlement's ditch.

'Ah,' Dewi mutters. 'I feared this,' he complains, and speaks rapidly to Sennicus. Sennicus' shock, I'm sure, isn't feigned. 'I believe they've no intention of allowing you to over winter within their settlement, after all,' Dewi suggests.

'By Woden's cock,' Eastmund grumbles. I share a strained look with Heafoc. We were, evidently, far too trusting of the agreement. A thousand thoughts rush through my mind. Most of them concerned with firing the settlement and killing the ungrateful bastards, but actually, my intention was to go to Uriconium for the winter and find some decent warriors to join my *comitatus*.

Sennicus' face has blanched, and he's rushed towards the

gate, shouting angrily. The large warrior looks aggrieved, but it's Osfyth who speaks what we must all be thinking.

'I didn't like the place anyway, or the people,' and without rushing, she goes to her horse, and mounts, turning the animal back towards the road that will take us to Uriconium.

'Arseholes,' Eastmund mutters, and I realise I should be grateful they didn't think to take our horses or Freki. But then, they've seen how we fight. They've taken a chance we'll accept what we came here with, as opposed to taking it from us. I find it's not a bad bargain, after all.

'Ask them if they want to come with us?' I direct to Dewi. The answer isn't long in coming, and quickly Sennicus, face still furious, is mounted on one of the spare horses, as is the large warrior. We might have a few nicks and cuts to show for our fight, and little else, but we do have two good warriors to add to our number. The third man's welcome to stay with his people. But he's not to keep the blade taken from one of his dead allies.

Turning my horse, I canter towards him where he stands, head turning from us to his gated home. I take the blade hanging loosely in his hand, and for good measure, offer him a kick in the stomach from my perch.

'Ungrateful bastards,' I mutter, thrusting the metal bear-like contraption towards him. I find I don't want it. Indeed, I'm pleased to be leaving this place. It reminds me too much of my former home. I really do look forward to enjoying a hot bath at Uriconium and seeing Gildas and Diseta again. And I have a task for Katourn to perform. If he will.

11

MEDDI OF THE EORLINGAS

'Seeress, there's news.' I turn from my task, and meet Madog's worried eyes with surprise. Outside, frost coats the land and I wear two cloaks within my workshop, as well as having a hearth fire burning merrily.

'From who?' I glower, standing upright and releasing the tension in my shoulders from my long work. 'I've heard no one approach.'

'Urien met traders on the road to Corinium. He says they've heard Elen has found a *comitatus* to fight at her side.'

'Who?'

'A warrior band. From the east.'

I lower my sharp knife, and wipe my hands on a cloth, before striding to meet him, closing the door behind me. I don't want anyone entering my workshop in my absence. The hemlock I was cutting can kill as well as cure. It looks much like parsley, which is much kinder on the body, but hemlock does have its uses, in the right hands.

'When did they hear this?' I hurry at his side, back towards the main villa complex, relieved to get within where the floor's been heated throughout the cold time of the year. I feel it begin to thaw my frigid toes. I've forgotten to stuff my boots with lamb's wool this morning, too intent on the task in my workshop. I need to be careful with my feet.

'A month ago, no more.'

'She's not wasted time,' I grumble, a shiver of fear doing more to chill me than the brisk wind.

'No, and neither have we,' he confirms, but I hear the same worry in Madog's voice I feel in my belly. 'Our allies have fine blades. The Husmeræ will fight with us, as will the Wocingas after my journey to tell them of the brewing conflict. We have the support of the Stoppingas women as well, don't forget that.'

'Will that be enough to counter a *comitatus*?' I ask, eyeing Urien, Kenal and Tudwal, where they've evidently been summoned to this discussion by Madog.

'How many warriors will stand with us?' Madog directs to Urien. Eyes narrowed, I see where he works it out in his mind.

'At least twenty, if not twenty-two,' he asserts confidently.

'How many in a *comitatus*?' I demand.

His shrug isn't reassuring. 'We've no way of knowing.' I gaze at Madog, he remains uneasy.

'We need more allies,' I pronounce into the heavy silence. 'We must be assured of our victory. We've the blades and shields. We also have new helms, and Madog's sword is almost ready.' Terricus has been busy throughout the short days of winter, making use of the excess charcoal from an abundant burn to forge a blade for my brother. I understand Hedrek has something special planned for the hilt. I know he and Sian have been whispering about it. I've resolved not to ask too many questions. They wish it to be a surprise. I'll allow it. Sian knows enough of our people, and my intentions for the future, not to make a poor decision with her lord's sword hilt.

'The local tribes stand with us, at least those still in existence. The Færpingas are finished, and those who once called Hedrek their leader, the Beansæte, look to us.'

I sigh unhappily. My brother's correct. We've absorbed people whose warriors stood against us, and we've firm friendships with Ladus and Padern, even if Riderch of the Wocingas remains a grumpy git. I consider my journey last summer. I'm aware there are many tribes throughout our island. Perhaps they could also be enticed to stand with us.

'We need our own *comitatus*,' Madog surprises me by announcing.

'What?' I startle, disbelieving his assertion.

'These warriors from the east. They know how to fight one another. We know how to fight amongst our own people. We should find a *comitatus*. Wasn't there news of one last year?' This he addresses to the room at large. I furrow my brow.

'Yes,' I admit unwillingly. 'We understood they were causing problems from Corinium and then northwards. We never met them, but we certainly saw the devastation they left behind. They left the dead to rot.'

'Then we should find them. They will, I'm sure, fight on our behalf.'

'No,' I dismiss. 'We must forge links with the local tribes not based on payment.'

'I suspect we lack the time to develop those ties,' Madog says respectfully. 'Our links with the Stoppingas, Wocingas and Husmeræ are long-standing. We shared grievances against Edern, and grief for their dead, as well as the death of Marchell. We don't have that with even those who live closer to Glevum. We do have wealth,' Madog asserts.

'And good blades,' Urien interjects fiercely.

'We've much to offer them,' Madog continues, acknowledging Urien's words with a determined nod and defiant look in his eyes.

'But they may be traitors.'

'We need to find them first,' Madog states slowly, his face twisted in thought.

'You wish me to hunt them?' I glower, shivering at the thought of leaving Villa Eorlingas at this time of the year. The warmer weather is still many weeks away.

'No. I'll find them,' Madog decides, nodding at his decision.

'No,' I dismiss. 'You're needed here. If you fear Elen's *comitatus* so much, you can't leave Villa Eorlingas.'

'I can, and I will,' he states, eyes narrowing at my angry expression. 'I'll know if the *comitatus* can be trusted. I'll know if they're good warriors.' He bows respectfully.

'No,' I deny once more, but I already suspect Madog has the right to it. He merely needs to continue to be so assertive and I'll relent to his request. I don't fear Elen, or whichever *comitatus* she's managed to coerce to her wishes, but I refuse to allow the Eorlingas to be overwhelmed by them. If it must be like against like, then that's what will happen. Elen thinks to better us by bringing a new threat, and one we've never encountered before, to the coming battle. We can nullify it by having our own *comitatus* to direct against hers. 'Very well,' I growl. 'Bring them here, to Villa Eorlingas, but only when you're assured of their loyalty. Then I'll perform my own tests to reassure myself of that as well. We'll not allow a wolf into our midst.'

My brother smirks at my choice of words, but bows his head respectfully. We might butt heads on numerous occasions, but between the two of us, we ensure Villa Eorlingas and all its inhabitants stays protected, and in good health. We'll continue to do so.

I look to Urien, challenging him. He inclines his chin towards me. He knows what I ask of him. I need not say the words aloud. He'll escort my brother. He'll stand at his side, and if necessary, absorb the full force of any blows directed against Madog. My brother must live until such time as Maccus can take his place. More importantly, my brother must live because I will it, and I need him. Together, we are the strength and wisdom of Villa Eorlingas. Together.

* * *

My brother leaves the following day, sheltered under three cloaks and with lamb's wool stuffed into his boots, and below his arse. Urien, Tudwal and Kenal go with him. The rest of the warriors are to remain behind and protect Villa Eorlingas in his absence. I watch them through the guarded entranceway, sighing unhappily as they make their departure, and then hurrying the men on guard duty to return the protection that blocks any easy passage inside, to keep us safe. It's a thankless task, to be sent here to keep watch for an enemy who'll be unlikely to attack during the winter, but the warriors are kept in firewood, good food and have the thickest cloaks to keep them warm. They acknowledge my presence. I turn aside, keen to return to my tasks, and to leave them with theirs.

I'll feel uneasy until Madog and his escort returns. I mutter softly beneath my breath, encouraging our horse-god to keep them company on their journey. It most certainly is the wrong time of year to be travelling, but that should give an advantage in this race to find the most allies and warriors to stand with us in the inevitably coming battle against Elen. I pause, within sight of the main villa complex. The familiar hot stink of iron ore being melted floods the air. It's as reassuring as the clanging of practice blades where those men not on guard duty hone their skills. A

nicker from Bronwen has me smiling despite the worry unsettling me. Villa Eorlingas is strong. Villa Eorlingas is wealthy. It
will remain so.

Unbidden, I find myself standing before the turf structure
into the sides of which my mother's remains have been placed,
and those of my father. I close my eyes, reach out and touch the
grassy embankment. A sense of contentment floods me. Many
might think it strange, to find comfort here, where my parents
and ancestors are interred. But it speaks of more than that. This
grassy rise, now coated with ice, is a sign of how long the
Eorlingas have held this villa. It reminds me Edern's depravations
might well have lasted for two decades, but in the time of our
people, of the Eorlingas, it's but the flap of a butterfly's wings. It
was inconsequential. For most, it has already been forgotten. We
will triumph. We always have in the past. This monument is a
testament to that.

12

WÆRMUND OF THE GYRWE

The heat's as welcome as I knew it would be. I allow it to thaw out my toes and bones. I sigh with contentment, and then half open my eye to discover what Heafoc and Bucge are complaining about now. The pair don't enjoy the cold weather. They tell me it's not been this cold in their lifetime. I'd dismiss the complaints, but Diseta, our guide and our translator, has assured me others are saying the same. Diseta, slight as she is, doesn't seem to feel the chill. But then, she's kept busy, assisting those who wish to trade with the inhabitants of Uriconium but lack the required language skills. When not doing that, she's our friend and ally.

Our return to Uriconium was welcoming, from Gildas, who was once held captive by Isarninus but who led us to Uriconium, to Diseta and even Gwladus, the stable owner, and a warrior of the Wreocensætan. Katourn greeted us warmly as well. I'm now the owner of a fine standard for my *comitatus*, and I've taken inspiration from Freki and the gift the boy pressed into my hand. And from the fact the wolf is beloved of my ancestor, Woden.

Our friends within Uriconium listened to our tale of events in Verulamium with mild interest and no concern. Verulamium, despite having an almost direct road to Uriconium, seems far distant to them. After all, Gildas was captive there for many winters and none knew. Perhaps, then, their settled way of life makes such distances seem vast, as opposed to my *comitatus*, who've followed the same path on a number of occasions, covering the distance in a short amount of consecutive days.

We've enticed a young man to our *comitatus* named Mato, as well as a few of the older women, Locinna and Totia, who like Gwladus were unhappy with being dismissed as inconsequential by their husbands, and are keen to learn a new skill. We have a force of fifteen, more than left my homeland. We fight well together. Heafoc has seen to that. But now I welcome the warmth from the baths and delight in knowing we'll have even more blades when we leave here, forged from the treasures we took from the Tomsæte enemy, or exchanged for better ironstone. Not that I yet know where we'll go. I suspect it's that which Heafoc and Bucge bicker over. Bucge endeavours to manage our store of wealth. It's not easy to keep so many fed and clothed when there's so little treasure to be earned. I've refused to allow her to sell my wolf emblem, and I've argued with her that the expense of having my wolf standard made was worth it. No one needs us to fight on their behalf within Uriconium, not even Gildas.

'We should go,' Bucge urges Heafoc, but he shakes his head.

'No. It's not enough recompense for the risk. And at this time of the winter.' I see him visibly shudder.

'We must expand our reputation,' Bucge counters. I think this is my concern, but Bucge's obsessed with growing our renown. I suspect she does it because she's the one to still be wounded. Her limp will never leave her. She wants to feel strong. But Heafoc's correct. The call for our services, coming from the far west of our island home, doesn't offer enough treasure to take the chance. We don't wish to fight no matter the risk. We wish to fight when the rewards far outweigh the jeopardy of someone dying in battle.

'Bucge, stop complaining,' Eastmund calls, while Maggenræd nods in agreement. She rounds on Eastmund, eyes flashing with fury. She's wild since recovering from her wound. Even Osfyth's often hard-pressed to control her spurts of anger. I fear they make her rash, but I've not yet scolded her for such anger. I'll see what Bucge does in a fight first. It's possible such rage will make her better. Equally, it might do the very opposite. I didn't see her fight the Tomsæte enemy. That she survived assures me only that she could contend with the feeble foes we faced.

'We must...' she begins, only for Diseta to appear before us. While I'm lounging in the steam of the bathhouse, she's fully clothed, a pensive expression on her familiar face that immediately has me worrying.

'What is it?' I demand, sitting upright.

'I believe...' she begins uncertainly, but then shakes her head and watches me firmly. I confess, I've enjoyed sharing her bed throughout the cold time of the year. She's fiery when in the throes of passion. I don't believe we've hidden our arrangement well from anyone, and Gildas is unhappy about it. He suggests we should be formally united. I don't believe Diseta or I want that sort of tie. 'There's someone here you might wish to speak with.'

'An enemy?' I reach for my waist, where my seax would normally reside, but of course it's outside, in one of the cubicles reserved for those using the bathhouse.

'No. Someone in search of a *comitatus* to defeat an enemy.' When I don't immediately respond, she comes closer, and leans down to whisper in my ear. I feel a spurt of desire, and she must witness it because a smile touches her lips. 'They're wealthy. I've never seen horses as fine, and Gwladus is drooling over them.'

'This I must see,' I announce, standing carefully, annoyed by the gentle laughter from Diseta. 'You'll aid me?' I question her.

'Of course. I'm here to fulfil your every whim.' She continues to laugh, and then evades my reach when I go to embrace her. Her laughter echoes around the stone building. I'm aware Bucge and Heafoc aren't the only ones to watch our departure.

'Heafoc,' I call through to him. 'This will interest you,' I comment, and for a fleeting moment consternation touches his lips. After all, he won't wish to see Diseta and me in another compromising position. 'And you, Bucge,' I further add. Now even Eastmund and Maggenræd are intrigued. I know they'll follow me.

I shudder at the sudden chill when I'm once more dressed. It's been a winter of enjoying our freedom and wealth. But the cold weather will only last so long. As will our current wealth, as Bucge constantly repeats.

All is crisp as I follow Diseta back towards the stables. I hear the nicker of my horse, and also the gruffer tone of someone speaking in a tongue I don't know. It reminds me of something, but I can't quite recall where I've heard the language before. I turn to Heafoc. Huddled within two cloaks, one rimmed with fur, he looks more bear-like than me. I see my wolfhound slink from within the stables and join me. He's still fearful on occasion, but I run my hand through his fur, and he settles. Gwladus and he have an understanding. He can shelter within the stables, provided he leaves the horses within alone, apart from mine. He doesn't mind Freki's presence. There are others within the settlement who don't like Freki. They fear him. They obviously don't know him as well as I do. Freki likes nothing more than to roll on his back and have his belly scratched. It's hardly the behaviour of a violent beast.

Gwladus watches our approach, but my eyes are drawn to

the four fine horses. I almost gasp in surprise. They're magnificent creatures. Taller than any horses I've seen before, and shimmering with good health. Their coats gleam and their eyes show far more intelligence than my beast ever does.

Immediately, Diseta begins to speak in the tongue of these people. I hear the gruff voice respond and then an astonishing man steps from beside one of the horses.

His moustache is so long it almost touches his chest, and around his neck he wears a shimmering torque that catches the winter sun so it's as though his head rests amidst flames. His eyes narrow as he sees me and my allies, and now I cast a look at Diseta which thanks her for not informing me of this. I should have come dressed as a lord of war, not as a man, red-cheeked from the steam of the bathhouse. She arches her pretty eyebrows, and I know I'll make her pay for this, later, in the comfort of our bed.

Beside the lead man are three others. Two are older, one younger. They're lean and dressed warmly against the bitter weather. Their leader isn't alone in wearing shimmering metal at neck and wrist. These people are indeed wealthy.

'Well, introduce us,' I direct to Diseta.

I hear my name being spoken, and incline my head towards the four men. Diseta then tells me another name. It doesn't exactly slide from her tongue.

'This is Lord Madog of the Eorlingas, and his men, Urien, Tudwal and Kenal. They seek the services of a *comitatus* to aid them in a coming fight against another of your ilk.'

'Another *comitatus*?' Heafoc's quick to question. I share his consternation. I wouldn't want to think there's another group like us. They might take the prizes we hope to earn. And the reputation we hope to gain.

'Men from the east,' Diseta qualifies, eyebrows furrowed in thought as Lord Madog further explains.

'We're not all from the east,' Bucge mutters beside me. Now I fix her with a steely glare and she subsides. That tells me much. She's impressed by the wealth of these people as well.

'And what will the recompense be for risking our lives?'

A knowing look enters the eyes of the two older men at Diseta's words, while the younger man watches us with an unfathomable expression. It's not fear. It's not relief at finding us either. I'm not at all sure what he's thinking.

'Horses like these fine beasts, and the services of a master bladesmith.' Now my eye is caught by the seaxes held at the waist by all four men. Even from here, I admire the craftsmanship of the hilts on the blades. They're finely wrought.

'We have a master bladesmith,' I dismiss, although the thought of owning the horses is exhilarating.

'You have a bladesmith?' Lord Madog asks, with the aid of Diseta. I see this unsettles him.

'Yes, but we travelled half of this island to find him, here within Uriconium.'

'So, there are no bladesmith's to the east, in your homeland?'

I shake my head, immediately realising the cause of his concern. I shouldn't have been quite so eager to deny it. I could have ensured we were recompensed more highly.

'No. The peoples in the east fight with old blades, aside from our lords, who can afford the services of those from our original homelands, far to the north of here.' This explanation seems to settle the four men. I consider what they've done to earn the ire of a group of warriors, who they think they can't overwhelm, despite their blades. 'Come,' I invite. 'We need not talk here, in the bitter cold. There's a tavern.' I point to where I mean. For a moment, I suspect Lord Madog might refuse, but after a heated exchange with one of the older men, he nods his unwilling agreement. Gwladus smiles and moves to eagerly take the horses. All four men reach for the bridles, and grip them possessively.

A hurried conversation ensues between Gwladus, Diseta and Lord Madog before he seems to understand what's happening. Unwillingly, Lord Madog directs his three companions to release the stunning horses into the care of Gwladus and the warmth of the stables. Then, together, we stride towards the welcome heat of the tavern, although Freki slinks away, with Gwladus.

'You must bargain for enough horses for us all.' Bucge steps close to order me.

'I don't think even our fine services are worth that much,' Heafoc counters from beside me.

'We'll learn more of their enemy before we set our price,' I confirm, pleased Diseta doesn't explain these words to Lord Madog. I'd welcome Bucge and Heafoc keeping quiet, but I admit, the thought of having a horse similar to the sleek-built one Lord Madog owns is enticing.

'Perhaps one for me,' I murmur, laughter rippling through my voice, while the other two snap down their arguments against. They're members of my *comitatus* and I'm their leader, and perhaps their lord of war, but even I know we fight together, as a collective. I'm not an imperious leader like my father was. I value the men and women who've given me their oaths too much. Even so, fifteen horses of such quality is far too high a cost, even for our services. I can't imagine they mean we can have a horse each. If we all live through the coming fight.

The warmth of the tavern's welcome, if not the stink of too many unwashed bodies. I'm constantly amazed by those who don't enjoy the bathhouse. The tavern keeper hurries to clear an area for us to settle close to the hearth. He's a thin, rat-like man, entirely bald, but with a thick beard that almost reaches to his crotch. He keeps a good house, and we've spent many a happy evening here. He likes the weight of our treasures.

He quickly brings beakers and jugs, and Diseta offers them to Lord Madog and his allies. The youngster sniffs the liquid suspiciously and dips his tongue into it, evidently surprised by the taste.

'We should warn him,' Diseta acknowledges, as he drinks the entire beaker in one swallow.

'No, we should not,' Heafoc replies with a gleam in his seasoned eyes.

I turn to Lord Madog and lift my beaker to him, before taking a small sip. It's a heady concoction. He samples the mead and barks an order to the others. The youth's eyes widen in shock. He hiccups and burps. The sweet smell reaches me across the distance.

Diseta is quick to intervene now, her speech rapid as she converses with Lord Madog. She nods along, asks more questions, and then looks me in the eye.

'Their enemy is a traitor to their tribe, who means to exact revenge against them, and steal their wealth. They've brought warriors from the east to their side, under false pretension. The Eorlingas already have a firm alliance of other local tribes, with over twenty well-trained warriors, but wish to have the skills of someone who knows how this *comitatus* will fight. They ask you to train them in the way of the *comitatus* and then stand with them in the coming battle, for there will be a battle, do not doubt that. In recompense, you'll be welcomed into the tribe until such time as the battle occurs, and you'll receive three horses similar to those ridden here by them, as well as more portable wealth. They would have offered you fewer horses and better blades, but you already seem to have good blades, similar to theirs.'

I run my tongue over my lips, considering the offer. It is a good one. A very good one.

'How far have they travelled to reach here?' I question, curious as to how many days we must go, and whether it's anywhere near Verulamium, where Elen is amassing a force to defeat us.

'Four days, using the old roads. It's to the south of here, near Glevum.' I narrow my eyes, and try to decide where I've heard the name Glevum.

'So not towards Verulamium?'

I sense a subtle shift from one of the older men as I state the name, but his expression immediately calms. I suspect it was caused by something else. Perhaps a fart because a terrible smell almost has my eyes watering.

'No, not towards Verulamium,' Diseta responds, having asked the question. 'To the south, almost towards where the River Hafren, which flows not far from here, leads into the sea.'

I look to Heafoc. He shakes his head, lips turned down. He can't comprehend the distance either. I consider my options. The weather will soon improve. Our wealth will not last forever. We have new members of the *comitatus*, and a reputation to grow.

'Tell Lord Madog he's gained the temporary allegiance of my *comitatus*. We'll teach him all we know, and fight at his side in the coming battle, and all in exchange for four fine horses,' I counter, eyes flashing, daring Lord Madog to disagree with me. For a moment, he hesitates as Diseta explains my terms. Then he nods, but Lord Madog's no fool.

'But first, he wishes to see what you can do with those fine blades you carry at your waist,' Diseta explains, chuckling darkly. I know where her thoughts have taken her.

13

MEDDI OF THE EORLINGAS

I eye Padern with unease. He's ridden to Villa Eorlingas, bringing with him five of his warriors. He offers me a smile. It's one I wish I could return fully.

'Seeress.' The incline of his head is graceful. Still, I distrust him. I distrust everyone in Madog's absence. I'm even wary of allowing the men and women of the Eorlingas into the nearby fields to prepare them for the summer crop. We're missing four of our finest warriors. I worry our enemy will have watched them leave and not yet return.

'Padern,' I reply without emotion. His mouth twitches. I think he'll castigate my reserve, only for the group of mounted warriors to open and reveal the slight figure of their new seeress. Now I understand why he's here.

The young girl, huddled within a thick cloak, offers me a cautious look, reaching for the spangles at her waist.

'Cadwysti,' she begins, mentioning the old woman I met last summer. But I forestall her with a raised hand.

'Please, come within. Be welcomed.' Quickly, I order my guard to clear the reinforced gateway. They do so eagerly, not having enjoyed barring the way for our ally, Padern of the Husmeræ. Padern rides within, and quickly dismounts, before bowing low, as do those who attend upon him. I realise now I've met all of these men before. The young girl stays mounted but relief flickers on her face. She must learn to school her expression and hide her emotions to become a seeress in the guise of her grandmother.

'Seeress Meddi.' Padern lifts his head to catch my eyes. 'You're most welcoming.' I feel my lips lift at the obvious lie. 'We thank you, and call upon our bonds of friendship. Our seeress seeks the benefit of your wisdom.'

'I'll ensure you're supplied with food and drink, during your stay. Will it be overnight?' Already, the sky's darkening, as another short winter's day comes to an end.

'If we're welcomed, then yes. We'd sooner be here, than camped with the bones of our enemy.'

Unbidden, my eyes stray to where the carrion creatures have finally availed themselves of all the suppurating flesh of the dead warriors from the end of last summer. Even I was surprised by how long it took for the bodies to become little more than a jumble of bones held together by remnants of cloth and not skin and sinew.

The younger woman looks relieved at such an open invitation, and quickly dismounts and comes to my side. Her eyes slide to where Padern waits, respectfully just far enough away he won't hear her muttered words.

'My name's Tangwysti.' She inclines her head to me. 'I hear things,' she mutters, voice filled with dread.

'About the Eorlingas?' I query, ill at ease all over again.

'I don't know. They're auguries, or so Cadwysti always told me. Alas, I don't understand them and my nights are sleepless with the horrors.'

'We'll go within, and find somewhere quiet to converse,' I inform her, my gaze straying towards Padern. He must know of the problem. His eyes tell me much. He's worried and concerned as well, but, I suspect, about his young seeress and not about the visions she's enduring. Tangwysti's eyes are heavily shadowed, her face pale, with lacklustre hair. I consider when she last slept well. 'Come.' I indicate she should walk with me. With her beside me, I realise how young she is. Her height's yet to overtop me, and I'm not very tall. Every step seems to pain her. Her breathing's too fast. I suspect she suffers from something aside from her auguries. I feel pity for her. The weight of being seeress is too much. Cadwysti should have chosen another, although, of course, our Gods choose who they want, and not vice versa.

Inside Villa Eorlingas itself, I take Tangwysti to a small room, the floor heated, the walls brightly coloured. She smiles with delight, and runs her fingers over the figures depicted there.

'They're so lifelike,' she stutters, marvelling at the images of horses.

'They are, yes. Someone who knew these animals well must have played a part in their creation. See, they catch the arrogant tilt of this mare, and the fury of the mighty stallion.'

She laughs, the sound not much different to Maccus' childlike giggle. She's too young to be seeress, but that won't mean she can't be seeress.

'Tell me of your dreams,' I ask her, when we're settled on two wooden stools and Rhiann's had a warming drink brought for us, redolent with last year's berry harvest.

Her spark of enjoyment leaves her face.

'I was named for my grandmother, but it's also meant people assumed I'd take her place. My strange dreams have furthered the belief and now I find myself without the steadying presence of my grandmother, while burdened with ever more dreams, which I'm sure warn me of a terrible future. Of death and contagion.'

'You see people you know dead?' I ask, eyes narrowed as I observe her.

'I see everyone I know dead. I see no one alive. I see the land dead as well, covered in corpses, animals and human. I can't see past it. Does it mean a time will come when all will perish?'

I reach for my spangles, unnerved by her cool tone when delivering such information. I thought her scared and fearful. Now, she appears as a harbinger of doom.

'The land will not die,' I say softly, eyes half closed as I seek a connection with my horse-god. It's tenuous at the best of times. 'It can't. It's been here for many generations longer than us.'

'People can die,' she replies dispassionately.

'They can, and they do. It's the way of all things. But not everyone, at the same time.'

'But it's what I've seen. Every night when I try to sleep, the scene plays out behind my eyes. All are dead. The horizon seems to burn. And there's a terrible, terrible smell that assures me all are decaying corpses, no matter how much I hope they're not.'

'You see this every night?'

'I see it before my eyes all the time. Now. At first it was just at night.'

'It must be terrifying,' I console, 'to only see devastation. You see no one living at all?'

'I see none who look like me or you, or our friends and allies. I see men with warrior helms crested with brightly coloured boar hair. They stride through the devastation and show no fear for the deaths of everyone else.'

I consider this. It's not my role to simply offer a reassuring response. I need to do more than that. I must forget she's little more than a child with a woman's place to fill.

'These warriors?'

'Don't look like Padern or Madog, no,' she confirms quickly.

'They must be *comitatus*? Those from the east.' I see her visibly shudder as realisation floods through my body. Madog has gone to seek such as these to help us beat Elen and her new-found allies. What if this simply invites them to steal all from us? Or worse, bring about our deaths?

'You believe you know what my dreams foretell?' she asks eagerly, the relief in her voice impossible to ignore.

'No, I believe I might know some of what you dream. But, I've yet to meet any of these people. I don't know whether we should fear them.'

'But everyone I know has perished in my visions, including Padern.' This she whispers, a worried look towards where we can hear the voices of the Husmeræ assures me she's not informed Padern of this element of her dreams.

'But did these warriors kill those you care about or do they come to help?'

Her mouth drops open in surprise. 'I confess,' she stutters. 'I'd not considered that.'

'No, I see that. And I understand why, but there are always multiple interpretations to our visions.'

'Then you'll stand guard over me this night. You'll stay awake and watch me sleep. I've been told I shriek in the night, but none can ever decipher the words.' I'm already nodding at her sugges-tion. I don't need her to know how desperate I am to understand the truth of her dreams. If Madog's walked into a trap, I'll never forgive myself for allowing him to leave here to find a *comitatus* to aid us. Equally, it might be that Tangwysti's foresights assure me I've done the correct thing.

It's almost painful to return to the others when we've finished talking, and share food and laughter with the men and solitary woman from the Husmeræ. I must know the truth of Tangwysti's visions, and what they foretell for my people. I simply must.

* * *

Tangwysti's slow to fall asleep within my workshop. From the main villa building, the sound of men drinking and sharing ale can be heard long into the night. The barks of laughter jolt Tangwysti awake time and time again, so she never falls into a deep slumber until I'm so exhausted as to be nearly asleep myself.

Tangwysti's taken the space where Marchell once slept. In the grey light of the single flickering candle, it's as though Marchell has returned to me. And when a voice rises from amongst the furs and blankets in the dead time of the night, it sounds like Marchell speaking with Tangwysti's mouth.

The noise has me startling fully awake, blinking to stay alert. Tangwysti lies entirely still, aside from her head, which tosses from side to side along with the stream of words pouring from her mouth. I listen with growing disbelief. Tangwysti's visions are a powerful statement of the future. I consider what she sees while sleeping compared to what I hear her state.

A final, plaintive howl ripples the silent settlement. It has the hair on the back of my neck standing on edge. Only then does Tangwysti subside to a more natural sleep, as I hold her arm and summon my horse-god to calm her. I sense the presence of my god, but it pays me no heed, concerned only with soothing my young guest.

When Tangwysti wakes, as daylight grows, and the shuffle of men and women can be heard within Villa Eorlingas, I've devised what I mean to tell her. It's not exactly the truth. It's not exactly a lie either, or so I reconcile myself.

'What did I say?' she demands. I offer her a soft smile. One name she spoke repeatedly. It's a name I've never heard before. It's certainly the name of a man who fights within a *comitatus*, I'm convinced of that.

'You said the name Wærmund. You spoke of him as an ally. You spoke of him as a killer of men. You spoke of him with some affection. Your dreams might be twisted with shed blood and broken bodies, but I'm not convinced he's the cause of them. You must return to your villa, with Padern and your men. Ensure all is well protected and none can steal away your wealth, cattle or women.'

'And then what?' She rubs sleep from her eyes. I see their startling vividness. I consider how I've not seen it before.

'And then wait for your warriors to be summoned to join us in the coming battle.'

'What, sacrifice our warriors to these helmed men?'

'No, they'll counter the enemy, but they must be well equipped to do so. More than Padern must have sharply edged blades. All must be able to fight with them, even the women of your people. I'll order the same here. Rhiann will be happy to support me. There's a reckoning coming, but your dreams don't portend failure. Remember that. Do all you can to make Villa Husmeræ safe and secure. When Madog sends a summons for your best fighters, dispatch them with your blessing, but only the very best. Those who are less proficient will protect your home. They don't need sharp blades, but merely the means to kill any who think to overwhelm them, with thrown stones and cooking pots if needed.'

'Is this truly what I said?' she asks, eyes narrowed, disbelief playing on her lips.

'No, you said much, but it was all concerned with this. Don't fear the enemy. Be eager to counter them. In that way, you'll prevail. We'll all prevail.' She nods confidently, and in that regal action, I see why she's been proclaimed the seeress of the Husmeræ. She has wisdom and calmness, she merely needs to understand it for herself. I only hope, when her vision comes to fruition, she'll remain an ally of the Eorlingas. I really do. Equally, I hope I've interpreted her dreams correctly. It is possible her visions foretell more than a single reckoning. It is possible they tell of a time of terrible dearth on the horizon. We've only just survived a string of poor harvests. I hope there's nothing worse to come.

14

WÆRMUND OF THE GYRWE

'You believe this is a good bargain?' Heafoc questions me quietly, as we arm ourselves and prepare to show Lord Madog our battle skills. No one else has thought to ask me the same. I think they're already convinced they'll benefit from one of the few fine horses we'll be paid with for our risks.

'I do. Don't you?'

'We know nothing of their enemy,' he cautions.

'We know they'll fight as we do?'

'And how do you know that?' he demands more acerbically. I offer him an appraising glance.

'I understood, from you, that people like us, from the east, all fought in this way.'

He grimaces and nods unwillingly. 'Of course,' he confirms, but I sense he remains uneasy.

'You still believe us ineffectual?' I don't ask the question with heat. It's important to know what Heafoc thinks about our skills. We beat the enemy of the Tomsæte, but they weren't the mightiest of warriors. We overwhelmed Isarninus. It was Elen and her new allies who caused us the most difficulties.

'No. But, we still lack the cohesion that will ensure we triumph over all. For instance, if we fight an enemy like your father and his warriors.'

'Which we won't,' I counter aggressively. 'He'd never leave his precious home. We've seen that. He sent ever-increasing numbers of men to beat us, but never came himself.'

'But if we were.'

'No, Heafoc. No. We're good at what we do. I'm not saying we're the best, but we're good. Our sharp seaxes assure us of victory, even if the fighting might be bloody and brutal.'

Unhappily, Heafoc stops arguing with me, and bends with an audible click of his back, to grasp his seax from where it awaits him on top of a wooden chest.

'Of course,' he exhales, striding outside. I pause momentarily. Is he right to be cautious? Yes, we've been overwhelmed, almost repeatedly, but we're now a much stronger force. We comprehensively beat the enemy of the Tomsæte. We've done little but practise throughout the long winter since then, learning to work together as a cohesive force with our new allies. We're good. I know we're good. Aren't we?

'Bloody bollocks,' I huff, hurrying to follow my warriors. Trust Heafoc to have me doubting myself. I'd welcome more effusive support for my decision.

Outside, the winter sun's vivid, if fleeting during the day. I wince against its brightness and eye my warriors, who are readying themselves. The intention is to fight against one another. We'll form up with two small shield walls, and reveal our skills in such a way. Admittedly, some of the damn fools might actually hurt one another. I've ordered them all to cover their blades, but someone will have forgotten. They always do. At that, I check my blade, and content its sharpness is tempered by a padded covering of wool before being wrapped in a layer of cloth,

I stride to where Bucge and Osfyth are testing their strength against one another.

Madog and his allies are also there, as is Diseta, and even Gildas. The old man grows ever smaller. I almost sense his release from captivity has accelerated his ageing. I hope he remains hale for many years yet, but I fear for him. Perhaps spending all of his time praying to his God is doing him no favours. Has he not done enough of that during his years of imprisonment?

'Warriors,' I call. All eyes turn my way. I smile at Eastmund who already sports a darkening eye. He offers me a shrug and a pointed glare towards Bucge. She shows no contrition for punching her friend and ally. I consider what Eastmund did to rile her this time. It might have been as simple as sneeze on her. Equally, he might have referenced her limp. She's like to respond with the same force. 'Now, we'll form up, shield wall against shield wall, and then prove our prowess.' I indicate who I want where, and then stride to stand beside Heafoc. He grunts a greeting. He remains unhappy with me. I consider if Heafoc has lost the desire to fight. Perhaps he's enjoyed his winter of comfort too much. It wouldn't be the first time he grew too accustomed to taking his ease.

Eastmund has Bucge to the side of him, as he takes his position next to me. I've forgotten that, but perhaps this is the best way to heal any discord between the pair of them.

Opposite me are Dewi and his men, and those from within Uriconium who've joined us, the two women and one man. The two from the Tomsæte, Sennicus and Mato, stand with one to each side of the shield wall. There are seven to one side, and eight to the other. It's a good number.

'Remember, seaxes should be covered, fists not so much,' I add, while a chuckle of laughter works its way along the two lines, not that Eastmund joins in. I hear him muttering beneath his breath. 'Shields,' I bellow.

I hear Diseta's higher tones speaking to Madog and his warriors. She'll tell him my commands, and only my commands. I berated her to ensure she does as I request, rather than toy with me and my new allies, as she did when we first met Lord Madog.

'Advance,' I order, and a thunder of wood hitting wood floods the air, and although I know these men are my allies, and my blade's not as sharp as it should be, I feel a surge of heat through my body. A tight smile on my cheeks tugs at my birthmark, and perhaps reveals my teeth to Dewi who fights opposite me. He's a big bastard, but so am I, these days. And the heat of battle takes me. Sweat quickly beads my face, making my helm slippery over my hair, as I take aim against Dewi and his blade. In the near distance, I hear Freki's howl, and understand the animal feels it too. No matter Heafoc's caution, and my stuttering steps towards this moment, I've been bred for war. A pity my father never understood that, but it is his mistake. I will triumph. I will be his death. One day.

* * *

It falls to Heafoc to shout an end to our mock battle. It should be me, but I'm too caught up. There are going to be many bruises amongst us, as we part ways, Heafoc's rich voice reminding me I do fight my friends. We're all panting, but everyone is also smiling. I'm proud to see my warriors enjoying the grunt of battle as much as me.

I turn to Madog. Diseta continues to speak to him, but I don't need her words to assure me he's impressed by our strength. I offer a tripped Eastmund my hand, and he hurries upright.

'Bloody Bucge,' he complains. I shake my head, while Bucge grins broadly.

'You were supposed to be allies,' I remind them, but neither seems to hear. 'Is this what Madog hoped to see?' I question Diseta, just to be sure. She wears an uncertain expression on her face. I consider if I've scared her, but dismiss it. She's known we were warriors since we first met.

'It is, Wærmund, yes,' she confirms.

I turn to Lord Madog, chest tight with the effort I've been expending. 'Tell him I'll teach his warriors how to fight like this, and he'll reward us with four fine horses, and access to the craftsperson who makes those hilts.' I jut my chin towards where Lord Madog's seax is on display. I confess, I'd like such a fine hilt for my seax. Katourn's skilled with crafting our blades, but the hilts are less than inspirational, even if they're lightweight and can be fashioned to our particular strengths.

Diseta must repeat my words to Madog, for he nods, solemnly, and then lifts his seax clear of its sheath. I know my eyes sparkle at the bone handle and the fine decoration on it. It's not gold or gemstones, but it needn't be. The depiction of a horse's fine head is impossible to deny. He holds it out to me, sharpened point towards his stomach. I don't believe he means for me to have the blade, but rather to admire the hilt.

I peer down, marvelling at the eyes of the horse, and how they sparkle more than silver in the bright light.

'It's beautiful,' I murmur. Madog speaks to Diseta.

'He says he'll gift you a wolf-headed hilt, alike to your beast, when you've aided the people of the Eorlingas against their enemy.'

A slow smile spreads across my face. I incline my head, aware my warriors are coming close to look at the hilt as well.

'I find I'd like that very much,' I confirm, and reach out with my hand to seal the bargain with a touch of spit. Lord Madog pauses momentarily, confusion on his face, and then he repeats the action. It's as good as sealing the agreement with blood.

I grin broadly, aware Diseta might not approve of this agreement, or indeed that Gildas might not, but both witness it all the same.

'When I have one of those fine horses,' I call to the woman who warms my bed, 'I'll allow you to ride it.' She grimaces, somewhat aghast at the thought, and turns aside. It seems I still have much to learn about how to please a woman. Eastmund chuckles darkly beside me while Gildas shakes his head with admonishment, although he shouldn't understand my words, and Lord Madog watches on with understanding flashing in his eyes.

I might have some of the best blades, and the most skilled warriors, but in some aspects, I remain a child.

'Oh well,' I shrug. 'We'll see if I can change her mind when we return.'

15

MEDDI OF THE EORLINGAS

'Bitch.' The word reaches me as though from a long way away. I can't comprehend it, even though it's spoken in my tongue and I know well enough what the word means. Immediately, Urien and Madog launch themselves between me and the wild-haired warrior who now rushes towards me, face twisted in fury, shimmering blade to hand, a wolf-shaped birthmark staining his cheek, just as a wolfhound hovers close to his legs. Blade glinting with such intent, it completely absorbs my attention. Is that one of Terricus' blades? I think it must be. I know of no others who can forge a blade that shimmers with such lethal intent, I swear I can hear it slicing the very wind.

But still, the wild-haired man charges at me. My eyes swivel back to him. I notice how young he is. His skin is winter-pale where it can be seen between his beard and moustache. His eyes have no lines surrounding them, and neither do his lips. He's but a boy. All this I absorb before he's forced to the ground by Madog and Urien, only for the remainder of the warrior band to menace towards us. Most of their faces are as twisted with fury as this young man's. I don't understand what's happening. I open my mouth to demand an answer, but bite it back, instead muttering to my horse-god to protect me. I refuse to fall. Here. Within the compound of Villa Eorlingas. I've protected Villa Eorlingas in Madog's absence. I won't falter now he's returned, bringing with him these crazed and hairy warriors.

Madog assured me he'd come back with allies who originate in the east and have iron as good as ours to defeat the amassing enemy under the control of the conniving bitch Elen. The woman who orchestrated the death of our mother. It doesn't seem they're our allies, however. Not now.

There's a further flurry of words between the man and those behind him, none I understand, even as I reach for my dagger, and hold it ready. They call one to another, and so do the Eorlingas. I sense Sian hurrying to protect me. Tudwal and Kenal as well. The shriek of outrage from the women of the Eorlingas is impossible to ignore. I even detect the furious shriek of young Maccus at seeing his seeress so threatened.

Every fighting man and woman of the Eorlingas has their blade to hand even as our new enemy do the same.

'Madog,' I finally cry, while Tudwal and Kenal step between me and the raving warrior. Whatever he's saying, I don't understand. I note he knows the word 'bitch' in my tongue, but nothing else. I look frantically towards the other enemy warriors. I thought they were our allies. I'm entirely perplexed, and fearful. Has Madog been coerced into bringing them here? Are they really Elen's allies, sneaking their way into the villa using subterfuge?

With a more rational mind I note the four women amongst the collection of fifteen warriors. Perhaps they're my age, maybe older. They wear expressions of fury, the one limping forward, even as another huge warrior moves to intercept her. He's as old as my father would be, had Edern not chopped him down in his prime. I know to fear him, even if his waist is sagging towards his cock.

He speaks a low rumble to the women. The one narrows her eyes, in thought.

'Seeress Meddi,' the giant warrior mutters. His tongue mangles my name. I understand his intent well enough. It seems, then, there's someone here who can speak my tongue, or at least who can do more than term me a bitch. 'Release my lord, Wærmund, please,' the man demands, arms held to either side, with no blade in them. Not that there needs to be. He exudes power and force. He could kill a child with his bare hands. Perhaps even a woman, if not a man. Certainly a lamb.

I swallow heavily, eyes switching between him and the fight taking place on the ground before me. There are wet thunks as punches land. At least, I think, there are no blades in hand. Not yet. I startle at the use of the name I'm convinced Tangwysti used while sleeping. Is this the man she saw? Is he, after all, the enemy? Did I tell her the wrong thing? I know I didn't inform her of the whole truth of what I fear her visions foretell, but I believed Wærmund would be an ally to the Eorlingas, and not an enemy.

'Madog, what is this?' I call to my brother, desperate to have some answers. But he doesn't reply. Thwacks continue to thrum through the air. The three men are fighting, bitterly, Madog's outraged huffs of exertion reach me even as Rhiann calls for her husband to be careful. Another of the enemy warriors, lips down-cast, comes forward, his eyes flickering from me to the warrior fighting my brother.

Tension thrums in the air. It need only take one wrong move here and all will be chaos. I turn back towards Villa Eorlingas. I know the weak are there. I know our strength is there. Our wealth. Our horses. But our men and blades are here, and we thought we had an ally but now don't. I suspect Elen's hand in this. How has she managed to undermine our endeavours once more? Does she know our thoughts even before we do? Surely not. I've always believed her assertion of the powers of a seeress was a falsehood. Did I err in that?

'Seeress.' The large enemy comes forward, his eyes seeking mine, even as he moves to stand beside the other man. The intent is clear.

'Madog,' I call again, my voice rising with urgency. Madog's beneath our adversary, Urien above him. 'Madog,' I shout, but he's too concerned with besting the man he fights. Abruptly, there's an unexpected sound. For a moment, I don't understand it, my head shaking with confusion. Another large man steps clear of the enemy warriors. Amusement ripples on his face, his lips pulled tight enough to reveal his teeth, or rather, the gaps where teeth should be. He looks like he could be a member of the Eorlingas, but I know he isn't, and never has been. Not in our time here. He certainly looks different to the vast majority of the warriors Madog has brought here. Perhaps he's one of our people, from a nearby tribe, and not from the east.

He speaks quickly. Very quickly. He gabbles to those he accompanies, and I can't catch what he's saying although I recognise the sound of the words. More slowly he addresses me.

'Seeress Meddi of the Eorlingas,' he calls, words thrumming with amusement, even as the other large man who tried to cool tempers speaks quickly to his allies. Their defiance falls away, weapons back on belts, and the fighting taking place between my brother, Urien and their man abruptly ceases.

I look between the three men with bloody noses on the ground, to the large, amused man standing, watching. He arches an eyebrow and bows low.

'Seeress Meddi of the Eorlingas, mistress,' he continues, tone jovial, as though the three haven't tried to beat one another to death. As though the shimmering sharpness of drawn blades can't be heard in the air. 'I fear my Lord Wærmund mistook you for a woman who looks like you. Mistress, we perhaps have the same enemy, one who shares your parentage?' The question hangs in the air. It restores me to the here and now.

'What?' I gasp, eyes sweeping from my brother, who aids the man he fought to his feet, both of them with chests heaving.

The one speaking bows low, eyes never leaving mine. It's similar to the way I approach the skittish horses. If I wasn't so confused, I might be outraged. Or amused. In his slow way, he continues to speak. 'I'm Dewi. This is the leader of our *comitatus*, Lord Wærmund of the Gyrwe. He is, I assure you, pleased to be here. These other men are Heafoc, Eastmund, Maggenræd, Cynin, Eli, Rhun, Blatero, Mato and Sennicus and the women are Bucge, Locinna, Totia and Osfyth. Bucge, especially, has no love for the woman who shares your face. Her limp was caused by Elen.'

The sound of my sister's name trips too easily from Dewi's tongue. I feel my eyes furrow in consternation once more, even as I reach for my spangles to ward off the use of her name. I'm right. Elen has reached them first. We thought our plan to find a *comitatus* would be a good one, and impossible to predict, but Elen has done just that. I open my mouth to shout for my warriors to bring their daggers and shields, their old armour and anything else they can find to defend Villa Eorlingas from this new enemy. Only, I snap my mouth shut immediately. His words have finally filtered through to my muddled thoughts. Instead, I listen to what's being said amongst the *comitatus*. I don't understand the words themselves, but perhaps I do the intent.

Wærmund speaks, lip already fattening from my brother's onslaught with his fists. Dewi nods, while the other giant shakes his head. I know his name is Heafoc because Wærmund says it repeatedly, and the large man doesn't try to correct him. I listen with half an ear, my gaze resting on Bucge, and the fury that tightens her lips. She's not unattractive, but I determine she spends her time fighting, not winning the love of men. I suspect she has something of a seeress about her from the way she mumbles beneath her breath. Certainly, she shows no fear now my calling and identity have been revealed by Dewi.

'Lord Wærmund would like to apologise for his outburst. He should have spoken before threatening you.' Dewi finally faces me once more. His hands remain devoid of weapons. Indeed, despite the size of him, of everyone here, I'm least frightened of him. He understands reason. He didn't launch himself at me, or immediately reach for his blades. No, he waited, and he watched. He comprehended the quickest that I wasn't Elen, as well. I suspect, although I don't know how, that he also knows Elen.

'He should, yes,' I continue, pleased my brother's mostly unhurt, although he limps. Hopefully, that will disappear soon. It would have been catastrophic had Madog and Wærmund wounded one another badly even before Elen and her collection of warriors make their way towards Villa Eorlingas. 'Tell me,' I demand, determined to re-exert my control over the situation. My people are turning quieter. Their rage has also diminished. If I'm prepared to listen, then so are they. 'When did you encounter Elen?' I hiss her name. I can't help it.

'It's a long tale,' Dewi responds. 'Best told over ale and fine food. Know this. We mean no harm to you. Indeed, now we know an old enemy is to be vanquished, we're even more pleased to make your acquaintance.'

'And you understand she comes with a war band from the east, with iron and sharp blades?'

'We didn't know she was the enemy you needed to counter,

but be assured, we have the same, if not better, blades, and we're largely warriors from the east who can fight another force from the east. And if not, our lord has taught us how to fight in a similar way to those from his homeland.'

I should, perhaps, be scared, but instead I'm fascinated by the weapons suddenly on display. All of them draw blades to reveal their strength, even Lord Wærmund. I turn to him. He offers me a bow and wipes the snot-filled blood from his nose with the back of his hand. I grimace, and he grins, showing his blood-tipped teeth as well.

It's Madog who's brokered this agreement. It's Madog who's found warriors to stand with the men of the Eorlingas. I look to him now. He offers me a rueful smile, and comes to my side, Urien hobbling beside him. I narrow my eyes. He bows as well. I shake my head. These men are like children arguing over the last of the sweet summer berries. I'd berate them, but I'm merely grateful all is as it is. If somehow Elen had reached these warriors first, I'd have been bereft. I'm pleased we're in control.

'Come, be welcomed.' Madog indicates the gateway, and it's as hastily cleared of the impediments blocking it, as it was filled when we all believed there'd be a bloody fight. 'You're welcomed to Villa Eorlingas,' he repeats. 'It appears we have much to talk about.' Dewi must repeat the words because the others walk towards us, Lord Wærmund leading them, alongside his horse, which, I fear, looks less than the best. At his side, the wolfhound stays close. I consider if he knows how much the animal resembles him, even down to its lanky movements. I would smirk, but I can't yet show amusement at this predicament. Instead, I peruse them with cautious eyes.

There are fifteen of them, plus horses. The animals are much shorter than our fine beasts. Beside Madog's animal, the other horses look like ponies. They'll increase the number of our fighting force by almost double. I hope they're worth the cost Madog said he'd pay for them. The horses of Villa Eorlingas are not to be given away without due thought. Three of the animals will be a high cost, even if they help us end Elen's life. Perhaps, if they hate Elen as much as it seems, Madog might be able to renegotiate the cost to something less onerous. After all, they imply they hate Elen almost as much as we do. And certainly, the woman who limps, Bucge, despises her. And, they already have blades as fine as ours.

I watch them as they enter Villa Eorlingas proper. They stride with confidence, but their eyes are everywhere. Madog has settled the terms, or so he told me. Admittedly, he looked uneasy. I hope he hasn't had to offer more than three horses. I should leave it at that. After all, they might also attempt to renegotiate, now they see our wealth before them.

As the last of them comes through the gateway, I turn to our warriors there.

'Block it tightly,' I urge, and only then hurry to follow my brother and his allies, with Sian at my side, Kenal also nearby, hand hovering over the hilt of his blade. I'd know more of their hatred towards Elen. I'd know more about them. I consider if these are truly the men young Tangwysti's seen in her terrible foretelling dreams. I confess, their leader shares the name she cried, Wærmund, admittedly said slightly differently by those who know him than she stated it. Is this the man she saw in her dreams? And if it is him, what does his presence at Villa Eorlingas truly mean? I must find out.

16

WÆRMUND OF THE GYRWE

I eye Villa Eorlingas with interest. I've seen enough of these villa settlements before to understand one that's wealthy in terms of crops and animals. Heafoc was unsure about this alliance, considering our earlier ones haven't always been fruitful. I see he's more pleased with it now. If not with me.

'Wærmund,' he berates. 'Perhaps you should have spoken before throwing yourself at the woman.'

'She looks so like Elen, I thought it was her. I believed this was a trap of our own devising.'

'Well, it's not. Now, look, the villa's large and there are many people. I see why others would covet the place. We'll grow wealthy here. Dewi says they're sisters, her and the bitch. There's no love between them.'

'I know the curse of family bonds only too well,' I confirm, grimacing as I feel one of my teeth. Lord Madog has good fists on him. But my eyes are absorbed by Meddi, not the villa. There's something about her I suspect others find unsettling. I don't. She's confident. She moves with grace. She, I sense, knows her worth to these people. I'm astounded there are those who'd think to better her. Although, perhaps not quite as astounded that the person is her sister. Vengeance, for that's what it will be, is a powerful motivator, as I know only too well.

Dewi speaks up then. 'It seems, Wærmund, you'll get to exact your revenge against Elen, while being recompensed to do so. You're lucky.'

I nod, absorbing this, and then my eyes narrow. 'Who stands at Elen's side?' Heafoc stills beside me. He must have realised what this means.

Dewi speaks to Lord Madog. I listen to the noises, but I can't decipher the words. I must learn more of this other language. Yet there's a pause before Dewi responds. It's so long, in fact, I stop leading my horse and Freki within the villa complex, and turn to face him. His face shows fury, and not a little fear.

'They don't know, exactly. She has allies, from the east. That's why they sought a *comitatus*, as you know. Better to have those who know how to fight one another facing each other.'

'You suspect Elen's ally is my father, don't you?' I voice the uneasy dread filling my mind, so contrary to my assertion my father would never leave his homeland.

'I do, Wærmund, yes. There are coincidences, and then, my friend, there are the workings of our gods. I sense their hand in this.'

For a moment, I know a feeling of trepidation. But this was always to be my reckoning. I killed my feeble brother, and many of my father's warriors. It was never going to end peacefully between us. If anything, this alliance with Lord Madog of the Eorlingas feels as though it's been writ into my destiny since Woden marked my cheek at my birth.

I offer a wolf-grin, casting a glance down to Freki, loping at my side.

'There's nothing to fear,' I lift my voice to shout. 'If it's my father, we'll best him, and the bitch. You're my warriors. We're *comitatus*. We'll prevail against all.'

My *comitatus* grins or smiles, or roars their agreement, but I sense Madog's scrutiny and turn to face him. I look at Dewi. He nods with understanding.

There's a flurry of words, a look of incredulity and then perception. Madog's lips set in a thin line of determination, his drooping moustache still despite the gentle breeze. Meddi too watches me carefully, although it's Dewi who speaks. I hold myself firm. I'm not scared of Meddi but I sense her power. It emanates from her. The torque she wears glimmers in the sunlight. Her other talismans, my gaze drawn below her waist, where an unusual collection of objects gently chime together, assure me she's as much marked by the gods, admittedly her gods, as I've been by Woden.

Lord Madog's the one to reply. His words lack heat. If anything, they reaffirm our already confirmed alliance. Dewi's translation doesn't surprise me, although I allow my face to broaden into a wide grin, and grimace as my lip hurts from my earlier beating.

'It seems, Lord Wærmund... that's how Lord Madog addresses you, not me,' Dewi offers with an arch of his eyebrows, 'that together we can right many wrongs foisted against us, and grow much stronger in the process. We welcome you, once more, to Villa Eorlingas, and are extremely pleased to discover you hold as much a personal grudge against our enemy as we do. United, we'll win.'

I stride toward Madog, my hand outstretched. For a moment, he hesitates, and I look to Dewi, nudging him with my chin to explain my intentions. He gabbles some more words. For a moment, Madog looks uncertain, but then he moves to run his hand over the firmness of my forearm, as I do with him, and we clasp, hand on each other's forearm, while all eyes watch on. Meddi observes the interaction through narrow eyes and steps to repeat the motion with me. I don't baulk. I don't hesitate. I offer the same warrior greeting I do to Madog. I feel her strength, and perhaps, if I squint and tilt my head to the side, I see the traces of long-healed scars on her face. Terrible scars, but I suspect, lost to all but the memories they've left on her body. Meddi's a warrior woman. She might also be a seeress, alike to Bucge, and like Bucge she'll not hesitate to shed the blood of her enemy, even if they're kin. I like her already, even if she shares a face with the bitch, Elen.

With our greeting concluded, we're received within Villa Eorlingas. The warriors there, all tall men, with moustaches similar to Lord Madog, assess us, just as we do them. Dewi provides an almost constant interpretation of Madog's words, but Heafoc's close. As much as Dewi's now my man, I trust Heafoc's distrust. He gives no indication Dewi lies.

I greet the warriors.

'Beli,' the one states. I clasp his forearm, and he mine. His strength is revealed in an almost pinch on my skin. I nod, pleased to meet a man of such firmness that even when his lord and seeress have accepted me, he conducts his own assessment. Behind me, Dewi does the same, Heafoc, Eastmund and the rest mirroring my actions.

'Idris.' A younger man leans in to make my acquaintance. He's tall and willowy, and perhaps only newly come to his warrior skills. He can't be much older than me. His moustache reaches only to his upper lip. It needs time to grow to maturity, just as he does.

'Well met,' I murmur in their tongue, checking with Dewi these are the correct words to use. He nods, and I move on. There are many warriors. They have excellent equipment. Blades shimmer from weapons belts, and there's a nearby collection of shields, some of which absorb my attention, so much so, the next man I offer a firm grip in greeting says something quickly, and a young scrap of a boy rushes forwards with one of the shields held before him so I can't see his head, only his feet moving beneath it.

Urien, one of the men I've already met at Uriconium, nods, and indicates I should inspect the shield. I lift it from the small boy. It's so light, it almost lifts into the air above my head without any effort on my part. My eyes narrow. But then I slip my hand through the shield handle and test the weight in my hand. My tongue pokes through my lips. I appreciate while this shield is unusual, it's not without merit. It's light, and large enough to cover a man's body. It is a piece of exquisite craftsmanship.

'Willow bark,' Dewi informs me. 'A treasured skill amongst the Eorlingas. It's one I thought lost. These people know it well.'

Still, I test the shield, and then stagger backwards, the thudding sound of a blow having everyone there reaching for blades. Only Urien laughs, and then looks shocked, as I lower the shield into position to protect my body. He has a stunning blade held before him, but I quickly realise, only intended to reveal the integrity of the shield. Worried eyes switch from me to Lord Madog and Seeress Meddi. A flurry of words, and Dewi gives one of his belly laughs, immediately defusing the situation, although Urien continues to look apprehensive.

'Apologies, my lord,' Dewi translates. 'Urien's keen to show you the strength of our blades. He should,' and here Lord Madog pauses and so does Dewi, 'he should have offered a warning.' Immediately, the tension lessens. I detect my warriors placing their blades back on their weapons belts. I nod towards Urien.

'I'm curious as to how these are made,' I say to Dewi.

Urien, relieved no doubt to not be facing more than a sharp reprimand from his lord, gabbles quickly.

'He can show you. When the battle is won,' Dewi assures.

I grin, to show I understand, and turn to Heafoc. Of us all, he's the one who's yet to replace his blade on his weapons belt.

'Put it away,' I admonish. He nods, but his face is pale, the beat of his heart, visible on his neck, too fast.

'Is this wise?' he murmurs. I don't even reply. Instead, I'm now being introduced to the women of the tribe. The first young woman is beautiful, even with a snot-filled baby daughter on her hip. At her side stands a small boy, mouth agape as he watches us come closer.

I bend low, wishing my back didn't creak as I did so, and meet his eyes. He reaches forward, despite a sharp hiss from his mother, and a careful hand on his shoulder. He runs his small hand over my face. I consider what it is that surprises him. He says a few words. I don't know what they mean, but I feel the sweaty heat of his palm over the purple mark on my face. His mother nods along with him, and I don't really need Dewi to tell me what the boy says, but he does so, all the same, his eyes going from me to my wolfhound.

'He says, like Seeress Meddi, you carry the mark of your god. He says, like Seeress Meddi, he hopes being here will make you better.' The words confuse me. I'd like to ask more, but I'm being forced upright, with more and more people desperate to make my acquaintance. Water, ale and wine are also brought, alongside fresh baked bread and chunks of meat that make my mouth water. We're truly welcomed into the heart of the Eorlingas, escorted to their main villa complex, and led inside. My eyes stray to the image on the floor, surprised when people walk over it without mention. There are two horses there, depicted in bright colours of red, green and white, making it clear a stallion and mare are intended. I didn't miss the fine horseflesh outside, in addition to that we've already encountered.

Villa Eorlingas is indeed a rich and vibrant place. If, as I hope, their enemy is also my enemy, I'll be pleased to aid them. I'll also be pleased to be paid handsomely for my aid. Evidently, the Eorlingas can well afford the services of my *comitatus*. I might have sold our services too cheaply. There could be a need to rene-gotiate but for now I'm content. Meddi wears the same face as Elen, but evidently hates her even more than I do. I must hear the full story of how that came about. But what I know is, for all her haughty appearance, and magiks, Meddi and I are very alike. That will serve us well. We will both get what we deserve. I'll ensure it.

17

MEDDI OF THE EORLINGAS

'He's younger than I thought he'd be,' I murmur to my brother. The warriors have been received within my home. I've muttered my charms, and spoken to my horse-god, but I don't fear these men and women. If anything, I'm less wary knowing women are amongst the warrior men. Women will not fight unless there's no choice. It's not the same for men. They're creatures of fire, not ice.

'Sister, as you should know, men build their reputations from a young age.' I laugh at my brother's affected aged tone. He arches an eyebrow at me, enjoying this moment of levity amongst so much prior fear and worry. 'They're good warriors. All of them. I watched them fight one another. Even as friends, they were brutal towards one another. They also hate Elen, as we've since discovered. That can only make their efforts to best her even more genuine.'

'They also seem to know who Elen's ally is, from the east. That does concern me.'

'I suspect they hold a personal grudge that must be settled, just as we do. We might be parting with goods and horses to pay them but men and women with the desire to even the score amongst their own enemies will always fight even harder.'

I pause with my spoon before my mouth, and allow a tight smile to touch cheeks once too scarred to make the movement pleasant. That hasn't been the case for some time now. 'You're right, brother. You've done well.'

'Let's not celebrate too quickly. We must still battle Elen and her *comitatus* from the east.'

Mention of her name turns the food I've already eaten leaden in my belly, but I shake my head and continue to spoon it into my mouth. Elen. My sister. How can a woman, with the same mother and father, be so very different to me? It's a question I've asked many, many times and still it puzzles me.

'We'll prevail. I'm sure of it.' My eyes stray to Hedrek. He doesn't sense my scrutiny. He's of an age with my father. He can still fight, yes, but not with the litheness of Madog and his warriors, nor with, I suspect, that of Wærmund and his, either.

'I know we will,' I confirm, thinking of young Maccus' interaction with Wærmund. I have hopes the boy will be a fine warrior and leader of our people in time. However, I can't ignore he also has some affinity for the magiks of a seeress. Perhaps, then, he'll be both. Certainly, I don't encourage him to know all I ken. Instead, I offer him wooden blades to practise with. If he perceives our horse-god, as I do, he must learn to defend her before he can know her.

Villa Eorlingas is filled with good cheer and the aroma of fine food. The smell of success and confidence hovers there as well.

'They'll come soon,' I remind Madog, where he sits beside Wærmund, and I sit beside him. Dewi, the large man who's evidently not a member of the same tribe as Wærmund, for he speaks my tongue well, is next to Wærmund, able to facilitate their conversation.

'Perhaps,' Madog murmurs. I feel my eyes narrow.

'What do you plan?' I demand. He meets my gaze and grins like a small child who's just found a worm in the soil.

'We don't wait for them to come here.'

'What?' I demand, wishing I could form more coherent questions, but I'm astounded by his idea.

'We send them word of our intent and arrange a place to meet. Somewhere to our advantage.'

'Why?' I further question, my joy in the meal, cooked exquisitely by Rhiann and the women of our people, dissolving.

'Do you wish to see Villa Eorlingas damaged? I don't. We've worked hard to repair it since the death of Edern. And, if we meet them away from here, there's less chance of them overrunning our home and stealing our goods when they realise they can't beat us and take it outright.'

For a moment, I'm speechless.

'How long have you been thinking about this?' I mutter.

'Lord Wærmund made the suggestion. He says, amongst his people, they fight their battles on borderlands. That way, the dead can be retrieved by either side. If they want them.'

'Hum,' I murmur, entirely unsure what I think of this suggestion. 'But what if they trick us and don't come to the battle site but here instead?' Madog, eyebrows arched high into his forehead, shakes his head, even as Dewi must relay our conversation to Wærmund. Wærmund replies quickly, his eyes flashing.

'It's not the way of his people,' Dewi explains. 'Honour's important. The victor must take everything by killing all, or have nothing but their dead at the end of the battle.'

I can't deny the idea has some appeal, yet I'm wary all the same.

'Come, Meddi,' Madog cajoles. 'Do you wish Elen to come here? I don't. She'll stain our home with her presence. Better she die far from here, her corpse left for the carrion creatures. She isn't welcome within Villa Eorlingas, even in death. She'll never be laid to rest with our ancestors.'

'Hum,' is all I murmur, turning to eye the people of Villa Eorlingas where they sit and feast, comfortable in the presence of these warriors because their leader and seeress have welcomed them. I hope that long continues, but a judder of unease rustles along my spine, as I'm reminded of Tangwysti's foretelling dreams.

I suspect the fight will come to Villa Eorlingas, no matter the plans of Madog and his hired *comitatus*. Whatever they intend to do, we'll have to prepare. I don't doubt that.

* * *

That night, the men and women of Wærmund's *comitatus* sleep within the dwelling set aside for them. It's been scrubbed scrupulously, the leaking roof repaired, and none would know to look at the space this was where the fool Edern once stored the magiks of making good blades, the tongs discarded as though useless. The wolfhound stays with Wærmund. He's not fond of my brother's hounds.

I don't miss that Lord Wærmund sets a guard over their door. Neither do I miss that Madog does the same, if from a discreet distance. For all our shared hopes, a sliver of unease remains.

I stride towards my workshop, following the familiar path and knowing where every stone must be avoided through my thin soles. I pass my hand over the lintel on entry and close the door behind me, grateful to block out the unwelcome chill of night. Once inside, I allow my rigid seeress stance to soften, and my shoulders to loosen. I peer into the greyness, bending low to touch the space where my daughter's bones lie. The movement reminds me of why we must fight for Villa Eorlingas, even if it is against my sister. Equally, it recalls me to the most violent day of my life, when my daughter was born and then taken from me. That day has marked me all my adult life, and I know Elen played a part in it, even though it was Edern who wounded me and killed our daughter. I judder at the thought of his hands on my flesh and wish I'd not thought of my daughter as something he aided me in creating.

But a sudden flash of memory, of watching Marchell within the workshop, quickly banishes the hideous thought. I see her standing there, bent over our working surface, carefully clearing away the roots of gentian to extract the goodness – or, rather, bitterness – from them. It's not that image which reinforces me, but rather the thought of Marchell herself. She birthed Elen. I lost a daughter through the savagery of another, but Marchell lived much of her life knowing the daughter she birthed was determined to ruin her own family. That must have pained her, perhaps even more than all the what-ifs I've experienced throughout my life. I must do this for Marchell, if not for me, although I must also do it for me. My horse-god has healed my physical manifestations of Edern's fury but I must repair the rest of me and there's only one way to do that. Elen must die. I must kill her. I vow there and then, while the fragmentary image of Marchell watches me, that I'll do so. I would never have let Marchell kill Elen. My brother wouldn't let me do so, when I first had the chance. But even he now understands the truth. I will end Elen's life, and in that way, put right all the wrongs inflicted against me, my daughter, my mother, my father and my people. I simply must.

18

WÆRMUND OF THE GYRWE

I sleep well enough, even taking the middle watch with Freki at my side, but wake when it's barely light, the sharp stink of burning rousing me, although I quickly realise it's from a forge and not a house fire.

With a slap on the back for Eastmund, on the final watch of the night, I duck below the door frame and walk outside, my ally loping at my side. Lord Madog assured us all we have the right to roam as we want and yet, at the same time, I know we're being watched. I admire his forethought. After all, we could be an enemy, although we're not.

I empty my stream into one of the pisspots set aside to collect the fluid for curing animal hides, and follow my nose to where the bladesmith labours. I've admired Madog's fine blades, so similar to mine, but where I've bartered for my blades, Madog has a man loyal to him who'll produce them in exchange for a home within the villa. It's Madog who has responsibility for securing and producing supplies of iron and charcoal. It's perhaps a better means of barter than the one I share with

Katourn. I wish I had the same, but I've no home such as Villa Eorlingas. Neither, I confess, am I sure I want one. Not yet.

The view I'm greeted with surprises me. In the sullen greyness, there are three busy figures, one woman and two men. I recognise them all from last night's welcoming feast.

The woman notes my approach, resting more on her left leg than her right. I recall now, she walked with a limp. She must inform the other two, but none of them move to intercept me. Indeed, they're not wary of my interest at all. I find a handy stone to perch on, and watch them. One of the men, the younger one, is busy with a raging fire, while the older man pumps bellows to keep the flames white-hot. The woman, off to the side of them, seems to sort through a pile of black stones I know to be charcoal. With barely a glance, she throws much of the burn onto a separate pile, keeping only a small portion from which, every so often, the younger man takes a small scoop and feeds the flames, causing them to spark and hiss. The aroma, I confess, is delightful. It reminds me of Katourn's workshop within Uriconium. It smells of power and success.

I sit and watch, as the day grows brighter and I hear the sounds of men and women waking and beginning their duties. But I don't hurry away. I don't feel the need to do so, but welcome a young girl bringing me a bowl of pottage sweetened with honey, as well as a bowl of raw meat for my wolfhound. He eats with as much relish as me these days, living up to the meaning of his name. The young girl does the same to the other three with the familiarity of a task performed routinely. They must wake early every day, or perhaps it's merely they must use the good light, while they have it. Or perhaps, it's the opposite. After all, they need light to illuminate their work, but even I know, if the daylight is too bright, Katourn would be unable to see the blade being forged in the heat of the fire.

Eventually, the bladesmith begins to bang and hammer, the larger man moving to a table where he has other tools. Curiosity raised, I walk towards him, Freki pressed to my side. He continues to work, and I realise he's making the bone handles for the blades the other man forges. He's the man with the skills I so admired when I first met Lord Madog.

'Wærmund,' I hear Heafoc cry. I look up, surprised to see the fury in his eyes. 'Have you been here all along?' he queries, face flushed.

'I woke early. I'm a curious man. Eastmund knew.'

'Eastmund's asleep now,' Heafoc complains. I grin. He doesn't return my humour but does come to see what I'm doing. I see comprehension on his face. 'Lord Madog does indeed have a bladesmith,' he states with awe, reaching out as though to touch the handles being made, only to stop himself before the other man slaps his hand away. He inclines his head in apology.

'Hedrek,' the man states. I take it to be his name.

'Wærmund,' I murmur. He nods and repeats it. I point to Heafoc, and introduce him. Now Hedrek does offer one of the handled blades. Heafoc touches it almost reverentially. He lifts it into his hand, testing the weight and, immediately, balances it on his forefinger. The blade wavers for a moment, but then stays in position. Heafoc's eyes alight and Hedrek smiles, the joy of a craftsperson who knows a chore has been well performed.

The woman, I notice, gives us a sly glance before returning to her task, but my gaze lingers on her. She's not beautiful, far from it. If anything, she reminds me of Seeress Meddi. She has the same aloofness about her. I admire it, but I'm grateful Bucge and Osfyth don't treat me with the same mild scorn. I imagine the woman believes all men think of little but satisfying their urges and killing their enemy. I'm better than that. I think. Diseta may argue with me but I've promised to return to her. I've left her in comfort within Uriconium.

Now Hedrek points to the bladesmith, and offers a name that sounds similar to Sennicus'. 'Terricus,' he mouths. I nod again, wishing Heafoc was less interested in the blades and could do more to aid me. I wish to know why the man has a name different to the others of the Eorlingas, but I don't have time to voice my question before Seeress Meddi appears.

She walks regally, back rigid, eyes assessing everything. She inclines her head towards me. I return the greeting. It seems, however, she wishes to speak with the woman. I'm sure she addresses her as Sian. Their words are as incomprehensible to me as ever. Heafoc, who I know understands many of them, makes no effort to follow the flow of the conversation. What I do, observe, however, is Hedrek's sudden reticence around Meddi. He offers a bow of his head, and I'm sure, tries not to watch her. I consider what there is between them. Surely he's too old to be her lover, but perhaps not.

With a comment aimed towards Terricus, which he answers without even looking away from his work, Meddi leaves us. I watch her swaying figure, still curious about her. While Osfyth and Bucge have blades and can fight, as do Locinna and Totia, I'm not as convinced Meddi could do the same. She's too slight. She appears too frail. But her position as seeress sees her revered and respected by the people of the Eorlingas. I muse on that.

Eventually, Dewi joins us, yawning wildly. He ruffles his hair, belches and then mumbles something to Hedrek. He answers swiftly. The two are soon laughing and joking. It's not a tongue Heafoc can speak, but he seems to laugh along as well. I feel excluded from this little conclave, and moodily stand and stride away. We've been given free access to the villa settlement. I decide to make use of it.

This place is so similar to Uriconium it surprises me. The layout, is of course, much smaller, but I can detect where a stone road perhaps once ran all the way to the main buildings, and how the remaining buildings were more than they are now. I also find the water channels intriguing. People greet me, some wary, some with wide smiles. Three small boys follow me, between them they all push one or other forward and then step away at the other's outraged and scared expression. I find a smile on my lips, and join them. As I stride around another set of buildings, I swivel on my feet and grimace at them, bending low. The three shriek, the one stumbling backwards and landing on the ground with a loud thud. The other two run and, feeling a little remorse, I go to him, smiling, and offer him my hand. He takes it, unwillingly. Once on his feet, he bobs his head and rushes after the fleeing backs of his less-than-loyal allies. I shake my head, and turn to find myself facing one of the Eorlingas' paddocks. My mouth falls open in shock. I knew they were rich in horseflesh. I didn't understand it was this rich.

Careful not to spook the horses grazing on the vibrant grasses close to their enclosure, I walk closer slowly. There are many mares, and a good collection of young foals. I try to count how many there are, but they keep moving and eventually I give up, content merely to acknowledge there are many of them. One of the animals, a white-coated foal, watches me with calculating eyes, hinting at more intelligence than the others. I'd like him to be mine, but I didn't make an agreement for any specific horses as recompense for fighting on behalf of the Eorlingas. No doubt, the horse is spoken for. It would be a superb mount for a loyal warrior. Or perhaps, the young son of Lord Madog.

It's here Dewi finds me. He alerts me to his presence by kicking a pebble which dashes against my boot.

'I knew you'd be here,' he murmurs, his gaze keen as he

appraises the horses. 'This is a fine place, isn't it?' he questions, although I do no more than nod in reply. 'The bladesmith and bone-handle maker are skilled men, although perhaps not as united in purpose as we might believe.'

'What do you mean?'

'Hedrek let slip he was once a lord in his own right. He, my friend, is the man who aided Elen in escaping from the Eorlingas' captivity.' I grimace at the unwelcome reminder of Elen. 'He's been punished most severely. He was once a slave to these people, although a highly skilled one. I don't think he lives in much hardship. But still, if you were looking to drive a wedge between them, he might be somewhere to start.'

'No,' I announce decisively, surprising myself. 'I don't wish to do anything to these people other than aid them in ending the life of Elen, and my father in the process, should he prove to be her ally.'

Dewi's silent for a moment. I turn to look at him. His expression is pensive. 'Heafoc said as much. But remember, you're only united in purpose for now.'

Now my eyes narrow. 'You're with us, aren't you, Dewi? You pledged yourself to me. You follow my commands.'

'Of course, Wærmund.' And he bows. I say nothing further, but suddenly I know to be wary of him. 'These seem to be good people.' He finally breaks the awkward silence.

'They're certainly wealthy,' I reply.

'Tell me, again, about your father,' Dewi surprises me by asking. He's never asked much about my father. I consider why he has such concern now.

'He loved my brother, not me. I killed my brother, and stole his wealth, and in return Isarninus of the Wæclingas stole that wealth. If my father allied with Elen, then no doubt, he's had it returned to him now.'

'Because you're marked by Woden?'

'Yes. He thought me a curse. He said I was gods-cursed, not gods-marked. He is, however, a good warrior, amongst my people.'

'He claims descent from your god, Woden, as you do?'

'He does, yes.'

'So, he fights with the same skill as you?'

I consider this. Have I become a skilled warrior like my father, or have I become a different sort of fighter?

'My father taught me little of how to fight. Heafoc has taught me more. And the people of Uriconium even more. So, no, my father fights differently to me, as do his warriors.'

Dewi considers this in silence.

'You fear him?' he eventually questions.

'I have feared him. When I first killed my brother, I believed he'd seek vengeance. I ran from my homeland, keen to outdistance him. He sent men to kill us. They failed. I no longer fear him. I'd say I respect him as a warrior, but not as a leader and certainly not as a father. More than anything, it is his death I seek, just as much as Elen's. I wish to take my father's life to prove how much he underestimated me. I will be a kin-killer once more but it will right wrongs foisted against me.'

'Then we'll triumph against him, if he's Elen's ally.'

'We will, yes, but it'll be bloody and brutal. And now, we must seek out Lord Madog and discuss battle tactics with him.'

Together, we stride towards the main villa building. From nearby, I hear the telltale sign of men fighting and hurry my steps, cursing my allies for fools. I come to an abrupt stop, my eyes quickly determining what's unfolding before me. It's no fight, but instead the warriors of the Eorlingas train with those of my *comitatus*. It's intriguing.

Lord Madog's there. I go to him. He turns to greet me, and speaks with Dewi.

'It came about by happenstance. The warriors all came together, without any orders, and have been testing one another's skills.'

I nod, somehow unsurprised. Heafoc battles against Madog's young warrior, Beli. It should be an unequal match. Heafoc has decades of experience, and Beli, with barely a moustache above his lips, clearly has only a few months. Curiously, the younger man doesn't make use of his greater speed to evade Heafoc, but instead fights in a very different way. He entices Heafoc on, meeting his jabs with his blade, not his shield. Heafoc takes the invitation and rushes him, thinking to overwhelm the youth, but now Beli uses his litheness to dash behind him, and offers a passing blow to Heafoc's shoulder blade.

I sense Heafoc's confusion, while Lord Madog grins, no doubt pleased with Beli.

'He's only become a warrior recently,' Dewi informs me of Madog's words. I don't immediately reply, my gaze drawn to where Eastmund battles Urien. He was one of those who escorted Madog to Uriconium. I realise, now, I should have asked Lord Madog to prove his warrior prowess before committing to aiding them. It's too late now, but luckily it appears these men of the Eorlingas are greatly skilled.

Eastmund and Urien should be more evenly matched, but again, there are small differences in how the two battle. East-mund's keener to hide behind his shield, only occasionally poking his head above it to sight a blow. Urien presses against him, quick, light blows on the shield, forcing Eastmund to retreat.

'We shall train everyone to fight in a shield wall, as is the way of our people.' Without waiting for Dewi's reply, I stride into the open space. It's perhaps usually cultivated, but for now the field is simply brown soil, the top layer likely to be picked up by the wind blowing inland from the sea.

Dewi follows me as I call instructions to my warriors, first bending to collect my shield from where it lies on the ground. No doubt Heafoc brought it here for me.

'Heafoc, Eastmund, Maggenræd, Osfyth, Bucge, Sennicus, Rhun, all of you, come on, shield wall.'

I'm aware Lord Madog questions Dewi, who responds quickly enough. Madog's own warriors step aside from mine, and watch us carefully. Many are panting heavily, and most have soil ingrained on their knees and elbows, from one fall or another.

Carefully, we make our shield wall, the wood overlapping with a soft shudder. Our positions are well versed now. We know whom to fight next to, and their strengths and weaknesses, as well as our own. As outside Isarninus' hill fort, Dewi and his warriors add themselves to the two ends, and Sennicus is also there, alongside Blatero, and the warriors from Uriconium, Mato, Locinna and Totia.

I watch Lord Madog. He speaks quickly. He and his warriors mirror our actions, so we face one another.

We should perhaps have wooden blades, or at least covered the ones we have, but I've not thought of that. Instead, I mean to test our respective strengths.

'We want no cuts, be wary of that. They are our allies,' I remind my warriors staunchly. 'Advance,' I call, confident the Eorlingas are ready.

I watch Lord Madog and his men. They've shields made of a variety of materials, some bronze, some willow. They're different shapes and sizes and don't overlap as ours do.

In ten steps, we come together, shield touching shield. Madog lifts his voice to offer a command to his men but I don't know what it is. Dewi's too engrossed to remember to tell me what the other man says. Immediately, I feel the strain in the back of my supporting leg, and in my ankle as well, but I also realise their shield wall isn't as strong as ours. I reach out with the hand I'd usually use with my seax and pat Urien on his head. He has no helm. Angry eyes glower at me. He surprises me by offering a swift jab with his fisted hand. I veer aside from it, although he retracts it before it can hit me square in the nose.

I don't have my helm on either, I realise, or my byrnie. These men wear leather coverings over their chests, or ancient bronze ones. Still, they're strong.

Again, I intend to pat Urien on the head, as a sign I'd beat him if I held my seax, but he evades my hand, ducking below his shield, and my arm can't reach that far.

Another cry from the Eorlingas, and now they press against us. My shield wall weakens. They're strong. We're matched in numbers, almost, but not in strength.

We jostle and grunt, Madog issuing commands, just as I do.

'Now,' I bellow. My warriors know what to do. We rush forwards, and immediately the Eorlingas' shield wall shudders apart, the men not expecting such a sudden reversal.

I drop my shield, and offer my hand to Urien frantically trying to move backwards on his elbows where he's dropped to the ground. I don't see Lord Madog, but I hear him, and also the sudden alarm from those of the Eorlingas who were watching us.

'Assure them we're only practising,' I order Dewi, but no doubt he already does, for no one comes against us. Instead, there's embarrassed laughter. Lord Madog strides towards me, his expression pensive but not angry. 'Tell him we need to learn to work together,' I direct Dewi. Heafoc's also doing his best to speak to the Eorlingas men and women. I realise language will be a problem when we meet Elen's force. 'We'll need to decide on some words for advance, retreat and all the other elements of the fight,' I muse.

With a little discussion, we once more take our respective positions in the shield wall, and try again. This time, the Eorlingas overwhelm us, and then we rout them again. Next time, Madog sends some of his warriors to fight amongst my warriors. I send some of mine to battle with his. The shield walls are immediately more balanced, and eventually Madog calls a halt when all of us are sweating and dusty. Laughter rings between the men on both sides, including from Bucge, Osfyth and the two women from Uriconium. I was concerned the Eorlingas might not like the women fighting but they don't even comment, as far as I can tell.

We're brought water in fine pottery jugs.

'They're good,' Heafoc huffs from where he sits on the ground, knees drawn up, swilling fluid into his mouth.

'They are. United, I suspect we'll be able to conquer all,' I confirm arrogantly. Heafoc glances at me, and shakes his head.

'Perhaps a little more time together before you make such a pronouncement,' he cautions. I grimace. I'm still guilty of making judgements too quickly. It's certainly caused me problems in the past.

I nod, acknowledging the advice. But once more, my attention's caught by Seeress Meddi. She stands off to one side, almost unseen in the shadow of one of the buildings, but I note her all the same. Her expression's inscrutable. I don't know if she's pleased by our efforts. I incline my chin towards her. But she disappears between one blink and the next, leaving me wondering if I saw her. And then I forget all about it, for Madog has brought Dewi to my side, and we engage in a long and detailed discussion concerning who should battle beside whom in the shield wall when we meet our enemy.

It takes much of the rest of the day, but eventually we have an agreed arrangement, one Eorlingas beside one of my *comitatus*, and then repeating the pattern. Our only slight disagreement is on who will take the centre position, because I want it, and so does Madog.

Dusty, and tired, we leave the field, now a churned mass of dust and mud. But just before we dunk our heads to clear away the dust, I remember something important.

'That is, of course, if our enemy brings a shield wall against us. It's possible they won't,' I admit, and Madog nods along, as Dewi relays my words. His response is quickly given.

'Tomorrow, we'll show you how we fight amongst our own kind,' he offers reassuringly. 'Perhaps a combination of both will be needed.' I grunt in agreement, reminded of the fight I witnessed when the Tomsæte fought my warriors earlier in the season. On that occasion, it descended into warrior against warrior. And in that, I suspect, the Eorlingas and my *comitatus* will find more differences than in the shield wall.

'I'd welcome that,' I acknowledge. 'I'm always keen to learn the secrets of how others fight.' Madog flashes a quick smile, but I sense some wariness. Perhaps, he suddenly fears he's invited the wolf into the henhouse. Maybe he worries we'll take all from him. I can't reassure him I won't, for why would he believe me? But I don't want to take this place from the Eorlingas. No. Yet I'm keen to learn their ways and secrets, especially how they manage the land and produce such fine horses. It would do me no good to kill these people. If I did so, I'd lose their skills along with taking their lives. I might still be headstrong on occasion, but on this, I know to be more restrained.

The Eorlingas are my allies. I must ensure all of my warriors remember that.

19

MEDDI OF THE EORLINGAS

I eye the sweeping location before me, unsure why Madog and Wærmund are so excited by it. Where are the walls, the ditches, the places where we can build barriers and prevent the enemy from overwhelming us? Where are the positions we can retreat to should the enemy prove successful? I'm entirely underwhelmed and open my mouth to voice my concern, but snap it shut once more. This is the furthest extent of any boundary our neighbours, the Husmeræ, might claim. To the far side of this summit, the land is claimed by another tribe, the Hendrica, one which is not our ally, or our enemy.

The two men are little more than boys. What experience do they have of warfare? But there are others there who know much more. I assess the older warrior, Heafoc, as well as Osfyth and Bucge. The three show no worry. Their faces don't echo my fears, but instead assess the place with eyes that see things differently to me. It makes me reconsider my initial complaints. I don't wish to undermine my brother and his new alliance with Wærmund's *comitatus*.

Instead, I listen to them. Madog's grown used to saying everything in his tongue and allowing Dewi to translate so Wærmund can understand. Dewi's another who shows no apprehension. If anything, all of them look at the chosen location with detached satisfaction.

I endeavour to place myself in their position and see with their eyes. After all, I'm a seeress not a warrior. What do I know of good places to stage a battle?

My home, Villa Eorlingas, is surrounded by a deep ditch and rampart, a single entrance point admitting people within, and out. It allows us to exclude people while ensuring our animals don't stray. This location benefits from none of those features. However, the terrain is different. Villa Eorlingas lies on reasonably flat ground, with the river nearby, and hills to the east, in the distance. The escarpment we're standing on is far from Villa Eorlingas. Here, we have a view to rival any I've ever seen, even that at Villa Husmeræ. I can see long distances from the peak. It's taken much effort to reach here. I sense the strain in my legs will take some time to stop aching.

If I turn towards where the sun will set, or rather, towards where I know Villa Eorlingas lies, I glimpse the sea, not quite a shimmering vastness in the distance, but rather the hint of it, the clouds high this day, although I feel as though I walk amongst them myself. Towards where the sun rose earlier I see the dips and hollows of this landscape, many of them shadowed by the vast hillside. The mighty peak gives way to lower ground much more quickly than I might expect. It reminds me very much of the path down into the Villa Husmeræ, only on a vastly larger scale. It is steep. So steep, I see why we came to it from a different route. The horses would not have made it up without injuring themselves. Potentially, neither would I.

The outcropping I stand upon is somewhat narrow. Yet it's wide enough I don't fear I'll tumble to the depths should my favoured mount grow difficult and buck me. I purse my lips. The enemy, when they come, will have to fight up this steep hill. I see how that will be advantageous to Madog and his allies. The Eorlingas will hold the high ground and be able to rain missiles down on our foes. My horse struggled up the slope. I was forced to dismount to allow the animal some respite. Now my calves burn with the pain of forcing my knees and feet almost directly vertical. This, then, is a huge advantage to have.

But surely the enemy won't be foolish enough to join us here. I listen to Madog and Dewi. I've learned more words the *comitatus* speak in our time together but not enough to understand everything.

'They're arrogant,' Dewi informs Madog confidently. He must speak of my bitch of a sister and her allies. 'They live in a hilltop site above Verulamium. They're used to fighting from the top but will forget the advantage it gives them when they see us here, flaunting our strength. They'll surge upwards, and it'll be their undoing, especially because, as I understand it, those from the east aren't used to this sort of ground.'

Madog nods with satisfaction. I open my mouth once more, and bite back the comment. It seems I need not make it. Another shares my concerns.

'The people once beholden to Isarninus will not be such fools,' Eastmund, one of the other warriors, questions, for Dewi to repeat.

All eyes seek him out but he looks unapologetic. I'm grateful he's voiced my worry.

'Those from the east,' Madog suggests, 'aren't used to huge hills, or so Heafoc has suggested. Will they realise their mistake or stumble into it?'

Slow understanding dawns on Eastmund's face. He nods willingly, his clouded features clearing.

'They won't allow themselves to be goaded, surely? Your father,' I incline my head towards Wærmund, 'if it is your father who supports the enemy, is a warrior of immense renown, isn't he?'

'My father,' Wærmund spits, 'isn't one to consider he has any weaknesses, and that's his weakness. His rage will drive him on. He'll be humiliated to discover I've such fine warriors with me. He'll not be reasonable.' Madog watches me with narrowed eyes. He must sense my unease but doesn't question me.

'Elen's an intelligent woman,' Bucge proposes, through Dewi. 'She'll realise. She's almost a seeress.'

I spit at Dewi as he repeats Bucge's words, even though my eyes are all for Bucge.

'She's no seeress,' I argue. 'She has her wiles, and little else. She's never killed in rage. She's always won with guile.'

'Seeress.' Dewi's respectful. 'Knowing our enemies' weaknesses will ensure we overwhelm them.'

'Then Elen's weakness is her utter belief in herself. She believes herself wronged. She believes herself right. Whatever decision she makes in the coming days will be the one she determines is absolutely the right one.'

'My father's the same,' Wærmund asserts, eyes blazing as I imagine mine do.

'Here,' Madog indicates the grassy plateau, spreading out behind us, with the breeze gentle, even so high up, 'we'll defeat our enemy. Here, we'll fight in the shield wall, warrior next to warrior, Eorlingas next to *comitatus*, and we'll triumph.' His words ring with conviction. All cheer them, even the *comitatus* before Dewi can rephrase it so they understand what he said. The warriors are all caught up in the idea of the battle. How they'll react when faced with blades that mean to kill, not just wound, I'm unsure.

I nod, trying to allow myself to become as swept up in the elation of finally gaining vengeance against Elen, who orchestrated the murder of my mother, although perhaps it was meant to be me who died that day. No doubt, she also knew of my father's death and disrespectful burial long before I did, but I remain unconvinced. I don't feel my horse-god at my side. That concerns me. I must find her. I must ensure she believes in what we hope to accomplish. The arguments of Madog and Wærmund have so far failed to convince me. Have they also failed to convince my horse-god? We're far from Villa Eorlingas, on land that owes its allegiance neither to the Eorlingas nor the Husmeræ. Have we misstepped in doing this? I understand the argument for keeping Elen away from Villa Eorlingas. But is this the right place to force the confrontation?

While the warriors talk, and then fall into place to practise their arrangements, wooden shields overlapping willow bark ones, and some old bronze ones, I turn aside, leading my mount to where the others have been secured, and then strike out alone.

As so often before, I seek a connection with the elements of air, earth and sky that surround me. I place my feet carefully, eyes open so as not to stumble, focused not on the here and now but on what my other senses tell me. The smell of the dew-soaked grass, the sound of the whistling wind, the feeling of the air through my fingers. I even stick my tongue through my lips and sample the location as well. It doesn't taste of home. It doesn't taste of much, the wind scouring all flavour away. The further I walk from the warriors, the more I become consumed by the escarpment. I almost don't hear the warriors any more, not the crash of swords and blades, and not the grunts of effort and pain. Neither do I smell them, which of itself is a relief. The *comitatus* certainly stink, no matter how many times their clothing is washed and left to dry in the breeze. They labour in their clothes.

It is on our behalf, so I should be grateful, but I would be more thankful if the smell was sweeter.

But still I search the viewpoint. To know we'll succeed, to understand what must be done, I endeavour to seek out my horse-god. Has she followed me here? Or does she protect Villa Eorlingas and the men, women, children, animals and wealth stored beneath the sun-baked tiles and between the stone floor and vaulted ceiling?

'Mother,' I murmur, hoping Marchell will come to me, but she doesn't. The memory of my father's physical presence has long since faded. My mother lingers. I see her in places I don't expect to, but she's absent here. Instead, my fists curl, nails digging into the soft pads of my hand. My sister. When I reach for my mother, for my horse-god, for my father, for my child, it's my sister I sense instead. How I despise her.

My lip curls. I need to banish her. The knowledge of her survival taunts me. It drives away my hard-won calmness, my acceptance of what happened to me. When I recall her survival, while Edern is over a year dead, my rage reignites.

I see her, as she was in captivity. Did I revel in keeping her in chains? Did I enjoy it too much? Is that why I'm being punished in such ways? I'd hope not. I wished her dead. I wanted her dead. My brother forbade it. I should have gone against him, but then the loyalties of our people would have been split. Madog must be the uniting force. I know that now, just as much as I did then.

I shake my head, angry with myself for allowing my rage to resurface so quickly. My thoughts scatter. For a short while, the smell of the grass absorbs me, the sounds of the *comitatus* and my brother's warriors fading away to nothing once more. I look towards where I've been told my sister commands the people who kept Wærmund captive two winters ago. She's a stranger in her hilltop fort and yet, somehow, she managed to insinuate herself into the good graces of Isarninus and now his son. She's also found an ally in a man all suspect is Wærmund's father, a mighty warrior from the east. I consider what she's done to accomplish so much. Has she used her body once more, as she did with Edern? Or has she been lucky? As a child, she was always luckier than I. From the simplest things, the juiciest berry, the tallest tree to climb, the fastest of horses. Her laughter, when I was angry about her triumph, mocks me even now. I grip my hand even tighter, aware I need to be careful, or I'll cut myself on my fingernails.

I grimace. I've never been the same with Madog. He was to be loved and nurtured, not battled against and beaten. Perhaps it's the way with close siblings. Wærmund and his brother, as I understand it, were the same as me and Elen. Madog, so much younger I could have been his mother, was an entirely different proposition. But no. That's not it. I'm convinced of it. Elen, my sister, has been sent to test me by my horse-god. I must ensure I survive and triumph against her.

I bite my lip and taste blood this time, considering all I know about her. While Madog and Wærmund consider the strengths and weaknesses of their opponent, I suspect I should do the same. More calmly now, sitting on a patch of grass dried by the building heat of the sun, I think about my sister, not as my sister, but as a woman and mere acquaintance. What do I know about her?

She's always been jealous and ambitious. She was thwarted and cast aside as a child, and then again, when Edern chose me first, and not her. When Edern died, she didn't have the support of Villa Eorlingas to take his place. I think it would have been easy to defeat the few warriors she did have even without Madog and his warriors. Without Edern to command, there was little loyalty left. In exchange for her losing that position, and being cast into our prison, she's chosen bloody vengeance. She believes she's always right. She believes we are wrong. Her weaknesses are many. And her strengths?

Jealous, ambitious, always lucky. How strange it is, I realise, to understand her strengths are also her weaknesses. I consider myself as well. Can I do so without refusing to acknowledge I'm not the perfect seeress I'd have others believe?

I can be cruel. I can be merciless. I can be without feeling for those who get in my way. I'm single-minded. But I'm loyal. I treated my mother poorly. I was harsh on my baby brother. I did all this to make the Eorlingas strong. Perhaps there were other ways to do so, but I lacked the wisdom to know what those ways would have been.

Wisdom. I pause and consider this. I'm wise. I know it. I ken things others do not. I ken things others don't even ponder. I'm a thinker, and a doer. Is this my strength or my weakness? Do I think too much?

'Meddi.' Madog's voice rouses me from my thoughts. I turn to smile at him, banishing my reflections.

'Brother.' He slumps down beside me, in a jangle of iron and wool. He huffs. His face is red with exertion. I suppress a grimace for the ripe smell emanating from his armpits. I'm astounded he doesn't smell it himself and remove his clothing.

'It's agreed,' he announces gleefully. 'Did you see us in the shield wall together? It was magnificent.'

'I did, brother, yes,' I reply, because he's so pleased and I don't wish to settle my contemplations on him. To triumph, my brother must believe he will succeed.

'It'll be a fine battle. We'll overpower all. I'm sure of it.'

'That's my hope,' I confirm, hand reaching for the new blade at my waist. I might not be standing in the shield wall, but I'll be watching and so I must be able to defend myself.

'It's what I believe.' My brother laughs. Today, he seems young and free. I envy him the confidence and belief in himself. 'Come. We'll eat and talk more of tactics. Wærmund deems the enemy will arrive soon. They received our message, delivered by Veda, the trader. Then there'll be posturing and showing of arses and then the fight.'

I narrow my eyes as I allow him to haul me upright, the strength of his arm impossible to ignore.

'Showing of arses?'

'Yes, yes.' My brother nods eagerly. 'These warriors will mock one another and then we'll triumph against them.'

'But still, arses?'

'It's better than cocks,' my brother giggles, reminding me of when all young children must be taught about their body parts used for creating children.

'It is.' I shudder and he chuckles.

We stride towards the collection of Eorlingas warriors and those of the *comitatus*. It's astounding to see how quickly they've bonded. Now men and women who don't share a common language laugh and tease one another, and all of it is done with good humour. There's no discord here. My brother chose wisely when he decided to ally with Wærmund.

Rhiann isn't here, and neither are the vast majority of the Eorlingas. The older warriors have been left behind to protect our people. I can't believe Elen will know to send people there when the warriors are here, but I argued for the necessity of protecting the villa, all the same. Ladus and the Stoppingas are also within Villa Eorlingas. It's better to have so many together. But we've brought others of the Eorlingas to ensure there's food and drink while we wait to battle our enemy. They aren't warriors, like me, but they have the means to defend themselves should it prove necessary. If the battle goes poorly, they're to retreat the two days' journey towards Villa Eorlingas taking the horses with them, and ensure there's no means by which the enemy can overwhelm those who remain. They'll also gather the extra warriors from the Husmeræ who now protect their home.

The warriors of the Eorlingas, the Husmeræ and the *comitatus* are to do nothing but practise and hone their battle skills, as they've been doing for upwards of a month now, while our intent to battle Elen was sent on its way to the hilltop settlement above Verulamium. Eagerly, I take the offered bowl of mutton from Sian and spoon it into my mouth and only then find somewhere to settle. The breeze rustles my hair. I feel it lift from my neck, and a shiver runs down my spine.

'Here, seeress,' Sian offers, bringing me a thick cloak which I gratefully slide around my shoulders, securing it with a horse-headed brooch. It's not an old object. Indeed, it's new, forged by Terricus to show he can do more than make blades and nails. He's a good man, and confident in his skills.

I listen to Urien where he laughs along with Eastmund. The two are very different, but their wiry strength marks them as the same. Bucge talks with young Tudwal, showing him some different ways of stabbing with his seax blade, as the *comitatus* name it. Kenal's with Dewi, those two sharing more than just a love of fighting. I should like to know more of Dewi but he and his three allies are the means by which we communicate easily with Wærmund and Heafoc. I won't upset them. Certainly, I trust them.

'Tomorrow.' The word rings through the temporary encampment and all look to where Madog and Wærmund stand together, pointing down the steep-sided slope, one of our runners panting beside them. I consider when he first saw them. It can't have been long ago. I stand and take myself to Madog's side, looking down into the shadowed valley. My heart beats a staccato of a horse at full gallop. I see a party coming this way, dust kicked up by the passage of their feet. There's no other reason for people to be here. Elen and her allies have taken up our offer of engagement. I knew she wouldn't be able to refuse. I endeavour to pick out her form amongst the collection of warriors and horses, but they keep a good distance away. Eventually, darkness begins to fall and I turn aside. Although I've not seen Elen, I sense she's there with the warriors as they build an encampment and set a campfire to feed themselves and keep them warm.

I know tomorrow I'll have my triumph and my vengeance. Tomorrow, my sister will die. I can hardly wait for the sun to set so it might rise again on my sister's last day on this earth.

20

WÆRMUND OF THE GYRWE

During the night, the men and women brought from Villa Eorlingas to keep us fed and to tend to the horses keep watch, allowing my warriors and me to sleep. I think I'll be beset by worries and fears of what tomorrow will bring. But I sleep immediately, my body cooling from a day of physical activity, so I sink gratefully into my cloak, wrapping it tightly to ensure I don't wake with sore shoulders and thighs.

It feels as though this day was set in stone even before I murdered my younger half-brother, ran from my homeland and encountered Elen, while escaping from Isarninus' captivity. Perhaps this is the work of Woden. Maybe it's not and I'm being fanciful. Certainly, I hope to meet my father in battle this day and we'll be equals. I've skilled warriors at my side to defeat him. I have the Eorlingas and their allies as well. Over the last few weeks we've forged a bond that will enable us to fight together, shield against shield. We can't lose. Yet I know not to be overly confident. The battle must still be fought. We must still sweat and bleed in the name of this alliance, and all in order to earn great riches, and more importantly, our reputation as a *comitatus* of high renown.

When I wake, the sky overhead is blue, the clouds scudding against the cobalt vastness. A prickle of excitement worms its way into my belly. Today my vengeance will be complete. I'll enact revenge against my father, and the bitch, Elen. Then I'll reclaim my lost treasures from the hilltop site Isarninus once made his home. I'll have all I've ever wanted, and my *comitatus* will forge themselves a name written in stone to be passed on to future generations.

'Come on, you lazy sod.' Heafoc's boot against the side of my body has me snarling and jumping upright so quickly he veers backwards in shock.

'You thought I slept? How could I still sleep when today will bring an end to my troubles?' Despite my words, my voice is calm.

'Don't be too confident, but equally, confidence is a good thing to own.' I narrow my eyes, trying to make sense of his words, but my gaze is drawn to the thin tendril of smoke weaving a grey pattern amongst the few white clouds. My father and his warriors have reignited their cook fire for a morning meal. They don't intend to rush this.

I watched the enemy warriors arrive yesterday. I understand Seeress Meddi was unable to pick out Elen amongst them, but I sensed my father was near. I didn't see him either, but the efficient nature of the campsite, the arrival when it was almost too dark to see, that has all the markings of my father to it. He is there. I will face him. I consider my battle standard, the wolf emblem, made of lengths of iron by Katourn, and based on my wolfhound and the wolf emblem gifted to me, and worn around my neck. My father has no such standard. It will terrify him to witness it when the sunlight grows bright enough. It is secured in the ground, held aloft on a long wooden pole. He'll see it and know it means I claim my birthright as a child of Woden's get. As though summoning him, Freki slinks close. He smells of death and blood mars his muzzle. He's been hunting already.

'I hope my hunt goes as well as yours,' I murmur, running my hand over his long body.

I take the offered food from Sian and eat it too quickly. The warmth hits my belly in a welcome burst of flavours. I feel any lingering lethargy leave my tall frame.

'Eastmund, wake up,' I hear Heafoc complaining to the prone form. I allow a grin to touch my cheeks. All is excitement and too-loud voices, all aside from me. And Meddi.

I see her standing on the edge of the escarpment staring down towards the source of the grey smoke, her focus intent. She appears terrifying, but I'm also intrigued by what she sees.

I make my way towards her, handing my bowl back so another can eat. At the side of the steep hillside, there's a collection of vicious-looking brambles clinging to the stony surface, until, about twelve horses' lengths away, it gives way to tufty grass, and then even lower, blooming flowers and a huge collection of weeds, which tumble down into the depths of the valley. It's from there the smoke comes. Small shapes move around. I'm surprised they've not sheltered beneath the strand of thin willow trees growing in a large block to the side of them. Perhaps, down there, it's not as windy as here. Maybe they didn't wish to hide from us. Their arrogance matches only ours.

One of the figures is immobile. A flash of recognition ripples along my body. Elen. I'd recognise the arrogant cast of her chin even from such a distance. Meddi hisses. I'm minded to do the same. I hear the clack of Meddi's strange, metalled objects that always rest against her legs, secured by a belt around her waist. She mutters beneath her breath. I hope it's a curse against Elen, and a promise for her painful death. I want to be the one to kill her. But I know Bucge and Meddi also wish to be the ones to end her life.

Only then another figure joins Elen's distant one. Now it's my turn to spit. I've assumed, since I was told of the threat against the Eorlingas, it was my father who supported Elen. Now I have it confirmed. For a moment, I wish I was closer and better able to see him, but I know him all the same. It would be impossible not to recognise the man who tormented my childhood. Unbidden, my hand reaches for the wolf emblem around my neck.

I consider what Wihtlæd knows of me and what he suspects I've become. Would he, had I simply run away and not killed my younger half-brother in the process, have esteemed me now? I'm Wærmund, leader of a *comitatus* of men and women and respected, and more importantly, recompensed by those who seek to employ us. No. I shake my head. My father has always despised me, ever since I murdered my mother while entering the world. Surely something he should hold the blame for, but which he clearly doesn't. I suspect I've always hated him too.

'Wihtlæd,' I mutter darkly. Others have joined us, Madog and Heafoc the most prominent. Heafoc growls low. Madog's silent. The two men are intent in menacing the enemy.

Meddi's words, when they're for our ears, are evidently commands. I look to Heafoc. He tries to listen, but she speaks too quickly. Luckily, Dewi's there to explain what she's saying.

'She suggests we take our positions.'

Heafoc shakes his head, but leaves it to me to call Madog back from summoning his warriors.

'If we get into position now, we'll grow tired and weak anticipating their first move. We hold the higher ground. We wait for them,' I caution.

As Dewi translates, Meddi casts a furious glance my way.

Madog reveals more wisdom, nodding sagely, and shouting orders to his warriors. They stop trying to eat quickly, and instead resume their slower approach to preparing for the day.

'It's all about making us wait,' I confirm. 'In this situation, anyway. But, have some of the Eorlingas deployed to watch our backs. I don't wish to be caught hissing and glaring at my father, while he sends others to slice open our backs.'

As if Woden has been waiting for my statement, there's a sudden shriek of outrage, and the unmistakable bang of a shield hitting iron. I hurry to see what's happening.

Ahead, the Eorlingas, with their cook fire, stand shocked, mouth agape as young Tudwal marches someone I recognise forwards. The figure's bleeding heavily from a slice to his belly, but Tudwal hasn't quite killed him. Not yet.

'Ah, Alric, it's good to see you again.' I smirk at the terror-filled eyes of the young man. He was once supposed to be my friend, but then he aligned himself with my brother, Waga. I'd not realised he didn't die when my brother met his death. That was an oversight, but it seems not one I'm going to regret today.

'Are there more of you?' Heafoc demands. There's a scramble to ensure there isn't. It's only then, as my gaze sweeps the plateau, I realise Meddi hasn't moved. She makes a forlorn figure, standing alone on the outcropping, the wind whipping her hair, precious objects hanging down her legs and dress swirling around her, but I don't call her away. She's not in harm's way, not with Bucge hovering to the far side, peering down to ensure no one else intends to take us by surprise. Bucge, I know, has her small trinket that once belonged to Elen. The two women, while not sharing a language, certainly share their desire to kill Elen.

'Wærmund?' His high-pitched voice takes me back to my childhood.

'Yes. How many of you are there?' I ask, aware his face pales.

He's almost slumped onto his knees. Tudwal's strength keeps him upright.

'I, I, I didn't believe her,' Alric murmurs.

'What lies has the witch been spreading?'

'She said you violated her and took her wealth.'

'Do I look like the sort of man so desperate for a tumble I'd bed a woman old enough to be my mother?'

His jaw slackens further, the drum of his lifeblood flooding my senses. He'll be dead soon. He means to distract me with his inane questions.

'How many warriors does my father have?'

'Thirty-three,' he gasps, only now looking down to see why he's so weak. He holds his hands against the gaping wound. I do him a favour I know he'd never have offered me. I slice his throat to make his death even quicker. His breath hisses and then he falls silent.

'Thirty-three,' I murmur, trying to determine if we have more or less than that number.

'Thirty-two now, so evenly matched,' Heafoc assures me, eyeing the body dispassionately. It's just the first of many who'll not witness the sunset, I realise. At least he was able to see the sunrise.

'Throw him over the side,' I instruct. 'Have my father know his plan has been discovered.'

It falls to Eastmund and Dewi to haul the bloody body away. With little care, they fling the corpse over the edge, in the direction of my father's encampment. We all hear the wet thuds as Alric's lifeless form falls sharply before coming to a stop on the grassy banks. I observe Meddi's response, but her gaze doesn't shift from where my father, and her sister, wait to join us in battle. She shows no reaction to the sound of the body dropping. Nothing at all.

'I admire her,' Heafoc huffs from beside me. He nods towards Meddi as though he needs to tell me who he speaks about. 'She holds her anger better than many.'

'It's been simmering for a long while,' I confirm, recalled to what I've heard about the falling-out between the sisters. I thought my brother bad enough, but Elen's allowed unimaginable harm to come to her sister. I imagine Meddi wishes Madog had been as forthright as I was in murdering my brother when they discovered Elen at their villa.

'Today she'll have her chance to seek vengeance. I doubt it'll be pretty.'

'She's not to fight with us?' I query, suddenly outraged at the thought. While I acknowledge Bucge's a warrior first and a seiðr only after that, Meddi's certainly a seeress. The tribe won't wish to risk losing her. I don't see they have a replacement. Not yet.

'I doubt any will be able to stop her, when it comes to it.'

'Then we must protect her.'

'Ah, my young lord, you have feelings for her?' Heafoc chuckles. I narrow my eyes to deny it, but realise he's teasing me.

That's when I see it out of the corner of my eye, and curse myself for being too young, too confident, and too damn arrogant, just as Heafoc warned me.

'Bollocks,' I huff, gathering my legs beneath me to dash towards Meddi's lonely vigil on the hillside, for Bucge has moved to ensure no enemy seek to reach us from behind, as Alric did. I feel Heafoc's mirroring actions as a rush of air beside me.

My father really is a bastard.

21

MEDDI OF THE EORLINGAS

My sister taunts me from below. I see how the wind buffets her long hair free from her neck, revealing some damn copper or golden torque settled there, in the hollow beneath throat and breast. I imagine seeing the swaying motion of seeress' spangles at her waist, and feel my lips twist with fury. Only some other-worldly force stops me from marching towards her and yanking both items from her arrogant posture. She's no right to wear the symbols of a seeress. She's never been one although, no doubt, in the way she's directed the course of my life, she believes herself one.

I breathe deeply, cooling my fury. I mustn't make a stupid mistake. Not now. I must remain cool and detached. We're so close to overwhelming her and bringing her life to an end. To stop that happening now would be foolish.

The first I know of any danger is when young Wærmund surges into me. I fall beneath his weight, and the stink of his warrior's body, to crash on the tufted grasses dotting the hilltop with a grunt of pain. The sound of something being hurled over where my head was mere moments ago has me gasping with understanding before I can voice my complaints at such an action from the eastern warrior.

The strength in young Wærmund's body rests against my more taut one, his hot breath rushing into my face.

I don't understand all he says to me, but I stay still anyway. The bastards meant to kill me by stealth. That must be at my sister's command. Wærmund assured us all, through Dewi, those from the east, bloodthirsty warriors that they are, would wish to meet us fairly. It would be a test of strength, warrior against warrior, not guile against guile.

Madog's the next face I see, above Wærmund's shoulder, and then Bucge and Heafoc arrive as well. Moments pass, while the three glare down at where I imagine my sister watches with a hint of amusement on her slick lips and swaying hips.

'Come,' Madog eventually announces, reassured the immediate danger has passed. I sense Wærmund's weight shift from above me, and for a fleeting moment I feel something I've not experienced for many years. A sudden thrum of desire in the parts of my body Edern marked and which have given me nothing but painful reminders of the day of the death of my daughter ever since. I sit upright, taking Wærmund's hand, and again feel a flurry of heat at his touch. I shake my head, and immediately march towards the spot I was standing in moments ago, determined to show my sister I yet live. Only Heafoc's large frame gets in front of mine, and Madog urges me to stand back, his long moustache blowing in the breeze, almost touching his eyes.

'What was it?' I question. Dewi's arrived to help us all make sense of our gabbled words. He holds a rounded piece of stone, smoothed by water or the passage of many hands.

'A slingshot,' Dewi informs me. 'Like the Uppingas use,' he further murmurs.

'Not our preferred way to fight,' Heafoc announces firmly, his fury evident in the look he passes between the stone and those down below.

'Then it must be those who were once beholden to Isarninus, the Wæclingas,' I glower, dismayed to find they almost wounded me so easily, and from such a vast distance. Would my death have ended this? Would it have made Elen triumphant? I hope not. My brother and his allies must do more than fight for me. They must battle for the future of the Eorlingas.

'Yes,' Dewi confirms, eyes narrowed, as he runs his fingers over the stone. It's a bright colour, almost green. I'm surprised he continues to hold it, and reach out to take it from him. He snatches it back. I don't believe any other notices. I'll need to ask him about it at another time, it appears. What, I consider, does he know of the Uppingas? They're a far-distant tribe to Villa Eorlingas. I notice those who are his especial warriors show no recognition of the stone.

'Come away,' my brother cautions me. Kenal and Tudwal have arrived by now, out of breath, faces white with fear.

'Check the perimeters,' I urge them. 'Ensure there are no others.' I turn to Madog. 'I thought they'd be honourable,' I grumble, more out of sorts than I'd like to admit at finding myself only moments away from being killed when I thought to leave here triumphant.

Madog nods. This we've both been assured, and indeed, the horror on the faces of Wærmund and Heafoc assures me they don't like this either.

'My thanks,' I direct to Wærmund. He nods, his focus remaining on the enemy down below us. We still hold the higher ground.

Before Madog can reply, a noise rushes upwards to us. I pivot, looking over Heafoc's bulk to see Madog was correct when he told me of what this day would bring. A collection of pale white arses greets us, others raising arms and fingers in ways I'm sure should offend. They taunt us, but I'd rather they mock us than have triumphed with my death. If this is all they have, it's a poor reaction to their failure.

A mumble of words from Heafoc. Then he speaks in my language.

'And so it begins,' he states. I take a deep breath. I've hungered for this moment ever since we realised we'd need more allies to face Elen and her warriors. Now we've come to it, I feel a surge of excitement, a belief we'll be the ones to leave here alive, and not her. I can hardly wait to see her cold, lifeless body. At my side, unseen by others, I sense my mother, and my father's presence. We're a long way from Villa Eorlingas, but they've come here to witness my sister's, their daughter's, final downfall. I only wish it had happened over twenty winters ago. Then, it's highly likely my father and mother would still live, and I'd never have become a seeress. Not, I acknowledge, I'd change that now. Not now. But there were certainly times I railed against what I was becoming. Perhaps, then, I've something to thank her for. Not that I'd ever admit it aloud.

* * *

'Come away,' I'm urged by Madog. I allow my steps to be guided towards where the *comitatus* and the warriors of the Eorlingas and Husmeræ prepare for war, on a wider stretch of the hillside, where the animals are being kept, as well as the supplies we've brought with us. Many of the Eorlingas women have formed a semicircle protecting us and our supplies from any more attempts by our enemy to attack us from that direction. In that, I sense the work of Elen.

The smell of iron and sweat is redolent in the air, the gentle breeze unable to dislodge it when over thirty men and women prepare to fight to the death. I look at those I know well, to those I've only recently met, and realise I want none of them to die on behalf of the Eorlingas, and yet I acknowledge not all will walk from here.

I know Wærmund and his warriors have made their barters with a god they name as Woden. They've struck good bargains to ensure we triumph. I've also spoken with the horse-god of the Eorlingas, although I still don't sense her presence. I hope she accepts my bargain. I don't believe she will deny me, not when my mother and father are here. But, still, her absence is concerning.

I stand beside the cook fire, with Sian at my side. The stern features of the remaining Eorlingas women who've escorted us to cook and tend to our needs while we wait for the battle remind me we're as martial as the men, when we must be. Sian aids me into my battered breastplate and shimmering torque, and then re-secures my spangles at my waist. I have my ceremonial dagger, handed to me through generations of seeresses, but I also have a new blade, a seax blade. The handle's firm in my hand, crafted for me by the now free Hedrek. We all benefit from such weapons. The spears are also tipped with new, sharp blades. We have shields, even me and the women who'll not fight unless they must, although they stand ready to protect us. It's the way of our people that the men fight for their women, but we all know women can perform the required butchery when the enemy lie dying and our men are spent.

I listen to the thrum of conversation between the warriors, although I don't understand all of the words. Some mutter prayers, others talk too loudly of past exploits. All of them are preparing for the roughness of the shield wall and the carnage to come.

I stand beside Madog. He looks resplendent in his breast-plate, blades ready on his weapons belt, a rough-shaped iron helm covering his head, similar to those Wærmund's *comitatus* have. I can't say he likes it but it's wise to protect his head, mouth and eyes as best he can. Around his neck he has a piece of rein-forced leather, placed there to protect his throat. He both is and isn't the man who rode into Villa Eorlingas and reclaimed it on Edern's death. He's a father now, a tribal leader, a lord, as the men and women of the *comitatus* name him. He's a warrior, honed as sharply as the blades Terricus has forged in the heart of the blue flames, sizzling with intent.

'Brother,' I murmur. He startles from wherever his thoughts have taken him, and offers me a wide grin.

'Sister,' he replies. His voice shows no fear. If he's doubtful of success, he masks it well. Not that he's arrogant either.

'Go well,' I instruct him. His grin broadens beneath his mous-tache, and then drops.

'Care for them all, if you must. He's but a boy but like you did for me, you can keep him safe until such time...' His voice cracks. I reach out and grip both of his forearms. His strength is evident in that touch. He's a strong man. A good man.

'You'll triumph, and return to them.'

He opens his mouth to argue.

'But if not, I'll be there, as will the entire people of the Eorlin-gas. We'll not falter now.'

He nods, licks his lips, and turns aside to make his way to the promontory, but I don't release my grip on him. He fixes me with a perplexed expression.

'Bring her to me. I'll make the final, killing blow.'

He nods quickly with understanding. I realise how wise he's

become. He doesn't argue with me. There was a time he would have done so.

Now I release my hold and watch him and Wærmund confer for a brief moment. Then both of them shout for their warriors to join them, as they begin making their way to the pinnacle down whose side our enemy wait to face them. The wind blows stronger, perhaps, I reason, it might even assist our foes to reach the peak more easily. Or rather, the sharp, keen edges of our blades.

I feel a stirring in my breast, my breath coming a little too fast. I tamp it down.

I've a part to play in this. I'll ensure the men of the Eorlingas survive this day, as well as those of the Husmeræ who've escorted us. And, I realise, I hope the warriors of the *comitatus* do as well. That realisation surprises me more than it should.

22

WÆRMUND OF THE GYRWE

I wince at the stab of pain in my right knee from tumbling Meddi to the ground. I peer down, sure beneath my trews my knee bleeds, but unprepared to reveal that to anyone. That would show the enemy had first blood, even if Meddi yet lives, despite their intentions. What cowards they are. I detect Elen's hand in the decision to enact such a tactic. My father, as much as I despise him, wouldn't countenance it. He might be many things, but dishonourable isn't one of them.

'Are you ready for this?' Heafoc whispers to me, as I bend to gather my shield and spear into my hands, having run my left hand along Freki's rough coat. He offers me a look and a soft whine, before heeding the call of Sian who's promised to keep the beast away from the fighting. In his absence, I touch my wolf emblem at my neck. With it there, I sense Freki will not be far away.

'Of course,' I murmur, but there's no heat to my words. Am I scared to finally encounter my father in battle? I find I'm not. I've allowed the idea of his retribution to follow me for much of the last two summers. I don't know why. I'm a good warrior. I can match him, and then some chance, something one of the Eorlingas will do, will allow me to exploit that and overwhelm him. I hunger to take the final killing blow. I wish to end his life, and that of Elen as well. 'Are you?' I ask just as quietly.

Heafoc has his own demons to lay at the feet of my father. He offers me a broad grin and slaps my back, making me grimace as the byrnie straps dig in deeply at my shoulder. 'Always,' he assures me.

I turn to assess the rest of my *comitatus*, absorbing their features. For once, we're able to make all the decisions about the coming battle. We'll not be set upon, or caught unawares. It makes a refreshing change. I note Osfyth and Bucge, reassuring one another their equipment is in place, and they have blades and shields to hand. Locinna and Totia mirror their actions. I see Eastmund and Maggenræd, laughing with Dewi. Eastmund's face is split as though there are two sides to him, the one showing joy, the other fear. Dewi and his three surviving allies – Cynin, Eli and Rhun – joke with Sennicus and Blatero from the Tomsæte, alongside Mato, the only man to join us from Uriconium. Indeed, there's a welcome joviality amongst my *comitatus*. It pleases me to see it. We've made our agreements with Woden, or whatever god we pray to. There's no fear, only iron resolve to aid our allies, and in the process, put an end to the pretensions of my father and his warriors.

'Come,' I call, and stride towards Madog. He's preparing with his warriors, and those who come from another tribe – the Husmeræ, I believe they're called. I hold my hand out towards him. He grips it. I feel his strength, and he mine. But he holds me for a moment longer than I expect.

'Thank you.' He says the words in my tongue. I nod. He speaks of Meddi and how I ensured she lived, when someone thought to kill her with a slingshot. Admittedly, they must have been very skilled to even risk such an action. Uphill, it would not have been easy to even sight Meddi.

'Victory will be ours,' I confirm, using his tongue. We share a grin and then a grimace as from below the bellow of enemy warriors can be heard. They've finally covered their arses once more. I'm grateful for that. A man doesn't need to see that, even if I understand why they determined to show them to us. 'Form up,' I cry, Madog echoing the order but in his own language. The familiar clatter and creak of leather and iron floods my hearing, the smell of people who are both excited and terrified adding to it.

I turn to face the men I'll fight between. It's not Heafoc and Eastmund, as I've grown used to, but rather young Tudwal and the older Urien. I trust them both. They're clever men and strong. They know how to skirmish with their blades and shields.

We share smirks of resolve and then lift our shields, to clatter the one over the other. I sense the same happening up and down the line of warriors, and find a broad grin on my cheeks, as the wind rustles my long hair and beard. This is what it means to be a warrior. It's this camaraderie I missed when my father banished me from fighting with his oath-sworn men. What a fool he was.

From the depths of the slope, I hear the same being set in motion against us.

'For the Eorlingas and the *comitatus* of Wærmund,' I bellow. I detect the deep response of Heafoc and the slightly higher ones of Bucge and Osfyth, and behind it all, I hear Meddi and her seeress' imprecations to the gods we worship. I think of Woden. I've made my bargain with him. Today I'll discover if I'm truly Woden-marked or Woden-cursed. Today, I'll discover if my father was right all along, or if, as Bucge has reassured me repeatedly, he was entirely wrong about me and my fate.

* * *

Steps in unison, we stride towards the edge of the summit. Below us, the vast expanse of deepening greenery greets me as the gentler slope forms. My gaze is all for my father's warriors and those Elen has brought from the settlement of Isarninus, above Verulamium. I hear the howl of Freki and know, while he's not at my side, he's willing us on to victory as well. He embodies my god, just as the metal wolf emblem, planted in position on the pinnacle of the slope, does.

Sunlight flashes off metal bosses on wooden shields, and on the spear tips held by my father's warriors. They're a seething mass of iron and wood, but they must first reach us. We've no plans on descending from this peak to meet them. My father must realise we have the advantage. He, or someone amongst the group, has endeavoured to win with guile and deceit. I consider if that pleases him or whether he thinks to win using his battle tactics. I suspect the latter. He's an arrogant arse.

The iron creature of a shield wall moving in tandem begins to stride towards us. They move quickly, with determination, and behind them all I seek out those who'll not join the fight, unsurprised one of them is Elen. Her lithe figure would be impossible to forget. I suppress a grimace as I see her in breastplate and with shield held before her. She'll not fight, but means to look the part. Then my gaze is drawn back to the others, their headlong dash slowing now as they reach the steeper parts of the slope. My father will be there.

I look along the line of the enemy shield wall. My father's not a tall man, but he's broad and powerfully built. I'm unsurprised to find him at the centre. He desires to take his vengeance against me and to drive his warriors onwards. I wish him luck with that.

I anticipate feeling a moment of fear as his eyes pick me out of the answering line of shields, but there's no such thing, as I sense his gaze. He's merely an enemy. And one I must kill.

'Hold.' I lift my voice to direct my warriors. Madog does the same. We've learned the most basic of commands in each other's tongues during the last month, but for now, we share the orders between us. It's reassuring, however, to know we abide by our predetermined plan. The enemy must come to us. We'll have the greatest opportunity to overwhelm them by disadvantaging our foes by having them fight uphill. That my father still advances speaks of his arrogance, or perhaps his determination nothing will stop him from gaining vengeance against the son he's always termed a bastard and Woden-cursed.

While I despised Elen's efforts to kill her sister with a sling-shot, we've come ready to throw stones down on our enemy. At least this is a fair fight. They've answered our call to battle. It was an opportunistic strike when Meddi was exposed and unaware.

'Hold,' I repeat. I hear Tudwal's breathing beside me. His shield arm shakes a little but I pretend not to notice where it overlaps with mine. He's brave. He must know being at my side makes it likely he'll face a concerted attack from my father. He makes no complaint and never has. Heafoc's to his side. It's as far away as he's allowed himself to be.

'Hold,' I hear Madog cry in his tongue. Beside me, Urien whispers beneath his breath. Meddi's chants are growing louder and louder. I breathe deeply, calmly, forcing my escalating heart rate to slow.

Below us, the advance of the enemy has decelerated. It doesn't surprise me. The slope's incredibly steep, more likely to be the home to birds than people. It startles me to hear my father's voice. I've forgotten how deep his tone is. He urges his men upwards.

'Hold,' I urge Kenal beside me, as I sense him preparing to

throw his stone at the enemy. 'Hold,' I say more softly, just for his ears, and perhaps for me as well. 'Not much longer,' I mutter, unsure if he'll understand that or not, certainly Heafoc will. We can't go too soon. We must make full use of our advantages to undermine their determined attack.

We need to be able to see eyes and mouths, not just the idea of these warriors, before we do anything. Spear tips continue to flash in the brightening daylight. I wince against the glare, blinking the brilliance from my eyes so I see more than shards of light dancing behind my eyelids.

And then it's time. I catch sight of my father's furious eyes, his belligerent chin and the greying beard covering it. I smile, not a joyful smirk, but rather a grimace.

'Now,' I expel.

As one, all thirty-two of us pitch our carefully hoarded stones over the side of the hilltop. Some go further than others, not every man and woman can throw well, but a reassuring clunk of stone hitting wood and iron rings through the air. Simultaneously, outraged shrieks and cries reach our ears as the enemy warriors try to evade the projectiles.

'Now,' I order, and another collection of stones follows the first wave. 'Now.' The third instruction comes even quicker. This time we all throw overarm, not underarm. While the enemy try to shelter from stones aimed at ankles, the final batch is intended to strike unprotected bodies and heads.

I nod with satisfaction as three of the final onslaught hit their targets. Men tumble backwards from the shield wall. I doubt the blow will be lethal but certainly one of them, thrown from the far end of my line of warriors, does strike one of the enemy on the head with a wet crunch. The man drops to the ground, lifeless. It is, alas, a bloodless death, as far as I can tell.

It was worth the effort of hauling the stones up the steep hill, despite the many complaints from all of us, me included.

'Now.' And our final wave of stones descends while my father fights to retain some semblance of order amongst his warriors and those of the Wæclingas who comprise his force. There are also some perhaps beholden to Elen. The three gaps in the shield wall are quickly closed, the wounded men abandoned, and all while our largest stones gain momentum as they near them. These strike once more at ankles and feet, and two of my adversaries falter, a snap assuring me one has misstepped and perhaps broken a bone.

A flurry of angry words greets me. The words 'bastard' and 'whoreson' the most pleasant.

'Hold firm,' I remind my warriors, sensing Urien and Tudwal are eager to break formation. We can't take this success and get consumed by it. We still need them to come to meet us. If we rush down the hillside now, all will be chaos. We have our plans. They'll hold until such time as it becomes impossible to stick to them.

Not that my father can exert as much control. A handful of men break free from the shield wall, surging upwards, their shouted words to one another those of Isarninus' people.

So far, much of what's happening has been well predicted. I hear my father shouting for them to return to the shield wall, but of course, rage drives them onwards. They're coming closer, much, much closer.

'Now,' I bellow. Those opposite the enemy scampering up the hillside, more akin to goats than men, as they scurry from side to side, handhold to handhold, stab out and down with their spears, seeking our foemen. Eyes focused only on where they need to place hands and feet and not on us, two of the fools are skewered with barely a sound. I hear Eastmund's crow of delight at killing one of our opponents, and also Dewi's. They've taken first blood, the madder-red shimmering brightly in the early morning air, and I'm not alone in roaring my appreciation. The remaining two foes belatedly realise how exposed they are. The one stands upright, faltering, arms circling wildly as he loses his balance and barrels down the hillside with more speed and force than our collection of stones. He might be the final projectile that wounds even more of his allies.

I see the final warrior assess his chances warily, from where he's almost on all fours. He backs up, slowly, mindful of stones dotting his route, threatening to trip him and following the other man in rolling down the hillside. There he waits for my father's warriors to join him. He's reabsorbed into the shield wall, even as three of the foes are forced to jump aside or risk being tumbled by the man who fell. They continue to surge upwards. I lick my lips. It's nearly time. It's so nearly time.

'Hold,' I murmur, more for myself than anyone else. I must not give the order too soon. I will wait until the enemy are within closing distance, and we can stab down with our spears, through unprotected necks, and end their lives. The urge to strike has my spear hand quivering. But still I wait. A moment more, perhaps two.

Below, a familiar command is given. 'Hold,' in my father's rich voice.

I swallow down my desire to attack.

The bastard intends to play me at my own game. I shouldn't have expected anything else.

23

MEDDI OF THE EORLINGAS

A rumble of unease from amongst my warriors has me stopping my chant, mid-flow. I blink, and refocus on where I am and what's happening before me. I've been summoning the horse-god of the Eorlingas, calling on her to allow my warriors success, and I finally sense her presence. She's keen to witness the end of the life of Elen and others who mean her people harm.

Why, I consider, haven't our warriors moved yet? Unable to stop myself, despite the staying hand of Sian on my shoulder, I step closer to the pinnacle, shield held before me. I won't risk the same twice. The enemy are close. Very close. But they've come to a halt, feet dug into the hillside as best they can, some also on all fours. Behind them, I see a scattering of immobile bodies and I hope they're dead and not merely wounded.

I quickly understand the problem. My brother and Wærmund were to wait until the enemy drew level. Our foe have finally perceived that and now they, in turn, wait, for my brother and his allies to grow tired of waiting and launch an inopportune strike.

A roar of outrage ripples from the enemy ranks. I don't understand all the words, but I ken enough to realise they mean to incite my brother, and more importantly, Wærmund to act irrationally.

'Hold.' I hear my brother's command and wait for Wærmund's reciprocal one but it doesn't come. From where I stand, with Sian behind me, I peer along my brother's shield wall and pick out stances I recognise but Wærmund's isn't one of them.

'Hold,' I order, the unfamiliar word of the *comitatus* tripping from my tongue.

'Mistress,' Sian commands, but I ignore her. The moment hangs. I scarcely breathe. Something will happen. Someone will do something, and all will come to naught. I can't allow it.

But what can I do? I've urged our horse-god here. I feel my mother and father, but this moment between Wærmund and his father is suspended. I've no skills to prevent it. Or do I?

What, I consider, do I know of Wærmund I can presume he's learned from his father? Both men must be arrogant, assured of their abilities, even if Wærmund was perhaps little more than a whiny fool before he learned to be a true leader. The same could be said of Madog. He's taken time to mould into the man he is.

'Do we have another stone?' I murmur to Sian.

'No, but I can find one,' she hurriedly determines.

'Do it quickly,' I urge her. 'And take it to the far side of the shield wall. Have whoever's there throw it at Wærmund's father.' I hear her scamper away. I murmur beneath my breath. I feel I should draw the eye of the enemy, even as I await Sian's completion of her task. But murmuring won't do that.

The enemy shout and bellow, but I know how to have them looking at me, and not at any other. I lift my voice, ululating as those amongst my people would do on the death of a loved one. I grip my shield tightly before me.

Shields lower from amongst the enemy, in a ripple of iron and wood, all eyes looking my way. Perhaps they've never seen this before. After all, Elen's no true seeress, despite her claims to the contrary. Bucge has informed me, those of the Gyrwe have a seiðr, but the man they now employ is no such thing. I hear Madog's heated demand I step aside, but I don't heed his orders. Instead, I continue, my voice carrying on the breeze, settling over the enemy as though a sleeping tonic. I sense the fury leave them, replaced by something else, hopefully terror. Not all will know what I say. They'll fear me.

I hear Wærmund's father's voice, undoubtedly ordering they all look towards the enemy, and not me, but I've a certain something about me. It's the way of all seeresses and, as though to compound it all, I sense the sun's warmth on me, illuminating my breastplate and torque. My horse-god watches me. Perhaps Wærmund's ancestor Woden is also here. I'm not sure my horse-god would walk hand in hand with Woden, but perhaps she might surprise me. Wærmund's wolfhound, a creature I've been assured is representative of his god, offers an eerie howl to match my ululations. I would laugh with delight at the animal's actions, but such would dispel the magiks I'm casting over my foemen.

An abrupt roar of outrage floods the air, and I understand Sian's been successful. A figure stumbles, the stone not hitting Wærmund's father, with his boar-crested helm, but the man next to him. He abruptly falls still, dropping as though a stone and not a body, with muscle and sinew to hold it upright. A shriek of ire and the damn fools are moving upwards, the order of their shield wall broken as they hunger to strike against Madog and Wærmund's force, in recompense for another of their own being broken by our warriors. And at the forefront is Wihtlæd, Wærmund's father. A man, I understand, who has always been cruel to his son. That marks him as a fool more than Wærmund's Woden-mark tarnishes him.

A man can only be cool for as long as he believes himself invincible. I've just proved Wihtlæd isn't invincible. All men must fall, eventually. Wihtlæd doesn't like that reminder. Not here. Not now. Not when he means to prevail against his son.

All men, I understand, not just Wærmund and his father, have one fear in common. Dying before they can accomplish their vengeance. I'll remember that, even as I note that men's fears are nothing compared to those of women's.

Madog and Wærmund are quick to relay their orders. A wave of the enemy endeavours to crash against their shield wall, but spears are busy, jabbing down. The scent of iron and rust floods the air as the two sides finally come together.

Some slip between the spears, scrambling up the final steps, while others hold their ground, projecting their spears towards my warriors. Shouts and cries, huffs and shrieks, flood the air, but I can't stop watching the terrible retribution unfolding before my eyes. I recall myself to my task, my ululations lifting up once more. To see such savagery reminds me men and women will die this day. I must do what I can to ensure it's the enemy falling beneath the harvest of blades and not my brother and his allies.

Sian rushes back to me, her limp somehow forgotten in the heat of the battle, face flushed, uncertainty reflected in her eyes.

'Mistress,' she huffs, trying to pull me back, perhaps fearing a repeat of what befell me moments before the battle started. I refuse to stand aside. Instead, my eyes swivel to where Elen waits behind her warriors. A long way behind her warriors.

Her cloak billows in the wind. Although I see few details of her face, I know she watches me, and not the battle taking place in her name. I lift my hands up once more, and call to my horse-god, and direct her ire towards the true cause of my father's downfall. Not towards Wærmund's father, acting on her orders, but towards Elen. The bitch that she is. She must die. I need only wait now and her last breaths will happen soon.

24

WÆRMUND OF THE GYRWE

Momentarily, I panic, as shimmering blades stab towards my legs, but then I remember all I've learned and arranged with Madog and our warriors before the fight even began.

'Lower shields,' I bellow. Seemingly as one, they're lowered, protecting shins and feet from the snaking spears held in the hands of my father's warriors and those who fight in the name of Elen. 'Strike,' I call.

With one hand on shield and one on spear, we aim towards the enemy. My weapon encounters nothing but air, until it doesn't. I can't determine what it impales, but as I retract the blow, it comes away shimmering with blood and matted hair, the distinctive scent flooding the air. Not that the warrior opposite me falls away. It'll not be that easy to kill men my father trained to his high expectations.

'Raise,' I cry, mindful the enemy redirect their strikes. It's only just in time. I hear the clang of iron on wood. A spear tip flashes before my eyes as it veers aside from the surface of my shield. If I had more hands, I'd grab it and yank it from my enemy's grip, but I must hold firm. I must remember our plan. 'Strike,' I bellow.

This time it's harder but not impossible, as our spears once more angle towards our foemen. I've no luck on this occasion. My spear tip encounters nothing. I consider if my opponent has fallen but doubt it. They've grown wise to our tactics quickly. It's time to change.

'Strike,' I command. My spear tip's bloody when it flashes before my eyes on this occasion. I also hear Tudwal's desperate cry as an enemy spear slides between his planted feet lacking a shield to protect them as our shields are so much higher. 'Hold,' I caution. His endeavours to evade the blow are unsettling the firmness of the shield wall. I feel it in the judder of shoulders and the mutterings of my allies, especially Heafoc to the other side of Urien.

'Wærmund,' he huffs. I can't turn to look at him, but I imagine his face is white with worry.

'Lower shields,' I order, but it's perhaps too late for Tudwal to escape injury. A shout of outrage from below and I realise the man has lost his spear, without Tudwal even moving. There's movement behind us. I grin. The women of the Eorlingas aren't warriors but they can pull spears from the hands of our enemy from behind us. They're fearless. No doubt, Sian, the respected confidante of Meddi, if any can be called as such, has ordered the women to such actions.

'Kill the bastard.' I hear my father's voice. I sense his rising frustration in the strangled tone. A stone's taken out one of his most trusted warriors. He means to reach me as soon as possible, in the mistaken belief it'll bring the fight to an end. He doesn't know Meddi's fierce resolve. She'll fight on alone, until all are dead provided her bitch of a sister dies this day.

'Strike,' I order.

The movements have grown more familiar. It's strange to stab down and not out, but down is where the enemy are. My spear tip encounters resistance. I push my weight against it. The assault from below is continuing but as far as I know, no one's yet been wounded, not even Tudwal's exposed ankles. Beside me, his stance is firm once more.

'Strike,' I repeat, Madog echoing the cry. Sweat beads on my lip and down my neck. Not even the breeze can stop me from overheating. My hands feel slick around shield strap and spear shaft, but I redouble my grip on both.

My father's nearly within striking distance. The heads of the enemy are visible. They're almost waist height, shields held outwards to prevent us skewering them.

'Strike low,' I call, this time using Madog's tongue so my father and his allies from the Gyrwe don't understand. I slide my blade along the ground as opposed to jabbing with it. The enemy shield wall bobs and fluctuates. They lack the discipline I've installed in the Eorlingas and my *comitatus*. Added to which, while I'm too hot, and sweat sheets my face, they'll be suffering even more from their exertions.

I retract the blade. It's nearly time to replace spear with seax. The enemy are drawing level with us. We hope to hold them, precariously balanced on the high summit, but if they make it onto our hilltop position, we'll still prevail.

More and more heads draw level with my shoulders. My father's boar-crested helm grabs my attention. He's stolen it from Isarninus, I'm sure of it. My father wouldn't have such an item. He certainly never did when I lived amongst the Gyrwe. He was an arrogant man but not as much of a fool as Isarninus proved to be. Isarninus cloaked himself as a great war leader in the ways of the long-departed Romans. How unwise he proved to be.

I recognise the men who face me. Men I was a child with, like

Alric. Men who were old when I was a child and still fight now. Men who were once discarded by my father as no longer effective but who've evidently been drawn back into his service because we've killed so many sent to hunt us down in the last year.

I sense my father's gaze. I luxuriate in knowing he's beneath me, on the hillside. If I can hold them there. If we can hold them there, we'll prevail.

'Attack.' The cry comes from Madog, in his tongue. I risk a sideways glance and appreciate some of my father's allies are in the process of forcing themselves onto the peak. I thrust my spear behind me, and grab my seax. The weight of the more intimate blade is comforting and familiar. A handspan of wood will no longer keep my enemies at bay. I bend low, over my shield, and my first strike opens up the exposed throat of a man who fights for my father. Gargling on his blood, eyes wild with fright, hands come up as though to stem the flood, his shield abandoned. His fellow warriors falter. He turns to them, blood landing on their faces with his struggles. He reaches for them as though they can aid him. He dies, but not before daubing his allies in his lifeblood, flooding the air with the metallic tang of blood. Terror shimmers in their eyes at their friend's death. Even I didn't expect it to be so easy but the blades forged by Terricus and within Uriconium by Katourn are more lethal than anything my father has.

My foeman's death has made strong men weak. His death has done half the task of defeating the enemy already.

My father encourages the others to continue fighting. With frightened eyes they heed the cry of their leader. I raise my elbow to stab and jab with my blade. Shields should protect them but the dead man's left a gap begging to be exploited. The one side of the shield wall bows outwards, one end coming closer than the other. At the far edge of our shield wall, my allies are engaged in a fierce battle against our foemen. Tudwal, Urien and I move almost as one being with three arms as we assault our enemy. I luxuriate in the ease of each stab or slicing blow. I detect strikes on my shield, but for now I don't need to duck aside from counterblows. Indeed, it takes all of Heafoc's grunted command to stay in place and not break free and descend into the ranks of our foemen. How easy it would be to do so, but no. Our strength is in working together.

My father's gruff voice encourages his warriors to greater efforts. Overhead, the cry of an eagle and the call of a raven assure me our fight's witnessed by other-worldly creatures as well as those who take place in the battle.

And then I feel the unforgettable sensation of cold iron on my leg and meet the upturned face of one of my father's allies, a man who was once pledged to me, but no more, Nothelm. His face is twisted with conceit. He thinks himself better than me. He believes he'll sever my lifeblood with such an action. But he wasn't a good warrior when he fought for me. And since then, my skills have increased. He's a damn arse. I'm glad he abandoned me. I wouldn't want someone as weak as him in my *comitatus*.

Tudwal's not slow to notice. He thrusts his shield forward, knocking into the man's face. Nothelm's blade immediately drops. I feel it with my foot and kick it behind me. Nothelm has no weapon to hand, aside from his shield. I stab above the metalled rim and I'm the one smirking with conceit as another of my father's warriors tumbles free from the shield wall. At the last moment, I snatch back my blade so it doesn't fall with Nothelm, and that's when I realise I have a new enemy.

'Father,' I huff, feeling his strength against my shield. He's managed to crest the hilltop but, in doing so, has disregarded his shield wall. He stands between his warriors and their shields and mine. I'll not be so foolish, even though I know exactly what his taunt will be.

'Woden-cursed bastard,' he hisses, unsurprisingly. It's been so long since he last spoke directly to me, for a moment I consider if he can recall my name.

'Father,' I acknowledge once more, bracing my back foot and considering how much force I might need to thrust my father over the precipice of the hill to have him falling to his death. Not much, I suspect.

'Kin-slayer,' he spits. 'Don't think your wolf banner means you fight in the name of my ancestor.' I allow his spittle to land on my helm. The smell of him is noxious.

'Father,' I retort again, pleased he's noticed my metal wolf emblem stuck into the ground closer to the encampment. 'I think you mean our ancestor,' I correct him. I've considered this moment for a long time. It's not at all how I thought it would be, and equally, it's exactly as I imagined. I don't fear my father. All he desires is vengeance for the death of his weak son. It makes him frail.

'Don't call me that,' he growls. 'You're no son of mine.'

'Very well, Father.' I grin and strike out with my blood-hued seax blade. The movement catches him unawares. As though realising how exposed he is, he endeavours to skip back into his shield wall, but it's closed behind him. As his back hits the wood held in the hands of his allies, a grimace of pain touches his bearded cheeks, for he's encountered wood and shield boss. Maybe he's lucky, all the same. Without them, he might have fallen from the height we fight at. 'Perhaps,' I suggest, quickly striking again, reversing my grip on the blade so I swipe back towards him, as opposed to across his neck in only one direction, 'you should get back into your shield wall, Father. It's a thoughtless warrior who abandons his allies.' How often I heard him say this. A flicker of recognition on his sweat-soaked, grey-bearded face assures me the recollection isn't lost on him.

'Bastard,' he menaces. I hear Madog encouraging his men to continue the fight. From the far end of the shield wall, I sense the men winning against our foemen. My father must know it. Still he stands, eyes holding mine, as though others don't jostle and battle to death around him. 'Not brave enough to fight me without the protection of your allies?' he derides. His arrogance no longer surprises me.

'Too brave, Father, to try and do it on my own. I am but one of many.' And I realise I've had more than enough of listening to him. It's a pity really that simultaneously I hear Elen's voice – or, rather, shriek – as she encourages her warriors to greater efforts, and then the thunder of iron against wood intensifies. In answer, I detect Meddi's more reasoned ululation. I know whom I trust more here. Meddi, not Elen. But Elen has some allure. Even I wasn't immune to it, as much as I wish I had been.

The distraction works. My father jabs his seax before my eyes. I find myself watching it, and not his arm, as I've been taught. A grimace, and he smirks as a thin shimmer of blood floods the air. He's wounded me. The sting on my lower cheek can't be ignored, nor the sliver of my beard floating free.

Rage thrums within me. How dare the bastard make such an assault against me? How dare he think I remain the young fool I used to be?

'Wærmund.' Heafoc's snarl recalls me to the here and now, grounding me. My fury dissipates, as I puff through my tight cheeks.

'That'll be the last blow you take against me,' I rumble. Once more, my blade flashes before my father's eyes. His head jolts back, exposing his throat as he hits the raised shields of his allies. It's a pity my aim's too low to flick the blade towards his throat. His answering strike is too slow in coming. Now I land a countering blow. It's deeper than the cut on my chin. Indeed, it's so deep, I see the flash of bone beneath the skin and feel my tense shoulders relax.

I can do this.

'Now.' The shriek comes from Madog. I repeat the order. As one, we press against our enemy. One step, then another, pushing them down once more. Some have drawn level with us, and some have almost been level with us, the shield wall bucking in the middle. We've allowed them to feel more secure in their footing. Now we intend to plunge them to their deaths over the side of the steep hillside. Well, all apart from my father.

I take one step, and then two. I'm crushed against my father's frame, the stink of him overpowering. He's never availed himself of a good bathe as we've learned to do at Uriconium. For a moment, he's fearful, his ally behind not realising what's happening.

I keep my gaze on him, watching the flurry of emotions covering his face, shown clearly in his too-familiar eyes. How he's haunted my life, even when I thought to escape him.

There's a moment. A tipping point. The enemy begin to fall away. Some scramble to stay upright as they encounter nothing but air behind their ankles. My father mumbles, his neck shimmering with flooding blood from his chin wound. I press my shield tightly against him, supported by Tudwal and Urien, with Heafoc never far away.

I'll beat my father. He'll plunge to his death, after all. Then, I'll find his broken body on the hillside and assure myself he's truly dead. Although I thrum with the conviction of this, I hold in place. We have our plan. We must enact it.

One step, two. Then quicker ones, three and four. My father's eyes no longer reflect haughtiness or anger at being wounded by his Woden-cursed son. No. They show his fear. I've never seen it before.

A crunch, a crash. My father disappears from view. One moment he's there. The next, he's gone.

I take a moment to regather my strength and suck much-needed air into my tight chest, reassuring myself I have my weapons. As one, we follow the enemy down the summit.

The path is steep and littered with bloody bodies. Men endeavour to crawl upright, or downhill. They're broken. They know it.

Elen's shriek of impotent outrage snags my attention. I risk a glance towards where she watches lower down the slope, mouth screaming in defiance. Meddi's more reasoned tone remains a counter. Men shriek and cry, or are preternaturally still and stiffening in death. I bend and impale a man through the neck. I doubt he lives, not with a neck bent in such a position, but I don't take the risk he might somehow still attack.

The corpse I seek is that of my father. Casually, I stab a man rising up on hands and knees, his seax blade in hand. He dies, gargling with my blade in his throat. And on it goes. My knees ache with the constant downhill movement. I'll regret having to crest the rise again when the slaughter's finished. I remain astounded my father determined to meet our attack when we had such an advantage.

Heafoc steps between me and another man surging to his feet. Our foe dies with a blade thrust upwards into his belly, and below his byrnie. I recognise the damn fool, his helm fallen askew. He was once a good man but then he became one of those who taunted me.

I see Bucge and Osfyth working together to slaughter men

they probably once bedded without so much as a second thought.

I hear Madog, encouraging his men to reap this harvest, but one voice is missing. Perplexed, I gaze upright and quickly feel a shiver of fear.

'Where's Meddi?' I call to Heafoc. He turns a furrowed brow towards me, sweat streaming down his face from the exertion of staying balanced on the perilous hillside.

'What?'

'Meddi?' I call, pointing my blood-drenched seax to where she was but moments ago. She's not there any more. 'Bollocks,' I huff, more than aware of her intentions. She was told to stay protected. She was instructed to do so by her brother. I thought that would be enough.

All thoughts of my father are banished. Wherever the damn arse is, he must be dead. He can't not be. Someone else will have finished the fight for me. I see almost no one moving on the hillside, aside from my allies. The vegetation is daubed with blood and the dead, as though an eagle has feasted on the young seabirds dotting the coastline, leaving nothing but their splattered corpses in their wake.

'She's going after Elen,' I roar to Heafoc.

'Bollocks,' Heafoc grumbles. He knows without me saying anything what we must do.

As one, we direct our steps towards Elen. She continues to stand, screaming her defiance, as though having the ability to rouse dead men. She makes no effort to escape, which is a relief. But as I scan the distance between her and me, I see a familiar figure making a determined descent from the hilltop.

'There,' I point, but I know, even as I watch, I'll never arrive in time to stop the fight. Meddi wishes to kill Elen. I don't deny her resolve, but she doesn't realise how deadly Elen is. After all, Elen nearly killed Bucge last summer with the severed sword hilt. I hurry my steps, cursing the scree-like slope. When I'm about to win free from the slaughter field, a hand wraps itself around my ankle, and I know without looking who it will be.

'Heafoc, stop her,' I bellow and turn to face the blood-stained, rage-filled eyes of my father, Wihtlæd, leader of the Gyrwe. Will the bastard not just die?

25

MEDDI OF THE EORLINGAS

She's there, waving her arms around as though that's the means by which she can talk to my horse-god. She always was a bloody fool. I pity the people who believe in her non-existent magiks.

The battle's gone well. Madog will be triumphant. Now I seek what I've needed to do for twenty winters, not only since I re-encountered Elen last summer. I'll bring her life to an end.

Carefully, not allowing myself to be distracted by the pounding of my heart and the pulse of excitement thrumming through my body, I pick my way down the steep-sided slope. I'm astounded once more the enemy fell for such a ruse. Surely they could have enticed us to fight them elsewhere, but they didn't. They were fools. Over-confident fools. Just as Elen is.

Her voice reaches me on the growing wind. I don't know what words she shrieks at the heavens above but they're nonsensical to me. I consider if she's always sprouted such nonsense or if this is something she's learnt from the Wæclingas. They might well have another god they revere, but if that's the case, they'll have no power here. Here, my horse-god and Wærmund's Woden prevail.

Eventually, the slope becomes shallower. I hurry my steps. My seax blade is ready on my weapons belt. I abandoned my ungainly shield on the peak for fear it would trip me. As I near Elen's encampment, I pluck another shield from one of the dead, who thought to flee but has succumbed before achieving it. The shield's heavier than my brother's warriors would hold, but I won't face Elen without one. I know Elen almost killed Bucge and Bucge's a fierce warrior, as well as holding the skills of a seiðr. I've watched Bucge battle my enemy this morning. I'll take no chances. I'll not dampen Madog's triumph by losing my life when he's victorious.

'Meddi.' My sister finally stops shrieking, and turns her twisted lips towards me. 'Bitch,' she spits.

'Witch,' I fire back. I see how her beauty has never dimmed, even now. She should be aged and lined, as I am, her hair turned to grey, but that's not happened. If I didn't know better, I'd believe her little more than twenty winters old, and not the near-enough forty she has.

'As are you,' she rounds. 'A hollow husk of a seeress with no true powers.'

I shake my head. I don't wish to engage in wordplay as warriors do. Neither will I show her my bare arse, as the men have done. I merely mean to fight and ensure she breathes her last.

'What, no reply to that?' she derides. I'm watching her. Beneath the cloak she wears, there's a breastplate of tarnished copper, matching the torque at her throat. I know she has blades, but they're inferior to the one I hold, forged by Terricus, and given its hilt by Hedrek.

'I think we both know the truth of who's the hollow husk,' I counter, deciding how best to launch my attack. She shows little concern as I come ever closer. Does she know something I don't? I can't imagine she does. She's simply always believed too much of herself. As I deliver the killing blow, she'll finally understand her entire life has been little more than air and fancies.

She surprises me by giggling, the sound rich and vibrant, as though a mere babe, similar to Madog's young daughter. 'You believe what makes you feel better?' she opposes, when her laughter abruptly disappears and her face returns to one of menace. The anger in her eyes is truly horrifying. I consider for how long she's hated me. I have my answer soon enough. 'You always had the best of everything,' she hisses. 'The love of our father and mother, and even bloody Edern. It took me a long time to convince him to hurt you as he did, when your newborn child was a girl.'

I shouldn't be surprised to find Elen was the reason Edern took against me so forcefully, and yet it does astonish me. I hate my sister, I don't deny that, but I didn't hate her before our father's death, and certainly not in the wake of it. I thought her my only ally when Edern forced me to his bed. If anything, I admired her. I'd wished I could be like her.

'Then you have my thanks,' I reply. 'His actions made me who I am.'

She laughs once more, directing her weaponless hand towards me. 'You think this is something to extol? You're weak and pathetic. You live through your brother, and his children. When you're dead, they'll follow you to the afterlife.'

'Who'll kill me, or them? Your warriors are all dead.'

'No,' she replies staunchly. 'They're not all dead.' At her words, I risk looking behind me. There's one warrior still fighting, Wærmund's father, with his distinctive boar-crested helm. But Wærmund will overpower him. Wærmund fights fiercely, lacking the rage that drives his father onwards, his face sheeted in blood. I see Heafoc hurrying this way. I bite down my frustration as I catch a glimpse of my brother, enjoying his victory, far up the hillside.

'One warrior will not overpower all,' I announce, turning back towards Elen, but she's taken advantage of my distraction and is no longer where she was a moment ago. 'Bitch,' I hiss, hurrying after her fleeing back. I realise she intends to escape, after all. She might say one warrior remains but she has no belief he'll triumph. She thinks only of her life, but I'll not let her evade me again. She'll die. Today.

There's no one here to help her. There's no Hedrek, no Wærmund, no Madog as would fight for me. And there's certainly no Wihtlæd to battle on her behalf. Wihtlæd's focus is entirely on besting his son.

I follow where Elen goes. She dips into the treeline of willow. With a glance behind me, assuring myself at least Heafoc knows where I am, even if it did frustrate me to be thought incapable of killing my sister a moment ago, I slip beneath the thin branches and allow the grey light between the trees to envelop me. Here, I feel even closer to my horse-god. Here, I know my mother, father and my daughter accompany me as I stalk my prey.

And it's not hard to follow Elen. She isn't quiet. Indeed, I suspect she stumbles over every stray rock and exposed root with a dull twang as she thinks to evade me, or lead me to where she hopes to overpower me. Has she thought this far ahead? I can't see it, but perhaps she has. I'll be wary, but resolved.

From far away, a roar of outrage erupts, and I think my name's bellowed by someone. I ignore it. If it was my name, I suspect it came from Heafoc. Elen won't steal away again. It can't be allowed to happen.

A spider's web covers my face. I welcome the soft touch of it against my cheeks. It reminds me of my old wounds and reinforces my already steady resolve. I move stealthily, evading the stones and roots that trip Elen. She'll know I stalk her, but not how quickly. A flash of her dark cloak, and pale hair ahead, and I watch her slip between two trees tightly pressed together, their branches combining so I can't tell which belongs to which. In her wake, the branches shiver, as though determined to shake off the sensation of her touch. In contrast, they welcome me, almost moving aside to allow me easier passage. Not that Elen stops. Again, she slips through more branches, always just out of reach. I could hurry my steps, but I don't feel the need to do so. I'll come upon her soon enough. Even the trees are trying to help me.

And then it happens. The tree branches open up around me. I step into a clearing. I blink the brightness from my eyes, and see Elen to the far side. She stands, gloating, a warrior at her side. I don't know him. He's younger than Madog. He looks uncertain, but there's something about him I recognise.

'I'm no husk,' she shrieks defiantly. 'This is my son, and the heir to the Eorlingas.'

My forehead furrows. Of all she might have said to me, I've not expected this.

'No,' I deny immediately. The young fool looks between Elen and me. He must see the resemblance. He doesn't speak, however. 'No,' I repeat. 'Madog's the leader of the Eorlingas.'

'No, he's not. My son, Macsen, named for our father. He carries the blood of the Eorlingas and of Edern. He's the true heir.' I can't help myself, I ask the question burning my tongue.

'How is he here?'

'I hid him away with the Uppingas. I'm no fool. Edern wasn't a kind man. I wouldn't allow him to hurt my boy. Not after what he did to your daughter. And not when...' And she leaves the sentence unfinished.

The boy certainly looks like Madog, and perhaps, in the

shards of bright daylight, he has the cast of Edern about him as well. But there's something else about him I find unsettling.

'Why doesn't he speak?' I realise I'm right in my guess as my sister snarls.

'He can't hear,' she counters angrily. 'Edern's seed was always rotten.'

'And so, what, you hid him from his father?' The boy's looking between Elen and me. If he understands us, he gives no indication. If he can't hear us, then he won't understand anyway.

'I hid him, yes. With those who would keep him safe, far from Villa Eorlingas, and far from me. But I've reclaimed him since the death of his father. He's mine now. He'll rule the Eorlingas.'

'No,' I counter immediately. 'No,' I repeat more softly. I see how he stands with blade and shield to hand. He might well be a warrior by training, but I see something else in him. Something that makes me smile, something my horse-god alerts me to with a gentle breath through my hair. 'He has another path,' I assert confidently.

'No,' Elen denies fiercely.

'Oh yes, he does. He's touched by our horse-god. You were unwise, Elen. You should have sent him to our mother, not hid him away to have him forged into iron for when Edern died and you needed another to rule through.'

'No,' she denies ever more protectively, her hands reaching for the warrior possessively. I shake my head. Elen has a true prize in her son, but fails to see it. She thinks only of herself, even now. To prove that, she directs him towards me, hands busy for a moment. I don't understand what she does. It's not an action of a seeress. She doesn't call upon our horse-god.

In response, his blade comes up, shield as well. It's all I can do to raise my shield in time to prevent him from ending my life with his first strike. My sister believes kin should slay kin even though I don't know the young man and have no need to kill him. He'll be a powerful seer. He'll be able to speak to our horse-god, in ways even Marchell wouldn't have been able to do. However, my sister's too determined on her vision of the future to appreciate his skills when she only wants to succeed for herself. In this, more than anything, she reveals her lack of knowledge as a seeress. She doesn't ken what is instinctively obvious to me.

'No,' I shout, shaking my head, hoping the boy will comprehend my desire not to fight. I wish to preserve his life, even while ending Elen's. I consider what she's told him, and how she's told him. He must be able to communicate, even if he can't hear.

But he doesn't understand me, of that I'm sure. While Elen watches on gleefully from a safe distance, he presses his weight against me. It's all I can do to stay upright. He pushes me backwards, backwards almost into the trees.

'No,' I bellow, holding as firm against him as I can, but not wishing to cut him with my blade. He has no such reticence. His blade jabs alarmingly close to my eye. I evade it. Then he slices and jabs. I should have worn a helm, and brought Madog to the fight. I came to battle Elen, not this young man who has my blood running through his body. And not just my blood, he has the power of a seer as well. It'll be unusual to have a seer and not a seeress, but it'll embolden my brother to have both at his command.

I see the boy's mouth moving. I don't hear any words, but abruptly his eyes open wide as a crashing sound from behind comes to a sudden end. I almost sag with relief on hearing Heafoc's familiar bellow of fury. He thrusts me away, and I sprawl onto the ground. Heafoc takes my place, fighting off the warrior. I recover my breath and focus once more on Elen. She howls wrathfully, and a flicker of fear shows on her hateful face, as she pulls a shimmering blade into her hand.

The boy's good. I doubt he's a match for Heafoc.

When I can draw enough air to speak once more, I shout to Heafoc. 'Don't kill him. He can't hear us.' Realising Heafoc won't understand, I shorten my command and speak slowly, although my heart beats so loudly within me, I fear I shake with it. 'Don't kill him.' I point to my ears and shake my head. Heafoc doesn't look away from fighting the boy. The clash of iron on wood rings through the air, as they fight, almost as equals. I direct my steps back towards Elen, who crouches, like a cornered animal, who knows her time is growing short.

'Bitch,' she hisses. I see true terror on her face as tall Heafoc battles her child. She cares for her son. What mother wouldn't? Heafoc's fierce, bloody and brutal.

'You can end this now,' I murmur, enticingly. 'Give yourself up to me. The boy will live, I promise.'

'No,' she screams, launching herself forward, blade extended towards me. Already spent from fighting her son, the abrupt advance has me retreating to evade the flashing edges of her blades. Her eyes are wild.

She slashes at me. Although lacking the skills with blades her son possesses, she's fast and unpredictable. One strike goes left, another right. Another jabs at my throat. With my shield, I counter the blows, but quickly, I feel my chest growing tight. She fights to protect her son, and just as I would have done, had my daughter lived, she'll give everything to ensure he isn't wounded. I can't look at Heafoc. I barely hear the crash of the blades and shields as they fight, as I focus only on Elen, and my blood thrums loudly in my ears.

Elen's as lithe as a cat and as tricky. She steps one way and then another. I can hardly follow her actions, and a line of blood wells on my forearm, while she gloats at such success. But I know how I can counter her. I risk closing my eyes for mere moments, while she thrusts her blades against my shield. Immediately, I sense my horse-god at my side. It becomes easier and easier the more I trust in my horse-god. How hard it once was to call her to my bidding. Now, the creature breathes hot air over my shoulder, informing me which way my sister will strike. Immediately, I step more fluidly, countering the blows easily. It's as though I no longer control either arm or my feet. I move as I'm directed. I skip and dance, and every one of Elen's blows misses me.

I reverse Elen's advances quickly. She begins to retreat to evade my more reasoned strikes. A sliver of her light hair falls into the air, severed by my blade. A slicing wound opens a deep gorge on her chin. Her tongue's bloody from biting it, when losing her balance as my shield presses against her. A line of madder-red opens on her arm as my blade caresses it. Another opens on her belly, slicing through the belt holding her spangles, for she has no shield to protect her body. The spangles land with a discordant clatter. I'm closer. I'm able to trip her with my front foot as she gasps in pain from her belly wound. She falls backwards onto a soft cushioning of grass, a shriek of fury surging from her bloodied mouth, as her head jolts painfully up and then down, momentarily losing focus.

My blade's at her throat, my knees on her chest, holding her steady, although she has no strength left to fight. The bloody wounds pulse with her lifeblood. She's trapped beneath me, but in that moment, when she must know her death is coming, she looks not at me, but at where her son fights. Her lips move. What words she mutters, I don't hear. What curse she evokes, I don't know. Her son, however, doesn't seem to notice his mother's predicament.

This has gone on for long enough.

With my eyes closed, calling on my horse-god once more, and with my mother, father and daughter close, Elen dies, with my blade in her throat, my hands slippery with the explosion of blood leaking from the jagged wound. Her final gasp is unsatisfyingly soft.

I blink my eyes open and watch hers turn sightless before me, a sense of triumph enveloping me, even as her legs drum beneath me. I think to luxuriate in the moment, to enjoy knowing my nemesis, my sister, my enemy, is at an end and can harm me no more. But a strange grunt grabs my attention.

Turning to where my sister's sightless eyes peer, I rush to my feet. Heafoc has my nephew held with a blade at his throat, while the boy opens and shuts his mouth, a strangled grunt coming forth as he witnesses his mother's lifeless form. The boy bleeds from cuts on his arms and face.

Unheeding of the danger, I place my hand on Heafoc's seax arm, restraining it although it takes all of my strength. I force the shimmering edge away from the boy. Heafoc stinks of battle and death. His confused eyes are filled with fury. I shake my head. 'No,' I instruct. 'No.' But while Heafoc heeds my warning, and retracts his blade from the life-ending thrust, the boy doesn't understand what's happening. He punches upwards, knocking Heafoc's cheek so I hear the snap of teeth banging together, as he thinks to seek vengeance for his mother's death, striking at me. His blow lands on my arm, opening another thin line in my skin.

Furious, Heafoc's blade is back at the boy's throat. Once more, it takes all of my strength to hold it aside, even as my blood drips onto Heafoc's wrist.

'No,' I pant. 'No.' Heafoc doesn't want to hear me, his eyes blazing with fury at the blow taken against me. Neither does the boy understand me. His eyes blaze with a desire for vengeance I know was my own for many summers.

Unceremoniously, I'm upended onto the grassy ground by

Heafoc, my entire body jolted, my eyes closing. I fear when I open them again, Elen's son will be dead, or Heafoc will be.

I'm scrambling upright, shaking my head, opening my eyes, desperate to stop the inevitable. Elen's dead, that's what mattered. I want to keep my nephew alive. I reach out, keen to grab Heafoc's arms once more, but find there's no need.

My nephew's immobile, on the ground, his head knocked to one side, eyes closed, but he breathes, while Heafoc moves to truss the young man's arms behind his back.

'Seeress,' Heafoc huffs, cheek bleeding, sweat beading down his face, eyes respectful. He looks from me to the boy. Sudden comprehension flashes in his eyes. I untie my waist cord. With a jangle of my metal spangles hitting the ground, I thrust the binding towards Heafoc. He immediately understands, and uses it to secure my nephew's hands so on waking he won't be able to fight us again.

'My sister's son,' I huff, but Heafoc doesn't need telling. Now, with him secure, and Heafoc safe, I stand proud, seeking my sister's body. I step towards where my sister lies, her body cooling, her hair tinted pink from her lifeblood, my blade still wedged in her throat. I sense the presence of my daughter, mother, father and the horse-god of the Eorlingas at my shoulders, and know this matter is at an end. My sister might leave her son, but he's no threat to my plans for the future. It might take time to have him understand that, but my task's accomplished. Elen's dead. I allow a tight smile to touch my cheeks, as I bend and collect the spangles she once displayed around her waist. She had no right to wear them in life. She has even less right in death. Tears form in my eyes, dripping without cease down my cheeks, running in rivulets, as though they track the wounds there that have been healed.

My sister. She caused so much hurt, so much pain. She took

so much and never gave anything back. And yet, perhaps, she wasn't without some redeeming qualities. She kept my nephew safe from Edern. That took bravery, or rather a fine sense of self-preservation not to be beaten and wounded as I was when I disappointed him. I'm grateful my nephew lives. How I wish my mother and father were here to meet him. How I wish my sister had never been inflicted upon us all. But I know I couldn't have the one without the other.

'My thanks,' I call to Heafoc, when I've taken a moment to compose myself. My voice is hoarse, my chest still heaving, my body thrumming with the moment of my triumph and the exertion it's taken to reach it. There's no reply. I turn back, startled by the sudden silence. In an instant, Heafoc's back on his feet and rushing through the trees. And I know why. It would be impossible to ignore Wærmund's anguished howl and the answering one of his wolfhound which echoes down the hillside.

26

WÆRMUND OF THE GYRWE

I stab down at the hand and try to wrench my foot free, but my father's grip is too tight. I stumble forward, my left foot just brushing the ground so I don't join him on the rocky terrain.

'Bastard,' I expel, sweat dripping freely down my face.

'Woden-cursed arsehole,' my father huffs, his other hand stabbing at my right leg as he holds me immobile. I finally get a good look at him. He's bleeding from many cuts, not just the one I gave him on his chin, but he's still alive. I reach for my seax and jab towards him. The blows land on his shoulder, but he doesn't even seem to feel them. 'You'll die, you snivelling shit. You'll pay for murdering your brother and bringing shame on my ancestor, Woden,' he growls, stabbing upwards, as though to drive his blade into my upper leg and kill me in an instant. I won't have it.

I reach out, and grasp for his fist and the hilt of his seax, but the weapon comes ever closer. I can't stop it. Wincing, I grip the blade, feeling the sharp slice of it into my hand and wishing there was another way to stop him from overwhelming me. My body's tangled. My hands and feet aren't mine to command.

I howl, the noise setting even the hair on my neck on edge. I sound desperate. My wolfhound echoes my cry. I won't have it. I will not be beaten. Not here. Not now. And not by my feeble father.

I risk putting all my weight on my trapped leg and kick my father in the face with the left foot. The strike's a good one. He releases his hold on my right leg instinctively, but my balance falters, and I windmill my arms to stay upright. By the time I'm steady, my father's shuddered upright, menacing me with his blade that oozes with my lifeblood, a delighted smirk on his face, more snarl than anything else. My left hand's all but useless, dripping blood with the thrum of rain. I might have exposed the bone beneath his beard, but I've cut myself almost to the bone as well.

From the corner of my eye, I see Heafoc crash into the willow trees at the base of the slope. He goes to aid Meddi in her fight against Elen, as I commanded him. That'll allow me to focus on killing my father. I can't believe the bastard still lives. He should be dead. I thought him dead.

My father feints towards me, but I hold my ground. I won't fall for the tricks I've watched him play on others throughout my childhood.

I hear Bucge and Osfyth shouting to one another, Eastmund and Maggenræd joining them. A clatter of falling stones assures me they're coming to help, but I want to do this myself. I must be the one to kill my father. Only then will I prove I'm not Woden-cursed but Woden-marked. My father will die and all will see me as the warrior I should always have been regarded.

'Snivelling turd.' He jabs towards me again. I lift my blade to drive his attack aside. I wince at the pain in my shoulder of having my arm thrust so far behind my body. I've had enough of this.

I barrel into him, allowing the slope to speed my steps so

they're almost out of control. We go down in a clatter of thuds and bangs. My head bounces uncomfortably on my shoulders, but stays in position, as does my helm. My left hand's bloody and almost useless, but I crunch it into a fist, howling at the pain as every cut is felt, to punch my father on his chin, where I've already wounded him.

His head snaps back onto the ground. I have him. I scrabble to sit over him, my thighs pressing into his chest. I feel his heat and chest rising and falling through my trews. But his eyes remain focused on me, all of his hatred reflected there. I knew he hated me. I never knew how much he hated me.

I punch again, bringing my other hand to the fight, forgetting I hold my seax in it. I punch and punch, the blade forcing cuts into his upper cheeks, close to his eyes. I feel the release of all my fury, rage and resentment towards this man who loomed so large over my childhood and who derided me for something I had no control over.

And still his eyes pierce me. He shifts from side to side, his arms pinned by my thighs, trying to wriggle free so he can defend himself.

'Finish this, Wærmund,' I hear Eastmund call. And I should. I really should. But I can't. Each blow feels like the release of a thousand hurts. Each dulling of his eyes, reinforces my belief he treated me ill. I want to luxuriate in this. I want to enjoy it. I want him to die slowly.

'Wærmund.' Osfyth's words are more gentle. 'We don't torture the animals we need to kill to eat. We end it quickly. Do it. Now.' I know she's right, but I'm not ready, not yet.

From far away, I hear more shrieks and cries. I detect Madog congratulating his men on their successes and hear his question about where Meddi is. All this I perceive, and still I punch and punch. My knuckles bleed on both hands now, just as much as my cut hand does. They're so slick, I have to be careful the blows aren't ineffectual, slipping free from my father's face without impact, and still I pummel and punch.

'Wærmund,' Madog shouts, stamping to my side, and breaking through my focus. 'Where's Meddi?' he demands. His voice is filled with fear. My father smiles, or at least I think that's what he does. His teeth tumble from his mouth beneath my blows. He fights me to win free, but he's growing weaker.

'There's something you don't know,' he spits, when I take a brief respite. At the same time, another scream pierces the air from the woodlands lower down the slope. 'Something you don't know that will bring your triumph to ashes.' I still at his words, trying to make sense of them. My mind's a fog of hatred and vengeance but I try to recall what's happened. Heafoc's chased Meddi. All should be well. But I hear the unmistakable sound of iron on wood ringing from beneath the trees nearby, and realise Heafoc can't protect Meddi alone.

I move to take the killing blow, to end my father's life and tell Madog where Meddi has gone, but he's already rushing towards the sound of the fresh violence. At the cry, Bucge and Osfyth follow him, as does Eastmund and Maggenræd, and indeed, all of my warriors. They know I'll triumph. Perhaps, they think, they'd rather not witness my wrathful revenge on my father. He's bloodied and bruised. He's trapped. I will kill him. When I'm ready.

But suddenly, my rage is undone. Somehow, my father gathers the strength to himself to overwhelm me. His hips thrust skywards. I overbalance, and I'm knocked to the ground, landing on my back.

He's on me before I can even open my eyes to understand what's happening.

Now his blade comes towards my open jaw, my father's sweat

dripping into my mouth. I howl once more. This time, the answering cry from Freki reflects his terror. I see my death in the bastard's eyes. I see it, and fear it. My father will overwhelm me. I batter against him with my blood-drenched hands, hardly seeing the madder-red knuckles or sensing my lifeblood dripping onto my face, as I punch upwards. He holds me firm, with just one of his hands, a testament to his strength while I feel weak, over-whelmed, and abandoned by my allies, even though they thought me successful.

'No,' I cry, voice hoarse. I must have been shouting for what feels like half the morning.

'Yes,' Wihtlæd states, haughty and smug with satisfaction. 'Yes, you bastard. You'll die for killing my beloved son. You'll die for the dishonour you brought upon your people. Upon me.' The blade, red-hued, held in his hand comes for me. My hands simply slip aside from his fist, too sweaty and too bloody to get a grip on his arms and arrest their journey towards me.

I hear the shriek of an eagle and a raven, accompanying the howl of Freki, and understand Woden has come to witness this momentous occasion between father and son, between enemies. Between his descendants. I'm all but helpless to prevent it happening.

I drum my heels on the ground, but I can't lift my legs to fight off my father for he's wise to such a motion. Still his blade comes closer and closer. I feel it on my neck, imagine the slicing blow that will sever my breathing tube and leave me gargling to death. I know when that happens I'll piss and shit myself. It's not the death I've foreseen. It's not what I've promised myself would happen, here today. It's not what was to happen. I am Woden-marked, not Woden-cursed. I was to prevail.

'Die, you snivelling turd. May your name be expunged from the list of our ancestors. May you die screaming as you did when you first ripped yourself into this world, killing your mother in the process.'

'Bastard,' I huff, still fighting, even though my arms are weak and my hands ineffectual. I won't make this easy for him. The blade caresses my throat. I feel the pressure. I try to swallow but I'm too fearful. I won't make his actions easier.

I can't even scream, not with the blade where it is. I can't close my eyes. I won't shy away from what's about to happen. In my mind, I barter with Woden. He's a tricksy fellow. He's promised me much. Does he mean to take it from me now?

I don't look away from my father's eyes. He'll watch my death. He'll know he did this. I'll taunt him with my final look for the rest of his life.

The blade presses even closer, even tighter to my throat. I know this is it. I consider what a fool I've been. I believed myself Woden-marked, not Woden-cursed, but evidently, I've been cursed since birth. What game has my ancestor been playing?

Abruptly, the pressure on my body disappears between one breath and the next. I scamper to my knees and then my feet, unsure what's happened. That's when I see my father, pinned to the ground by a blood-soaked but grinning Urien, his blade to my father's throat, my wolfhound breathing heavily to the side, jowls bloodied, although whether he's bitten my father I don't know. But there's no need. My father's eyes are closed. His chest continues to rise and fall, but he sees nothing, his head knocked against the rocks, allowing a madder-red stain to halo him.

I stride towards the pair, aware there's no one left but me and Urien, and my unconscious father.

'My thanks,' I huff, offering him my hand. Urien takes it and stands unsteadily. His knees bleed, his hands as well, from where they've knocked against the rocky slope. He grins, showing me his grey teeth and pink tongue. He kicks my father dismissively. I embrace him, beyond thankful for his intervention. That I still live is all down to him. Freki comes close. I run my hand through his fur as well.

Reminded we're alone, I peer towards the woodland. All of the Eorlingas and their allies and my *comitatus* have rushed to Meddi's aid. I know a moment of unease. They abandoned me too easily, but then they anticipated my success and not that of my father. I wasn't alone in believing his death was just a matter of moments.

I lick my dry lips and look down at Wihtlæd's face. Asleep, all the elements that have always mocked me are gone. He's like a trusting babe sleeping in his mother's arms. I hunger to kill him, but I'm not that weak a man. I'll end his life when he wakes.

'We'll tie him up,' I huff, peering around for something to do just that. I stride to one of the lifeless bodies of a man I grew to manhood with, and rip his tunic from his body with the aid of my bloodied seax, wincing at the action. The cloth comes away with a struggle, and as quickly as I can, mindful I don't wish any more cuts on my body, I cut it so I can secure hands and feet. Urien eyes me uneasily, his gaze turning time and time again towards the woodland, where the sound of a fight can be heard. With my father's hands bound, I nod towards him and the woodland. 'Go,' I huff. My father isn't waking up anytime soon. 'Go and ensure all is well.'

A sudden thwack of wings and a flock of birds surges into the air, followed by shrieking and grunting. Without a second thought, Urien hustles to follow where all others have gone, my wolfhound loping at his side. I shudder to my knees, exhaustion weighing me down more than my byrnie, weapons belt and shield.

A lifetime of abuse from my father has brought me to this

moment, and now, for the first time ever, he's under my command. What happens to him is entirely up to me.

I bend to tie his ankles. If I was less tired, perhaps I might have noticed the twitch there, but I don't. The next I know, I'm staring at the sky once more, blinking repeatedly, the blueness of the sky distracting me so I forget where I am. Only as I roll to my feet, reawakening every hurt in my body, leaving bloody hand-prints on the ground, do I realise my father is gone.

My howl is more akin to Freki denied a tasty meal. Damn the bastard. And damn me for being the biggest fool of all. Again.

27

MEDDI OF THE EORLINGAS

All is chaos as I crash back through the trees. The boy's immobile. His mother's dead, but others hurry towards me as I rush away towards Wærmund. We meet in a tangle of limbs and branches, of shouted orders and reassurances. I see my brother, and his worried expression lifts immediately. He glances over my shoulder, as though Elen might appear there.

'She's dead, brother. Very dead. I took the killing blow. I heard her last breath. She will not rise from the ground. Now, where's Wærmund? Didn't you hear his shout?'

Madog shakes his head. I realise his desire to reach me has clouded all.

'Come, we must aid him,' I urge, turning Madog back the way we came. We erupt free from the trees into the bright daylight. The branches hid my fight with Elen, and the shock of the revelation that she had a son. Now, I face the carnage of the rest of the battle against the men beholden to Elen.

I collide with Urien as he surges towards me. I steady myself against his tall frame.

'What's happened?' I demand. He shrugs his shoulders,

opening and closing his mouth, although no sound comes forth. I seek Wærmund on the slope stretching upwards before us. It's easy enough to find him. Nothing moves that doesn't have wings, apart from him. My forehead furrows, reminding me of the dried blood there, as my lined skin cracks it open. I crave hot water to wipe it from my face, even as I luxuriate in the knowledge it's Elen's blood. My sister is dead. At last.

'What's happened?' I repeat, as Madog joins me. Quickly, he assesses the situation, just as I do. He doesn't move. I'm unsure whether I should run towards Wærmund or not. He continues to howl. Like a wolf denied its prey. Like a wolf denied everything it ever desired. The sound vibrates within my belly, his wolfhound mirroring the sound. I don't like it. I sense the hair on my arms rising, and I suppress a shudder. A hand on my shoulder startles me, but it's Urien. He's regained the ability to speak.

'Mistress, seeress. His father, Wihtlæd. Wærmund had him. He must keen for his death, which surprises me. I thought he wished him dead.'

'No,' I deny immediately, shaking my head, my spangles clattering around my waist as I sway. 'This is something else. A son who wished to kill his father wouldn't react in such a way. It's not anguish he howls to his Woden-god. But fury.'

With barely a thought for Elen's corpse, abandoned in the woodland, I stride upwards, feeling the strain in my feet, ankles and calves. It's a bloody steep hill. I'm astounded once more that the men of the Gyrwe and those of the Wæclingas could be enticed to fight up it. Bloody fools. All of them. They've paid with their lives for such arrogance.

When I near Wærmund, I'm not alone. Heafoc dogs my steps, his ragged breath rattling in and out of his exhausted body. The wolfhound has beaten him to his master's side. Urien's not far behind. He too calls to Wærmund, using our tongue, not the one Heafoc employs.

Heafoc shouts to Wærmund. Neither elicits a response. Yet all can see Wærmund lives. Bloodied, admittedly, but very much alive. I assess the nearby ground. There's splatters of blood, a lot of blood. But where is his father's corpse?

I march to Wærmund, and grip his shoulders. I force him to meet my gaze. His eyes are crazed. Still he howls, his wolfhound growling now, perhaps weary of howling. What lunacy has claimed Wærmund? Heafoc bellows again. The sound is so loud it's as though thunder rocks from the sky above our head. Slowly, Wærmund speaks, blinking furiously, his hands opening and closing. I wince to see the deep lacerations on his hand, the bloodied knuckles as well. I don't know many of the words he directs to Heafoc. A single one leaps out at me. 'Gone.'

'Who is gone?' I frantically query, hand reaching for my seax as though we're threatened despite all evidence to the contrary. 'Is his father gone? Is he not dead?' I demand of Heafoc. I turn, seeking Dewi, but he's still down the slope and too far away for me to shout for an explanation. Impatience wars within me. 'Be alert.' I bark an order to Urien and Tudwal, who are with me. Madog has gone. I don't know where. Perhaps he knows where Wihtlæd is. All the time, Heafoc talks to Wærmund, although he nods in my direction. Heafoc hears my questions too.

'He's gone. Wihtlæd is gone. He was tied. Immobile, but alive, and now he's disappeared, as though plucked from this place by an eagle and taken away.' I shake my head at finally receiving an explanation. Even as one who can communicate with the gods, I don't believe in such an act. It's impossible. Even for the gods. There's no eagle large enough to steal a man. Perhaps a hare, maybe even a lamb, but not a man.

'No. He must be here. Urien and Tudwal, check the corpses.

We must find Wihtlæd.' Wærmund's fallen silent, but the rise and fall of his chest is laboured. I reach for his bleeding hand, and bend to rip my dress, catching sight of my bleeding arms at the same time. I'm happy the wounds are little more than scratches. I tie the cloth around the terrible gash, wincing as I do so, although Wærmund doesn't seem to notice. His blood has pooled beneath where his hand rests. He must be careful or he'll grow weak.

A clatter of feet over the rocky incline, and I watch Bucge, Osfyth, Eastmund and Sennicus turn the corpses, while Heafoc stands at Wærmund's side, hand resting on his seax. Urien and Tudwal do the same. I ordered them to find Wihtlæd, but in the absence of Madog, they protect me instead. It quickly becomes apparent Wihtlæd is not here. Where has the bastard gone?

So frantic are our efforts to find Wihtlæd, I hardly notice when Madog leads one of the enemy horse's with Elen's corpse strung on its back free from the woodland. Or when another horse follows with my nephew similarly tied, although still breathing. I almost don't hear Madog's questions as I seek out the enemy of my ally. Suddenly, it's not enough that Elen's dead. All those who fell beneath her spell must also perish. If not, her desire to overwhelm the Eorlingas might well continue. I can't allow it. I've learned a triumph must be complete. This is half accomplished.

'Sister.' Eventually, I've checked every corpse and peered into every crevasse on the hillside, forcing Urien and Tudwal to aid me. We've still not found Wihtlæd. My brother grows impatient with my continuing ignorance of his presence, and marches up the steep incline to where I've returned to Wærmund and Heafoc's side. 'Sister.' His voice thrums with frustration.

'What?' I shout, vexation welling in me. Why are younger brothers so infuriating?

I thought today we would be victorious. I feel angry I've been denied the satisfaction of knowing this is all at an end. Urien implied Wihtlæd was bound, and wounded. Where can he have gone? Clenching my fists tightly, I have to consider that Wihtlæd has truly been taken by some other-worldly force. Has his Woden-god come to take him away?

'Who is he?' Madog's softer question finally draws my attention, as he points to my nephew. I see my sister's son has woken. He's been allowed to stand beside his mother's body, all of his blades taken from him, while Beli and Idris stand beside him, hands on weapon hilts, ready to act if needed. They're bruised and bloodied, and Idris favours his left leg.

In the daylight, my nephew's resemblance to Edern is even more pronounced. I'm startled to realise I can look at him without hatred. While he carries the arrogance of Edern, there is much, much more of my beloved father in his intelligent eyes.

'He's our nephew. Our sister's son. Macsen, named for our father.'

If Madog's astounded, he masks it well.

'He doesn't speak, or seem to understand us,' Madog continues.

'He doesn't hear at all,' I counter quickly, 'according to Elen.'

'Who is his father?'

'Can't you tell?' I whisper, only to recall my brother didn't know Edern as I did. He never even saw the man alive. 'He's the son of Edern. My sister hid him away from Edern's malice. She believed he'd make a warrior but he won't. She believed, after Edern's death, he'd secure her position as the leader of Villa Eorlingas, but Macsen's lack of hearing means he can communicate with our horse-god.' Despite the disappearance of Wihtlæd, and Wærmund's continued anguish, I revel as I tell Madog, a smile once more playing on my lips. Elen was always unwise, but she did the right thing in keeping Macsen's presence from his father. Macsen is a rare find, to be prized even more highly than our sharp blades.

'Yes, but how are we to communicate with him?' Madog persists.

'What?' My forehead furrows. My brother's questions distract me from my triumph and my excitement at discovering Macsen. From seeking out Wihtlæd.

'How will we talk to him if he can't hear us?' Madog says more slowly, as though I'm the fool for not appreciating the difficulty.

'I don't know. Elen must have found a way,' I murmur, wishing my brother's concerns were directed towards finding Wihtlæd.

'I can help.' Dewi surprises me by striding towards us, from where he's also been seeking Wihtlæd amongst the campsite of the Wæclingas. Dewi's hued in battle glory, blood on his fore-arms, and a nasty cut on his left cheek. He looks terrifying, as his chest heaves with his prior exertion, yet his words ripple with respect. 'I can help,' he repeats. 'Come, I'll show you.'

Quickly, I follow him, with Madog, as Dewi strides towards the captive youth, where Beli and Idris menace the hulking figure of my nephew, who leers at them although he has no blades with which to fight.

Hardly understanding what's happening, I watch as Dewi uses his hands to make some complicated patterns in the air, almost as though summoning my horse-god, although aloud he says, 'My name is Dewi. An ally of the Eorlingas.'

Abruptly, comprehension dawns on my nephew's face, although he watches Dewi's hands. Macsen nods eagerly. Almost so quickly I can't watch everything happening, the two engage in what must be an energetic conversation using their hands. Dewi continues to speak.

'We are the allies of Seeress Meddi and Lord Madog from Villa Eorlingas. We mean you no harm.'

Macsen's eyes narrow at the news, and his gaze sweeps towards Elen's corpse. I grimace. Perhaps Dewi chose his words poorly, although I intend no harm to come to Macsen. Macsen uses his hands, and Dewi speaks again, turning towards me.

'He asks what's to happen to him now Elen's dead.'

'Does he not name her as his mother?' I ask softly, head turned away so Dewi hears. Dewi shakes his head, and slow realisation dawns on his features.

'He doesn't, no. He believed her someone he was pledged to protect in this fight. He asks what's happened to the men of the Gyrwe and the other Wæclingas.'

'Ah.' I see my sister was playing her games until the very end. Would it be a kindness to explain the relationship, or better to leave it as it is?

'Tell him we mean him no harm. Tell him the others are dead, and he's now one of the Eorlingas, should he wish to join us.'

I turn aside. The conversation between Dewi and my nephew no longer absorbs my attention, although Madog remains behind. Dewi, I suspect, knows something of my nephew. I recall his mention of the Uppingas tribe. Is that where my nephew has been all these years? Was it my nephew who threw the sling-shot at me, the stone which Dewi recognised?

My brother's still shocked at the revelation. I feel I should be, but there's no time. I've many questions I wish to ask Macsen, but they can all wait. For now, we must find Wihtlæd. Hastily, I stride back towards Wærmund. The hillside is alive with our allies checking all of the dead, turning them so we can see sightless eyes.

'Tell me,' I direct to Heafoc, on reaching him and Wærmund,

the wolfhound at Wærmund's side. I'm pleased Wærmund's hand no longer bleeds so copiously. 'Where do you believe Wihtlæd's gone?'

'He was wounded,' Urien interjects dejectedly. 'Badly. On the head. I delivered the blow myself. It can't be far.'

'He'll run from here, surely? Are all the horses accounted for?' I gaze upwards once more, seeing some of the Eorlingas' women peering down at us. I can't shout to them from here because the distance is too vast. Not even Sian will understand what I want, and she knows me the best of us. I see no sign of fear on their faces. 'More likely to take one of his own?' I suggest. Elen and Wihtlæd and their warriors came with many horses, as well as warriors.

'I don't know how many there were,' Heafoc mutters, indicating the camp. Sennicus and Blatero have made their way there. I see them hurrying to check beneath every cloak and fur covering, in case Wihtlæd hides beneath them. Beli and Idris, no longer needed to guard Macsen, have gone back beneath the trees, to see if Wihtlæd has gone that way.

Wærmund has at last fallen silent. His face is pale. I watch Bucge and Osfyth, turning another body. They shake their heads. It's still not Wihtlæd. Angrily, I strike back down the hill. Wihtlæd must have gone this way. He must be hiding somewhere. Any moment, I expect to hear the cry of Beli and Idris as they alert us to having found Wihtlæd.

'He wouldn't come this way,' Madog huffs beside me. 'We were all here. He would have gone away on foot, or over the peak of the hill, but he didn't go that way. Our people would have seen him. The wolfhound would have followed him.'

I grimace, nearing the horses that carried our enemy here. They're mediocre animals. They lack the breeding of my mares. Frustratingly, I don't know how many were brought here. I didn't watch them arrive, but there are certainly fewer than one horse for every warrior killed on the slope. I reach out a hand, muttering nothings to the most inquisitive animal. She whiffles my hand without fear. I slide it over her ears and attentive gaze. No doubt she hopes to extract a treat from me.

'Wihtlæd didn't come this way,' I grudgingly admit. 'We need to take the horses to our encampment. And anything else we might find useful.'

Those scouring the hillside are gathering a collection of treasures. Some have even collected hempen sacks from those at the peak to make it easier.

'What of the dead enemy?' Madog asks. I look at him. His shimmering eyes reflect our triumph, but I also see weariness weighing him down. It's still not the latter part of the day.

'We leave them,' I announce firmly. 'All apart from Elen's. Few will come this way. It'll be a feast for the animals who do make this place their home. Next year, we'll gather what bones remain and inter them beneath the ground, as we did with those who attacked us, the Færpingas. For now, we take the horses and rejoin our allies on the summit. We'll eat and drink and then decide what to do about Wihtlæd. Perhaps by then we might even have an idea of where he's gone. We might be able to spot him from so high.' I know it's unlikely, but I can't give up yet. Our vengeance must be completed. All of Elen's allies must die.

Together, Madog, Sennicus, Blatero and I halter the horses and lead them up the incline – well, not quite directly up it. There's a gentler path, not much gentler admittedly, but it means we need not walk through the field of corpses. They're turning whiter, bluer and even greyer. The dead are to be pitied but they don't scare me. Macsen joins us, and Beli and Idris have also given up seeking beneath the trees, and trudge up the slope as well, aiding others with their heavy sacks of treasures.

At the top, breathing heavily, I turn to Sian.

'Everyone is here and every horse?'

'Yes. The Eorlingas are all accounted for. What's the matter with Wærmund?' She indicates where he still stands, Heafoc at his side.

'His father escaped. Did you see it?' Sian unhappily shakes her head, and then her forehead furrows as my sister's son crests the summit.

'Who is he?' she gasps, hand fumbling for the blade at her waist. Like me, she must see the resemblance between son and father quickly.

'He's my sister's son. He has no hearing. He'll be coming home with us. I suspect he can communicate with the gods. For now, Dewi uses his hands to tell him things.'

'Does he now?' Sian muses on this strange development. The news Elen had a son doesn't surprise her as much as it did me. I consider if she knew. After all, she lived at Villa Eorlingas. The knowledge Macsen can't hear our words lessens her apprehension of the tall warrior.

'Treat him kindly,' I instruct. 'He's ignorant of who his mother and father were.'

This surprises her. Her features soften.

'Allow me to ask Dewi to teach me how to speak with him. I'd welcome such knowledge.'

'Of course,' I agree quickly. Wærmund, with the aid of Heafoc and Eastmund, is being brought to our encampment. I watch him carefully as he labours up the steep incline. I'm disappointed Wihtlæd has escaped, but it's nothing compared to Wærmund's devastation. He appears shrunken.

I stride towards him.

'We'll find him,' I reassure. Wærmund doesn't seem to hear me. I reach out to shake his shoulders. He rounds on me, hands reaching for bloodied blades before he realises who I am. I hold up my hand to prevent Eastmund and Heafoc intervening, and hold Wærmund's gaze.

'We'll find him, and finish this,' I repeat slowly. 'I waited over twenty winters for the deaths of my enemy. A day longer will be acceptable.' The fury in his eyes is quickly replaced with understanding, although it takes Heafoc's halting words to ensure he understands me.

'I hope it's no longer than a day,' he mutters, through Heafoc, before slumping to the ground. Exhaustion has him in its grasp. I must ensure it doesn't become despondency, even as I appreciate his wounded hand must be further treated for, already, the bandage is saturated with his life blood.

* * *

The mood's celebratory, but muted. From Wærmund's metalled wolf emblem, the treasures of our enemy have been hung. They speak of our triumph, and I'm astounded by the wealth on display. We're tired, and we have four allies to mourn. The men will be missed. The Eorlingas are now less three good men while Wærmund doesn't seem to have noticed one of Dewi's allies is dead, so consumed with his failure.

My sister's son, Macsen, initially uneasy, settles amongst us. I watch him turning his head constantly and wonder what it must be like to live in a world without hearing. He and Dewi remain close to one another. I must know more about that. I knew Dewi was aware of who my sister was when he first met Wærmund, but what part has he played in my nephew's life? What did he know of the smooth stone he took from my hands? I play with the name Uppingas on my tongue. I must question him about it.

Eventually, many roll in cloaks to sleep, with three good fires lit to keep us warm as the temperature drops, and overhead stars twinkle from the dark masses of the vast space. I wish I understood what they were.

Madog and Heafoc arrange watches but for all my exhaustion, I remain awake, gazing into the flames of the fire closest to me. I don't know what I seek, but at the moment, I'm looking for something. Strangely, I suspect it's not Wihtlæd. There's a void where my enmity towards my sister has always been. I'd not realised what a part in my life she'd played. So often absent from me throughout my adult life, I thought her death wouldn't affect me. It seems I'm wrong about that. Eventually, I must sleep, for when I wake it's to an outcry. And one I feel I should have anticipated had my exhaustion been less complete, and my thoughts less focused on myself. Our vengeance wasn't complete, and despite the musings of others, no man can simply disappear.

28

WÆRMUND OF THE GYRWE

I'm too tired to sleep. A strange sensation has my legs jangling. My cut hand pulses with pain. Meddi's cleaned and bound it with the aid of Sian. She's also tended to my bloody knuckles, and any number of other cuts and bruises on my body, but whatever she's tried to get me to drink to dull the pain, it's simply made me more agitated. Not even the comforting shape of Freki, asleep at my side, can soothe me.

Frustrated, I stand and stride to where Eastmund keeps watch from our peak, leaving Freki to leave. I'm careful as I make my way towards him. The strip of land's narrow. I feel as though I walk on the clouds. I'd be foolish to fall into the voids to either side in the darkness, where even now I can hear the carrion creatures feasting on the dead, the crunching of bones assuring me some of them have very sharp teeth. The fires we shelter around will keep them away from where everyone sleeps.

'Get some rest,' I instruct him.

Eastmund doesn't argue, which surprises me. 'Be mindful of the bloody birds,' he calls over his shoulder. 'They smell the corpses and if you sit too still, they come for you as well.'

I nod, grimacing as I get a nose full of the pungent aroma from down below. I consider if we should bury the dead, or rather, the dead of the Gyrwe and the men who once fought in Isarninus' name, but I shake my head. Meddi's correct to order only our allies are buried respectfully, aside from Elen. I know Meddi has plans for Elen's corpse. The rest can feed the local creatures. Their lives should amount to something, even if it's only allowing the animals and birds to flourish with their passing.

I replay the events of the morning, running the hand with only bleeding knuckles over my head to feel the pulsing bruise there. My father hit me with something. How, I don't know. I thought him bound. I thought him under my command. I'm a fool. I should have killed him then, as opposed to trying to elongate his death for longer. I should have killed him rather than allowing my rage to flood from me, seeking recompense for every hurt he inflicted upon me. My failure, and it is my failure and no one else's that haunts me. I desired to prove my father wrong, and in the process succeeded only in assuring him of my uselessness. How he must be laughing now, wherever he's escaped to. I doubt he'll run skulking from here, but rather, with thoughts of revenge once more dominant in his mind. He'll return to hunt me down, with fresh allies, and endeavour to kill me once more. He'll not let me live. He wishes to have his vengeance, just as much as I need mine. For either of us to live our lives, the other must die.

I slump to the ground where, moments go, Eastmund kept watch. My arms and legs thrum with exhaustion but my mind's abuzz. I don't wish to constantly berate myself for such failure, but it seems I can do nothing else. In time to the beat of my heart, I mutter the same words, 'He should be dead. He should be dead.' I can't think of anything else. I can't mourn the loss of Dewi's man, or marvel at the son Elen told no one about and somehow kept a secret for almost twenty summers. Or even consider what my *comitatus* will do now we've aided Meddi and the Eorlingas. We'll be paid well, but what to do with that wealth? Should we hoard it or spend it prolifically and then seek another patron next summer? I hardly know. All that matters right now is that my father isn't dead and I craved his death. As much as he craved mine.

I repeat his words in my mind.

'*Woden-cursed arsehole. Kin-slayer. You'll die, you snivelling shit. You'll pay for murdering your brother and bringing shame on my ancestor, Woden. You weak arsehole.*' Even now, even here, he thinks me a curse and not a warrior. But, and I pause in my circular arguments with myself, he said something else as well. He told me there was, '*Something you don't know that will bring your triumph to ashes.*' I smirk with the memory. No doubt he spoke of Elen's son. How little he knew. Elen's son is to be welcomed into the Eorlingas, not as a warrior, but as a seiðr. Elen's son will not be fighting against the Eorlingas.

I sense Woden's amusement at my consternation. Did he know this would happen? Did he think to test me again? Will he never stop testing me? And all the time, all I can think is that my father should be dead. We've killed his allies, and the bitch, Elen, is dead. Even now, my wolf emblem banner carries the treasures of those we've killed. We will share them out, eventually.

I peer upwards, seeking solace in the vast expanse. The stars appear timeless. They, I reflect, must have witnessed many a family rift such as ours. What would they tell me if I asked for advice? Would they advise me to leave it, or to hunt down my father? Would they instruct me to allow the wounded man to live? I bloody hope not.

Eventually, and despite everything, I must nod in sleep. I wake with a hand around my mouth and a blade at my throat.

The stink of my father's wounds and sweat is overwhelming. I can't see him in the darkness, but no other would attack me as he does. The blade at my throat promises me a quick death. I open my eyes, seeking out Woden in the pattern of stars overhead, but wherever he is, his games have yet to come to an end.

'Put your weapons down, stand up, and come with me, you cowardly turd,' my father commands in a harsh whisper. His breathing's fast. I consider how I'd not heard his approach. Or any other, especially Freki, but of course, I left Freki to sleep. For a moment, I'm confused. Why doesn't he kill me here? Why not leave my corpse for my allies to find in the morning? But then it all starts to make sense. My father doesn't wish to kill me where the people of the Gyrwe will not witness he's had his vengeance. No. My father needs something else, and that might well give me an opportunity to survive, provided I play by his rules. Just as I needed to ensure his death was slow, and entirely at my pleasure, he needs to do the same. Perhaps I'm not the only bloody fool. Slowly, I release the grip on my seax blade. I've been holding it in my left hand, my right hurting too much. I wince at the unmistakable sound of iron hitting stone. 'Quietly, or you die now,' my father growls, pausing to ensure no one else has heard the noise.

Thighs shuddering with the motion, I stand upright, my father's hand and blade staying where they are. He pushes me forward with his hips, his hand remaining at my throat, the heat of his body against mine. He wishes me to descend the slope, with his blade in place. Perhaps I should purposefully misstep and end this, allowing his weapon to slice my throat. But no. I desire to live through this. My allies, I hope, will come for me. My wolfhound, I suspect, will be able to find me easily when he's awake. I should have woken him and brought him with me. At my side, Freki would have alerted me to my father's approach. He might on occasion appear meek, but Freki can hunt out the smallest mice in the largest fields. I need only wait for that to happen. And then I'll be able to kill my father and bring this to an end.

Carefully, neck straining against the cold bite of iron against it, I move down. It feels as though I step into nothing, but my foot eventually encounters the rocky incline. I'm sure someone will hear the noise my feet make on the scraggly surface. No matter my father's hissed complaints in my ear, I can't see anything in the darkness, and can't even risk looking down with his blade at my throat to attempt to see where I place my feet.

Eventually, painfully, aware I have small cuts on my neck from where my father's arm has shaken, or I've stepped too closely to it, the terrain levels out. My father walks with unnerving confidence, as though he can see even in the dark. Perhaps his god, Woden, directs his steps. Perhaps my god, Woden, directs mine.

All I know is he makes me walk all night, our feet having to work in unison to prevent us tripping one another. Never once does his grip release, not until, as the greyness of a fresh day begins to make itself known, he leads me to two tethered horses Meddi must have missed when assessing the strength Elen brought to the fight. As I eye the two animals, reassured by their presence, my father finally releases his stranglehold on me, but if I think I can escape now, I'm proved wrong. Blackness descends, and my knees give way beneath me. My final conscious thought is that my father is, and always has been, a complete bastard.

* * *

The pulsing in my left hand wakes me. I cough aside horsehair from where I'm slung over the animal's back and strain to peer upwards and blink into the bright day. My body's jolted by every step the horse takes. I can't see my father, but I hear his horse and realise he leads my animal. I strain to find out where I am, but from this position, it's difficult to see a great deal. My entire body hurts and, if I try to arch my back, I'm prevented from doing so.

My hands are bound behind my back, my feet tethered in such a way if I endeavour to push myself upright, my neck's pulled down, the rope circling the horse's belly, just as surely as I do. I could spin here, and I doubt the horse or my father would care if my head was beneath the horse's belly, head pressed against its stones, or above it. Uncomfortable, tongue stuck to the roof of my mouth, I resolve to stay still. It's easy to look down, and so I do. We don't move over the ancient roadways, with their familiar drainage ditches to either side. Instead we travel through grasses and growths, through fields of harvested and still-growing crops. The longer grasses tickle my nose. It takes all of my willpower not to sneeze.

I know my father's taking me back to my homeland. I sense it, although I can't determine which direction we move in. Sweat beads my neck from trying to hold myself in position. It feels impossible. At some point, I'll slide. I almost wish myself unconscious once more. I seemed to do well enough then.

Eventually, the forward movement of the horse stops. I sense my father dismount and take the longest piss I've ever heard. It has me wishing I could do the same, but instead, I'm forced to relieve myself where I am, the sharp stink of my piss making me wrinkle my nose, as it drips down the horse's coat and dribbles onto the ground.

'Disgusting arsehole.' My father's feet appear below my eyes. I don't risk looking up at him.

Unceremoniously, he releases my bindings. I fall sideways off the horse, straight into my pool of piss. My hands painfully jolt behind my back. I bite my tongue with the unexpectedness of the movement. My father moves around the horse. His haughty eyes disdain me. He slaps me, hard, just because he can.

He surprises me by holding out a water bottle. I drink as deeply as I can as he allows me to tilt my head backwards. As much water rushes down my throat as it does down my chest. He snatches the bottle away when he believes I've had enough, and drinks more leisurely himself. The two horses have ambled away. I smell a stream nearby. They must drink themselves.

'You always were a disappointment,' my father extols, and if I think I'm going to be able to reply to that, he moves quickly to gag me. The material he places in my mouth stinks of horse and tastes of it too. He pulls me backwards, hooking my bound arms to propel me. My feet scrabble beneath me, as I try to stand, but it's impossible. I find myself secured to a thick oak tree trunk, which at least removes me from the bright daylight hurting my eyes by shielding me with the leafy branches.

Wihtlæd doesn't speak again. Instead, he brings the horses beneath the spreading branches, starting to crisp and turn brown, before pulling food from a sack and eating hungrily. My belly rumbles but he doesn't offer me the same. Quickly, he rolls in his cloak, and his loud snores flood the small space. The two animals, secured for the night, pay me no heed.

My hands pulse, and my body aches. I look upwards, realising I'll spend the night awake, while he sleeps, and all I'll be able to do is curse myself for being a bloody fool once more. I need to find a means of escape. I refuse to be taken back to the lands of the Gyrwe like a pig about to be slaughtered. And even worse than that, by my father, whose only intention in keeping me alive is so he can take me home, and end my life there, where all will stand as a witness to it.

29

MEDDI OF THE EORLINGAS

'Wærmund's gone,' Madog informs me, shaking my shoulder urgently, his words sharp.

'Gone?' I blink grit from my eyes and turn to assess the encampment. I grimace at the mass of blackened eyes, bloody teeth and gaping mouths on display, but I can't miss the unease on everyone's faces, or the whine coming from the wolfhound. 'By the gods,' I glower, stumbling upright, and shrugging off Madog's helping hand. I'm not some old crone to need assistance to get to my feet.

Eastmund and Heafoc are engaged in a ferocious argument, one so threatening Bucge and Osfyth stand to either side of them, evidently determined to stop them from coming to blows, while the wolfhound paces beside them, whining. The creature looks half crazed, eyes wide, a constant whine thrumming from its long, thin body.

'Where's Wærmund gone?' I query, seeking him as though he might appear from taking a piss or some such. Perhaps he's merely reclaiming his treasures from his wolf-shaped metal emblem stuck into the ground close to the peak. My mind isn't sharp enough yet to understand what's happened.

'No one knows. He left his seax.' Belatedly, I begin to understand the urgency infecting everyone.

'He wouldn't do that,' I say slowly, realisation dawning. Madog nods, wincing as he does so. The movement must awaken his aches and pains from yesterday.

'Exactly.' He nods swiftly again, following me as I make my way to Heafoc and Eastmund. I don't understand the argument. It's taking place too quickly for me to follow the words, and of course, Heafoc's the one who usually converses in my tongue, albeit slowly. I look for Dewi, but he's not there.

Frustrated, I lay a hand on each of them. They pause mid-argument to look at me. A flicker of contrition on Heafoc's face lasts only long enough for him to take a deep breath and continue haranguing Eastmund. I don't know why the two quarrel so fiercely. I peer over the side of the summit, still somehow convinced Wærmund must be close. I turn back to the camp, picking out Beli and Sennicus, Mato and Totia, Maggenræd and Rhun. I realise then Eli is missing and remember he gave his life so we might triumph yesterday. The smell of decay reaches me, sickly-sweet. I gaze towards where Elen's body lies, waiting to be burned. I feel some relief to see it still there. She, at least, hasn't been restored to life, although I already suspect Wihtlæd is behind Wærmund's disappearance.

'Get Dewi,' I growl to Sian, as Eastmund and Heafoc persist in shouting at one another without explaining to me what's happening.

'I'm here,' Dewi says tiredly. I face him. My nephew's behind him, expression confused and fearful. 'They argue because East-mund was on watch duty. Wærmund replaced him. Heafoc blames Eastmund for Wærmund's disappearance because he must have disappeared in the night. That's where his blade was found.' Peering down, I see what I suspect is a glimmer of blood. Wærmund's hand still bleeds. That's not good.

'Tell them to stop. It's not helping.'

Dewi does as I command, and two pairs of furious eyes look my way, even as Dewi communicates with Macsen. There's so much I wish to know about Macsen and Dewi but, for now, I can only think of finding Wærmund. I hold the gaze of Eastmund, who bows his head quickly enough, and Heafoc, who takes longer before quelling.

'We must search for Wærmund. I suspect, however, we all know what's happened.' As Dewi repeats the instructions, Madog speaks.

'We must find him. He's our ally.'

'We must find him, yes, but we mustn't act rashly. Everyone's tired.' I grimace as I realise I'm correct to urge caution. We can't rush after wherever Wærmund's been taken. The damn fool should have been more careful. As much as I'm grateful for the men of the Husmeræ protecting the Eorlingas in our absence, our warriors are needed at home. We must mourn our dead, and see to the rites for Elen as well. All need to see the threat she presented to the Eorlingas is gone.

'Meddi,' my brother seethes.

Already Osfyth, Bucge, Sennicus, Maggenræd and Totia gesticulate wildly as they argue about who will go where. Someone needs to take control or we'll all do the same thing. I bend and collect Wærmund's blade into my hand from where it's fallen. A sudden pulsing works its way along my hand. I furrow my brow. I've never felt such a connection to the blade, aside from the one containing some of the core of my father's shattered one. Is this similar? My mind's busy remembering all I've learned about Elen and Wærmund's interactions before she tried to kill Bucge. Is this the other half of the blade Elen stole? A slow smile spreads its way across my face. I suspect my quick determination is correct.

'Meddi,' Madog repeats urgently.

'What?' I glower angrily.

'What are you thinking?' He lowers his voice, moving me aside from the others.

'I'm thinking the alliance is at an end. We have what we want. We pay them, as we arranged, and they can find Wærmund. If he lives. We return to Villa Eorlingas with Dewi and Macsen, and Elen's body.'

'No.' My brother's outraged at my statement.

'Why? This disagreement between Wærmund and his father isn't for us to resolve.'

'You told me every one of Elen's allies must die.'

'And they're nearly all dead, so I'm content,' I state, wishing I didn't feel the wrongness of the statement on my tongue, and it wasn't so contrary to my true thoughts on the matter.

'No,' Madog repeats angrily, snatching the blade from my hand. I watch the flurry of emotions on his face, and realise he feels it too. 'What is this?' he hisses.

'I suspect it's the other half of our father's sword, embedded in Wærmund's blade. We know they had blades made at Uriconium.' The name sits ill on my tongue.

'Then it's ours,' Madog asserts, only to shake his head just as quickly. 'No, it's Wærmund's. It means we're bound by more than our alliance. We're bound by something akin to blood. Our father would demand we aid Wærmund.'

I growl. Madog's words ring with more conviction than mine

did. 'If that's true, I must go and seek Wærmund. You must return home,' I decide unwillingly. I long for my bed, and the comfort of Villa Eorlingas, and to be amongst my people who understand all of my words, and not be reliant on Dewi and Heafoc to aid me in talking to the *comitatus*.

'No,' my brother denounces, shaking his head firmly, and lifting his chin high. He adopts the guise of our tribal leader, but in this I see him as my young brother, and not my lord.

'Yes,' I say softly. 'This is the way it must be. I see it. I have half the blade. Wærmund had the other half. I must unite the two halves to bring our agreement to its conclusion. You must see that, brother.' I use guile, and soften my voice. With the wind lifting the hair on my neck, almost as though a whiffle of hot air from my horse-god, I witness Madog's uneasy acceptance of my decision.

'As you will, sister, but should you fail in this and meet your death, I'll come for you and haunt your afterlife.' His threat can never be fulfilled, but I admire him for saying it all the same.

'I'll return to Villa Eorlingas,' I assure Madog. 'In my absence, take Macsen, and burn Elen's body and scatter her ashes on the wind. All must see she's dead. I promise I'll return to Villa Eorlingas and then we'll continue to build the strength of our people, using Terricus' skills with iron and heat, with Hedrek's ability with bone and hilt, and we'll be esteemed by all. This, Madog, lord of iron, I promise you.'

His soft sigh of resignation is the only answer I receive.

* * *

It takes too long to resolve the minutiae of who will go where. Wærmund's *comitatus* doesn't possess the patience to wait, and they stream their way down the hillside, taking the wolfhound with them, nose to the ground. Kenal, Tudwal and I eventually start our journey to follow where they've gone.

I've bid farewell to my brother, and my nephew, although he still doesn't know that. Dewi goes with him to Villa Eorlingas, although the two surviving men, Cynin and Rhun, who joined Wærmund alongside him, have rushed away with the others of the *comitatus*. I still don't know Dewi's part in my nephew's survival, although I note that Macsen now holds the smooth stone Dewi took from me. I realise my sister tried to have my nephew kill me. She truly had no thought for the retribution he would face from our horse-god for such an action. I vow to discover more when I return. I sense I may have Dewi to thank for keeping my nephew safe for at least some of his life. And, perhaps, the Uppingas people as well.

In the meantime, Elen's body is to be taken to Villa Eorlingas. She will be burned and her ashes scattered on the wind. She doesn't even deserve a traitor death of having her body exposed and then her bones interred. She'll be dispersed on the wind, her fleeting life forgotten about, despite all the hurt she caused.

'Mistress, are you sure about this?' Kenal calls to me. We're on more level ground, and can mount our horses. I refused to ride from the peak. It would have been too easy for Bronwen to wound her legs or hooves. I can't risk her being lame.

'No, but I sense this is what must be done, as uneasy as it makes me.' Tudwal's more restrained, and far more determined to find Wærmund. The two, I realise, have struck up a friendship.

Kenal lapses to silence. Ahead, Bucge and Osfyth emerge from beneath a line of branches. They both have their horses and although I think Osfyth's keen to be on her way, Bucge waits for us to catch them. The pair offer me a nod in greeting. Osfyth shakes her head to show she's found no sign of Wærmund. I look down at the grassy path we follow, but there are so many hoof imprints, it would be impossible to say whether Wærmund went this way or not. We took the enemy horses and merged them with our own once we were victors. A pity we didn't realise some must have been missing.

In a rare flash of calm, Heafoc informed me it would be many days' journey to the lands of the Gyrwe. He said they live towards the rising sun, and close to the sea. It startles me to realise how wide my homeland is. I hope we encounter Wærmund and his father before then. I wish to go home myself, but acknowledge something binds Wærmund and me together. Heafoc forcefully denied the worry Wihtlæd would simply kill Wærmund now he has him. Wihtlæd, Heafoc confidently stated, would be taking Wærmund home and only then killing him. With so many of his allies dead, Wihtlæd must reassert his control of the Gyrwe by ensuring they witness the death of the man he blames for bringing such calamity upon them. I already didn't like Wihtlæd, now I despise him even more. He's Wærmund's father. He shouldn't wish to prolong his son's impending death, although it will allow us time to prevent it. I hope.

Quickly, we move to a canter, the horses able to maintain such a speed over long distances, the wolfhound leading the way. As we journey, more and more of the *comitatus* join us. I see where they've been searching beneath the trees, in caves and along the bed of streams, even the wolfhound stands ahead, urging us to follow him. The surviving *comitatus* show consternation for what's befallen Wærmund. Eastmund and Heafoc, thankfully, have determined to work together. In that way, I hope they'll keep their argument about how this was allowed to happen to themselves. At least, without Dewi's presence, I won't be able to understand much of what they say.

Around my weapons belt, I keep Wærmund's blade in close

proximity to mine. Heafoc demanded I hand it to him, but I refused. I wasn't quite able to explain the connection between me and Wærmund, but Heafoc eventually stopped arguing with me.

Now, with the daylight growing weaker, after a long day of searching, we hurry to cover even more ground. Ahead, the wolfhound continues to encourage us onwards. I know we'd all feel much better if we could find even the smallest sign that Wærmund came this way. But so far, there's been nothing obvious, apart from the wolfhound's determination, nose pressed to the ground from time to time, scenting his master. I don't sense Wærmund is dead. Heafoc's correct. Wihtlæd wants him alive. That in itself speaks of Wihtlæd's arrogance. Like I did with Elen, he should have killed his enemy and simply taken his corpse home.

Eventually, as dark clouds cover the sky, obscuring the moon and all the stars, a halt's called for the night. We make camp beneath an overhanging rock. If the wind changes direction it'll not provide much cover, but no one's prepared to spend more time looking. We must get what rest we can and then be on our way. Kenal and Tudwal show no unease that there are only three of the Eorlingas amongst the remaining members of the *comitatus*. I imagine my presence is reassuring. I wish it comforted me as well.

We eat supplies given us by the Eorlingas before we parted ways, Sian ensuring we had the best food remaining. Forcing myself to eat, I wrap myself in my cloak, determined to sleep. I know Heafoc will wake us as soon as it's light. And he does so. He's bellowing at us from the saddle before most of us are fully awake. Wærmund's wolfhound is already loping onwards.

Hastily, we resume our positions of yesterday, and continue along the path all believe he's taken. Osfyth's shown me the splatters of blood on the roadway that the wolfhound seeks with his

keen sense of smell. Heafoc tells me it will lead us to Verulamium, eventually. I know that's where Elen allied with
Wærmund's father. I'm far from convinced it's where we need to
go, however. The homeland of the Gyrwe is not near Verulamium, as far as I can determine.

We ride all day, the mood sombre as men and women veer
aside to check caves, streams and beneath trees and behind
hedgerows, despite the wolfhound's determined tracking, and
Osfyth's argument the wolfhound knows best, but there's no sign
of Wihtlæd and Wærmund. I sense Heafoc growing angry at
Eastmund once more. That night, when we seek shelter from
heavy rain clouds, I resolve to seek out my ally with the aid of my
horse-god, hoping there might be some connection between us,
forged by the twin blades we possess. Or rather, which I possess
but with one belonging to Wærmund.

While most sleep, including the wolfhound, who, having
paced backwards and forwards through the temporary camp, has
finally succumbed to the need to rest, I settle myself out of the
driving rain, and focus on the world around me. Sennicus keeps a
wary guard on me, and on the expanse surrounding us. But all is
thunderous rain and dripping branches, the drum of the downpour lulling me so I reach out for the other-worldly connection
I've only truly experienced throughout the last year.

The scent of fresh rain removes the traces of everything,
leaving me alone with what I can only describe as a visible line
heading northwards as though cast from lightning, or even the
magiks released from ironstone through heat. Startled by the
immediate answer to my problems, I blink open my eyes. That's
when I realise it's not just a figment of my mind. I truly see a
light, but it's not heading north, wavering beneath the heavy
onslaught, but towards us. And I'm not alone in seeing it.
Sennicus calls a warning, and that's when everyone jolts awake,

grabbing weapons, because a *comitatus* like Wærmund's must always have more than one enemy. I was foolish to forget that. We were unwise to overlook we're enemies in a hostile land, and there are those who've seen our wild advance, and now, they too have vengeance to seek against the *comitatus*. And alas, that includes me, Tudwal and Kenal.

30

WÆRMUND OF THE GYRWE

I curse my allies. Where are they? Why haven't they found me yet? Two days have passed and I've remained my father's prisoner. He doesn't treat me cruelly, but he's not kind either. I am but an animal being led to slaughter. I don't like it.

He rarely speaks, which pleases me. I can't speak to him. My mouth remains gagged aside from when I'm permitted a little water and some food. I am, at least, allowed to ride mounted as opposed to slung over the horse's back like a sack. My wrists pulse in pain, and the smell from the left hand assures me the wound rot's taken hold.

Still, this is the third day of my captivity. Where's Freki? Where's Heafoc? He's wise enough to have pieced together what must have befallen me. I consider how fiercely he'll have berated Eastmund for allowing me to take his position on watch duty. I doubt the two are speaking.

And then my thoughts turn to Meddi. Will she bestir herself to find me? I doubt she'll allow Madog to join the chase although I know he'll want to do so. Meddi, I'm unsure about. I thought her a cold woman, lacking a heart and only determined on vengeance. If that's the case, she won't think of me. But, having saved her life, perhaps she'll feel duty bound to do the same for me.

My father travels during the night, sleeping during the day. It means I move through darkness, no moon illuminating the way. If I could see where I was going, I'd feel more comfort in knowing my allies still had time to reach me, but instead all I sense is my homeland coming closer, a place I vowed never to visit again.

'I have a new son,' my father states while allowing me to drink. Surprising me by breaking the silence that categorises our new relationship. 'The child's well built and will rule the Gyrwe after me.' I almost choke on the water being dribbled into my mouth. My father's old. I pity the young woman forced to endure his grunting efforts above her to bring forth a new child. 'He'll know what happens to traitors.'

I don't respond. A flicker of fury on my father's face, and I brace for the impact. The slap's hard and sharp on my cheek. My father comes close enough for me to see where his skin fails to heal on his cut chin. He needs to do something about it or he won't see the child's first birthday celebration, let alone see him attain the age of fourteen winters, which our people have always considered means a boy has reached manhood.

Wihtlæd pulls forth my brother's rusted ancestral blade from where he's been keeping it safe behind his saddle. It was, no doubt, restored to him by Elen before she met her death. 'The boy, Waga, will have this blade and rule our people.' It seems my father's replaced his murdered son with a new babe. I think he mocks Woden in such a way. One son named Waga born to a father is surely enough.

I consider if my father has the rest of my treasures, lost inside Isarninus' stronghold. For now, I see only the rusted remnants of a once mighty blade, and one I once hoped to have repaired. Now

I've lost my new blade, as well as my old one. It's a pity my father didn't realise its worth. Then, I could have found a way to get my hands on it, and end his life. Then, I could have forced my way to freedom without needing my allies at all.

'You made many enemies,' my father continues. I sense his relief as the journey home grows shorter. He talks far more than when we first began. Then, he startled at every crack of a snapped twig. 'They'll come and watch your death, just as the people of the Gyrwe will. You left behind nothing but destruction. In the ruins of that, the Gyrwe have grown stronger; all that's needed is your death to resecure us in the eyes of Woden.'

I'd like to ask him about all those who've died to bring about my capture, from Wædel to Cenbryht to Alric. How has that made my father stronger? He can't have enough men to replace all those who died. How will he explain that to grieving families when he alone of all the Gyrwe returns to his homeland? I doubt he's given it much thought. He wished only to apprehend me. Perhaps, in his absence, others have moved to replace him. My father, I'm rapidly realising, has always been unwise. Before, he had warriors to stand at his side. Now he has nothing but an adult son he means to kill.

While Wihtlæd sleeps during the daylight hours, I stare upwards, through the branches beneath which we shelter. I'm once more tied and bound to the tree. I can barely wobble from side to side to relieve the pain in my arse from sitting on a stone without pulling my wrists or my ankles. I detect Osfyth's teaching here. She's shown my father how to tie a beast together well. A pity for me he actually heeded her lessons. I don't believe he's ever been good at listening to others' advice. I admit, I was once the same.

I watch Wihtlæd's chest rise and fall, and grimace as I see flies flocking to the bloody, flapping piece of skin on his chin, now devoid of any facial hair. Would I tell him to be careful if he allowed me to speak? I'm not sure I would. Yes, I wish to kill him with my blade, and not watch him wither away through the wound rot, but if he were weaker, it would aid me. But no. He must be the warrior he always was. I wish to kill him man to man, son to father, as is only right. Perhaps, then, I should tell him of how infected his wound is. Not, of course, that he gives me the opportunity. If I open my mouth to do more than drink or eat, he smacks or punches me. I've more bruises from being his captive than from fighting in the shield wall. I reassure myself that by constantly keeping my hand wound from scabbing over, leaving what I hope is a splatter of my blood for Freki and Heafoc to follow, I'm ensuring the wound rot doesn't develop, although it's a pity it rained so much during the night. Still, I force the scab aside once more, wincing at the pain, and allow the iron and rust smell of my blood to smear the tree I'm bound to.

My father, well, he really is a bastard. His wound won't heal. He'll grow rotten and weak. I hope I have the opportunity to kill him before that happens.

31

MEDDI OF THE EORLINGAS

Tudwal and Kenal are alert before Sennicus or I need to rouse them. So are the warriors of the *comitatus*. I blink the bright light from my eyes and focus on what's happening before me, as opposed to what my seeress' sight shows me.

'Who are they?' I call, but Heafoc's too busy ordering everyone into position to answer. Above us, all is darkness, but the enemy bring brands with them to blind us. I try to see how many there are, even as I hurry to get behind the line of warriors, scrabbling for shields, seaxes and anything else they might be able to reach beneath the deluge. Some have helms. Some do not.

There's a flurry of words between the two peoples as the enemy line up to face us. I can't believe they mean to battle us at night, during a storm, but perhaps that's their strength. Maybe they can see in the dark, although the presence of the flickering brands suggests it's not the case. It would have been better to sneak up on us, without light, and hold blades to throat. The heavy rain would have masked their steps.

'What do they say?' I growl, feeling incompetent not to be

able to determine what's happening here. The rattle of iron on wood, and the menacing growls coming from the enemy assure me that, although I see only the odd eye, nose or piece of equipment threatening us, in the half-light, they mean us harm.

'Stay behind,' Kenal barks. I'd take exception to that, but the sharp sound of iron hitting iron floods the air. I swallow back my shriek of dismay at finding ourselves attacked when all we wanted to do was find Wærmund. The *comitatus* evidently made many enemies as they moved around our island. They should have realised others would seek vengeance. We should, perhaps, have moved with more caution through the landscape.

I hear a startled whinny from Bronwen and rush towards her, worried the animals are being stolen from us. The terrified eyes of my horse greet me. They reflect the dancing flames of the brand. The animals are all shuffling forward and backwards uneasily, while the rain continues to fall. The smell of wet horse is to be compared with that of wet dog. A sudden cloud of smoke covers me. I turn to determine why. The enemy have thrust their brands into the ground. Now the smoke drifts at head height as opposed to higher, the rain keeping it low. The continuing clash of weapons joining and sundering apart, and the outraged and heated complaints of my warriors and the *comitatus*, flood the damp air.

With fumbling, wet hands, I reach for my sack of supplies, and pull it towards me. I don't wear my breastplate, and I should. I hurry to find it, the bindings tight in the damp, slipping it over my cloak in my haste and then releasing my horse from her tether, and mounting up.

I detect Osfyth's roar of anger, Bucge's shriller shriek, as well as Locinna's and Totia's. Eastmund growls while Sennicus urges Blatero to greater efforts. Even Maggenræd roars like a beast. The wolfhound has resumed his eerie howl. That, more than anything, unnerves the horses.

I might not know who these people are but surely they must respect a seeress.

Quickly, I lead Bronwen towards the row of heaving warriors. Above the low-level drifting smoke, it's as though shimmering blades stab up and down without anyone to direct them. If I weren't so concerned, I might find it amusing to watch. But these foes intend to kill my allies. I can't allow that to happen. I must find Wærmund and fulfil whatever destiny it is that brought us together, the warrior from where the sun rises, and me, from where it sets each night.

I lift my voice, ululating as I so often do to garner the attention of my horse-god and the enemy. I don't sense any eyes on me, but hear the angry exclamation of Kenal as he realises what I've done.

I bang the seax blade against my breastplate, the sound swelling and overriding all else. I lift my head skywards, water pooling into my eyes, seeking some evidence my horse-god walks at my side, but I find her absent. For now. Perhaps, like the rest of us, she's getting some rest.

A shivering blade surges out of the smoky cloud. I hear it whizz past my ear. I grimace. The damn fools mean to kill me too. I won't allow it. Fury drives fear from my body. I ken I must do more than sit on my horse. My mind returns to the attack on the Eorlingas when I used our horses to trample the enemy. Should I risk such again? The brands will drive them crazy but, already, the unease caused by the wolfhound's howl threatens to cause injuries.

Quickly, I return to the animals and dismount. Eyes wide with terror, they fight against my endeavours to cut them free from their halters, even as the roar of battle intensifies. I'm nipped and stamped on, and the first two horses rush away from the fighting and not towards it. The next I encounter are Kenal and Tudwal's mounts. They're more comfortable with me. Uneasy, they stay where they are, too terrified to move or determined to obey my instructions, I'm unsure, but it aids me. The other animals wait, and now I turn back towards the bitter fighting.

I don't even know who the foemen are, but they know the *comitatus*, or at least, I assume they do. While we were busy seeking Wærmund, we were unaware that we were being hunted by the enemy.

'Come on.' I mount once more, lean down to pat the shoulder of Bronwen, before directing her towards the fighting again. I'm sure the ground's relatively flat. I don't wish to push the animals to a canter when they might trip or slip on the wet grasses, but another roar of outrage from Heafoc assures me the *comitatus* is hard-pressed. I must do something, or everyone will be wounded, or worse, die here.

Bronwen takes my command easily enough. I reach for the other horses, slapping their backs and arses to have them pointing where I need them to go. Our foes, as far as I know, don't have horses. They arrived on foot, at least. Do they even know we have horses? But then there's no more time for thought because, ahead, I see one of the enemy warriors, wearing a helm of blackened iron, or so it appears as the flames don't dance on its surface, rushing through the press of the shield wall, war axe raised. I need to act, or I'll meet my death here, and that isn't to be my story, I'm sure of it.

'Come on, girl,' I urge Bronwen. Suddenly she's less compliant. I sense her dig her heels in, and she'd move backwards as the warrior comes closer, if only there weren't more horses behind her preventing the action. 'Come on,' I soothe, running my hand along her wet shoulder.

As terrified as I am, seeing this creature of darkness and flame rushing towards me, I know I can't hurry my horse. If she senses my fear, she'll refuse to move. If I kick her sides, as I've seen others do, she'll equally reject my orders. I must make her believe this is her idea.

'Come on,' I whisper, my heart beating ever faster. I'm struggling to take my eyes from the sliver of shining metal coming closer, the rain making it glimmer even more than with the brand alone. I've never known such terror as this. Always rage has driven me on. Rage to avenge all the hurts visited on my father, daughter, mother and on me. But, with Elen dead, the rage, I realise, has left me. I feel weak, powerless, unable to act. I can't summon my horse-god, not here.

I lick my lips, tasting my sweat mingled with the rain water, clawing at the old fury I feel should still be within me. But it's entirely gone. Instead, I tremble, my words faltering as I endeavour to perform my rites. The blade comes closer and closer. I don't even hear the roar of the battle above the frantic whisper of blood in my ears, and harsh breathing as fear makes me pant.

I catch sight of the cruel eyes, of the disdaining lips, of the utter conviction he'll prevail, and I know him to be correct. Abruptly, the wolfhound steps between me and the enemy, growling fiercely. The warrior registers the new threat, assessing eyes looking from me to the wolf, before turning and running back towards his fellow warriors, not prepared to take on the might of the angry wolf.

'Move.' A sharp slap on my leg restores me to myself, as I blink and breathe deeply now my enemy has gone. Kenal stands beside me, Tudwal in front of my horse, the pair dripping wet. 'Move,' Kenal repeats. 'Then we can mount.' He tugs on my horse's reins when I fail to act. Only then do I realise he means me to run from here. More and more of the *comitatus* have mounted, some limping and being helped to their horses. The wolfhound gives a yip of pain and I hear him, rather than see him, lope away. With the whining stopped, Bronwen moves at Kenal's command, her first steps uncertain, and then quicker and quicker, as I feel the firmness of a stone road beneath her hooves and we can move more quickly, even though it's dark and still very wet. The rush of water in the drainage ditches masks my harsh breathing. Kenal's immediately at my side, his horse hurrying to match Bronwen's speed. I spare a thought for Tudwal. Does he continue to fight the enemy, or is he behind?

Other noises make themselves heard, my breathing and heart rate slowing as I realise we'll live through this. Heafoc shouts to the *comitatus*, his voice rough. Osfyth replies, breathless, and the thunder of hooves almost drowns out all else, including the deluge that's drenched us, but in the distance I hear an other-worldly wail of anguish and I know we've lost some of our allies. They've sacrificed themselves to ensure we lived. I only hope Tudwal isn't amongst those we must mourn when the sun rises. From ahead, the wolfhound howls once more, and although Bronwen momentarily shortens her gait, soon we're rushing ever onwards. I realise I should be grateful the wolfhound lives. The animal will aid us in finding Wærmund. It's a pity he didn't hear our enemies approach, but then, neither did we.

* * *

'Who were they?' I demand later, when grey daylight has begun to lighten the darkness of night.

'I don't know,' Kenal replies. His voice is querulous. I turn to get a good look at him. He survived the battle on the hillside with little more than bruises, but I see a deep cut on his arm still bleeds in watery lines. It needs binding.

'Where's Tudwal?' I request, reaching for his arm, as the horses ride closely together, no longer at full gallop, but a more gentle canter that can be maintained over long distances. He snatches his arm away.

'There'll be time for that when we stop, and I don't know where Tudwal is.' His tone is sorrowful.

I turn to survey those who've escaped the attack under the cover of darkness. Heafoc's there, as are Osfyth and Eastmund. I don't see the two men who were allies of Dewi, Cynin or Rhun, or indeed, many of the other warriors who ride with the *comitatus*, including Sennicus and the two other women. I risk looking behind me, but we're chased by the night, and it's impossible to see if we're being followed.

'Did they have horses? I don't think they did.' I answer my own question. I feel safer, but I'm still concerned we might be followed. I remain furious with myself for not being able to do more to aid the warriors when they were attacked.

'No. They didn't,' Heafoc replies from ahead. He's slumped over his horse. He must bleed, although I'm unsure from where. It's not light enough to determine everything. Finally, the rain has stopped, but now we're all wet and the smell of damp is pervasive.

'Bucge?' I don't catch the rest of Osfyth's words, but she's evidently concerned about her ally.

'Who were they?' I finally question.

It's Heafoc who replies, of course, bringing his horse to a stop ahead, and turning to face us. The animal's head is low to the ground. Heafoc looks like he might tumble off his horse too. 'An old enemy of ours,' he huffs. 'They've learned to fight since we encountered them.'

'Do you think Wihtlæd set them on us?'

The question startles him. He doesn't immediately reply. From behind, more and more of the tired horses come close, more than half of them lack a warrior on their back, their manes damp. I don't see Tudwal or Bucge, although Tudwal's horse is there. I feel a pang of remorse for the brave young man. He'd become a competent warrior of late. His family will miss him, and so will I.

I attempt to dismount, to lead Bronwen to the nearby stream, but tangle my legs in my cloak as I do so, and more fall than descend. I land with a huff of pain, and if not for my horse, I know I'd have tumbled into a heap. Head low, her nose twitches as we reach the water. I allow her to drink, as I attempt to make sense of where we are. The landscape isn't familiar to me. In the very far distance, I suspect there are hills, but they're shrouded in the black of night still. The daylight coating the land does so too slowly for my liking.

'I don't know, Meddi, but what I do know,' Heafoc eventually announces, 'we're not amongst friends any more.' His words aren't at all reassuring from someone who comes from the east. Perhaps I should have realised how many enemies a *comitatus* would have. No doubt, I've been foolish to think none would wish to take their vengeance against them. I have to hope that oversight doesn't see me meet my death here. My brother would be most aggrieved, and I can't help thinking that, although Elen is dead, and gone from this life, she'd still be triumphant if I never returned home to Villa Eorlingas.

32

WÆRMUND OF THE GYRWE

Three days after the night of my capture, my father surprises me. He doesn't stop the horse to rest after daylight grows as a thin red ribbon on the horizon, but instead carries onwards. His shoulders have lost their tension. I quickly realise why as we pass landmarks I recall from my time escaping my father's wrath. I know we'll soon be amongst the Sweordora and then it won't be long until we reach the settlement where we killed Dægbeorht. I consider if the animal skulls still mark Dægbeorht's land, or if all have perished since his death.

I risk looking behind me. My father notices the motion and grins.

'No one will rescue you, you damn bastard,' he assures me. 'Not here. Tomorrow at the latest, we'll be home, and then I can kill you where everyone will witness it.' I don't allow his words to unsettle me. My allies will come, I'm confident of that. Heafoc won't abandon me. Freki will not leave me to this fate. He'll have smelled the bloody trail I've left behind me and will bring my allies to me. My father erred in not killing Heafoc, Bucge, Osfyth, Eastmund, Maggenræd, my wolfhound and all the others, before taking me captive. I need only await their arrival, even if it is delayed longer than I'd hoped.

The wind's grown in intensity, and now, every so often, I detect the salty stink of the sea. More than anything, it assures me I am, indeed, nearly home. My father endeavours to hurry the horses but they're exhausted, and poorly fed. Despite how uncomfortable it makes me feel, I force myself to sit more upright. As we move onto the stone road, and away from the trackways my father's used until now, more and more people will see us. I refuse to show myself as a subservient, even if I'm tied and trussed to the horse. These people might well know of Wihtlæd of the Gyrwe. Whether they'd heard of Wærmund's *comitatus*, I'm unsure, but they will. Soon. My father's arrogance and belief he'll take me back to my childhood home will be his undoing.

Around midday, my father calls a greeting to three women and four men busy in a field to the side of the road. I narrow my eyes. They're no doubt a family grouping. I consider if they'll know who I am. I consider if they see a proud warrior before them, or just a dirty traitor. I have my answers soon enough.

'Do you have bread, in exchange for payment?' I hear my father's belly rumbling from here. He's decided to forego eating on our journey now the food he did have has run out. Until now when it won't involve hunting, but rather, barter. I turn, assessing my chances of escape. They're not good. The stone road's bordered by the drainage ditch and thick hedgerows. There's nowhere for me to go. Not at the moment.

Warily, the seven eye him. I'm unsure if it's through lack of understanding, or if it's because while my father rides a fine horse, his appearance is ragged, his chin wound seeping obnoxious yellow pus. Evidently, he has a prisoner with him, or he's stolen the fine horse from me. It's quite possible the seven won't welcome involving themselves in something like this. It's sure to end badly for them.

'Who are you?' one of the women demands, assuring me they do understand him. It's simple wariness then, or at least, it was.

'I'm Wihtlæd, leader of the Gyrwe.'

'Are you now?' she replies, although it's obvious she's heard of the Gyrwe. 'And who's that?' She jerks her chin in my direction. I notice they speak my tongue. It's been a long time since we moved through peoples who could understand us without having to rely on Heafoc's rudimentary understanding or Dewi's more rounded ability to communicate. Or even Diseta. I realise I've not thought of her throughout my time as a captive. I thought I loved her. Perhaps not, then. Or maybe, I've been trying not to think about what I might have left behind. Could she be with child? I really don't know.

'A traitor.' A flicker of sympathy touches the woman's lips. I doubt she'd truly feel remorse for me if she knew who I was. My father must sense it. 'He's a kin-slayer,' Wihtlæd announces firmly, as though that should make her hate me, as he does.

'Hum,' she replies noncommittally. And then strides towards us. I sense my father's immediate disquiet, but she simply walks to the side of the field they're tending and bends to retrieve something from a basket. 'You can have this,' she states, showing the flat brown bread to him, 'in exchange for his horse.' Again, she jerks her chin towards me, to indicate my horse, and not me.

It's a terrible exchange, but once more my father's belly growls. No doubt, he'd be happy to see me walking along in the trail of his horse's shit, even if it might make our return slower. I can't imagine he has any loyalty to the horse.

'Done,' my father decides immediately, dismounting just as quickly. He releases my binding from the horse, and despite my best efforts I slide to the stone ground, lips jolting together painfully, although the gag ensures I don't bite my tongue or lips. Winded, it takes me a few moments to right myself, and by that time, the horse has been handed over in exchange for the food. And my father has consumed all the bread. As he chews, his gaping chin wound pulses. I grimace away from the sight of it. I can't believe it doesn't pain him.

'You need to tend to that,' the woman says, running her hand along the horse's flank, where she's walked onto the road to take control of him. The animal's in need of a good brush and a lot of water. Its coat is matted from my piss and sweat, my father not allowing me to ever stop when I needed to force what little extra moisture from my body I had.

'What?' my father questions, his eyebrows furrowed.

'Your chin. It needs cleaning, packing and stitching. Can't you feel it?'

My father's grubby hand runs across his chin. He visibly shudders, eyes widening in surprise. Has he forgotten I did that to him?

'Can you help me?' he demands.

'No. Only in exchange for the other horse,' the woman laughs. For a moment, fury tenses my father's chin. I'm unsure if she notices. With the flapping skin, it's more difficult to understand his expression. Wihtlæd could kill her for that, but does he really wish to fight these people when he's alone?

'Done,' he decides without further thought. If the woman's surprised, she doesn't reveal it.

'Come with us. I need hot water, and some healing herbs. You can ride the horse there. Then he'll become mine.'

My father nods. I feel eyes on me. I've not yet managed to stand. It's impossible to do so with my ankles bound as they are.

'He's not going anywhere,' the woman calls, already moving away with my mount. Ahead, I see a glimpse of smoke and smell food being cooked. It really isn't far. Uncertainty wars with my father's need to have his wound tended to, and eventually, he surprises me by leaving me as I am. I rock myself more upright. It's bloody painful. Three pairs of eyes watch as my father and the woman, with three of her friends, walk away. Deciding I represent no threat, they return to their task. I listen as they talk amongst themselves, and occasionally hum a tune I don't recognise.

I remain gagged. I can't speak to them. They evidently have no interest in helping me escape my father's captivity. I try shuffling around a bit but everything hurts, and eventually as perfect an opportunity to escape as this seems, I appreciate I can't get anywhere bound. I could perhaps make it to my feet, but I'd not be able to lift my head to see where I was going, or even move very fast. My feet are too tightly tied.

I close my eyes instead, listening to the sound of the day. Birds call high overhead, the thwack of wings alerting me to a flock of sparrows rushing on their way. I envy them such freedom. I'd sooner be flying free than captive. When my father returns, he'll have to allow me more liberty or he'll not be able to move me from here. Without his horse, he'll be forced to walk as well. It'll slow our progress, and hopefully allow my allies more time to reach us.

Surely it can't be much longer? With their swift horses, they can travel quickly along the road. It's not exactly difficult to determine where my father means to take me.

I must nod off, for the next I know, my father's returned, his chin criss-crossed with far from small stitches. At least the yellow pus has been removed, but in its wake, my father looks to be in pain. Was the wound truly so numb he couldn't feel it before now?

'Get up.' He kicks me. He's released my feet from their

binding to my hands and now my hands are behind my back. I can at least hobble on my feet. But, with the gag in my mouth, it's difficult to get a deep enough breath to steady myself. 'Come on,' Wihtlæd instructs, tone brokering no argument, although I still take my time.

The remaining men and women have taken themselves away. We're alone. Could I attack my father now? My hands are bound, yes, but I have the most freedom I've enjoyed so far.

'Don't even think about it,' Wihtlæd menaces, blade to hand so it pricks my chin and leaves a sting in its wake. I stagger upright. I didn't enjoy being bound to the horse. I enjoy my father leading me by the halter he slips over my neck even less. He compounds my growing fury by clicking his tongue between his teeth as though I'm little more than a horse. If I were free from my bindings, I'd enjoy gutting him from head to toe. He must know that, for he chuckles, forcing me to walk faster than my bound feet can comfortably allow. For now, the roadway's smooth enough but, should it deteriorate, I'll fall to my knees. Without having my hands to intercept my fall, I'll no doubt knock myself insensible, as I almost did when he released me from the horse. That would slow my father down even more.

All seven of those who helped my father, earning two good horses in the process, watch us as we walk past their settlement. Both horses drink deeply from water troughs, in a small enclosure with a few sheep and a milk cow. They weren't very prosperous before my father came this way. If my father lives to return to the rest of his warriors, I'm convinced he'll come here to repay them for their exploitation of his desperation. Should I live, I'll give them two more of my father's horses for ensuring my allies were given more time to catch us.

The older woman watches me. I'd smile in thanks, but it's impossible with the gag in place.

'You should let him drink,' she calls when we're almost past them. 'He'll not get far if not.' I almost taste the water she speaks of, but my father merely grunts and continues. I slow my steps as much as I can even while he tugs on my halter. I feel weak from lack of food and water. I'm content to make my father use more of his reserves to drag me to my homeland. The weaker he is, the greater chance I have of managing to escape, when the time finally presents itself.

Ahead, the distinctive smell of rotting flesh fouls the air, and it consumes me so much I'm coughing and choking, even as my father endeavours to drag me onwards. The maggot-strewn body of a deer comes into view, and bile floods my throat as well. I can't breathe, I can't swallow, I can't do anything. I thud to the ground, awakening every hurt, as I feared would happen. I peer upwards, eyes streaming, taking what I believe might be my last sight of this world after all.

My father hauls me onwards, until he doesn't. I close my eyes, gasping, and sense his presence as he stamps to my side, and yanks the gag down over my chin. I open my mouth to inhale air, but all I get is the rancid smell of rotting flesh. I turn, pushing myself upwards, saliva dripping to the ground, belly heaving. I need to get away from the dead animal. I surge to my feet, and scurry away, to where water gurgles. My father's shouts follow me, but he's released his hold on my halter. I reach the water, crash to my knees and thrust my face into its clear surface and lap at it because my hands are still behind my back.

Wihtlæd kicks me on arrival. I fall into the deepening water, face entirely submerged. I consider staying there, and for a moment, I don't fight. Only my father wants me alive. His rough grip on my bound hands hauls me free. I sense an opportunity might have presented itself, as I rest on my knees, sucking in air.

Wihtlæd's furious, his trews drenched, as he pulls the tunic from his back and rings the water from it. His weapons belt remains in place, but he's not paying me any attention. As quietly as possible, aided by his disinterest in me and virulent complaints about how this is all my bloody fault, I surge upwards, knees shaking, and rush into him. He falls into the water. I'm on him as he splutters, trying to get his head above the water. I kick him as much as I can, which isn't much, with my feet bound. He's squirming like a fish, bubbles from his mouth breaking the surface of the water, as I get my knees over his chest to hold his down. The water's just deep enough to keep him covered, but I need to hold him there. Somehow.

While I might have his body held as immobile as possible in the bubbling, froth-filled water, his hands are free. He claws at my face. How I wish I could place my hands around his throat, and squeeze, or better yet, stab into him with my blade. But I can't. Water seeps along my body, and despite my best intentions to keep my father under, he manages to surge upwards by digging his elbows into the swirling muck beneath him and gasp a much-needed breath.

'Bastard.' He wastes that breath on spitting at me, endeavouring to thrust his hands in my eye sockets, but I veer backwards, evading him, allowing him to spring free from where I've been holding him down.

'Bollocks,' I huff, stumbling upright as the water swells around me, but he's on me in a moment. Now I'm the one being held beneath the water, and I've half as many weapons at my disposal. My feet are bound, my hands as well. But his fingers are slick around my neck. He can't quite grasp me. I buck, shoving my hips upwards, endeavouring to plant my feet to get some purchase in the thick mud.

My luck holds. My forehead impacts his only just treated chin. He roars with animal savagery, reaching for me again. Even consumed by rage, he's wiser. His hands hold my chest under, as opposed to trying to strangle me. My feet kick once more. I won't let him end my life here. I bloody refuse. I twist and turn, wishing I had my hands and seax at my disposal, as he does. But I don't.

Once more, he holds me under, for a long time. I feel the strength in my body waning, and my feet kick less and less, and I can't wriggle any more. I'm desperate for a breath, just one more breath. But I'm not to get it.

Until, I do.

33

MEDDI OF THE EORLINGAS

We've barely had time to regroup and Heafoc has us rushing onwards. Tudwal's still missing. I'll mourn him. When there's time to do so.

'We must find Wærmund and return to Villa Eorlingas,' I growl, unhappy at the calamity that's befallen us. I turn to Heafoc. Ashen-faced, he rides beside me. 'Is there anyone you didn't upset on the wide expanse of this damn island?' My tone's too sharp. I don't apologise.

He turns to me, an arch of his eyebrow, and the faintest hint of humour on his lips. 'We're a *comitatus*. We don't often get invited to the feast,' he counters. I swallow my unease at his statement. Our numbers constantly deplete. Bucge's missing. Tudwal's gone. I don't know if Dewi's fellow warriors have simply run off or whether they're also dead. Sennicus and Blatero are missing, so are the two women from Uriconium, and Maggenræd. Right now, our number is small, Osfyth, me, Kenal, Heafoc, the wolfhound and Eastmund. We go to battle Wærmund's father and we barely have the numbers to counter a single fighting warrior, let alone whatever force Wihtlæd can command. We do have the better blades, I acknowledge. I feel driven to find Wærmund, no matter my unease. I sense a connection between us, one holding me firmly to this course. However, I wish the damn fool hadn't managed to get himself captured, I really do. I feel lost, and entirely dislocated. I don't know where we are. It feels strange to me, and very wrong. Here, I don't sense my ancestors, or my horse-god.

'Who were they?' I question. I still don't know the answer.

'I believe they were the Hicca, or what survives of them.'

My forehead furrows. I've heard the name before. 'The people you betrayed to Isarninus?'

'The very same,' Heafoc confirms. 'Or rather, Wærmund betrayed them. I was against it.'

'And are there more we'll encounter, aside from Wihtlæd?'

Heafoc shrugs, but Osfyth answers. Her tone's filled with sorrow for Bucge. 'Yes, the Sweordora and perhaps others, who were our allies momentarily. They'll not think twice about striking us down.'

I growl angrily. We've still seen nothing to indicate Wærmund has even gone this way, aside from the wolfhound's determination. If I mention it, the others will shout me down. And we've come so far now. It doesn't feel right to turn around. I sense he's alive, if only we can find him.

'Wonderful.' The word ends on a yawn. I'm exhausted. The horses are tired. We're all struggling to stay awake. When we find Wærmund, if only his father protects him, I still fear we won't be able to retrieve him.

'We'll not stop,' Heafoc announces, even though I've not asked to do so. 'He's close. I know it.' I furrow my brow. I don't sense the same but I'm in a strange land. The others, aside from Kenal and the wolfhound, have been this way before.

I lapse into silence, trying to shake the fatigue from my body, but despite Bronwen's speed, I feel my eyes closing. I blink them open. To fall asleep now would be problematic. I'd fall from my horse.

Ahead, a settlement comes closer and closer. There are plumes of smoke rising in the air, and people run from us, desperate to be behind their ditched enclosure. They need not fear. We've no time to even stop and ask them if they've seen two mounted men coming this way.

The gentle breeze begins to intensify, and along with it I suspect I smell the tang of the sea, not that I see it. How far inland does the smell spread? I know on windy days, it can be a long distance. The *comitatus* shout to one another in the tongue they understand and I don't. I turn to Heafoc but he doesn't tell me their conversation. It must be nothing more than the complaints of warriors tired from fighting and fleeing. I yawn once more. My horse stumbles. I grip the reins tightly, but it's not enough. I find myself slipping over her head. I land, with her looking down at me over her long nose, winded and panting.

No one stops, aside from Kenal, and those horses looking for any excuse to have a rest.

'Mistress,' he shouts, worry flavouring the word. I struggle for a deep breath, winded, and then it finally comes, as he peers down at me.

'I'm fine,' I wince, wishing I felt the words were true. 'My mare,' I murmur, hurrying to my feet. The horse stands patiently. Bronwen sweats from our exertions, but doesn't seem to limp.

'You should take a different mount. Rest her. We've enough.'

I nod, grimacing again, and pat my horse's nose. She nickers, perhaps an apology. I take myself to Tudwal's horse. The animal isn't the finest, but he'll suffice for the time being. Gingerly, I mount and we follow in the wake of the others. They rush so fast, we can't catch them, even though our stoppage was only brief. Eventually, I turn to Kenal.

'We should let them go. Better to travel at a speed the horses can maintain.'

'But then we'd be alone,' he cautions, eyes sparkling with fear, surveying this strange land.

'Yes, but we've many horses. We can escape. I'm sure we'll catch them come nightfall anyway,' I try and console. I don't wish to tell him each jolt of the horse causes me pain down my back. He'd only worry and we have a task to complete.

'Very well,' he acquiesces, and only just in time, for ahead the others have slipped out of view. I suspect they merely follow the stone road's route, but we'll discover soon enough.

A cry ahead catches my attention. I peer around. I see nothing moving, but the sound's very human.

'Who is it?' I demand, but no reply comes. Kenal has his blade to hand. I have mine too and the other horses are spooked.

The cry comes again. Perhaps a buzzard on the hunt, and not a person after all. I see no settlement and nothing that makes me even believe the fields are used for cultivation. Still, I slow my pace, nose scenting the air like one of the hounds.

The noise repeats.

'What is it?' I mutter, feeling Tudwal's horse shudder beneath my legs, and that's when I realise what it is.

Ahead, a collection of hunters merge onto the roadside. The lead man doesn't see us, but the next to follow him certainly does. He calls a warning in a guttural language I don't understand.

'I don't like this,' Kenal murmurs, quivering beside me. They've a boar strung up on two wooden poles and held between the shoulders of four others. They look strong, mean and determined.

'Stay back,' I urge Kenal. I've made a mistake in allowing us to become distanced from Heafoc and the others. I hope it's not the last one I ever make.

I sit upright, casting my cloak to one side so my breastplate and torque are visible. These men should know they've encountered a seeress, but quickly I realise they don't see a woman who can commune with her horse-god, but rather just a woman. I'd recognise the sound of interest from men anywhere.

'Retreat,' Kenal advises me. I cast a glance over my shoulder, keen to do that, but the horses are in the way. They crowd the back of Tudwal's stallion and Bronwen looks as though she wouldn't get very far at all if I changed my seat and urged her to a gallop.

'Stay steady,' I urge him. I hear his tut of anger and disagreement. For a moment, time stops. There are too many men for Kenal and me to overpower. I know what men like this will think when they see a woman such as me. I won't endure their attentions. Never again.

The lead man slips a smile onto his bearded face, with its crooked nose and receding hair. He says something to his followers. I don't know what it is, but I hardly need to because they place the dead boar on the ground and walk towards us.

I swallow down my unease.

'We should make a run for it,' Kenal orders. He's no doubt correct, but at that moment a scurrying from behind assures me they've thought of that. I shouldn't have delayed. Disquiet makes my hand slick. I fear I'll lose my grip on my blade before I manage to slice their necks open. 'By the gods,' Kenal hisses. He moves to dismount.

'No, stay on your horse,' I urge him, trying to turn Tudwal's horse to see how many there are behind. A glint of something catches my eye. I feel my forehead furrow. Surely not two enemies in one afternoon?

There are only four men behind us. They have blades, but they're not a match for that I have. I see the pitted rust stains from here. Again, my gaze twitches upwards.

'Hold firm,' I order Kenal. 'Just hold firm.'

'Escape, when you can,' is his reply, as the sound of men laughing and joking comes ever closer. They believe this will be easy. I have to ensure it isn't.

Again, my eyes flick to the horizon as though help will come from that direction, but of course, that's not to be the case. Instead, I must escape when I can. I'll not allow these men to take me captive. I'll not endure such against my body again, not now Edern and Elen are dead, and that part of my life is finally over.

34

WÆRMUND OF THE GYRWE

Rough hands haul me upright. I blink into the daylight, seeing my father floating without moving in the water. It's the woman and the others from the settlement. She pulls me clear, and I sit, dripping on the riverbank.

I'd have felt much better if they didn't also yank my father clear. His chin's bleeding once more. His eyes are closed. Whatever she hit him with, he's insensible.

'Who is he to you?' she demands, cutting through my bindings with one of my father's blades so my hands spring free with a surprising amount of pain. I hurry to release my feet as well from the tangled ropes. She aids me by cutting them. When my father wakes, I need to be able to run from here.

'My bastard father,' I mutter, considering whether I can reach my seax and kill him before someone can stop me.

'A loving relationship,' she offers with a cackle of delight. I find my gaze drawn to her.

'Who are you? Why did you stop him?'

'This is our water. We don't want it fouled with a body.'

'Is that the only reason?'

'Well, you can also pay us for helping you. Your father was generous.' She screeches once more, holding her hand towards me, seax edge showing. I grimace. She laughs again, before expertly twirling the blade so the hilt's towards me. 'Take it,' she advises. 'Take it, and one of the horses, and get far from here. We don't want this particular family argument staining our land.'

I watch her, eyes narrowing. This must be some sort of trick. But at that moment, I notice my father's finger twitching. He'll be awake soon enough.

'Thank you.' I struggle upright, wishing I had food to eat and time to drink the water, but I don't. On trembling legs, I dash back along the road, to the dwelling there, and quickly reach for one of the horses. But the animal's tired. His head hangs low. I debate with myself whether it's a good idea to take the horse or not. With a glance towards the stream, where there's still no cry of outrage from my father, I make a decision I hope I won't lament, and slip out of the back of their enclosed area, not making use of the road, or the horse, but instead trusting to my unsteady feet and the belief my father will think me too stupid not to take the most obvious of routes.

I regret my decision almost immediately. The ground I run over, or slip over, is rugged, the soil churned over as though ready for planting crops. I more fall from one foot to another than run. I'm panting heavily within only moments. I set my sights on a small rise in the distance. I convince myself I need only get to it and I'll be safe from my father. I strain to hear his furious complaints against the people who stopped our watery fight, but I can't hear anything above my rasping breath. Before I reach the trees, I find something else that might offer me more help. There's a stream. I don't think it's the one I fought in, but it might be. It shimmers beneath the sun. I dip my finger in, try it on my tongue, having sniffed it, and convinced it's not water from the sea, I allow myself to drink my fill, using my grubby hands to pull it close to my lips. I thrust my head beneath the water when I'm finished, welcoming the feeling of it on my face. I'm filthy, despite being dunked in the water by my father. It would be good if I could dispel the scent of piss from my trews.

Standing, I eye the trees once more, but the stream continues inland. The water isn't much above my shins. It's easier to walk through it than make myself return to the uneven ground. With my breathing calming, I pause to listen and, hearing nothing but the shush of running water, I strike out inland. I must return to my *comitatus*. I will find them. But, more than anything, I must evade my father when he wakes. His rage will be immense. Not that I plan on allowing him to live, but I want my warriors at my side, and my seax in my hand. Then I'll kill Wihtlæd. I will bring this to an end, and I will be victorious.

* * *

Later, I'm too exhausted to continue. I followed the stream as far as I could, and when it dried to little more than a trickle, I forced myself back onto the uneven ground. It's been hard going. Now, as darkness coats the land, I seek somewhere to shelter. I've managed to evade any animals or people. I have to hope my luck lasts throughout the night.

I'm still ravenous. I've not paused to find food. I've welcomed a handful of glinting berries, savouring the sweetness and cursing the birds for beating me to the majority of the crop. Now I'm slumped down in a hole in the ground. I can't call it anything other than that. The rich, dank smell of the earth almost covers me. It's the best I've found in the growing gloom. I wish I could get deeper beneath its embrace. My father would never think to find me in such a place.

I shiver, cold now the sun's settled below the horizon. I ignore my grumbling belly, and close my eyes. I need to sleep. If I don't rest, I won't be able to keep on moving. I only hope I find my allies soon. They can't be far behind me. Provided I catch them before they find my father, we can all flee from this place once he's dead. I don't want to think what might happen if they stumble upon my father before I find them.

* * *

I'm woken by mud hitting my face. I freeze, ears straining as I'm reminded of my predicament. I don't hear people, only the furtive movements of animals. Carefully, I raise my head, startling a huge hare, who eyes me, as I eye him, and then makes a run for it.

I remain low to the ground, peeking above the long grasses. I see nothing moving on the horizon, I hear nothing but bird call. I force myself to my feet and stand to look once more. I piss and yawn widely, before turning my back on the rising sun, and continue walking. I lick my dry lips. I need to find water again. There must be some nearby for the birds and hares to drink. Not that I find it. The day's cooler than yesterday. I don't sweat as much because I'm cold. I've no cloak to keep me warm, and when I look at my wrists, I see large cuts where the hempen rope has been too tight, and I've rubbed them raw. My ankles look little better. My hands are still bloody from the initial fight with my father. I knock the scab aside, and allow the blood to drip once more. I forgot to do that yesterday.

I find another handful of berries, savouring the juices, licking anything that spills down my chin. Abruptly, I hear shouts coming from nearby. I turn, eyes narrowed. It's cooler, but the sun remains bright. I don't believe there's a road nearby, but there must be as, otherwise, I wouldn't hear people bellowing at one another.

Catching sight of glinting iron in the distance, I war with myself. Surely, it would be more sensible to stay far from any trouble. I'm weak and have only my father's blade to hand. But curiosity drives me towards whatever's happening. Making use of the thick hedgerow containing berries, I slide closer to the sound. It takes a long time for me to make sense of what's happening, and when I do, my anger pools within me.

There are many men, all of them armed with spears, and one single woman, on a horse. I recognise the woman very easily, and the single man trying to protect her. It's Meddi and Kenal, with numerous riderless horses. Where the others are I don't know. Have they abandoned me? I feel a trickle of delight that Meddi has come to find me. I suspected she might not. I can't believe only she has come, however. I fear for my friends.

Licking my dry lips once more, I eye the backs of these enemy. There are many more of them than there are the three of us, but their focus is entirely on Meddi. They think her a prize to claim. They're damn fools. I'll enjoy ensuring they don't lay a finger on her.

The horse she rides isn't her mare, and the animals are unsettled by the men. My eyes narrow because there are many horses there, but not many warriors. I'm unsure what's befallen them. Are my warriors dead? Is there only Meddi who still seeks me? I hope that's not the case, but I mustn't consider that until I've rescued her.

I slip through the backs of the horses, speaking softly to them so they know not to fear me. The enemy warriors almost surround Meddi, but there's one gap I can exploit. Bending below the body of one of the animals, wishing my body moved more fluidly and without the aches and pains, I erupt between Meddi's mount and the man who menaces her with a rusted and pitted seax. The damn arse. He dies with my father's blade in his throat, and a startled cry half formed on his lips.

I see relief flicker on Meddi's stern features, but the next man rounds on me. He's had more chance to prepare. He stabs towards me. I've no shield for protection, but I do have my body. I reverse into him, shoving my arse into his groin and gripping his seax arm tightly. At the same time, Meddi stabs down from her mounted position. Blood once more shimmers in the air.

The horses are unhappy, as are the remaining warriors. Kenal's to the other side of Meddi, and we labour together to overwhelm the enemy. Three more men die with bloody wounds in throat, belly and under the armpit until the rest slip away after a barked order from whoever commands them.

I pull myself onto one of the animal's backs, bloodied once more. Kenal gasps on seeing me. I don't know who he thought fought beside him, but it was evidently not me. He gabbles in joy at seeing me, but I don't understand the words.

With more assurance and a calmness that belies the danger she faced only moments ago, Meddi reaches across the divide, to hand me the seax I left behind on the summit where we first battled my father and Elen's men. I take it gratefully, enjoying the weight of it in my right hand, despite the pain I feel on clenching my fists. I don't deny the shuddering sensation holding the hilt once more causes. I narrow my eyes, and I see Meddi watching me fiercely. Some part of my reaction seems to please her. A rare smile touches her cheeks, and in the shimmering daylight, I once more see the traces of long-healed scars. I narrow my eyes against the glare of the sunlight, and only just stop myself from running my bloodied hand over my face.

Meddi sees my bleeding hand, and a wince replaces her smile. This time, her actions are more brusque. She pulls a piece of linen from her saddlebag and quickly binds it, all the time shaking her head. I consider if she knows how I've been using my blood as a trail for Freki to follow. But my wolfhound isn't here. I survey the horses. It's frustrating not to be able to communicate.

'Where's Heafoc?' I question, even though Meddi won't understand. I remain confused as to why she has so many horses. Have they been in a fight? Are my friends dead?

Meddi must recognise Heafoc's name, and she turns to point the very way I've spent an entire day and night running from in the opposite direction.

'Bollocks,' I huff, even as she hands me a piece of stale bread. I'd thought to evade my father until I found my allies, but it appears that was never going to happen. Heafoc and my warriors must be found. When that once more brings me into conflict with my father, I must be triumphant. I know I will be, with my seax in hand.

35

MEDDI OF THE EORLINGAS

Wærmund's arrival has saved me from the warriors who thought to take me captive. Or to do worse than that. I can't say he looks pleased to be continuing on the road towards the rising sun, however. He's bruised, bloodied, his hand wound in need of careful ministrations, and he stinks of piss. Still, I'm grateful he could aid me and Kenal. If not – well, I don't like to consider it. As I passed him his seax, I saw the look on his bruised face. He felt it too. The same connection. His seax, I'm absolutely convinced, holds at its heart half of my father's sword which Elen stole. In his hands, provided we survive the next few days, I'm confident he'll do much good. Perhaps not as the leader of a *comitatus*. Hopefully, as more than that.

Mounted, Wærmund doesn't look much better. I offer him what food I have, and he eats it eagerly. I wish I could ask him where he's been and how he escaped his captivity. Does his father still live? I suspect he does from Wærmund's appearance. Were he victorious and his vengeance satisfied, I'm sure he'd be mounted and riding confidently, rather than skulking through our horses.

'Sorry, seeress,' Kenal calls. He's carrying a bloody gash on his left arm, while his right hand gleams madder-red as well. I don't think it's his. His horse is initially unwilling to allow him to ride because of the stink of iron and rust, but eventually the beast calms.

'It's not your mistake,' I reply. It isn't. We've ridden into an enemy land, losing sight of our allies. It's my fault for moving so slowly. But then, if we'd been quicker, we'd not have found Wærmund. Or rather, he'd not have found me. We'd have missed each other.

Ahead, the landscape's very flat. It makes it difficult to determine how far we've travelled and how much further we might have to go. I wish we'd not dropped off the back of chasing Heafoc and the others.

We travel on for some time. Every so often, one of us emits a cry, something catching our eye on the horizon, but it's never our lost warriors. The further we go, the unhappier Wærmund grows. His head constantly swivels. I don't think it's because he's made an enemy of those we encounter. No, I presume he followed this path with his father. He suspects we'll come upon Wihtlæd soon. I reach for the comforting hilt of my blade where it rests around my waist.

'There, mistress.' I look where Kenal points, and this time I do see Heafoc's familiar shape. Our allies are stopped, not far ahead. I don't rush the horses, however. The three warriors aren't facing this way, but instead along the road, towards the horizon. Beside me, Wærmund sighs wearily, and unhappily. As we get closer I realise why.

Wihtlæd stands there, face suffused with rage, anger pouring from him like a torrent from the sky. He's not alone either. Confused, I look to Wærmund, but his eyes are focused on his father, who has at least ten warriors at his back. I don't need

Heafoc's aid to understand Wærmund's outraged cry of 'bastard' as we draw closer.

Heafoc must hear and turns towards us. His face furrows with confusion, and then relief on seeing Wærmund at my side. I see the glint of triumph on Wihtlæd's face, even as Heafoc and Wærmund shout frantically to one another, gabbling their words. Heafoc doesn't tell me what they speak about, but Wihtlæd makes his intention clear in a shiver of drawn blades. The background noise of low growling stops. The wolfhound surges towards Wærmund, a satisfied grumble coming from the animal's throat. Wærmund bends to rub his hand over the animal's furry head, where it slides close to his mount. The horses are very used to the tall wolfhound.

'Mistress,' Kenal cautions warily. I swallow my unease. We've fought one battle this day. Now we must fight another.

Ahead, Heafoc, Osfyth and Eastmund dismount. Wærmund hurries to join them, the flat of his bound palm cautioning his wolfhound to stay away. I also hold Kenal back.

'What, mistress?' Kenal demands, voice high with excitement. He's eager to aid Wærmund and the others.

'You must stay alive,' I caution him. 'I can't lose both of my loyal warriors.' He offers me a grin of reassurance before hurrying to join Wærmund. I remain mounted, endeavouring to bring as many horses close to me as possible, keeping the wolfhound nearby too. The horses of the *comitatus* aren't used to me. They wish to stay close to their riders. I doubt that'll last when the blood starts to flow.

The shield wall facing Wihtlæd's pathetically small. The enemy could wrap around it easily and attack them from the front and the back, but I do notice how the *comitatus* and Kenal move smoothly together. The same can't be said for Wihtlæd and those standing at his side. These men didn't come to fight on behalf of Elen. Are they even Wihtlæd's followers or has he summoned them while travelling home? And how did Wærmund escape him? These are all questions I know won't be answered until Heafoc has the time to tell me.

The crash of shield walls joining barely ripples through the air. If anything, Wihtlæd's the one to look uncertain, although of course, I can't see Wærmund's face, only his back.

I wait for the fighting to get nasty, but instead the enemy seem content to hold against the *comitatus*. Do they mean to wait until my warriors are too tired to fight? It seems possible. I doubt Wærmund will allow that to continue for long.

Yet no one moves, not until I see one of the enemy peeking over his shield with a wry smile and slipping to the side. I watch, waiting for one of the others to notice, but they don't. A cry of outrage, and Kenal's being attacked where he stands close to Wærmund, his grunts of effort almost assuring me he'll prevail. Gripping my seax, I reach for my shield, and dismount in a clatter of spangles and breastplate. I'll not allow Kenal to be wounded.

I rush forwards, determined to prevent the attack on my one surviving warrior. I stab out with my blade, careful to ensure my shield protects me, but I've stopped too soon. I encounter nothing but air. Moving closer, mindful of Kenal's back foot supporting him, I jab once more. This time, my blade comes away bloody. The enemy warrior snaps towards me, his face reflecting pain and fury.

I don't know what he spits at me. His intent is clear enough. He slashes with his blade, forgetting about Kenal. I thrust the shield between us, wishing it didn't weigh as much as it does. His strikes come quickly. I can't risk moving my shield to attempt to wound him again. I'm forced to retreat, one step, two. I'm braced for another blow, but it doesn't come. Slowly, I lower the blade, to find the man lying in a rapidly swelling pool of his own blood.

Kenal offers me a look filled with fury, and then returns his attention to the shield wall, his blade flashing maroon, dismissing me.

But my actions have given me an idea. I'm but one person. I can sneak around the far side and attack the enemy, similar to their intentions. They won't be expecting it, and with the one man dead already, there's no one to shout a warning.

I falter, however. Kenal's aid helped me. Earlier, Wærmund's intervention saved me, and of course, he stopped me from being hit with the flung stone at the site of our battle. I'm a seeress, not a warrior. I must remember that. I cautioned Kenal not to die. He'd say the same to me.

Admitting my shortcomings, I retreat to my horse, watching the shove of the shield wall, although not mounting up. Wihtlæd's shouting orders. I can't tell if they're being obeyed because I don't understand them, but the *comitatus* holds firm, even outnumbered. I decide to see what happens before taking any further risk.

Seax blades flash in the bright daylight, but I can't determine if anyone else has been wounded yet, aside from the foe Kenal killed. The grunting of the warriors tells me while it looks as though they merely hold one another upright, it's difficult going. Wærmund's barely eaten for days, it's evident from his gaunt appearance. This will be all about who can withstand the assault the longest.

From behind the enemy shield wall, I detect movement, and hurry to mount to see over the heads of the warriors. There's a small collection of women and men. They're not armed. They're merely bystanders. I can't hear them shouting for one side or another. I don't know who they are. However, I don't believe they mean to interfere.

Abruptly, a sharp crack of wood on iron floods the air. Before me, the shield wall of the *comitatus* gives way. Each warrior faces two of the enemy. I swallow down my cry of fear and worry. The *comitatus* must prevail. I call upon my horse-god to aid them, reaching for my spangles to run them through my left hand. They certainly need some intervention as I realise Wærmund faces not only his father, but two of the other enemy warriors as well. I reach for my connection to the magiks I ken, determined to bring my allies every advantage I can. I half close my eyes, desperately trying not to listen to the frantic cries of Kenal, Heafoc, Eastmund, Osfyth and Wærmund. I pull my seax into my right hand, chanting as I do so. Here, far from home, I summon my ancestors to come to my aid.

36

WÆRMUND OF THE GYRWE

Fighting my father is one thing, fighting these men of the Sweordora as well is quite another. I don't know how my father managed to entice them to his cause since yesterday, although I have an idea. Their desire for vengeance, however, will be their undoing.

I know I'm weak from my privations of the last few days, but I'll not allow my father to overwhelm me. The discord between us must be settled. One way or another.

When the shield walls break, my father comes for me. His face is twisted with fury, no doubt because I stole his seax, although I've abandoned it for mine, handed to me by Meddi, with a frisson of something I sensed connecting me and Meddi in a way I'd not realised before. Not that I have time to consider what it means. I crash my superior blade against his shield, not to wound, not yet, but to assure him I will do, as soon as his two allies are gone. Do they think my father too weak to overwhelm me, or are they merely too eager to take their revenge against me?

The two other foemen grunt as they crash their blades

against my shield. The weapons aren't as effective as mine. Or as good as the one my father had. He's not thought to gift them better weapons, or more likely, hasn't had the time to do so.

I counter their blows, punching out with my shield, and jabbing around the side of my protection, and all the while, ensuring they can't get behind me. If they surround me, I'll have to decide who to battle first. Kenal, I see, is to the side of me, and Heafoc to the other. They have their own foes to face. Until they overwhelm them, I'll hold my own.

Not, it seems, that my father's minded to wait.

A thundering crack against my shield has me surprised it remains in one piece. My wounded and bound left hand trembles. I slide my blade down the side of my shield, looking at the feet of my enemy to tell me where they are. A huff of pain alerts me I've been successful against one of the Sweordora's warriors. It does me no favours, however, as his rage intensifies. His wild strikes force me to move my shield to prevent them striking home, and now my left side opens up. My father stands there, waiting to rain down blows upon me.

'Bollocks,' I huff through tight lips. I jab out with my shield. The other Sweordora warrior is thrust back against one of his allies. Their legs tangle and both fall to the ground in a jangle of metal and flesh. I doubt they'll stay there for long. It gives me a small opening to continue the fight against my opponent. Quickly, I move my shield between my father and me, and advance on the other foeman. The fool grins, black teeth showing through his thick beard, believing it an easy fight, but straight away his smile drops as blood sheets from a deep cut on his cheek. Almost immediately, it has a matching partner. I thrust my elbow back and jab into his throat and all before he can get his shield in place. I kick his flailing body so he slides from my blade, landing with a crack amongst the limbs of the two inter-twined men.

If my easy success concerns my father, he doesn't show it, as I round on him. I'm aware some of the Sweordora are dead or dying. My allies will be able to contend with the others, while I focus on Wihtlæd, the bastard leader of the Gyrwe, and my father.

I feel we've been here before. This time, we both have similar tools to employ. It'll be a true test of our skills.

'Woden-cursed bastard,' my father huffs. His breath is rank.

'Same,' I counter, but I don't want to trade barbs. That was my mistake last time. I want him dead. Immediately, I flash my seax towards him, stabbing repeatedly. He thrusts a shield between us. My seax skids off the rounded surface, even as I jab my shield towards his seax hand. His response is furious. I lift my shield to batter aside his borrowed blade. His blows are thunderous. His blade doesn't slide off the surface of my shield, but instead skims the top and almost takes a slice through my hair.

Grunting, I veer backwards, placing my feet firmly. The ground's awash with shed blood and piss. It's slippery.

I focus my next attack on his seax arm. My strike's slower, more carefully aimed. He darts his arm aside at the last moment. I leave only a scoring mark, although he crashes into my shield. My balance falters. Wihtlæd chuckles, his blade nipping my chin, perhaps in mimicry of the blow I wielded against him when last we battled. I growl, angry to have been thwarted, but not wrathful enough my next strike is less well timed.

Dropping my shield, I jab towards his chest, closing on him quickly, giving him no chance to retreat. A deeper flood of blood erupts from above his breastplate. He grunts in pain. I'm aware the ferocity of the battle surrounding us has quietened. I don't risk looking, but I suspect my father's alliance has been extremely short-lived.

Wihtlæd forces up his blade, holding my seax away from him. He thrusts his shield against me, perhaps hoping my weapon will cut me, but the tangs are too closely intertwined. The shield bounces harmlessly against me. Extending my arm to the side, knocking my father off balance, I step towards him and use my forehead to whack against his already wounded chin. He howls in fury, hot spittle landing on my face. Now my blade's free from his. I bring it closer to his chin, flicking it against the stitches to spring them open, in the process releasing a foul stench.

Wihtlæd's howls grow louder. I punch into his shoulder, all of my weight behind my bloodied right hand. The seax buries itself deeply, slipping effortlessly between leather and skin.

Wihtlæd stumbles backwards, swaying. His face is sheeted in sweat but he's far from finished. While I grip my seax hilt to retrieve it, he punches towards my throat with his shield, I'm forced to duck down to avoid being winded. I feel my blade slide from my grasp because of his slippery blood.

'Bollocks.' I reach for a blade abandoned by one of the dead enemy. Better to have something than nothing, even if it is far inferior. But I don't have time to grapple with it before my father's on me. He's removed my bloody blade from his shoulder. Eyes wild, mouth open with fury, he hammers against me. It's all I can do to get my hastily reclaimed shield between us and stop him from visiting the same wound on me.

But I don't lift my shield quickly enough. An icy burn works its way along my seax arm. I'm shocked to see madder-red shimmering there, while my father chuckles darkly. He follows up his success by almost running into me, so I'm forced backwards. My feet slip on the slick surface. It's only when I feel another steadying foot, I stop. I don't have time to look, but someone's behind me, adding their strength to mine. My father doesn't realise. He continues to chase me down. Now I can't move backwards. The shields held between us grip my chest, refusing to let go. My father's angry and confused face is directly in front of me. I smell his rankness. I see where his teeth are bleeding or entirely missing. Nostril hairs peek from amongst the bloody mass of his nose. I suppress a shudder for whichever young woman was forced to endure his advances.

A blade slips into my hand. I grip it, and immediately feel a connection to it. I lift my elbow, and slide it above my father's shield rim and into his neck. The drumming of his blood flooding to the ground blocks his final exhalation, but my seax, wielded by him, is almost in my right eye.

I hold myself steady, waiting for the bastard to realise he's dead.

In that flickering moment, shock's replaced by something else. I take it to be grudging respect. He drops. The sound's horrifying. It's not a clatter of bone on stone, but a thud of lifelessness, as even more blood oozes from his many wounds.

I gaze down, panting heavily, not prepared to wrench my eyes away until all life is extinguished from his eyes. I must see him die. I must assure myself he's finally gone. My eye flickers to the blade that killed him. I know a moment of recognition, even as I snatch the blade created for me from my father's lifeless hand. I have both seaxes, forged from the heart of the sword that once belonged to Meddi's father, I'm sure of it.

A murmur from all around me swells, but it's Meddi's singsong ululation that assures me my father is finally, without doubt, and undeniably bloody dead. The howl of Freki raises the damp hair on the back of my neck, but in this I also appreciate the work of the gods has been accomplished. Woden is here. As is Meddi's horse-god.

I sway to the ground, catching sight of Heafoc behind me, the man who gave me the steadiness to stop my father's attack, and Meddi, who handed me the blade to end his life.

I've much to be grateful to them for, but right now all I can do is concentrate on the breath in and out of my body, luxuriating in something my father will never enjoy again.

37

MEDDI OF THE EORLINGAS

I eye the dead man. Wihtlæd's eyes remain open, but he sees nothing aside from his god, Woden. Not that I anticipate him being here to welcome Wihtlæd into whatever afterlife these men believe in. No god would wish such a man amongst them after death. Was Wihtlæd brave to take on his son like that? Undeniably, but he was foolish too. He believed the stories of his strength rather than knowing them for himself. Despite Wærmund's skills, his father believed him but a child he could easily overwhelm. He paid for that oversight.

Wærmund's slumped on the ground, almost as immobile as the lifeless corpse beside him, but I know he's well. Now a flurry of conversation springs up between the members of the *comitatus* and those who came to witness the fight.

Eyeing the warriors warily, the bystanders come forward, hands snatching to take what they can from the dead. I'm not minded to stop them. I want nothing the dead had. Not even their rage towards someone they sought vengeance against. I've held enough rage within me for too much of my life.

What I want is to see Wærmund enjoying his victory, and

more importantly, I wish to start the journey back to my home-land. From what Heafoc's saying, I don't believe that's going to happen anytime soon.

Heafoc's embraced me warmly, his hot-sweat smell unpleas-ant, but for perhaps only the second time in my adult life, not reminding me of Edern's assaults on my body to be held in such a way by a man. He grins broadly, laughing although he's evidently exhausted, as he steps back from me, and moves to Eastmund. Kenal's also collapsed to the ground. I remain standing, assessing my allies, and those people who didn't sway the battle either way, but now mean to make good on the spoils. The older woman who seems to lead them reminds me of my mother, and if not my mother, then certainly Cadwysti of the Husmeræ. She has wisdom beyond even her many winters she's lived through.

Osfyth stands next to Wærmund, blade on display, as though she doesn't quite believe the attack's entirely over. I consider if she's correct to remain wary. Surely Wihtlæd can't have any more allies? So many of his men have fallen beneath the blades of the *comitatus* and the warriors of the Eorlingas, it's ludicrous to think there could be more.

'My thanks,' Wærmund huffs, both seax blades in his hand. Madder-red drips to the ground. I startle to see my blade, which I slipped to Wærmund, and his own, held side by side. Both shimmer in the daylight. I realise how similar they look, even though different bladesmiths crafted them, and the two hilts. They could be a pair by design, although they're not. Wærmund seems to be entirely without understanding of what he's accom-plished. It will come. Eventually. For now, he's concentrating on breathing.

I incline my head. I did very little to help him. But perhaps giving him the means to take the final killing blow was enough. This was the work of my horse-god and Woden working together.

Now Wærmund calls to Heafoc and the others, his voice ringing with jubilation. Does he, I consider, exalt in his father's death, as I did Elen's? I'd think no less of him if he did. If he doesn't, I might have cause to consider my reaction to my sister's death.

Heafoc replies quickly, his words muffled from where he's finally managed to force Osfyth away from her guard to embrace her. When he lifts his head, he speaks in my tongue. The words slow, halting, perhaps making sure he says exactly what Wærmund desires.

'You have our thanks, Meddi of the Eorlingas. Our father's death releases me from a terrible burden, as I'm sure Elen's death does you. Now, we will return his body to the kingdom of the Gyrwe. I may have hated him, but he deserves to lie with his ancestors. And his people deserve to live with the futility of his death.'

'No,' I retort. I don't wish to go further into these lands, ruled by men who think only of fighting.

'You will not accompany us?' Heafoc questions. I sense the scrutiny of all I've fought beside these last few days.

'My place is with my people.' Wærmund watches me. He obviously understood my 'no'. He speaks again, quickly, agitation on his face.

'Wærmund wishes you to meet the seiðr.'

'Why?'

'He believes he advised his father, and his people, poorly. And more than anything, he wishes to show his people how much he's changed.'

I shake my head. The reason doesn't seem good enough to risk elongating our time away from the villa. And I must hunt for Tudwal, even if all I find is his body. He must be taken back to his people.

'He wants to show his victory to those who demeaned him. He wishes to show you off,' Heafoc offers, more softly now. I breathe deeply, and then cough on the stink of rust and iron, on the salty air. Is Wærmund correct to exalt in his triumph and ensure the people who treated him so poorly know of it? Should he truly risk riding to where people hate him? I don't know. 'It is but a day, perhaps two at the most,' Heafoc further reassures me. I share a glance with Kenal. He gives me the slightest nod. I'm not often one to take advice from others but perhaps Kenal's correct. I should like to see the home of the people who cast out Wærmund, and worse, who heeded the call and allied with my bitch of a sister.

'Very well,' I concede. Wærmund, having risen to his feet, walks to my side, and offers me an arm clasp. I accept it, seeing the shimmering triumph reflected in his eyes, as he hands me back my seax. I grimace at the skin, blood and hair adhering to it, but take it all the same. I feel more complete with it in my hand, although I'm no warrior, but the seeress of the Eorlingas.

It's finally time to accept everything has been concluded. My sister is dead. At last. Wærmund's father is dead. At last. We need not know one another for much longer, but in that time, we can both acknowledge we'd not have succeeded without the other.

I offer a rare smile. Wærmund grins, and I wince away from his mouth filled with blood. His grin broadens. He moves aside to take the acclaim of his standing allies. The absence of those who've fallen on our journey is keenly felt, but it would dishonour their memory not to take pride in what has been accomplished. We are triumphant. We've taken our vengeance. And our gods undoubtedly approve. If not, we'd be the ones lying stiffening and cooling on the stone road.

* * *

We leave half of the horses with those who stood as bystanders to our fight. We allow them to take the dead Sweordora back to their tribe, using the animals. We don't need to slow our journey by going there. Neither should it be for us to dispose of the bodies. Their own people can do that.

Wihtlæd's corpse is flung over the back of his horse. The animal's skittish with its burden, and further unsettled by the presence of the wolfhound. Despite everyone's exhaustion, Wærmund encourages us onwards while the daylight remains. We shelter for the night beneath a solitary tree, standing proud and visible for a long distance. I should feel uneasy, here in enemy land with so few warriors, but I don't. The Sweordora warriors are dead. Wihtlæd's dead. Wærmund's *comitatus* might number only a handful of people, but they wear their triumph proudly. People would be encouraging their own deaths to start a fight.

In the morning, Wærmund's again keen to be on his way. Heafoc's slower to be ready and he rides at my side, telling me about the landscape we ride through. It's far from inspiring, and the buzz of insects quickly grows frustrating. I slap one of the annoyances aside when it stings my arm.

'They are a pestilent irritation,' he confirms knowingly. 'They're worse at night.'

'I don't welcome that,' I mutter, grimacing at the constant droning noise. Bronwen's unhappy as well, her coat dotted with as many bloody welts as my arms. Kenal's just as angry. 'I'll be pleased when this is done,' I confirm, eyes peering all around me. The landscape's flat and riddled with the sound of running water, none of it, I'm informed, good for drinking.

Eventually, with the sun high in the sky, Heafoc speaks again. 'There.' He points. I narrow my eyes against the glare, anticipating seeing a hilltop location rising from the flat land, or if not, something like the villa I live within. I don't expect to see a collection of round houses rising upright from the landscape, smoke billowing through roofs, and with barely a deep ditch or rampart surrounding the settlement.

'That's it?' I hear Kenal murmur. I'm not far behind him. It's hardly the sort of home I expected. It reminds me too vividly of the hovel we lived within after Edern took Villa Eorlingas from us, having first murdered my father and abandoned his corpse to rot in a traitor's ditch.

'That's it,' Heafoc confirms, taking himself to ride beside Wærmund. Osfyth and Eastmund are there as well. They intend to protect their lord of iron as he faces those who were once his people, with his father's lifeless corpse.

A scurry of activity takes place ahead. I see an entranceway into the settlement being hastily obstructed while five men, with spears in hand, block easy access.

They watch Wærmund, his warriors, and his wolfhound with disbelief, as do others who can be seen through the barricades. Frightened eyes peer at us. With a slap to the horse's rump, Heafoc encourages the animal to keep on walking, but no one goes any closer.

The five men look uneasy, and from behind another greybeard pushes his way through to the horse, where it comes to a halt, head hanging low.

I hear Wærmund's hiss, and decide this man is the seiðr he spoke of. I sense nothing other-worldly about him. I can't see he has any connection to Woden. I can't see much through his tangled mass of dirty grey hair.

He moves to the lifeless body, turning the head so he can see who it is. Horrified, he takes three swift steps back, crashing into the five spear-holding men. A keening noise erupts from within the settlement, followed by crying from a babe. Even the bloody hounds howl.

It seems they didn't realise we brought them the body of their dead leader.

There are angry gesticulations from the six men standing outside the settlement. Now Wærmund and his allies move closer, the wolfhound at his master's heels. I can't see they have anything to fear from the armed men, or the seiðr, but all the same, I reach for my spangles, and begin the task of summoning the protection of my horse-god once more. She'll be far from home, but she won't abandon me. I listen to Wærmund shouting to the people of the Gyrwe. I'm unsure what he says, but can imagine it easily enough.

His words are met with dismay and, I suspect, angry denial although the truth is before them. Do they seek their men? The warriors who died on the hilltop far from here? They must. Only after some considerable time do those within truly understand their men aren't going to return. Wihtlæd's the only one who'll be treated in death with whatever burial rites these people use to commemorate their lost loved ones.

Kenal grows uneasy beside me, the buzz of the insects setting my teeth on edge as well. I distract myself by eyeing the seiðr. I know he assured Wihtlæd that Wærmund was Woden-cursed. I also believe he was the cause of Bucge losing her position of honour amongst the Gyrwe. I consider if those who remain will realise the folly of believing a man can commune with the gods over a woman's innate skill? There is nothing about this seiðr to set him apart from any others. Unlike my nephew, he possesses the ability to hear, and speak.

Finally, the horse is allowed within, as the impediment is cleared momentarily, but still, these people make no effort to welcome Wærmund. Not, I realise, that Wærmund wishes to lead these people. I believe he'll return to the west with me. He's discovered there's more opportunity there than here, in these fetid swamplands.

Now the keening intensifies, as all can see Wihtlæd's cold body with their own eyes.

'Can we leave now?' Kenal calls to me. The sharp slap of his hand on exposed flesh reminds me of the bloody insects. I sense them all over my body, as though little seax blades, probing my skin.

'We wait,' I reply, trying not to scratch my skin where angry red marks are already appearing. 'We leave together.' We've come so far together. I won't abandon the surviving members of the *comitatus* now.

I sense I'm under scrutiny, and meet the gaze of the seiðr. He continues to stand between Wærmund and entry into the settlement. He speaks to the man next to him. I don't know what he's saying, but suspect it concerns me.

'Heafoc,' I call to him.

'Mistress.' He turns.

'What does he do?' For a moment, Heafoc's confused. 'The seiðr.' I stumble over the word.

Heafoc's silent as he observes the man. He leans towards Wærmund. I sense unease prickle my spine. I don't like being unable to understand him. My hands are busy on my spangles, Bronwen quiet beneath me. I lift my nose, as though I scent whatever mischief he intends. Only now does Heafoc reply.

'He's all piss and wind,' he chuckles. 'He knows what you are. He must be careful in the presence of someone who truly has understanding of the gods.'

'So he doesn't mutter curses against me, or you?' I'm unconvinced.

'He can do nothing against us. He has no skills.'

I'm far from reassured, but eventually I see something being brought towards Wærmund. I inhale sharply. A woman comes this way, shoved through the crowd and blockage by those behind her. In her arms she holds a squirming babe. She can be little older than a girl herself. I don't know if she's more terrified of Wærmund or the wolfhound. Her gaze flickers from one to another.

'What's this?' I demand.

'Wærmund's brother,' Heafoc explains. The seiðr calls the woman to him, and then speaks quickly, hands busy. I see her shudder, but straight-backed, she walks towards Wærmund, the child held tightly, her bottom lip wobbling with terror.

I'm unsure what this is all about. I doubt Wærmund wishes to meet his baby brother. My eyes narrow, my imprecations to my horse-god coming more quickly. This could be a trick. I'm astounded when Osfyth, Heafoc and Eastmund allow the woman close to Wærmund. She might carry a seax. She might have been sent to take the ultimate revenge on Wærmund.

I hold my breath as she comes to a stop. I get a good look at her. She's incredibly young, and evidently terrified as she holds the baby up to Wærmund. Her arms shake with the effort, but she holds still, even as the wolfhound growls. If I could see the beast, I'm sure it would be showing the girl its teeth. My forehead furrows.

'What is this?' Kenal mutters. Heafoc finally replies.

'They offer the child to Wærmund. Wærmund's the leader here now.'

A flurry of words, and Wærmund's reaching for his seax. A horrible premonition unsettles me. Without thought, I hurry Bronwen through the crowd to where Wærmund remains mounted.

'Tell him no,' I call to Heafoc. 'Tell him the child must live.'

I don't immediately hear Heafoc relaying my words. I reach out to snatch the babe from the girl's hand, but Wærmund already holds the child. The boy's legs are fat and chunky. His mother might be young but she feeds him well.

I reach out, to stop Wærmund, but he surprises me.

He doesn't move to stab the baby, as perhaps is his right when faced with someone who could contest the leadership of the Gyrwe when he were older, but instead nicks the child's cheek with his seax so a small burst of blood wells on the pale flesh. The babe screams and kicks. Wærmund almost does more damage by dropping the wiggling child, but he retains his grip, handing the child back to his mother with a flurry of words. For a moment, she's immobile, as though not hearing him, but then she gathers the child back into her arms. With a terrified glance in my direction, she turns and rushes back to the safety of her people.

Only then does Wærmund move aside, his wolfhound turning at the same time.

'This is done,' I hear him mutter. I don't need Heafoc to offer me a translation to understand he's content the matter is at an end. He's triumphant but, still, he abandons these people. Behind us, I hear the shrieks of the Gyrwe. They've no adult leader to guide them. They've no warriors but old men with bent backs to protect them.

Wihtlæd has gone and they're left with nothing but a babe marked in a very similar way to Wærmund, derided as Woden-cursed throughout his life, but clearly beloved by Woden after all. Woden-marked, not Woden-cursed. They can make of that what they will.

38

WÆRMUND OF THE GYRWE

'Why?' Heafoc questions me. I don't truly have an answer, as we turn our horses and our backs on my father's home. I feel the weight of a life spent trying to please a man who despised me lift with every step the horse takes. I'd been unaware how much his presence had been a constant niggle at my side, even when I was far from him.

'Why what?' I reply absently. I wish to breathe deeply, and extol my new sense of freedom, but here, in the lands of the Gyrwe, I can't do so. The buzz of irksome insects and the stink of the brackish water hold me in their grip. I'll need to wait until I'm further away.

'Why did you harm the child?'

I shake my head. 'I don't know. I thought it best to mark it with a scar. Those fools believed my father when they said I was Woden-cursed. Now their future leader is as well. It felt only right.'

Heafoc merely huffs. It's evident he doesn't understand. Neither do I. Did these people think I'd try and lead them in the absence of my father? Did they believe I'd kill a babe who's done no one any harm? Yet.

Ahead, I see Meddi turning more than once to gaze back at my former home. I encourage my horse to hers, pleased when Heafoc joins me, and Freki streaks on ahead.

'What is it?' I call to her.

'The man. The seiðr.' She replies through Heafoc. 'He still means you harm.'

'What can he do?' I question. 'I'm triumphant. He has no warriors to fight against me, and no true knowledge of Woden.'

Meddi's silence is telling.

'Does he?' I question. She shakes her head before Heafoc's finished speaking. Her reply is quick. I notice her hand remains entangled with the spangles around her waist.

'He has no ability to speak to the gods, no. But he won't necessarily need it. He hates you.'

'They all hate me,' I dismiss, my eyes on the way ahead. I see a layer of smoke rising from where I suspect the Sweordora now live. They must have decided to burn their dead. My father, in contrast, will be laid to rest in splendour, even if he's brought disaster on his people.

Heafoc and Meddi continue to speak, but I pay little heed. There's somewhere else I wish to visit before I leave this place forever. My brother's home, where all this began.

It's not far and none of the others argue as I turn slightly towards the north. Quickly, my father's settlement is out of sight, but it's difficult to find where my brother lived. I realise why as I'm faced with the charred remains of his home, the ditch overgrown with nearly two summers of vegetation. My lip curls as I see my father turned this place into a burial ground for his favoured son. The dwellings that didn't burn as we rushed through the settlement on that fateful day have been cleared. Now a large mound fills the centre of the place.

I ride my horse over the overgrown ditch, reaching out to hold the covering of grass growing over the mound. My father was always a fool where Waga was concerned. This testament to his useless life reminds me of where Meddi's ancestors have their remains placed. But I know beneath this great mound there'll only be one body, or rather, part of a body, for much of Waga must have been consumed by the flames before anyone came to pull his corpse clear.

'Well, brother,' I murmur, 'your father will have joined you by now. I hope you enjoy the afterlife, knowing I live and thrive.'

But, of course, there's no reply. There was never going to be one. I feel nothing here. It's a dead place. I consider what treasures my father gifted to my brother in the afterlife. Do I want them? No, I realise, I don't. I don't want anything that marks me as of the Gyrwe. I'm Wærmund, not of the Gyrwe, but Wærmund, lord of my *comitatus*. I'm a lord of iron now, nothing else. I couldn't be happier.

'Come,' I shout over my shoulder, keen to be as far from here as possible before night falls. 'Come. We're done with this place.' No one argues with me, and Freki once more leads the way towards the west. Even Meddi's lost some of her consternation against the seiðr who encouraged my father's hatred towards me and the belief I was Woden-cursed. I hope the remaining people of the Gyrwe do the right thing and kill the damn fool before he can do more damage. I think it unlikely, but someone amongst them might well realise much of the tribe's downfall can be placed at his feet, as well as those of my father.

I encourage my horse to ride more quickly. I'm desperate to be away from the heavy air, and the buzzing insects. I'm anxious to mourn my lost allies. They deserve more than to be abandoned on the slaughter field where they met their death fighting the Hicca, or so Heafoc believes.

Quickly, I find myself back on the route I once took to escape the only homeland I'd known then. It feels like a lifetime has passed and not merely two summers. I'm much changed from the boy I used to be, and more importantly, I'm not arrogant enough any more not to realise I'm still foolish and make bad decisions, but with Heafoc, Eastmund and Osfyth at my side, I'll grow my *comitatus*. We'll earn more battle glory yet. I can already feel the weight of future accrued treasures in my hand. Laughter floods from my mouth. I'm finally free from all my father imposed on me, with the willing aid of his loyal seiðr. I hope the people of the Gyrwe see him for what he is. A liar who can't commune with Woden as I know Meddi can speak with her horse-god.

I reach for my seax, feeling the power contained within it. The core has given me much, and Meddi holds the other half of that power. It seems strange to find us so connected, but then, we both hated Elen. Our desire to discover the lost magiks of forging iron are perhaps not surprising after all, even if we came from opposite sides of this island.

We rest that night close to a wide river, having walked the horses through the shallows, allowing the water to reach almost to the top of their bellies. It was at least clean of the taint of brackish water. For all our knowledge our enemy is dead, Heafoc insists on setting a guard over us. He offers to take the middle watch, Eastmund the first and Meddi suggests she has the final one. I eye her just before I roll in a cloak Heafoc's given me. She appears distracted, but then, she's a long way from home. I think nothing of it. Exhaustion has me asleep before my head hits the ground. I'm aware of voices around me, but only briefly. Meddi and Kenal speak in soft tones, lulling me to a deeper sleep with their familiar, but still often incomprehensible, tongue.

When my eyes blink open into the darkest of nights, it takes me a moment to remember where I am and to determine what woke me. Only the sound comes again, and I'm on my feet before I've finished yawning away my lingering tiredness.

'Meddi,' I shout, tripping over the sleeping form next to me, who growls angrily. 'Meddi,' I shout once more, desperately trying to determine where the shriek comes from.

I hear others waking and scrambling upright. I lift my chin to the sky, as though scenting the air, Freki doing the same beside me, and then Meddi screams once more. I dash towards the river-bank, convinced she's there, the scamper of paws assuring me the animal follows.

There's no light to see by, only the faintest shimmering from the surface of the water, where it catches the smallest specks of light from the stars overhead. I turn my head from side to side, and then grasp my seax tightly. I see Meddi, and she's embroiled in some desperate fight.

I don't have time to consider who would try and attack her, here, before I crash into the figure. The smell tells me all I need to know, as I surge upwards, seax stabbing down, but entirely missing the man.

He scrambles upright, reaching out for Meddi with a blade glittering more menacingly than the water. I don't understand why Meddi can't protect herself. Where's her blade? She can be no match for the old seiðr who told my father exactly what he wanted to hear.

My foot kicks something, and then I understand. Meddi was caught unprepared, or has been disarmed by the man I always thought frail. Now, as he fights to get to Meddi, furious words streaming from his mouth, I appreciate he's stronger than I suspected. Either that, or desperation has him managing to over-power her. More and more footsteps rush towards us, Kenal's the most frantic of all. Osfyth, unsurprisingly, has more forethought than the rest of us. She's kicked our fire to life, plunged a bundle of cloth into it, and now stalks towards us, illuminating the immediate area, her face revealing horror at finding Meddi under attack.

I reach out, but encounter nothing as the seiðr slips through my hands. I hear Meddi fall beneath his wild attack, the sound wet as the riverbank absorbs her.

'Bollocks,' I huff, kicking out to find him, and then bending to grip his shoulders so I can haul him upright. But he wriggles free from my grasp. Kenal barges into me, sending me wide.

I scoop up Meddi's blade, and endeavour to make sense of the writhing mass on the ground. Even with the flames, it's impossible to tell where the seiðr ends and Meddi begins.

'Bloody bollocks,' I huff, but feel a frantic hand grabbing my ankles. I follow it to where Meddi's entirely beneath the seiðr. I place her blade firmly in her grasping hand, as she did for me in the fight against my father, and watch with satisfaction as it dances in the leaping light of the flames Osfyth has commanded to blaze. The blade joins the dance, rising and falling, rising and falling until the seiðr falls still and silent.

I kick him aside, wincing at the wet, gurgling sound coming from his open mouth as he flops over. I reach for Meddi's hand. She grips it tightly to haul herself upright. Her eyes are wild, her face, I believe, covered in the blood of our enemy, but for all that, her demeanour is calm, as she bends and spits on the cooling body of the seiðr.

She calls words upwards into the sky, as though seeking her horse-god or perhaps Woden. It falls to Heafoc to explain what she says, even as he helps Kenal to his feet. Kenal's weeping. Meddi places her hand upon his bowed head to calm him.

'She accused the gods of this place of being craven and tricksters,' Heafoc huffs. 'She warns all should worship the ancient gods of this island, and not those who've stolen their way here.'

A smile breaks on my face, now the danger has passed, and I believe it has gone. There's no sound of others being here. The seiðr thought to right his mistakes by ending Meddi's life, believing, rightfully, she's aided me in seeking vengeance against my father. He's only served to prove how weak his skills were. Or, perhaps he foresaw that only one of them would live.

'You think it funny?' Heafoc demands, his tone betraying his unease.

'No. I think her wise, and clever. She extols her horse-god while casting down ours. Perhaps, my friend, her horse-god, who never walked this earth as ours did, holds more power after all.'

I don't need to be watching Heafoc to know his mouth drops open in shock. I grip his shoulder.

'I didn't say I no longer worshipped my ancestor,' I quickly reassure. 'But, perhaps, there's always room for more than one god.'

His lack of response makes me grin wider. I look down at the seiðr. I wish Bucge were here to take her revenge against him. She'd have enjoyed witnessing his failure. How I mourn her, for she must be dead in the fight with the Hicca. There's no other reason for her absence.

Glancing towards where the sun will rise shortly, I appreciate the night will flee soon. I don't believe any of us will sleep again.

'Come,' I shout. 'Let us leave this place to the dead. They're welcome to it.'

39

MEDDI OF THE EORLINGAS

I don't deny the attack unsettles me. I'm grateful to Wærmund for his aid, and realise our bond isn't one that will break easily, after all we've accomplished together.

I wash my face in the water, determined to remove the stink of iron and rust from me, and stride to Bronwen, ensuring Kenal comes with me. He continues to weep with fear and failure. He won't stop, even though I've commanded he does. Bronwen, who I know was sleeping well before the attack, greets me eagerly. I check her reins and then mount quickly. Like Wærmund, I've had more than enough of this place. The people here might look similar to the Eorlingas, but they aren't like us, or them. I'm convinced of that.

We ride through the shadows, outpacing the coming day for some time. We reach a road, and Wærmund seems to know the way. I allow my horse to pick her speed. We've a long way to go, but I sense Wærmund keeps a good speed for a reason.

It's been a few days since the battle against the enemy. He knows how many more died there. He must hope to reach them and treat their bodies with the respect they deserve. If we manage to find Tudwal's body, for I fear him dead, I'll order a cremation for him and then return his remains to the Eorlingas.

Kenal's sullen beside me. Eventually, I can endure it no more.

'Kenal, I don't blame you,' I state blandly. I still feel the seiðr crawling on me, and every so often the wind brings the stink of him to my nostrils.

'I blame myself,' he mutters, refusing to meet my eyes. 'And Lord Madog would have blamed me too.'

'He wouldn't. He knows I make my own decisions. He's always known that.'

'That man almost killed you.'

'But he didn't. Look at me. I don't even have a wound on my body. Not from fighting him.'

Kenal finally looks at me, and the worry on his face clears quickly. 'Not a single wound?'

'Not a single wound. And before we left, I took this from him as well.' I hold out the item I've secured to my collection of spangles. I've seen it on some of the enemy warriors. I don't know what it means, but it must be something to do with their gods. It's a heavy item, perhaps made from iron, or silver, and by someone even more skilled than Terricus. 'I'll wear it from this day onwards to show I have no fear of Woden. If he is even a god.'

'Why would you say he's not a god?'

'He walked this world, or so they say. How else could Wærmund claim Woden as his ancestor? Our horse-god is more than that. She was never made of flesh. In that way, she'll survive forever.'

'Seeress,' he sighs, but I hear his reverence for our horse-god, and he sits straighter, riding more confidently. Or at least, he does until we find the first body.

Wærmund calls a halt as soon as he catches sight of a horse ahead. We've ridden all day and covered a vast distance. The riderless animal hasn't gone far. I grimace on seeing Tudwal's lifeless form. But he's been dead for some time.

I dismount and go to him. His body feels warm beneath the gentle sun, but his skin is so white as to be grey. His death occurred some time ago. I swallow my grief, while Kenal retrieves the horse he rode here, its pale sides shimmering with Tudwal's dried blood. The animal's keen to be reunited with horses it recognises. It once belonged to a member of the *comitatus*.

'We must burn him,' I inform Heafoc.

'We should take him from this place. There may be more.'

'They won't be Eorlingas,' I argue softly, but I know he's correct. Tudwal managed to travel a long distance before falling from his horse. I know he died from a bang to the head, for his skull is sticky with days-old blood. But he had other wounds too, ones that made him fall from his horse in the first place. 'You're correct. We take him from here.'

It takes much effort, but eventually Tudwal's slung over one of the other spare horses, the mount he rode to the place of his death, too spooked to be able to take the load.

We travel until darkness tinges the sky in a ribbon of deepest blue before coming upon more bodies. We're drawing closer to the slaughter field now. Without needing to allow the wolfhound time to scent, we move much more quickly. I know Wærmund's been demanding answers from Heafoc. He should, I realise, have asked for them long ago when so few of us came to save him. Did he not wonder where Bucge was?

There are three of them, close together. I suspect they died from wounds gained during the battle. In the dying light, dark patches surround their bodies, and there's a trail of it leading onwards towards where the battle was fiercest. I see Bucge's bloodied corpse, and sorrow for her has me cursing the seiðr once more. If not for him, she might not have been here. If not for him, she'd have continued to serve Wihtlæd as opposed to leaving with Wærmund, although, of course, perhaps she preferred the journey she took with Wærmund. It's not my place to pity her when she died a good death, protecting what she believed in.

'We'll stop here,' Heafoc informs me, his voice heavy with sorrow. 'We'll set a funeral pyre.'

'Will it not bring the enemy, the Hicca as you named them, here once more?'

Heafoc's eyes glint as he acknowledges my comment. He speaks to Wærmund, the conversation not without heat but spoken in subdued tones, to honour their lost warriors.

'If they come, we'll ask them to join us,' Heafoc states. 'Wærmund always intended to offer reparation for deceiving them. It'll be an opportunity to do so.' I swallow my unease at hearing that, but quickly dismount to aid the others in gathering wood for the pyre. My horse is led to water by Kenal, tears stinging his eyes. I leave him to his mourning. I know where his thoughts will have taken him. It seems wrong to him that he lives while young Tudwal is dead. I can offer no explanation. It's the way of such things. Our horse-god has deemed that was to be Tudwal's purpose in life.

It takes a surprisingly long time to collect enough wood and sticks to burn the dead. In that time, Heafoc's discovered more corpses. The fighting was fierce here, as people tried to follow the road north. By the time the first flames rustle along the thankfully dry wood, there are eight bodies. I name them as the flames grow and billow in the wind: Bucge, Tudwal, Sennicus, Maggenræd, Locinna, Totia, Cynin, and Mato. I lift my voice to ululate and to ensure they journey to the afterlife quickly and are welcomed.

We stand a guard, as the flames leap along clothing and spark on hair, as the scent of roasting flesh fills the sky. The fire's brighter than Terricus' forge, and I blink away from it, unsurprised when I see hazy images of my mother, father, child and even Bucge, against the smoky outlines of the funeral pyre. I incline my head towards them, allowing tears to drip down my smooth cheeks.

It is done. It is over.

* * *

Our return to Villa Eorlingas is greeted with joy, although we've watched more of our former allies burn on our journey here. We know the fates of Blatero and Rhun now as well. I dismount quickly, embracing my brother, forgetting I should present myself as seeress and not sister.

Kenal's quiet. I see immediate understanding on the faces of Tudwal's expectant family that he's not with us. Somehow, I suspect they knew. They'll mourn him. I still mourn him.

Madog's frantic words have me realising I must offer an explanation, as to why only the two of us return, and the *comitatus* is also absent.

'Wærmund's free, his surviving allies have journeyed to Verulamium. They mean to retrieve their treasures and gift them to a tribe they wronged. Then, they'll come here,' I state loudly enough so all can hear. There are cheers, and my brother looks pleased at the resolution. Only then does he realise one of my warriors is missing. Grief shrouds his face, and he grasps his wriggling daughter tighter.

With Bronwen taken away, and Kenal absorbed by his warrior allies, Urien most prominent amongst them, my brother takes me to one side, still holding his daughter. My young nephew, Maccus, sits astride his horse, Rhiann keeping a wary eye on him.

I see how the boy has grown in my absence, and how Gwynmarch is attentive beneath him. The boy will make a fine rider and warrior one day.

I notice Madog carries his fine sword held in place along his leg. I catch sight of eyes peering at me from the hilt which Hedrek must have crafted. A small smile tugs at my cheeks. There's an eagle there, not a horse. It seems only right to find such a creature adorning my brother's sword. For he is a lord of iron now, and in his wake, he leaves feasts for the carrion creatures, the eagle amongst them.

'Tell me, sister, is it truly at an end?' His words are wistful, his gaze resting on his daughter.

In the last few summers, the responsibilities my brother has shouldered have made him into the very image of my father, although with a slimmer build.

'It is, brother, yes. Villa Eorlingas is safe. Her enemies are dead.'

He absorbs this, perhaps determined not to accept my summary. I know he wants to believe but it's difficult to accept everything has been resolved. I decide to convince him.

'Our father has been correctly buried beside his ancestors, my mother as well. His sword has been used to create two new blades. Terricus can forge the best blades from our iron ore, as I see at your side. Sian can choose the best pieces of charcoal, and Urien knows how to perfect the art of making charcoal. We even have a good source of fresh ironstone from the Stoppingas, including more of the small horse-shaped objects which must be broken down to ensure our blades are the sharpest and strongest. Our horses are strong and healthy, our crops grow well. Your son and daughter thrive.' I tick off each item on my fingers as I speak. Even I'm astounded by the summary of what we've accomplished in two short summers. 'Our nephew is here, with us.' I've noticed

Macsen, standing close to Dewi when we first arrived. He acknowledged me with a quick hand conversation with Dewi. I still need to discover the truth of their knowledge of one another, but I suspect I already know. Dewi's family were murdered by Edern. Perhaps he was briefly a prisoner. I'm unsure. However, he evidently came into contact with my sister when she most needed someone's aid. She, it seems, managed to inveigle another to carry out her commands. I don't think any less of him for falling under her spell and raising her son in her absence. I'm curious to know what happened after, and where Macsen has been while Dewi's been with Wærmund, but I have all the time I need to ask these questions. I must also inform Dewi of the deaths of all of his allies.

'And what of Wærmund and his *comitatus*?'

'They'll rebuild. Our connection will remain strong.'

'Will it?' It seems my brother's determined to be contrary.

'Lord Madog, you're a lord of iron now, and Wærmund shares a bond that can't be broken. Within his seax blade lies the other half of the core of our father's blade, stolen by Elen. He's bound to us, as we are to him. You're both lords of iron. Now, enjoy it.' And I embrace him once more. 'We're all where we should be,' I huff into his shoulder, and for once he doesn't argue with me. How wise he has become.

Later, I discover how wise I've become as well, as I see Sian and Hedrek sharing a tender look as they work together, while I make my way to my workshop. The door creaks open on new hinges Terricus has forged in my absence. He really will attempt anything now. I step inside, smelling the essence of my mother, closing my eyes to recall my small daughter, not as she was when broken and beaten, but as she was fresh at birth. She was perfect. Her being here, and not within the tomb of our ancestors, is fitting. She's still with me, even now.

I run my hands over the worktop where I laboured with my mother, hand rubbing the double horse-headed torque around my neck to elicit the connection I share with my horse-god.

I'm Meddi, seeress of the Eorlingas. It's been a long and troubled journey to reach this moment in my life when hatred has bled away to nothing but a dull ache where the life I thought I'd have has a child has failed to come to fruition. But I would change nothing, aside from the loss of my daughter. I should have liked to have her at my side, but in her place, I'll train another, my nephew, Macsen, the embodiment of my father, provided I look at him in the right light.

I'm Meddi, seeress of the Eorlingas. With my brother, and his family at my side, my nephew, and Sian, we will thrive. My horse-god wills it, and so do I. Villa Eorlingas has been reclaimed, physically as well as within my being. It will long continue, and for all the work I must still undertake in training the future seer, and future warriors, my story is almost concluded.

40

WÆRMUND OF THE GYRWE

The horses take the slope easily, unlike the last time we were here. Freki hardly seems to notice the incline. Even weighted down with the treasures the pack animals carry, and with the slower cattle following on behind, we make good time. I'm aware we're being watched from the peak of the Hicca's homeland.

We found Isarninus' stronghold abandoned by all but those too weak or old to walk from the place. We didn't take more from them. We only retrieved our stolen treasures that remained. And, in all honesty, I left them with the means to buy food to last them throughout the winter, provided they can find someone to barter for it with.

Now I must make reparations for my most foolish mistake, and one that set me on the path that took me to Isarninus, even if those men and women have thought to take their vengeance on me by killing so many of my allies. I don't expect to see anyone I recognise on the Hiccan hillside, and I don't. I know they're there, but they remain hidden.

I pause, and turn to Heafoc. He knows my intentions.

'People of the Hicca. We return that which was stolen from

you, and beg the forgiveness of your gods for our part in what happened here, and at the slaughter field. We hope you'll accept our endeavours to recompense you.'

Silence greets his pronouncement. I know the words he speaks, even if I don't understand them. Eastmund flicks me a furious glance, but I dismount, and lead the three packhorses forward, the five remaining cattle as well. There are three older females and two young calves. The animals could do with fattening up, but aside from that, they appear healthy. The smell of their shit tickles my nostrils, and when I tug them with their halters, it rubs the hand I so badly cut fighting my father. It's healing, but the work is slow, and often undone by my impatience.

Without weapons to hand, I stride towards the enclosure encircling the Hicca's hilltop settlement. In my hand I carry the small depiction of the wolf, gifted to me by the boy I bartered for Eastmund's life with. Bucge told me it would give me protection and ensure I was welcomed. It's a pity she didn't have the same. The Hicca killed her, but no doubt she killed many before that happened.

The Hicca are, admittedly, a different tribe, but it might work the same here, if needed. I should perhaps fear them, but I don't. Not with my breastplate and warrior's helm in position. The others say I look like an arse in Isarninus' boar-crested helm, which my father battled me wearing, but I'm not a complete fool. I don't wish to die now, when I'm so close to fulfilling my intentions of making restitution towards those I acted foolishly against, aside from the Sweordora. They deserved my wrath, and they received it.

I stand, holding the halters, unsure what else to do. I don't wish to release the animals and then have to gather them together again. Now I do feel foolish, stood in the garb of a warrior when I have five cattle beside me, and three horses just a little ahead.

A sudden loud noise fills the air, startling the cattle as well as me, and two figures step through the very heavily protected enclosure. There's a woman and a man, perhaps of a similar age. It's not Boddw. Not that it could be. He died in the fight that took place between Isarninus and them. One we took part in, much to my shame.

The woman moves with the most confidence, the man limping heavily. They come closer, but not close enough I can hand them the halters.

Behind, Heafoc calls in their tongue, and understanding flashes on the woman's face. She takes another step, but the man holds out a hand to grip her. She says something. He reluctantly releases her. Closer now, so close she grimaces on seeing the mark on my face. I doubt people will ever stop doing that. Mind, it's hardly served me poorly these last few weeks.

'Here.' I walk closer, holding out the halters. The cattle move unwillingly. I see her stop abruptly. 'If I let them go, they'll escape,' I huff. Comprehension flashes on her face, although Heafoc offers no further explanation. She strides ever more confidently, and I offer her all five halters. She takes them eagerly, licking her lips with a thin tongue. I think she'll simply walk away, but instead she pauses, turns back, and reaches out hesitantly to run her free hand over my Woden-marked cheek, while Freki sits silently beside me. Her touch is rough but light. She offers me a smile, and with a click of her tongue, the animals follow her, momentarily enveloping me in the stink of cow shit.

I grimace, and watch the animals being welcomed into the enclosure, where more and more people show their faces.

I retrace my steps to Heafoc, Freki keeping pace, and mount up, but don't immediately move, although Osfyth and Eastmund have already turned aside. Osfyth carries my wolf standard, retrieved from our battle against the enemy on the hilltop. In the absence of Bucge, I think she welcomes the distraction of riding with the heavy standard.

'Well, Wærmund,' Heafoc questions, 'does this settle your unhappiness at what happened here?' That he speaks without rancour, and reminding me he didn't agree with the decision made on that fateful day, says a great deal about why I so admire him.

'It does, yes,' I murmur, pleased in being able to bring these gifts. 'It really does,' I agree, and then turn my mouth, grinning towards Heafoc. 'Where now, my friend?' I question. 'Another battle, or back to Uriconium for a good soak in their baths?'

Momentarily, I think I've upset Heafoc, but then he breathes deeply, and opens his mouth to reply.

'Well, Wærmund, lord of iron, I suggest you decide what you value more highly. New members of the *comitatus* or scraping all the crap and filth from your body. Or conversation with Gildas, or exchange of a different sort with Diseta?'

'I don't see why they can't all be done,' I reply, laughing, and Heafoc nods.

'Very well, Wærmund, lord of iron, to Uriconium it is, although we must also visit Villa Eorlingas for our payment along the way.'

I encourage my horse onwards, Freki able to match the speed of the horse.

I've become the man I always believed myself to be. How wrong I once was, when I was simply arrogant and angry, but at least, unlike my father, I've allowed myself to learn much. I've become a lord of iron, as Heafoc termed me. I've a new family now, a connection with the Eorlingas which can't be broken, through our paired seaxes, and a loyal wolfhound at my side. I've lost much, and I'll always mourn those who died fighting on my behalf, especially Bucge and Maggenræd, but I'm who I was always meant to be. I feel my ancestor, Woden, as well as Freki, dogging my every step. I'll make my legend now, for I'm Wærmund, lord of iron, and my story has only just begun.

* * *

MORE FROM MJ PORTER

The first instalment in a brand new action-packed historical adventure from MJ Porter is available to order now:
https://mybook.to/HouseMerBackAd

HISTORICAL NOTES

This cast and the events in this trilogy are all fiction (apart from Gildas, although some suggest he may have died earlier). However, I was somewhat delighted to discover while reading Max Adams' new non-fiction work *The Mercian Chronicles* that the monastery at Peterborough, named as *Medeshamstede* at the time, was so-called because there was a spring there called Medeswæl (p. 46), or Medi's Well. The scene where Meddi encounters the seiðr of the Gyrwe is placed there, somewhat hazily. This is one of those delightful bits of information that assure me, while I might be writing fiction, there are always elements that could just be historically accurate, if only we knew more.

Every series needs a 'hook' to build upon. For this trilogy, I decided to use the idea (so eloquently presented by Robin Fleming in *Britain After Rome*, and I'm sure elsewhere as well) that the presence of newly worked iron is so largely absent at this time, preventing such things as coffins being constructed as they would have lacked nails, and no doubt hinges too (I hope you noticed that near the end). The more I examined this idea in the trilogy, the more seemed to make sense about what was happening, particularly in this mostly undocumented sixth century. We have a vast amount of tribal names from a later source that are beyond difficult to locate let alone date and it's only in the next century that the Saxon kingdoms as we recognise them begin to truly form. How obvious this suddenly seems. Without the means to overwhelm an enemy (or an ally) how could these kingdoms form and, indeed, become kingdoms with a king leading them offering their warriors high-quality weapons, etc? Historians can be somewhat guilty of forgetting the 'lived' experience of the past. Archaeologists, often sifting through rubbish to find evidence of our ancestors, meet them in a very different context. I would suggest that for the time being, the archaeologists are who we should be listening to about events in the true Dark Ages. A close look at the information available, and emerging, certainly highlights the great variety amongst the people living on this island at the time. Our obsession with the Saxons, Angles and Jutes overlooks what was already here. In that we do err. And indeed, the lack of ironworking in the aftermath of the Roman withdrawal might provide many more answers than previously suspected.

The production of iron also appears particularly complex when you realise how many different elements were required to forge a blade. Not just the skill with heat and ironstone, but the ability to create that heat and then to make the blades themselves, as well as finding the iron ore in the first place. That's not to say older relics weren't still being used. The Romans, we're told, were good at recycling, and this certainly continued, but a blade can only survive so long being constantly sharpened before it becomes too thin.

And that is another element that's been further highlighted for me while writing this trilogy. The Roman era seems so alive with information, with visible remains, with written records. The sixth century, by stark contrast, lacks almost all of that. It's jolting to go from scouring written records to reading archaeological reports. It does feel as though the period is regressive, although I doubt people thought that at the time. I'm sure they wouldn't have been concerned about leaving written records (aside from the historical Gildas). Their concerns would have been with living their lives. They were evidently successful at it. Admittedly, those who could write perhaps all died from the plague which was ravaging communities at about this time as it wasn't a one-off occurrence (as my brother-in-law reminded me – one day I might tell you who he is. He's certainly an expert on the period). It's worth remembering how tenuous life could be and how susceptible all populations are to the sort of drastic change plague could bring. While it's often stated the plague arrived in Britain after the 540s, this dating is now being questioned. It might have arrived much earlier. See this article for details https://www.cam.ac.uk/research/news/justinianic-plague-was-nothing-like-flu-and-may-have-hit-england-before-constantinople

As I've said before, the timing of this trilogy was carefully considered. I didn't wish to force my characters (and my readers) to live through plague years when we've so recently had a very real reminder of how difficult that situation would be. I have, however, allowed the young seeress, Tangwysti, to foretell the coming of the Saxons to the west of Britain and the plague (sorry if you didn't pick up on that). For those who know, I hope that's enough. For those who don't, this is sadly what's in store. However, the coming plague years would have enabled those with blades to hand to triumph over those weakened by poor harvests and loss of valuable members of their community. And indeed, in 552, we hear of the Battle of Searoburh where Cynric defeats the 'Britons,' as well as other details of battles fought between the Saxons and the 'British'. In 577, we have the Battle of Deorham near Bath, when Ceawlin of Wessex was victorious over three 'British' kings, and 'took' Gloucester, Cirencester and Bath. Gloucester would certainly not remain in his possession as this is where the Hwiccan kings were based. These entries in the *Anglo-Saxon Chronicle* are, of course, suspect, pertaining to a period long before the entries were actually written, but they are interesting.

If you've not quite comprehended the link, Wærmund is one of the names mentioned in the Mercian genealogy, dating to the eighth century (I think). The genealogy claims descent from Woden, as most of the Saxon genealogies do. How Saxon warriors came to rule 'Mercia' is worthy of consideration, and of course, it doesn't strictly point to these 'lords' claiming Mercia from the beginning, but are more likely to have ruled elsewhere and then expanded into new territory. Wærmund might have been the first; equally, perhaps he was merely the father, grandfather or great-grandfather of the person who did. The home of the Eorlingas, which I've placed close to the River Severn, would come to be part of the kingdom of the Hwicce, which also came to be part of Mercia. The origins of the name for this kingdom are much debated, but it might have a Brythonic (like Meddi) origin.

My characters have perhaps not behaved as I thought they would, or as you suspect they might have done. This is the delight in creating characters the way that I do. With all the discussion regarding concerns about AI in writing, I'm far from convinced anything could be made to think in the same way I do. My writing style bends itself to obscure twists and turns in the narrative. Every time I write, I make thousands of little decisions about what my characters will say and do and then sometimes change them again. I would apologise, but as many of my readers have been with me for a long time, I suspect you enjoy it as well. I hope, in *Lords of Iron*, I've sought an ending you're pleased with for these characters. Meddi and Wærmund have been a joy to write. Even with these endings, my characters fought me to the bitter end. I sense they had more stories to tell, but first, they needed to resolve their inner conflicts.

Thank you for being my readers.

ACKNOWLEDGEMENTS

The Dark Age Chronicles should perhaps have followed a more 'expected' storyline, perhaps even an Arthurian one, but the Arthurian legend is exactly that, a legend. I wished to tell this story of what 'might' have been happening at this time, through the eyes of others, allowing the delightful mix of people and places, Latin, Brythonic and Saxon naming conventions. For that, I'm grateful to my publisher for supporting me, and especially my editor Caroline. I also want to give an enormous shout-out to my copy-editor Ross, who engages with my projects with such enthusiasm. When he says 'Yes!' I know I've nailed the storyline.

I also wish to thank Shirley, my proofreader, who manages to catch all those words I consistently manage to spell incorrectly, as well as ensuring I maintain consistency. (I am not good at consistency.)

Huge thanks to my narrators for this trilogy, and a grateful nod to my cover designers, who I've never met, but who do such a fabulous job of portraying, visually, what my stories are about.

Another thanks to Christine Rauer, for lending her language skills to my narrators. Who knew you said Bucge like Budga, and Eastmund like Estmunda.

As always, thanks to my family for supporting me (read there – putting up with me when I'm distracted by writing) and an especial shout-out to my brother, and my other half, for venturing to historic sites with me. I know how to have a good time!

And finally, a big shout-out to my publisher, Boldwood Books. Knocking down barriers, making publishing fun, and quite frankly, showing that women can be just as fiery as warriors in all their many guises too.

ABOUT THE AUTHOR

MJ Porter is the author of many historical novels set predominantly in Seventh to Eleventh-Century England, and in Viking Age Denmark. Raised in the shadow of a building that was believed to house the bones of long-dead Kings of Mercia, meant that the author's writing destiny was set.

Download your exclusive bonus content from MJ Porter here:

Visit MJ's website: www.mjporterauthor.com

Follow MJ on social media:

 x.com/coloursofunison

 instagram.com/m_j_porter

 bookbub.com/authors/mj-porter

ALSO BY MJ PORTER

The Eagle of Mercia Chronicles

Son of Mercia

Wolf of Mercia

Warrior of Mercia

Eagle of Mercia

Protector of Mercia

Enemies of Mercia

Betrayal of Mercia

Shield of Mercia

The Brunanburh Series

King of Kings

Kings of War

Clash of Kings

Kings of Conflict

The Dark Age Chronicles

Men of Iron

Warriors of Iron

Lords of Iron

WARRIOR CHRONICLES

WELCOME TO THE CLAN ✕

THE HOME OF
BESTSELLING HISTORICAL
ADVENTURE FICTION!

WARNING:
MAY CONTAIN VIKINGS!

SIGN UP TO OUR
NEWSLETTER

BIT.LY/WARRIORCHRONICLES

Boldw♾️d

Boldwood Books is an award-winning fiction
publishing company seeking out the best
stories from around the world.

Find out more at www.boldwoodbooks.com

Join our reader community for brilliant books,
competitions and offers!

Follow us
@BoldwoodBooks
@TheBoldBookClub

Sign up to our weekly
deals newsletter

https://bit.ly/BoldwoodBNewsletter